TRIAD

BRITTANY WEISROCK

For Peyton, may you always know how much I love you. And Tara, remember in darkness, there's always light.

Praise for Triad

"TRIAD is a sexy, romantic, and suspenseful twist on the tried-and-true genre! It will build you up and break you down in the span of one book, leaving you begging for the second installment. It's a definite must-read, and I highly recommend it to Paranormal fans!"

— Mary A.J., author of Vagabond

"You will want to keep turning until the very last, heart-wrenching page. If you like Dead Until Dark, Buffy, or Supernatural, you will devour this book as I did, and your inner wolf will howl for more!"

—Nick Starling, author of Oil and Water

"I loved so much about Triad – the romance, the strong family bonds, the suspense, the action, the love, the heartbreak, and that amazing and shocking ending! Did I mention the fantastic (and steamy) romance? I so enjoyed the story and can't wait to read the next book in this series!!!"

—Julie Petitbon, Book Reviewer for One More Book

"This book is fabulous! Complex and very detailed. Definitely up there in the realm of Charlaine Harris with the paranormals. That ending of 'Brittany Weisrock's' KILLED it! Was not expecting that at all!"

—Rachel Talavera, from Yours Truly Book Services

PLAYLIST

Want to listen to music behind and featured in Triad?
Check out the playlist on Spotify

QUOTE

"A man might befriend a wolf, even break a wolf,
but no man could truly tame a wolf."
George R. R. Martin

PROLOGUE

Twenty-Four Years Ago

*Under the first Full Moon of Winter Solstice and Fae frost, a
prophecy comes to life—Lupin Dragona
Three children brought forth by wolf and fire—a Triad.
The first of their kind, with one born to lead them all.
She is the key—the bringer of fire and ice.*

Their power unknown, but their story foretold.

With their magical gifts comes great loss.

To save the Unseen and humanity, they must pay—in blood.

CHAPTER 1

I rarely ask for permission. It's overrated.

At least, that's what I told myself upon sneaking out. Again.

I looked down at the ground and jumped from the window.

The heels of my shoes crunched gravel as I landed.

I glanced over my shoulder for what felt like the hundredth time.

Behind me, the front door clicked faintly.

Goddess. I'd never get out of here without them. A twig snapped and feet jogged to catch up to me. An enormous hand grabbed me from behind.

I brushed it away, growled, and scowled deeply—the untamed rumble sounded more animal than human.

"Move, Atlas. I won't tell you again," I snapped at my brother. I was in a grim mood, further exacerbated by this detainment.

Earlier, I'd gotten into a heated debate with my father. I suggested an aggressive approach in locating a demon: sending out the guard, having our human agents investigate some seedy buildings I'd heard hosted supernaturals and humans.

My father disagreed, calling me overzealous and stubborn.

Apparently, his plan comprised of doing nothing. Now, I had Atlas and Anders on my case, both pestering me to tag along on this investigation. We all knew they'd be a distraction.

"Thea, come on. We're best when we're together, you know that! I'm not trying to order you around. Just hear reason." Atlas pleaded.

My brothers were the only two I'd ever permitted to call me Thea. Even if Atlas and Anders were my Betas, they were my brothers first. And because I loved them, I tended to cave when they got to whining like a bunch of pups.

"Lower your voice. I don't need anyone overhearing and objecting to my little outing," I whispered.

"You know he's right," Anders chimed in, racing to get in front of me. "We're the Triad. That means three Thea, not one. If trouble shows up, we wanna be there." Another common ploy—ganging up. They always used the two against one bit, pretending it overpowered me.

"I'm tired of this argument," I sighed, my irritation already fading as it always did with them. I pulled out my keys, flipping them into my palm, the metal clinking together.

Atlas shot me a look from his big, brown eyes, a fake pout on his lips.

"Fine," I rolled my eyes.

"There, wasn't that so much easier?" Atlas laughed, doing little to stifle his rueful smirk. His wide mouth curved upwards, revealing his too-pointed teeth. He eased his posture, assuming he'd won this quarrel. Perhaps he had, but I wouldn't let him know that. I shoved him forward. He turned to look at me, walking backward to the large garage attached to the manor. "You could always try listening the first time."

A tight pressure grew behind my eyes. I knew the sensation all too well. My eyes glowed, brilliant, fluorescent green.

"You were saying Atlas?" A ball of fire manifested in my hand. I tossed the reddish-orange orb around like a baseball, staring Atlas down, daring him to continue gloating. *I swear—if they weren't mine to protect, I might kill them both.*

"Dammit, Thea. Chill, ya show off!" He hollered as he jogged away up our paved driveway back toward the house and Anders. Another step, and the security lights would flick on, alerting our guard and family that we were up to something.

Anders clapped his hands together, howling with laughter. "You idiot. Never know when to quit, do you?"

Atlas pushed Anders in front of him. He ducked down, pretending to use Anders as a shield. *How theatrical.* All three of us knew my threat didn't alarm Atlas. If I did—he'd manifest his *real* shield. One of Atlas's abilities allowed him to release a force field around himself or whoever he chose if they were within so many feet. It proved his greatest defense against my talent with fire. One I made him test often in our frequent rows.

With a tilt of my head, I grinned. "Oh, but brother dearest, I'm helping you train your shield," I quipped, feigning innocence. I put my hand to my chest in a dramatic swing and bowed my body back in a fainting motion.

"Last time we trained with your fire, I left with burns." Atlas gestured to his stomach, lifting his blue shirt as if to show scars. I laughed. He didn't scar—none of us did, courtesy of supernatural regeneration and Anders.

"Shh," I quietly chuckled, putting a finger to my lips. "Your dramatics are one of a kind, Atlas. Anders healed you literally ten seconds later." I let my fireball evaporate. Smoke seeped and swirled through the cool night air.

"Are you two done? We need to get moving before the guards hear your incessant bickering. You know Mother and Father don't approve of these little excursions," urged Anders—always our peer mediator and voice of reason. He routinely sought to diffuse situations, maybe because he was the middle child, if only by moments. Being younger than me and Anders by minutes offered Atlas the title of '*the baby,*' and he was all too keen to use his skills in whining or picking to get his way—a prick habit of his, if you asked me.

Anders shrugged out of Atlas's grip and narrowed his icy blue eyes. He gave Atlas a solid shove toward the large garage and received a sock to the shoulder for his troubles. Most days, those two couldn't go five minutes without trading joking blows.

"Cut it out, and let's go then," I scolded as the over-sized wood panel door finished opening. I pointed to the jet-black car, sleek and ready.

The sound of pebbles grating together grabbed my attention. Footsteps. Someone was coming.

"Just get in already," I hissed.

We hopped in my Jeep Grand Cherokee and pulled out of the garage with the headlights off, hoping to further avoid being noticed. It's not like we weren't adults or possessed a curfew. Hell, most things that went bump in the night feared us. But—the fresh edge in my father's voice when he'd told me to *drop it* this morning was a warning I had no intention of heeding. King or no king, I knew I was onto something, and as future Alpha—I took orders from no one.

I hit the gas at the end of the driveway and sped down the winding road towards the Barrier. From the rearview mirror, I saw my father's beta, Logan, and a few members of the guard watching us tear down the driveway.

"*Ha-ha. Hasta la vista* baby," Atlas howled out his open window.

Anders scoffed and reached behind him to pull Atlas back in the car. "You're still quoting The Terminator? Get in the fucking car already."

I swatted at Anders. "*Já chega!*" Both brothers settled in their seats.

Before we hit the highway, Logan would likely tell my father we left, and not a single drop of me cared.

I pulled my phone from the console, tapping on the music icon. Music always helped the time pass quicker. We were heading past the Barrier, not for a clean-up or dispatch scenario, but to observe. I intended to research a few rumors, determined to gain as much information and evidence as possible. Perhaps then, my father would listen to me. Either that or I'd make him.

The Barriers kept the human world from the Unseen. To my knowledge, they existed for over a millennium. I wasn't entirely sure anyone knew how or who created the Barriers, but they allowed us to stay *"unseen"* from the human world, giving our realm its namesake. It was an all-pervading cloaking spell, keeping humans from passing into our realm while letting us pass freely into theirs.

All citizens or magic folk knew humans existed. Most supernaturals never saw one—let alone interacted with one— while others enjoyed the thrill of mingling with humans or *naturals,* as we sometimes called them, going back and forth through Barriers. Sometimes passable supernaturals lived full-time outside the Barriers. I didn't understand it, suppressing our nature. To what? Live with humans? I shook my head. I found humans curious and a touch small-minded. I understood my duty and protected their existence, yet most humans couldn't bear the idea of supernaturals from their *'faerie'* tales being real. Still, I wanted to familiarize myself with their complexities and gain a general knowledge of their behaviors.

Humans. My eyes rolled at the thought. *Oh,* to live in a bubble of ignorant comfort. I chewed my lip. Maybe part of me resented the hiding, but it didn't matter. I had a job to do, and failure wasn't an option.

I believed Xercarus, an ancient blood demon, had returned. Whispers of missing humans and supernaturals swirled around the Unseen, but I had no concrete proof to indicate if I was right. Even thinking the demon's name left a bitter taste in my mouth.

My hands twisted against the leather steering wheel. I'd only had the misfortune of reading about the bastard scourge in our record books. The blood baths. So much death. Xercarus and his filthy mutated horde slaughtered millions, ravaging their bodies, consuming them.

Our tutors forced us to read the human history books. *The Plague*. Such a poor lie. The fourteenth century was a damning time. Wolves, vampires, fae, elves, humans—they all died by the hundreds over the years as the battle waged on, but one day it came to a halt. My lips pursed as I recalled my favorite part of the literature—when the Fire Warriors joined the cause, rising against Xercarus using their dragon forms. Their fire sent him running back to the hellish portal he crawled from.

Rotten bastard deserved worse.

As for warriors, they didn't fare well either. Shifting into dragons cost them their lives.

They lost their energy in the transformation, leaving them helpless to move or shift back. Over time, they turned to stone. Our people erected a grand temple around their statues out of respect and gratitude for their sacrifice. As children, we often visited their resting place with our parents, leaving offerings. One of those statues was an ancestor of mine, the reason I was both wolf and dragon. I shook my head, wanting out of the memory. Wisps of black hair caught on my lashes, making me bat them. I couldn't think of my youth or father while I disobeyed him.

Anders and Atlas hadn't looked up from their phones, both of them mindlessly engrossed in some game about candy. I almost chuckled, but that'd draw their attention, and I needed the quiet of my mind for a while longer. My hands tightened on the leather steering wheel as I sped up the car.

I had my sights set on a club, one where humans, vamps,

wolves, and other creatures mingled—humans just didn't know it. Besides finding some answers, I had a bigger challenge: corralling my rambunctious brothers. They knew how to find trouble and left me to clean up the messes from their less than graceful human interactions.

Flicking my eyes up, I peeked at Atlas in the rearview mirror, and I felt a smirk spread on my lips. Atlas and Anders were, by nature, *boisterous*—Atlas more so. He lived to make my temper flare with his juvenile commentary and his lack of a sense of urgency over anything. That broody pout and bad-boy exterior were mostly for show, though that did little to make him any less aggravating. My jaw tightened, thinking about the last time Atlas pissed me off.

I glanced over at Anders, still swiping away. He mirrored Atlas, almost twins in appearance. But Anders possessed these amiable blue eyes he'd inherited from our father, along with an equitableness about him Atlas could never muster. Anders always kept a more level head than either Atlas or me. Then again, we rarely left him with much choice.

"Thea?" *Ah, dammit.* Anders sensed me looking at him, then slid his phone away into the pocket of his jeans and began his questions. "Where are we headed on tonight's human stakeout?"

He shifted his torso to face me as I watched the curving road. He tapped his leg, waiting for me to respond. When I didn't offer a quick answer, Anders leaned in closer on the leather armrest between us and squinted his blue eyes at me. I pretended not to notice his staring and pushed down on the gas, accelerating the car forward. My shoulders felt tight. I couldn't put my finger on this impatience bubbling beneath the surface of my skin. It roamed through my pores, and unease coiled in my belly as if I was expecting something. I rolled my head from side to side, my hair tickling my neck.

Atlas spared no time in filling the silence. "Ha! You know

she loves to check out those dive places. The darker, the better, I say. Nothing is harder to look at than humans," he snorted, slapping his hand against his leg from the backseat.

I narrowed my jade eyes, clenching my teeth to keep from grumbling. Anders had gotten in the front seat first, calling shotgun, which left Atlas with only the opportunity to bug me with commentary from behind. A tense smile graced my lips—thank Goddess for small miracles.

Anders laughed, his shoulder shaking up and down. "Brother, you are utterly cruel. You know they can't help how fragile they are, or their smell." He and Atlas twisted in their seats to high-five, thinking they were both such clever comedians.

"Tell me again why I agreed to take you two along?" Annoyance from Atlas's and Anders's flippant remarks tainted my tone, making me sound shrill. Neither of them carried too high of an opinion of humans, and why should they? They were, for the most part, weaker and hard to keep alive. Sometimes, I found it difficult to disagree with those assessments. Humans were capable of so much less than wolves or supernaturals in general. Yet since the beginning of time, we'd protected them and let them throw around their power as if they owned the world. There was a time when I wasn't sure if I believed humans deserved our unknown protection, but I had it ingrained in me for so long. I stopped giving it much thought and continued to guard them as you would helpless children.

Anders exaggeratedly cleared his throat. "Because if something should happen, we're better together. We know, we know. You're the fastest, the biggest, but as the—"

Before I could stop myself, I swung my palm up, interrupting my brother's well-rehearsed speech. All my life, I followed rules. I served the Unseen without complaint, but I couldn't hear our prophecy one more time—*the Triad.*

"Anders, stop. You're a damned broken record. No need to

remind me again. The *almighty Triad*. We've heard it our entire lives, yet here you two are, mocking humans. The people we're supposed to protect." I paused, giving them time to absorb my words.

I adjusted the rearview mirror, allowing myself to glare at Atlas. "And so help me, if you two don't behave tonight, I'll singe both your hides!" I snarled, curling my lip up to bare my teeth. That ought to drive my point home.

"*Whoa*. No need to go to Alpha mode, T. Damn. Okay, we'll behave." Atlas bowed his head, appeasing my inner wolf and dragon. And my, oh my, the dragon had a *fiery* temperament.

"Good. I knew you'd see it my way." I raised my eyebrow and looked from Anders and again to Atlas in the backseat.

Silence held my brothers' tongues for a while, giving me a moment to ruminate. I thought back to the time when my brothers had been on the receiving end of my dragon in full form. It was only once, and it was years ago. We were impulsive youths; they were still trying to get a handle on their abilities. Not me, though. I learned fast to channel my aggression, honing my skills with fire. I pushed myself without hesitation, and in time, I'd become a better warrior than anyone expected. Killing became easy. Rogue hell spawns and ogres learned to fear me. I'd become lethal, a dealer of justice and killer of those who wouldn't fall in line or threatened the Alliance.

Being female, the packs underestimated me at every turn. They clung to an antiquated idea of only a male being able to rule. I snorted out loud—*only a male could rule. Bullshit.* They all saw what lurked beneath my fleshy exterior, the animal beyond a mere wolf.

Anders glanced over, giving me a wrinkled brow expression over my unexpected noise. He said nothing but offered a shake of his head.

A song by Trevor Danial played. I hummed along, letting myself relax into the notes.

Sensing my mood had cleared, Anders tried again. "So, where are we going?"

Not looking away from the road, I fiddled with the radio, searching for another song. "We're going to Zephyr. It's a newer club. Supposed to host a lot of vampires and wolves."

"Vamps, humans, and wolves? *Nah.* Vamps seldom keep their fangs to themselves," Atlas blurted, shaking his head from side to side. I frowned. He wasn't altogether incorrect.

Vampires needed blood to survive, but some enjoyed the thrill of feeding—the hunt. I didn't understand the appeal, toying with humans or the blood. I hated the metallic, earthy smell.

Before the Alliance, some vampires killed humans indiscreetly, not caring how many bodies piled in their wake. Over the years, my grandfather, Asher, and then my father had remedied this. They enforced the laws by penalty of death or disembowelment, though to my knowledge, we put few supernaturals to death. Those that had were mostly before my father's rule. I'd only dispatched several over the years. Justice served if you asked me.

"That's exactly what I'd like to find out. If laws are being broken, it's my responsibility to resolve it." I lifted my head higher and tapped the steering wheel with more force than necessary. I looked from Anders to Atlas. They understood the rules as well as I did.

Anders cleared his throat, interrupting my train of thought as usual. "*Our.* It's our responsibility."

One law stood out from the rest. It was simple: *Don't kill humans without cause.*

Which meant vampires and sea nymphs could feed on humans. It was a biological necessity for vampires, but sea nymphs did it for amusement. The reasons didn't matter if they left the humans unharmed and unknowing of the event.

Vampires often used their *trance*. Trance allowed a vampire to lure a human in, to seduce their mind. It also gave them the power to make the memory fade away. I possessed that same lucky ability—well, Anders did.

From what I'd learned, humans often enjoyed the tryst, and by morning all knowledge of what occurred was long gone. Vampires nowadays preferred to go unnoticed, but there was always the loose cannon who'd tear into a human in a social setting. Since bath salts and other hallucinogens entered the recreational drug use scene, media easily explained it away to the human tabloids. *'Crazed madman high on altered drugs eats woman's throat.'* Humans bought that trash hook, line, and sinker. Over the years, we'd only taken a handful of irrational vampires back to the Unseen in silver manacles. And only on one occasion had I given a vampire their true death.

Atlas popped his head between Anders and me. "Why would wolves hang around humans or vampires anyway? I mean, I know why vampires enjoy humans, but wolves?"

I shrugged. "Not sure. That's what *we're* going to find out." Atlas sighed and sat back in his seat.

He asked a solid question. Wolves didn't hate vampires per se or vice versa. We just didn't keep close company. I'd trained with several vampires; they made excellent sparring mates. As for humans... *oof.* Too breakable for most wolves to befriend.

Wolves had a tendency to be rowdy and prone to finding trouble. Our raucous nature was often hard to stifle. This disruptive behavior resulted in fights, trashing venues, and the occasional hospitalization of humans. Occasionally, there was a fatality. *Goddess,* the paperwork, and intervention required for that kind of infraction was miles long, and I hated paperwork. Such an unenjoyable experience for all parties, living or deceased.

The silver lining to group animals like wolves was our

nature required us to defer to a higher pack member or Alpha. It was almost too easy.

Wolves—such unruly hotheads, though I was one to talk.

"I guess we're off to save the humans from the likes of us again. *Ah*, an Alpha to the very end. Always looking out for the little guys," Atlas teased, giving a strand of my dark hair a tug as a child would do.

"*Har har*." I fake laughed, turning up the music, letting 'The Reaper' by The Chainsmokers blare through my Jeep speakers. My head bobbed as I sang along.

I adjusted the rearview mirror as I sang, looking at my green eyes. We were triplets, though my brothers looked far more alike. I was the odd one out with black hair I'd inherited from some relative long gone. Anders had focused blue eyes, the same shade as our father's. His slender muscles wrapped around every inch of his tall stature. He had sandy blonde hair, always kept neat for being a little long, either tucked behind his ears with care or tied up. He looked so much like our father, but when you observed him close enough, you saw the cupid's bow of his lips, which was an exact match for our mother Illiana's, and his eyelashes were too dark for someone so fair. His skin tone leaned more toward our father's, but long days in the sun gave him the ability to tan.

Glancing over my shoulder as I turned the wheel to go around a curve, I glimpsed Atlas. He looked much the same as Anders but possessed soulful brown eyes plucked straight from Illiana. They could warm you like being in the rising sun... when he wasn't running his mouth. Even with linked minds and emotion, I often wondered what secrets Atlas tried so hard to hide behind those mysterious brown depths. A breath passed through my nose as I watched Atlas adjust his tall frame against the seat. His height matched Anders's, but his build was a touch larger as he fancied lifting weights far more than Anders did. Atlas also kept his hair shorter but never out of place or out of style. He often accessorized with a wrist cuff, a ring, and occasionally, an earring if he felt like stabbing himself. For wolves, earring holes healed up once you removed the jewelry.

To my relief, they finally abandoned picking at me and focused their attention back on their devices. *Thank the Goddess.* I shook my head and rolled my eyes a little. At least they looked dressed for a club.

CHAPTER 2

Two hours later, we pulled into an almost full parking structure. I circled the first level, checking the surrounding cars' license plates, all from California except a few.

One open space near the back wall remained. Driving past it, I shifted the car in reverse and backed into the tight space, not needing to look behind me. I turned the engine off and we got out, shutting the car doors behind us. The sound echoed off the dank cement. Mildew and dampness tickled my nose. I stuffed my phone into my back pocket, jogging ahead of Atlas and Anders.

'Zephyr' blared in red neon lights. Blacked-out, solid metal doors obscured the entrance to the establishment, making it impossible to see inside. That seemed odd for a nightclub. Most had glass doors, allowing its potential patrons to see the fun inside.

I approached first, giving the air another sniff—the husky bouncer was a wolf. Flashing my eyes and our IDs, I growled low, causing him to fumble while moving the rope to the side. Our presence flustered him. *Good.*

One rumor confirmed: wolves did indeed run here. How curious to have one placed right at the front door...

Interesting, I mused to myself, intrigued by Zephyr and its frequenters already. I ran my tongue along my teeth. Maybe I'd actually find some entertainment along with answers here. It'd been months since I'd properly chewed on anyone. Everything had been a bit too peaceful in the Unseen. If I was honest, a little mischief couldn't hurt.

Walking through the dim entry, the overpowering odors of vampires, humans, and wolves filled my nostrils—and... something else. *What was it?* A fresh aroma of salty beach waves ignited my nerves. A hot and cold chill rang through me all at once, and goosebumps lined my arms. My white, billowy crop-top and distressed black denim pants itched my suddenly too sensitive skin. Sweat beaded at my hairline, sticking long black strands to my forehead. Lifting my hand, I wiped it across my brow and tossed the rest of my hair over my bare shoulder. I fidgeted, hoping this daze would pass, but it didn't. The chill moved farther, creeping down my spine and settling in my bones.

We weaved through crowds of bodies, evading swaying limbs, and made our way to the packed bar. Neon purple back-lighting illuminated the rows of liquor bottles covering the wall. I sniffed again, inhaling deeply and trying to pull myself together. Anders pulled a chair out for me, and I took a seat on the stool. My head fogged, making my thoughts unclear. I lost my balance, fumbling to regain my bearings on the bar stool. The noise pounded so loud it rattled my chest. My heart raced with the music, pumping blood in my ears and chest. 'Roses' by SAINt JHN blurred around my head.

What was going on? My brothers' heads snapped in my direction before they took seats on the stainless-steel chairs. Another gift of being the Triad: linked minds and emotions. We possessed a heightened awareness of one another. It was a bond meant to keep us safe, but right now, it betrayed my accelerating haze to my brothers. Atlas and Anders froze, staring at me suspiciously. Their heartbeats came faster along with mine, and they sniffed the air, searching for a hidden threat.

Ignoring them, I waved my hand in the air, signaling the too eager, young bartender. He licked his lips, looking me up and down. He didn't bother to disguise his blatant staring at my breasts through the keyhole of my top while he shouted over the music to ask what I wanted.

"Three shots of Patron," I ordered, slapping a one-hundred-dollar bill I'd pulled from my phone case onto the glass and lacquered bar.

Both their voices pushed into my head, linking my mind.

Thea. What's going on? Anders asked, leaning in closer to me.

Nothing. I brushed them off. I had zero desire to explain to them what was coming over me when I didn't know myself.

Anders backed off, pursing his lips, and took a seat to my right.

The bartender set the three shots in front of me. Tequila sloshed onto the bar as he tried to crack my hard exterior with a hopeful smile. "Can I get you anything else? Like my number?" He winked while I suppressed a warning grumble. *My number. How ridiculous.* If I didn't believe in the laws and Alliance, it might've tempted me to leave my number on him in teeth marks. Did the male species actually believe this was an efficient way to draw us in?

I pushed the money closer to him. "No. Thanks." And slugged back the first shot and slammed the empty glass to the counter.

Atlas side-eyed the vest-clad bartender, sending him scurrying to the other end. He reached for a shot. In no mood to share, I snatched it up, downing it in front of him.

My head pulsed. I felt dizzy and even more uneasy.

Dammit, Thea. What's wrong? Anders asked again, refusing to let me ignore him this time.

My eyes wandered to Anders and back to the crowded dance floor. Heat rushed over my cheeks. Wrong wasn't the word I'd use, but I had no others to explain the unknown sensation.

I'm... not sure. We got out of the car and I... feel—

I didn't finish my sentence. The smell became too strong, floating like a cloud in the air, moving directly to me. It was alluring, almost seductive, and it overpowered the odor of human sweat and pheromones. *Hm,* this smelled of all my favorite scents: wildflowers, crackling logs on a fire, a cool breeze coming off the ocean all rolled into one. *But how?* There definitely wasn't flowers or ocean in this congested club, crammed to capacity with clammy, inebriated bodies.

You're scaring us, T. First your heart, now you stopped... I put my finger up to silence Atlas. His lips weren't moving, but I heard him regardless. I focused on the scent and an interior, compulsive desire to locate where it emanated from. Another long breath in, and a delightful tingle prickled up my spine, spreading across the surface of my entire body.

"*Shh.* I smell..." I spoke out loud this time. I pushed out of the chair; it made a scraping sound against the polished concrete floor. Following instinct, I moved towards the scent, my wolf yipping. I lifted my head, sucking in more air. The more I inhaled, the more hypnotized I became. It drowned out my good judgment and swallowed me up. I wondered if this was what it felt like to be under a vampire 'trance'. Alphas weren't susceptible to that trick up a vampire's sleeve, so I had no way to know.

I pushed through the swinging crowd, dodging waving arms and rocking hips. The lights above the dance floor weaved patterns as I walked.

There it was.

Only, it wasn't an *it*. It was a *him*. I stood motionless, watching for a moment. Dread filled my heaving chest. My heart made its way to my throat, locking in place. Confusion racked my mind.

"*No*," I mouthed, my lips sticking on the "o." My brothers, quick on my heels, flanked my sides. Alert and ready to shield me, except this feeling wasn't something they could save me from. What I was experiencing was a natural incident in wolves. The scent and who I blundered upon was not a wolf.

Human.

The man sat in a booth drinking with four other male friends. All of them laughed and clinked their pint glasses together. One of them, a blonde with a lanky build, tapped the mystery man and gestured to a group of three women. I noticed all the women admiring the handsome stranger as well. *Good, they can have him.* My wolf snapped in my head in sharp disagreement. I winced. What was this feeling... *jealousy?* No. I didn't get jealous. Of anyone. I watched the man run his hand through his too-perfect disheveled hair and laugh.

It wasn't hard to read his lips as he talked.

"No, thanks," he told his friend, laughing and looking away as he did. "That's not my thing anymore." He took another sip of his drink. I watched as he adjusted his body, angling it away from the women who gawked at him in a less than subtle manner. They lifted their phones, each one taking turns snapping quick photos of him.

I tilted my head, watching him smile and talk, moving his hands. He clapped his other friend on the back, then rested his hand on his thigh, picking at a frayed string. For someone so confident looking, his absentminded picking suggested he wasn't too invested in being here. So why was he? *Odd.*

He wore distressed light-wash jeans with well-placed holes, focusing my eyes on a spot on his thigh and several around his knee. The exposed skin made me shiver, wondering what it felt like. I wanted to slap myself at the thought.

I knew I should leave. Just turn around and go, but I remained frozen. My knees quaked, threatening to buckle from under me—until he looked up, catching my eyes. He held perfectly unmoving, almost like a deer, and kept my gaze. A small smile formed on his full pink lips. Was he smiling at me? That was a mistake. He had no business grinning at me with such bright-eyed curiosity. I bit my lip, expecting to snap myself out of whatever this was. I'd never found a man so appealing and so human.

No, I said again. *Oh, Goddess, why?* I clutched at my bare midriff, trying to dig the feeling out. I didn't want this.

My brothers' eyes widened, searching my face for a clue, and then they followed my gaze.

"Shit." Atlas cursed beneath his breath.

Ignoring Atlas, I continued watching the man. My heart whacked against my chest walls, struggling to beat in rhythm. The man reached his hand up. Long fingers tousled his dark hair away from his eyes again. *Blue.* They were blue, and even in the low, flashing light, I could see them clear as day now—pools of cerulean. I could swim in them, dive in deep, and forget everything else. I listened to his heart fluttering on and off, indecently dashing to match mine.

"Athena!" Anders shouted over the music. He reached his arm out for me but stopped mid-stride, realizing he couldn't evade what was transpiring.

Atlas looked over at Anders. I felt them both eyeing me and the human with grated suspicion. "Fuck. This can't be happening," he said again, more worry saturated his tone. Like me, Atlas must have believed the more he denied it, the less real it might be.

"I didn't know it could happen with one of them," Anders sputtered, rubbing his jaw.

Anders and Atlas felt a fraction of it too. A bond-forming before their very eyes. Nothing could undo or prevent the emotions currently developing, and to interfere with this bond would cause me pain. And if I experienced pain, they did too.

The dark-haired man pushed off the booth, moving around his friends, and approached. An invisible race between us, moving in real-time. His blue eyes fixed on my bright green. My wolf bounced inside; she had no qualms displaying her elation. Her sureness almost startled me.

My great dragon lifted her head. She breathed from the shadow of my mind, never one to interject. Unlike my wolf, she seemed to always have some input I didn't ask for.

But how? He's mortal. This doesn't happen...

I shook my head.

No. Nope. This can't be, I said to them, begging for these feelings to be false. What had I ever done to upset the Goddess to deserve such a fate? I'd followed all the rules, and she saw fit to leave me with—

My wolf paced, her exuberance countering my denial. My body no longer listened to me and walked to him. Sweaty bodies collided on the too-crowded dance floor. Somehow, they parted, clearing a direct path to the man I wanted so much to avoid. I'd never realized time could stand still, yet for him, it did.

One of the pretty young women, a petite brunette, used this opportunity to break from her friends and approach the oncoming Adonis. I laughed at my reference like a mad wolf. I was Athena, and Adonis, a lover of the Greek goddess Aphrodite. *Ah*, the irony. I watched him with the anticipation a cat reserved for a canary. He stopped and cocked his head, listening to what she had to say, never taking his eyes off me. His mouth moved again. He told her he appreciated the offer; it was sweet, and maybe another time.

That brief encounter offered me the chance to run, but I

couldn't. His eyes were mesmerizing, compelling me to stay despite me trying to dig my heels in and avoid him.

Stopping inches from me, the mysterious blue-eyed man spoke first. He bit his lip, his nerves getting the better of him. "Hey. I don't mean to be weird, which is what every guy says before doing something completely creepy, but... I feel like I know you from somewhere."

I was tall, reaching six feet, and I still had to look up at him. With my mouth seemingly glued shut, I didn't say anything. Perhaps if I could keep from speaking, he'd take the hint and leave me alone. *Run along, mortal.*

He rocked on his feet from side to side before continuing. "That's such a line. I get it, but you're... beautiful. Not beautiful, like bewildering or something. Is that even a word? Wow..." His voice was like silk, tangled up with my favorite melody. How utterly odd...and tantalizing.

Tilting my head, I examined him further. His high cheekbones and clean-shaven face made him almost too pretty to look at.

I glanced down, proud of myself for not having said anything to him. *Keep it up, Athena. You can do this.*

"I'm not makin' this any less awkward," he said while taking a step back to give me space.

I reached for his hand, wanting to ease his discomfort away. Why? *Damn me.*

"You're not awkward." My skin connected with his as his hand caught mine. The contact was electrifying, sending jolts through me. My skin vibrated, buzzing all over, and I felt nauseous—in a good way. Was that possible?

My surroundings slipped away until all that remained was us. I heard his heart; the thrumming filled my ears, dazzling all my senses at once. He squeezed my hand, sending another striking blow to my nerves.

"What's your name?" he asked, his smile open and inviting.

His blue eyes gazed at mine, boring into me, and he licked his lips lightly. The action made me shiver.

Walk away, Athena. I told myself. *Don't say another word to him.*

"Athena. Athena Whiteridge," I answered, my breath hitching in my throat. *Traitorous body.* I got more pissed at myself the longer I stood in front of him and those translucent blue eyes. "And you are?" My voice shook. I'd never sounded so weak and unlike me. *Was that* want *I heard in my tone?* How disappointing this display was, a future Alpha simpering to a human. I tried straightening my posture, which kept bowing towards him.

"Kalen Ryan. I'm sorry, but I have to know you. This is crazy." Confused, Kalen wrinkled up his nose and pulled his eyebrows together, which I could barely see through the thick hair covering them. "Your voice even sounds familiar, like I have it memorized."

Kalen lifted his other hand to caress my face. His fingertips left an ardent trace wherever they touched my cheek. I leaned my face into his palm, his every stroke igniting another fire along my skin.

"And your eyes... they're the most marvelous green. Such a peculiar shade," he said, breathy and winded, while he tilted his head to get a better look.

It was then I could hear my brothers. Their intrusive hollers reviving me back to full reality.

What are we going to do? Fuck, Anders. This is bad. Atlas's voice swamped Anders's and my head. I frowned, clenching my teeth.

I dunno. I really don't. Dammit, if I don't feel like this guy is... I felt Anders's eyes on me, stuck watching the scene unfolding between Kalen and me.

Oh, Goddess, help us. No one ever said this would affect us too.

This is bullshit. Atlas grumbled. I looked back over my shoulder to see Atlas palming his face in frustration.

Kalen released my hand, bringing it to my other cheek. The world stood still again. "This is—I'm sorry. I can't seem to stop apologizing for myself. This is super forward, but can I kiss you?" he asked, bringing all his courage to the surface and swallowing hard. The flashing lights above us couldn't hide his trembling lips as he awaited my reply.

Absolutely not. What's he thinking, asking a stranger to kiss him? This human is insane. My rational side tried to remain firm in her convictions. My mouth, not listening to logic—did otherwise.

"Yes." I let out a slow breath, ignoring my better judgment. Kalen's face drew nearer, his jaw flexing with eagerness. I closed the distance and my eyes, curious to know what his full mouth felt like. My lips touched his, warm and gentle. I parted my lips to greet his tongue. *How could something so soft feel explosive?* His lips erupted fireworks behind my eyelids, causing me to brace my hand on his expansive chest. I curled my fingers into his shirt, pulling Kalen farther down to me. The influence of him pumped through my veins as my heart thrummed faster, wanting more of him.

Um, Thea... We. Need. To. Go. People are staring. Anyone who isn't human is gonna know something's up. Anders's voice was lower, more tentative about interrupting time. I saw him shuffling closer to me from the corner of my eye.

Yeah, T. Let's bail and leave the lovesick puppy behind before he follows us home. We don't need the dead weight, Atlas said, adding a snort at the end to ensure his annoyance with Kalen was clear.

I pulled back from Kalen, touching my mouth as if I could wipe away the connection along with the kiss. Our very public display of affection was out of character for me. *Why couldn't I control myself?* This wasn't me. I didn't need a mate, nor did I want one—especially one so fragile and ignorant of my world. A low growl flowed from my throat, demanding otherwise. My wolf had a mind of her own, and she very much wanted Kalen —human or not.

My brothers looked down. *Thea, please...* Anders said, clenching his hands at his sides.

Turning my head in their direction, I grit my teeth. "I'm trying. I just can't seem to," I said aloud, trying my best to throttle my aggravated and protective wolf inside. She was putting up a fight, and, like me, my animal nature did not take well to being restrained. But he wasn't for us. He couldn't be.

"Leave?" Kalen choked out, confusion raising his brows into his hairline.

"I have to go." I forced myself to rip my palm from his.

His body went rigid. "Can I at least get your number?" he asked, scrambling to his side to retrieve his phone. Pulling it from his pocket and unlocking the screen, he thrust the device into my hand.

When I failed to move, he drew up our hands close to him. Our bond hit him hard, decimating his ability to think straight —*to think of anything other than me.*

I understood as well as any wolf, the undeniable pull of the bond. It was irrefutable, but that wouldn't stop me from trying. I pushed the phone back to Kalen and attempted to turn away, but as his hand once again grasped mine, I stopped. His proximity threw me off, and I swayed backward.

To walk away would hurt me, and worse, hurt Kalen, whose eyes turned down and glazed with a muddled longing. My senses kicked into overdrive, feeling his building anxiety like it was my own, and my heart begged me to provide him solace. To shield him from the ache enveloping my chest each time I thought of leaving without him.

Nothing prepared me for this. Not now, and certainly not with a human. This was unfamiliar territory. All my life, I'd trained for battles, worked with magic, and pushed my limits past any boundary possible. I was strong, impervious—ready for any obstacle thrown my way...

But I possessed no skills to fend him off.

The way his high cheekbones shone under the flashing lights; the curves of his lips, the bottom slightly fuller than the top; his almost black hair grazing his forehead... Damn his face and the Goddess for making me yearn for him. If I could get away, put some sort of distance between us, maybe I could ignore this binding call.

"Kalen." I sucked in air, holding my breath. "I need to go. Family business." My heart sagged, and the animal in me snarled and howled, fitting to rage an epic, wolf-sized tantrum.

We'll find him again. I did my best to lie to the wolf. I didn't want to find this man again. A man who lessened my control and threatened the composed exterior I'd worked too long to refine.

Kalen's eyes narrowed to slits, and his head snapped over to Anders and Atlas. "Why? Is it because of them?" Kalen puffed, broadening his stance. Though Kalen was every bit of six-feet-four-inches, he paled compared to my taller, heavily built brothers. Kalen was a poor match for them in their human form. Should they shift, they were deadly to him.

My heart wrenched, and a painful queasiness threatened to push bile up my throat at the thought of my brothers hurting Kalen. I saw Anders and Atlas both wince and glance away. They felt it, too. Kalen's well-being concerned more than just me.

Atlas recovered, shaking off whatever emotion he didn't care to share. He cocked his eyebrow while Anders began laughing.

I shot Anders a look, then turned back to Kalen. "No. They're my brothers. Atlas and Anders."

Kalen's posture relaxed, and he shook his head. He

extended his arm past me, offering it to Atlas. Atlas creased his brows together but gave Kalen his hand.

"Atlas." A brief shake and Atlas dropped Kalen's hand like he'd touched something unpleasant. Atlas looked away, sniffing the air. He wrinkled his nose and pressed his mouth in a hard line. He wasn't taking this any better than I was, and it showed in his tight posture and terse tone.

"Kalen Ryan." I detected a note of irritation in his voice, and it sent a shiver up my spine. Fighting for my clarity, I backed away from Kalen, needing distance from the energy he emitted.

Meeting his stare, I blinked several times, trying to break the growing connection. "I'm sorry, I need to go," I said again, though my chest felt wounded. If I could gain enough distance between us, I could walk away, or run. I'd need to run.

"I apologize for being weird and clingy. I'm not that guy, I promise." He hesitated, eyes darting, thinking of his next move. "Maybe we can go someplace quiet and talk," Kalen fought with his words and ran his hand through his hair, "Fuck, what am I even saying? I can't imagine how much you must wanna run away from me right now." Kalen's voice shook. He wasn't wrong. I wanted to run away. And at this very moment, I knew I never would. I couldn't. I'd likely do whatever he asked, and it maddened me.

What was he doing to me? Frustrated, I fisted my hands at my sides.

I was about to respond when an attractive blonde bounded over, laying her hand on Kalen's shoulder, her pink painted nails digging into him. If her goal was to piss off my wolf, she succeeded massively. She stormed around my head, and claws extended from my fingernails. I dug them into my palms, hoping to slow the spread of her fury.

"Kalen, there you are! The guys are waiting for you. Who's this?" Her high-pitched slurring would've annoyed me on a normal evening, but today, with her touching Kalen, I might eliminate her where she stood. My wolf refused to back down, pushing herself closer to the surface. I rolled my shoulders and neck, trying to regain the upper hand.

"Hey Jenny, thanks. The guys can wait." Kalen's eyes never left mine. "Yeah, this is Athena." Kalen lifted his shoulder and pulled his arm up to politely maneuver out of Jenny's grip. Jenny, unphased, kept tugging at his shoulder. Her thin mouth tread too close to his ear while she used him as a crutch to balance herself.

The dominant being filled my head, demanding action. My self-control hung by a way too thin thread. A rumble came from my chest, incensed by my wolf's ire.

Oh fuck... Thea, said Anders.

T, don't lose your cool. Breathe, she doesn't know. None of them do, Atlas continued on, and as he did, I felt Anders place his hands on my shoulders, increasing his pull.

Move back, Thea, you can do this. It's gonna be fine... Anders attempted to calm me further, rubbing my shoulders. Harnessing what willpower I had left, I backed up several steps, following Anders's lead.

Oblivious to the battle waging inside me, Kalen added gasoline. "Hey. Wait, a damn minute!" Kalen raised his voice, removing Jenny's hand from him completely. He made his way towards me, unaware he wouldn't persuade my brothers of anything.

"W-who cares, Kalen? Let them take whatever her name is. She's just another stupid—" Jenny twisted her mouth in disgust. She muttered *'groupie'* under her breath, thinking I wouldn't hear. I smelled her heat, the pure jealousy she harbored toward me. In that second, Jenny struck a match, throwing it on the gas and igniting my anger. She wobbled on her heels, spilling her fruity, colored drink down the front of her top.

I threw my head back and laughed, a devilish grin dancing across my lips. My palms twitched, itching with fire.

"Ah, damn, almost," Atlas sighed, biting his lip. His eyes rolled freely as he continued to mutter under his breath. "Woman couldn't leave it well enough alone. Drunks. My favorite type of human."

Zigzagging out of Anders's vice-like grip. I squared up, broadening my shoulders and getting close enough to use my imposing height against her. "Jenny, is it?" I clicked my tongue, looking her over. Her petite stature and athletic build suggested she was into things like yoga and salads. Her breath told me she guzzled vodka.

I leaned into her, my voice low but still loud enough to hear over the commotion. "I suggest you not say another word. I also suggest you keep your hands to yourself. He clearly isn't buying what you're selling." Venom laced my words, forcing my lips to curl up in a sneer.

"Who do you think you are, anyway, bitch? Kalen's here with me," Jenny shouted, the alcohol thick on her breath, hitting my face like fog. She staggered forward, then stumbled backward with drunkenness, attempting to point her finger at me—a finger she was moments away from losing. My teeth came down, and claws pushed out where my fingers were, ready to give Jenny a preview of who she spoke to.

This time it was my dragon who filled my head. She tired of this game. Burning from inside seeped into my pores. The fire traveled from my palm, tingling the tips of my fingers. I felt pressure from my eyes as they roared to life with a glowing green I couldn't contain. I lifted my shaking hand, about to snap my fingers, and set Jenny ablaze.

Kalen sidestepped around me, putting himself between us. I jerked my hand down. "Enough. You know what, Jenny? I tried to be polite—really, I did. But you're not getting it. We aren't together anymore if you could even call what we had a relationship. Now, go. Just go." Kalen backed up into me and shrugged off Jenny's reach. He frowned, then he grimaced with hostility to match his sour words.

My chest heaved up and down. "Thea, your eyes," Anders said in a hushed tone. They were glowing. I already knew. *Stop, stop, stop!* I hollered inside my head, hoping to calm the blaze bubbling inside.

"We gotta go. Now," Atlas urged and tugged me by the hand in the exit's direction.

"Athena?" Kale hollered and cut through the crowd. "I'll go with you..." Kalen trailed off. "Wait... what's happening to your eyes? "

I scrambled for a reason. My brain felt like mush. "Shit. Um... " I snapped my eyes closed. I couldn't lie to Kalen, so Anders did.

"She has allergies. It's the lighting in here," Anders said. His tone wavered, unconvincing, as his own blue eyes finally met Kalen's.

"It's not fucking allergies. Athena, look at me, please?" Kalen moved past Anders and brushed his hand across my cheek. My insides thundered, acknowledging the sensation of his touch. I couldn't refuse him. I opened my eyes, which I'd been squashing shut. Batting my lashes, they fluttered open at his request. The unnatural flickering continued.

Kalen tilted his head to the side, moving his face closer to mine. "See, I told you. The most marvelous green." Kalen smiled and tucked a stray hair behind my ear.

"What are you?" he asked. Any normal human with a sense of self-preservation would run in the opposite direction, but Kalen didn't budge. Our forming bond was suppressing the natural trepidation he should have felt.

I moved my eyes around his face, searching for the right answer. Instead, I noticed the dimples nestled near his mouth. "I...I'm," I struggled to reply. What kind of Alpha was I—tripping on words, making my wolf submit, bending to someone else's will. Kalen messed with my mind, my concentration. All my rationality told me to flee, to forget this entire situation. Even if I overlooked how my body reacted to Kalen, leaving him behind was no longer a valid option, but telling him the truth... far more dangerous. Humans weren't ready for us.

But *maybe* Kalen's different.

"You know what?" Kalen declared, breaking through my inner monologue. "I don't care. I'm coming with you." He touched my face, holding it with sensitive precision. The growing affection passed through his hands, leaving a permanent, invisible hold on me.

"Why? You don't even know me."

"I dunno. A feeling, I guess. You say I don't know you. I find that hard to believe. Every part of me tells me I do," he replied. My sanity screamed at me not to take him with me as Kalen pulled us farther out into deeper and more hazardous waters.

Throwing away whatever sensibility I possessed, I grabbed Kalen's hand, letting our fingers entwine together. His hand felt warm, like the soft glowing comfort of a crackling fireplace. I started leading us to the door, moving almost too fast. My impatience to get out of this crowded club and into the fresh air elevated by the second.

T...We can't. Atlas popped in my head. I already knew he wanted no part of this. I growled at his disapproval, and both brothers heaved a collective sigh. Anders and Atlas continued to lead the way, weaving through dancing bodies and veering around sticky tables.

Persistent, but they reminded me of another issue. *How do we get him through the Barrier?* Anders walked faster towards the exit. Anders rarely panicked, but his speedy pace and the tension bubbling off him was a dead giveaway.

I wanted to share Anders's fear. "I'll get him through the Barrier. I know I can." I had obviously never attempted what I proposed, and Anders's logic should've been enough to dissuade me. Instead, I tugged Kalen's hand.

"If this is about a passport ID for the border, I have one." Kalen chimed in. I looked at the man to my side, his ocean eyes gleaming at me.

Oh, sweet human. If only it was an ID you needed.

If this doesn't work, Thea, we'll all suffer. You know that. He's bonded to you. Anders hesitated, *And to us.*

His concern was dead on. If I failed—if I couldn't lift the Barrier around Kalen—it'd kill him.

I know, I said, swallowing my knotted nerves and a sourness that crept up my throat. *But it's a risk I have to take.*

CHAPTER 3

Callouses brushed my knuckles as I held on to Kalen's hand, squeezing it intermittently. The contact gave me a profound rush, fueling my preternatural senses. Pushing the door open with one fast shove, we exited Zephyr and looked toward my Jeep. The fresh air hit my face but did nothing to lessen the aroma that rolled off Kalen.

"I'll drive." Atlas put his palm out, signaling for the keys. I plucked the little black key fob from my pocket, tossing it in his open hand. He pressed the remote start, and, even at this distance, my ears detected the vehicle's engine roaring to life. Taking point, Anders and Atlas moved in front of Kalen and me.

Rhythmic music poured from the oversized doors as they continued to open and close, letting new people in. Noisy bodies lined the sidewalk, almost around the corner, all clamoring to make it past the velvet ropes. I didn't even see their faces blurring as I walked; I thought of nothing besides getting Kalen out of here. I wasn't sure what was going on within Zephyr, but my gut told me it wasn't good.

Various colognes laced the air, mixing with human pheromones, vapes... and something unpleasant and dark I couldn't quite put my finger on. Something ominous hid in the shadows here, but where? I'd let myself become so distracted and unfocused by Kalen, forgetting my true purpose. I looked down for a moment. The wall of a bouncer we'd met at the door stepped in my path, putting his square hand on my shoulder too hard for my liking. A normal woman would have bowed under the force of his hand.

I was anything but normal.

A subtle growl came from my chest. It was a warning.

"You can't take him." His tone was gruff as he touched his wired earpiece, buzzing with someone's voice.

Kalen tried to interfere, dropping my hand, and jabbing his finger in the bouncer's face. "Hey, man. Get your fucking hand off her. What do you think you're doing?"

I touched Kalen's arm, my fingers buzzing, "I've got this, Kalen." A placid smirk churned on my lips. The bouncer's massive size and shifter background was not enough defense against me. I glanced down at the hand on my shoulder, grinning at the burly man, then flashed my eyes up at the wide bearded face. Anders and Atlas were ahead of us, chuckling, knowing this wolf was in way over his head.

"Either you remove your hand and get out of my way, or I'll do it for you." I eyed him, raising my brows, issuing the ultimatum. I curled my lip up, baring my teeth. I clung to whatever fragile strand of patience I had left from my encounter with Jenny.

He furrowed his thick brows, leaning down to whisper in my ear, "And I'm telling you, you can't take that human from here."

I cracked my neck, giving over to my feral side. "Option two it is, then." I nudged Kalen farther away with my hip, not wanting him hurt. In a fluid upwards motion, my hand was on the husky bouncer's throat, and I yanked his large hand from my shoulder, squeezing it between my fingers until I heard cracking. The man winced. His eyes watered, and his knees buckled in pain. I snarled in a very unladylike manner, letting my wolf venture out, gripping his thick gullet harder. I should kill him for his disobedience, but there were too many witnesses.

"I could snap your neck without even trying." He needed to know who was in charge here. My wolf growled again, and I let my claws sink into his skin. The male turned an unpleasant shade of violet. His eyes bulged, and his head fell into a bow before me. From the corner of my eye, I saw Kalen jump away from me. His hand clamped over his mouth, then he jerked again, his fists clenching at his sides. *Fear.* I smelled it ebbing off Kalen. He was afraid of me. Good, he ought to be. Underneath my docile human skin dwelled a savage wolf and, beyond her, an untamed inferno I could release whenever I pleased.

Atlas grabbed my arm, still clamping on the bouncer's throat. "Uh, Thea. We're gaining an audience. Finish him, and let's go." Atlas extended no pity to this strange wolf, and his dismissive remark to finish him suggested he agreed with removing the bouncer's esophagus.

Settled then.

"Thea, you've made your point," Anders urged. "Don't listen to Atlas. Come on, let him up."

Fine.

I released the bouncer, dropping his heavy body to the asphalt. He gasped for breath and stumbled to his feet, clutching his shattered hand. "You can't do this. I'm notifying," he threatened, voice hoarse, clutching his neck and attempting to retreat. With preternatural speed, I caught up to the bouncer, pushing him to the ground with ease and putting my foot on his back.

"Next time, you cross me; you won't be so lucky," I said and pushed the dark-suited wolf down harder. My foot pinned him to the ground like an anchor.

Wipe his memory, I linked Anders.

Anders sped to me and picked up the doorman, putting his palm to the faltering male's forehead. A goofy smile spread across the bouncer's previously sullen face. He got up, dusted himself off, and walked away, taking his place near the door. His hand and arm would heal, and he'd remember none of this. The onlookers went back to their phones, most of them wrapped back up in social media.

Kalen, however...

His heartbeat hammered in my ears.

"What the fuck just happened? What are you?" Kalen's voice shook, and the alarm he should've felt right away overtook him. He paced in front of me, looking from his feet to me, throwing his hands in the air. Maybe now he'd see me for the dangerous creature I was.

Run, human, run.

I knitted my brows, watching him, knowing I caused his fright. Atlas and Anders pushed into my head. Both of them insisting we needed to go, especially since I'd assaulted a man double my size in public.

Kalen feared me. *Good.* He needed to. He needed to understand I'm not of his world. Yet, the idea of him never seeing him again churned my insides. My need to be near him buried the dislike I wanted to feel for him. Instead of encouraging him to leave, I moved closer to him and reached out my palm. *Goddess be damned.*

"I'll explain everything. Anything you want to know, but we have to go now." Why? Why did I still try to convince Kalen to come with me? I knew better, and my mouth did it, anyway. I glanced down at my feet, wishing they'd move away. Goddess, I was an internal mess. The tug of war continuing in my head gave me a migraine and fractured my reserve.

"She's right, *tick-tock* lover boy." Atlas's tone bordered on rude, and his unamused face did the rest. He cocked his eyebrow and tightened his lips while glaring at Kalen.

Kalen stared at me, conflicted. His pupils dilated. "I don't think I can do this, whatever the fuck this is." He pointed to the three of us. His heart was a flurry of palpitations, reminding me of hummingbird wings.

I felt like a knife burrowed in my chest, but I'd let him go. I swallowed hard. This was for the best. Nothing about us was compatible; we weren't even the same species, and *yet...*

"I understand," was all I managed without my voice cracking. *No. I won't cry. Tears solved nothing, and Kalen made the right choice.* He had no business coming with me—a human and a wolf. I needed to let him go, live his life, and I'd figure out the rest.

Anders walked over to me, grasping my shoulders with his hands. "Come on, Thea," he whispered, leaning his head down to mine. I wanted to tell Anders I wanted Kalen gone, to never look back, but he'd know I was lying. This stung my brothers, too, though they hid it well. Neither of them wanted to make Kalen's absence any harder on me.

Anders turned me towards the concrete structure, and the same musty smell invaded my nose. Our footsteps echoed through the garage. I darted my eyes, making sure we were alone and taking in how many cars remained parked. Atlas was already inside the car, hands on the steering wheel. I reached for the door, but Anders leaned forward, opening it for me.

"Athena!" I heard Kalen calling, his feet hitting the pavement. "*Ah*, damn it. Wait..."

Hand on the car door, I stilled. Kalen sprinted, his shoes scratching the grit as he skidded to a stop in front of me. He put his hands on his waist and breathed heavily, chest heaving up and down under his shirt. Anders stared for a second, let out a snort, then walked to the passenger side and got in the car with Atlas.

I turned to face the man I'd been ready to abandon. His blue human eyes strained in the useless, low lighting. He reached in his pocket, pulling out a pair of glasses. The squinting made sense. Glasses. This human didn't even possess decent vision. I hated to acknowledge it, but the glasses made him look even better. The way the dark frames sat on the bridge of his nose. Only a human could pull off making an imperfection attractive.

I shook off the stupor he was lulling me into. Annoyance pricked my skin. Why wasn't I strong enough to push him away?

"What do you want?" I asked.

"To go with you." Kalen shook his head. The certainty of his words didn't reach his eyes. "This is a terrible idea, but something tells me you're worth it."

Again, I went against my common sense. "Are you sure? Don't you have a family or something to go home to?"

"Yes. No. I don't even know. What are you doing to me?" A strand of hair fell in front of his glasses. I blew out a breath. At least he had no one waiting for him at home.

Kalen took my face in his hands. "Kiss me again?" he asked, his voice velvet soft and lyrical, but his earlier hesitation lingered around the edges of his question and in the slight trembling of his hands.

My body responded to his request, and I inched up, finding his lips. Feeling all his warmth and heat, my stomach flipped and twisted as my body hummed. His mouth parted, taking my bottom lip between his. I shuddered. I could feel Kalen's indecision wavering, losing its hold the longer we kissed. His lips planted a fierce longing deep in my belly, rousing the beasts lurking beneath my skin. He brought them to the surface, calling them without a word. I pulled on all the command I could muster to keep them trapped within me, refusing to set them free. As our lips brushed together again, I gave into acceptance—I'd fallen into our bond right along with him. There was no escape. The knotting connection devoured us.

He pulled away, eyes still closed. "*This.* This is why I'm coming with you. It's like witchcraft." He grinned wide as his hands moved from my face to hold my hand again.

I cast my eyes down, heart racing. "You have no idea."

And he didn't. A pang of guilt stabbed my neck. He truly didn't have a clue what he was getting into, and I'd let him come along, leading him straight to the wolf's den...

Releasing Kalen, I pulled the door open farther, offering the seat to him. Kalen's eyes met mine as he climbed in, and he smiled widely. "I've never had a woman open the door for me, thank you," he said, shaking his head, grin in place. My skin prickled, and I sensed him drifting deeper into the connection. He wasn't even trying to fight it. For a human, he had a poor sense of self-preservation.

I offered a tight-lipped smile. "Well, I can guarantee you've never met a *woman* like me."

"Athena." Kalen's voice triggered a faint blush to rise up my cheeks. "The moment I saw you, I already knew I'd met *no one* like you before." I shivered. I knew damn well he had no clue how accurate his comment was.

I shut the heavy black door, cursing myself all the way to the other side of the Jeep. Kalen was turning me into a puddle of emotions, and the reasonable side of me wanted to hate him for it. I touched my grinning cheeks.

Irrationality won.

I slid into the SUV.

A loud guffaw interrupted the moment. "*Oh,* Goddess. If I have to endure this the entire two hours, I may be sick," Anders said, dragging a hand down his face.

I rumbled a growl in response, snarling my lip up.

"Okay, okay. Relax." Anders shook his head and furrowed

his brow. Brooding wasn't his best attribute. Atlas was always the better pouter.

Kalen tilted his head, angling his torso to face me. "Why do you growl? Don't get me wrong, I find it kind of hot... and a little scary." Kalen was staring at me, curious and wary. I could feel him analyzing me, his eyes moving up and down my face. He was trying to figure me out—or, more accurately, was trying to figure out what I was.

"Do you really wanna know?" I asked him, raising my eyebrows. My desire to test his fascination coursed through me. *What would he think?*

Thea... Atlas warned.

Not bothering to open my mouth to speak, I replied, *Yes, Atlas. Something you'd like to say?*

You're not going to tell him the truth, are you? Atlas replied, his eyes never leaving the street.

I say, tell him. If he thinks we're lunatics, oh well. We'll knock him out and figure it out later. Anders didn't bother to look up from his phone while he shrugged his shoulders a bit. His motions matching his nonchalant tone. He was pretending to be indifferent, but I knew better.

No one will hit him.

Come on, Thea, that was a joke... mostly. Anders smirked this time, covering his mouth and turning his head to look out the window.

Kalen interrupted our unspoken conversation. "Athena, are you okay? I asked you a question, and you just phased out. You're obviously not telling me something. After the scene at Zephyr, I know you're different. I took a chance coming with you. I deserve an explanation." Kalen cocked his eyebrow and embraced my hand tighter, thumbing my knuckles. His touch clouded my thoughts, and I struggled to find the right words.

I straightened my back and turned to face Kalen more

directly. "I'm sorry. I was looking for how to say it. Since I can't think of a good way, I'm just gonna tell you."

I took a deep breath, attempting to continue on. I'd never been this nervous in my entire life. *Never.* My leg bounced up and down, my body searching for a way to release the pent-up energy. It was a foreign feeling for me, an uncomfortable and unwanted reaction. Is this what it was to have a mate? To feel this kind of nervousness and fear? I hated it. I hated this help-lessness. If he rejected me... it would tear me apart.

My brothers felt me coming unhinged, picking up on my racing heart and short, quick breaths.

Thea. Stop overthinking. If he's really the one, he'll accept what and who we are, Anders said.

Definitely. If he's meant to be with you and our family, he's gotta know sometime. Now is as good a time as any to tell him that the big bad wolf is real. Atlas, while making a joke, made a valid point.

I know I don't say it often, but..... I looked between my brothers in the front seats, both their heads watching the cars go by through the windshield. The sources of much irritation, but more often support. *Thank you both.*

Don't go gettin' soft on us now. Atlas's famous half-smirk pulled up the corner of his mouth.

Shaking my head, I adjusted again in the seat, putting my hands in my lap, and looking at Kalen sitting across from me. *One more deep breath and...*

"I'm a shifter, Kalen."

Kalen's eyes widened, then narrowed, "You're a what?"

"A wolf..." I told him. "More than a wolf. I'm what supernat-urals call an Alpha." I kept eye contact as I spoke. It was best to tell him as much of the truth as I could.

"Wait, like a werewolf?" His eyes nearly bulged. "Come on..." He dragged his hands through his hair, letting them rest on the back of his neck.

"Not exactly. It's more like a separate entity living inside me.

I growl because sometimes my wolf needs to be heard, and that's how she communicates. She'll never hurt you. *I'll* never hurt you."

Kalen blew out an unsteady breath, shaking his head and pressing it to the headrest. I saw the indecision pouring over his face like sweat. "Is that why I'm drawn to you?"

I took his hand in mine, feeling his skin growing clammy. "Kind of. You feel you know me because you're what we call... my mate. Means we're meant for each other. Kind of like fate." I loosened my grip on his hand, releasing him. Time slowed as I waited for him to pull away from me in terror and demand we let him out of the car. I glanced out the window, bracing my heart for rejection I knew had to come. It was like walking a tightrope with no net, and his words could send me careening to the ground.

Atlas and Anders were silent. Kalen was silent. There was nothing, just the radio. 'The Less I Know, The Better' by Tame Impala thrumming along seemed appropriate. No human wanted to know this, especially in close quarters with no simple escape. I bowed my head down for the first time in my life, waiting for what I knew was coming. He'd think I was utterly crazy and run away. I didn't blame him, and a small part of me wanted him to go to release us from this unknown. Anders readied himself to wipe Kalen's memory, turning around to observe Kalen.

Kalen raised his brows and pushed himself up on the seat, putting a limited distance between us. "*Huh*, fate? Like we're destined to be together..."

"Yes."

He adjusted his glasses, then rubbed his hand over his mouth, looking out the tinted window and then down at his hands.

"And this wolf, that's how you took down that bouncer?"

"Yes."

"*Hm...*" was all he said, his body going stiff against the seat and his eyes opening and closing.

Nausea took over, making my mouth water. Minutes ticked by in slow motion. I'd never told a human what we were, never needed to, and this waiting killed me. What killed me more is that I cared...that part of me wanted to know his response. He said nothing for what felt like an eternity. I stared out the window, watching the surroundings blur by. Anders would make Kalen forget—forget this entire ordeal.

But then, I felt warmth. Kalen's finger slipped beneath my chin and drew my eyes back up to his. "Show me."

A smile twitched at the corners of my mouth, and my eyes flared to life, shining green like they had at Zephyr. I let my wolf venture forward, her power rippling beneath the thin barrier of flesh covering my bones.

"What I'm feeling for you right now seems unreal." He pulled my body towards him. I curved into his embrace. It felt like nothing I'd ever experienced before. Anxiety dispersed from my mind. Kalen was like home, but more. "Why shouldn't you be magical?" He kissed my forehead. The fireworks I felt were unbelievable. Magic was an appropriate word. He was right.

This was damn magical.

My brothers let out the breaths they had been holding. The acceptance washed over them, too. They felt relief sink in, as much as I did—almost content. For the first time, they remained quiet. Soon I could sense Atlas and Anders doing their best to tune out, disconnecting from my mind and emotions. It was a tiny veil of privacy. I used my slight freedom and leaned up, catching Kalen's lips in mine for a quick kiss.

Kalen matched my enthusiasm, not missing a beat. I pulled away, breathless yet again. "Give me a moment. I need to think, and I can't while your mouth is near me." I huffed in a tizzy. Glancing out the window, I watched the city whip by.

"Sorry. I don't normally behave this way." Kalen's eyes clouded with longing as he apologized, and his cheeks flushed when he remembered we were far from alone. I felt my brothers' antagonizing amusement, both smirking nearby.

"Don't apologize. I'm as new to these emotions as you are. But I need to figure out a way to get you through the Barrier," I replied, shaking my head, trying to smother the craving that was building between us.

"The Barrier? What's that?" Kalen asked, looking at the three of us.

It was Atlas who answered. "It's a spell enforced veil with entrances throughout the world, concealing our realm from the prying eyes of the humans. Barriers to The Unseen exist wherever they need to for supernaturals to come and go as we please—hidden and guarded against humans, for your protection."

Atlas looked up into the rearview, catching eyes with Kalen, and continued explaining, "We can't have you wandering into the Unseen and creating panic because you saw a vampire or Faerie flying about. Humans are a little sensitive that way."

"Right. I understand. At least, I think I do. And what happens if I can't pass the Barrier? " Kalen continued with his questions; his calmness was eerie and very inhuman.

"That's the thing, if I don't get this right—it'll kill you. Your body is unable to withstand the impact." My heart ached again, thinking of a world without Kalen. Having just found him, the thought of losing him seemed unbearable.

"That won't happen. Thea's excellent with spells," Anders said, giving a brisk nod.

"Thanks," I said, forcing a smile, and I sat back against the seat, hoping I'd absorb some extra confidence from him.

"Kill me. Great. This keeps gettin' better." Kalen rubbed his hands on his thighs, digging into the denim. "Spells? So, tell me. What's waiting for me beyond this Barrier?" Kalen asked, looking at each one of us.

I explained the prophecy—the Triad. I told him how Anders, Atlas, and I were born during the Winter Solstice twenty-four years ago under a full blue moon. He listened intently as I described my affinity for magic and fire and how we kept the balance between both worlds.

Kalen continued to ask many questions, never balking much from the answers. I told him of our abilities and of all the creatures that existed in the Unseen. I enlightened him on just how often we protected humankind and of our one true law. Like an eager student, he kept his eyes on me, listening intently to each word I disclosed to him. Curiosity and what looked like wonder played in the blues of his irises as he probed further into our lives and world.

Every now and again, he would look at me with the caution reserved for a predator but then reach for my hand as if to soothe himself. The contact gave us both jolts to the stomach, like riding an adrenaline high. I heaved a breath each time. It was only a matter of time before this unnerving ball of sensations got me into trouble.

It was time. The Barrier was a mile away. I'd gone over a variety of spell combinations—invisibility, transfiguration, sleeping—but couldn't pinpoint one that would leave a lasting effect or fool the Barrier. Magic was, to the point, limited in lasting effects. I used enchantments, but only on objects. Kalen wasn't an object, and I did not know if I could enchant a human. That kind of magic was wielded by elves and fae.

I'd decided blood and scent were the keys. I'd concluded maybe I could fool the Barrier. I'd give Kalen a touch of my blood and scent, and it might be enough. If I was wrong, we'd all pay the price.

"Do it," Kalen said firmly, bracing his back against the leather seat.

My eyes shifted. "This is going to hurt, but the pain will pass. I promise. Just hold as still as you can."

I let my canines venture down, sinking into my palm. Blood flowed, pooling in my hand. I'd heal soon—I had to move fast. I glanced at Kalen one last time. He faced forward, and I observed his profile. A slim, perky nose and a jaw that looked handcrafted and chiseled to perfection from the finest of marbles. *Goddess, help me.*

"I trust you. Just do it." His breath came faster, and he worried a woven bracelet on his wrist between his fingers. He extended his hand to me, and I bent my head to his palm. I nipped at Kalen's skin with more precision than I had my own. He hissed, his blood trickling down. I grasped his bleeding hand in my own, pressing them together. Our blood mixed, connecting us.

Now for the scent. The only plausible way I could think of to share my scent was to *mark* Kalen. For my kind, marking another was an act of passion and heated emotions—nothing like the current predicament. Between the presence of my brothers and our time constraint, marking Kalen was going to be a survival tool, nothing more.

My stomach churned with a nauseating mixture of butter-flies and knots, both battering my stomach. Between wolves, marking a mate would bring amplified pleasure for both of us, but Kalen was human. To mark him would be an unprece-dented feat and the idea of probable pleasure diminished, sinking into a vast ocean of the many ways this ritual could go wrong. Kalen was likely to experience immeasurable pain, but pain was more favorable than death.

"I'm ready," he said, turning his head, tilting his chin up, and baring his neck to me.

I felt flushed. *Not now. Not now. Focus.* I pushed him back on the seat. My breath hit his neck, and he moaned ever so softly, the noise beckoning me to have him in ways unsuitable for an audience. *Shit.* This was awkward with my brothers so close. I couldn't think about them right now. We needed this to work. I let out a warm breath on his neck to warn him. Kalen trembled, his skin prickling with goosebumps. I found something stirring in me beyond fear and anxiety, an awakening I didn't want to acknowledge.

With my canines down far enough, I opened my mouth, placing my teeth on the base of his neck, right above his shoulder. Kalen gripped my waist, digging his fingers into me. That did it. I bit down. He gasped, and I released him, trying to shake off and fight the euphoria threatening to overtake my body, causing us both to quake. I moved off Kalen in a swift motion, unnerved by the ease of marking him. I'd done it, and hoped it was enough. It all felt too simple and far too good.

"Quarter of a mile, T," Atlas announced, straining on the steering wheel.

This was it. It had to work. Here came the Barrier. I put my arm in front of Kalen, ready to pounce on anything that dared hurt him.

Nothing happened.

We went through. The car drove along, passing into a familiar landscape. A lush forest with the greenest of pine trees so tall they ventured up the sky as if to kiss the stars. Our atmosphere was brighter in the Unseen. Twinkling stars scattered across the blue-black skies. The full and brilliant moon cast enough light to illuminate our faces in the night.

My wolf was ecstatic, running around in my head.

"Holy shit. It worked!" Atlas took one hand and slapped the steering wheel.

"You did it!" Anders hooted. Fists pumping in the air at my triumph.

I hugged Kalen close to me, squeezing his warmth to my chest. "Athena... you're squeezing me...t—too hard..." Kalen gasped for air.

"Oh, Goddess, I'm so sorry." I released him, pushing my body away from him and chastising myself. I can't be this careless, not with him. How could this ever work? I could accidentally kill him at any point out of excitement or relief. I bit my cheek, and a metallic tinge hit my tongue as my blood trickled in my mouth. This body, my greatest weapon, used against me.

A familiar pain sent a wave through me. *Hurting him.*

Don't be so hard on yourself, Thea. This is new. Atlas skipped the opportunity to mock me and sought to comfort me instead.

"What, what is it?" Kalen asked me, his face full of concern. "I hate that they always seem to know what you're thinking, and I'm left grasping at straws. Just tell me. You can't scare me away anymore."

I leaned my head back against the seat, blowing a breath out. "I'm afraid of hurting you. I'm stronger than you, and I'm not used to your... humanness. My strength has always been my power, but with you..." I said, pausing, giving Kalen time to understand how different we were. "It's a weakness. I'm not used to feeling out of control. And Kalen, if I'm not careful, it will be this power that harms you." It all flooded out too quickly. Again, I felt exposed, an emotion I'd not experienced until tonight. I didn't care for this sensation either. These feelings were far outside my comfort, and yet I kept seeking to address Kalen's feelings, rather than my own.

"You can't hurt me. Not really, Athena. I know I don't understand what's happening, but do you think for a second if I felt that you'd willingly harm me, I'd have left with you or let you mark me or whatever?" I opened my mouth to answer but closed it again as when he went on. "I don't know what you're capable of, but hurting me, isn't it." He sighed hard, rubbing his temple, and his glasses moved on his cheekbone. I didn't understand how he could be this certain of me.

Anders chuckled. "Kalen, man, if you're exhausted now, just wait. You haven't met our family yet, and boy—are you going to be a fucking surprise!" he said, turning around and clapping his hands together. It never ceased to amaze me how my brothers managed to be amused at the most inappropriate of times. The animal inside rumbled.

Atlas could barely contain his glee. "Ha. Athena may lord over us, but you seem to have quieted her, even if it only lasts a minute. That's something even our father can't do. This is gonna be epic."

Looking up and into the rearview mirror, Atlas eyed Kalen. "All kidding aside, Thea may be your mate, but we're connected to her. You're like a new brother, and we'd like to welcome you to our family." For once, he shelved his picking. Kalen meant something to him. Not like he did to me, but they'd protect him as they did me. I didn't always see eye to eye with my brothers, but when it mattered, they never let me down.

Kalen's laughter shook me from my thoughts. "I hadn't given any of this much thought... Hopefully, your parents like me," he stated.

Smiling, I patted his hand. "No time for backing out now. We're here." A slow grin crept over my lips; nerves buried beneath the excitement. If I was to present him to my family, I'd need to be fearless.

One thing rolled around my head, plaguing my mind: the odor outside Zephyr, it smelled of darkness and sulfur, the unmistakable scent of decay. Death lurked somewhere near that club, and I needed to go back there to find it.

CHAPTER 4

We turned down our partially paved driveway, lined with tall sycamore and evergreens that enclosed our estate in picturesque beauty. The car rolled to a stop as we parked in the driveway, car doors swinging open simultaneously. It wouldn't take long for our guards and neighboring Pack members to realize a human was here. My scent covered Kalen, but not enough to mask his humanity.

Sprinting around to the backside of the car to meet us, Atlas playfully shoved Kalen's arm. "Welcome to Whiteridge Manor! *Mi casa es tu casa*, brother!"

Kalen absorbed the shove and took a long view at our sizable log home. "So, you guys are, like, rich then?"

Having grown up in the house, I regarded its grandeur as rather unextraordinary. But seeing Kale's face, I realized it must be impressive to an onlooker who hadn't spent their entire life here. The stones and heavy cedar beams with grand bay windows overlooked a huge blue-green lake with towering pines in the background set against an always expertly lit scene.

The more I gazed at our home, brushed by a starry night sky, it looked as though we plucked from a cinematic masterpiece or one of those calendars humans purchased with pretty photographs of places they'd never been.

Kalen's eyes stayed on the house, his mouth gaping in astonishment, and I let him take in the architecture a moment longer. I stifled a laugh as I pondered his question. Nobody had ever asked me that before.

"By human standards, yeah, I suppose so. Our parents run a lucrative investment firm. Titles afford us extra comfort, so to speak."

"Titles?" Kalen's eyebrows shot up. "Question answered."

"*Ha*, bro! Thea's a princess around these parts. As for me, I'm a prince, but you can just call me 'Your Highness.'" Atlas indulged with a loud laugh. Anders shook his head, joining in on the chortling.

Kalen shrugged out a laugh, mustering as much humor as he could on short notice. "A Princess? Of fucking course you are. Why wouldn't you be?"

I eyed Kalen, tilting my head to the side. Despite his chuckle, he curled his hands into fists deep in his pockets and turned to face the car.

"You're not angry about that, are you? The Princess thing is a formality, really." My 'Princess' status didn't make me entitled. If I couldn't earn my place, I didn't want it.

Continuing to fidget, Kalen grinned, striving to recover from his perceived slip-up. "Not angry, Thea. Intimidated, maybe. You're like a faerie tale. Something straight out of Narnia or Once Upon a Time. What can I possibly offer you?" Kalen took his hands from his pockets and tossed them in the air, and walked away from the house, his head staring up at the glistening stars.

"What can you offer me?" I let loose a chuckle. "You. You offered me you, with little hesitation, without knowing what or who I am. That's more than enough." Kalen stood in front of me, bearing his vulnerability, and suddenly I admired his unpredictable gamble on me. He wasn't afraid to show me what he was feeling, making him, unlike any other human I'd met. Bond or not, Kalen should've concerned himself with my ability to tear him apart, but no part of him feared me anymore. *Strange.*

That crooked grin I'd knew took its place back on Kalen's reddened lips. Walking back to me, past the car, he bit his lower lip and smiled again. He gathered me into his arms. "I got *you.* I'm the lucky one here, Princess." He winked, picking me up. My feet dangled, and without thinking, I placed a small kiss on the corner of his grin. My determination to keep away from Kalen was rapidly dissolving. The chemistry between us was undeniable, much as I had wanted it not to be.

I leaned my head onto him, letting myself sink into his embrace, but our bliss was short-lived. Light footsteps and the scent of fresh linens moved around. *Oh, Calliope.* She apprehended us. "What is this?" She bellowed.

Startled, Kalen set me down gently, removing his hands from my torso.

"Children! What have you done?" Her voice brimmed with concern rather than anger. It didn't matter how much we aged; the term 'children' stuck. We'd probably be a hundred and still called "children." The word normally aggravated me, but they meant it as a term of endearment.

"Relax, Calliope. He's one of us," Anders said, sidling up to Calliope with an innocent smile and trying to charm our way out of this.

She put a hand to her chest and turned her mouth down in disgust. "He most certainly is not. He's human," Calliope informed, sniffing in Kalen's direction. Her face wrinkled up like she'd gotten a whiff of something rancid.

"Cal, we're well aware of what he is, but, come on, stop and think..." Atlas attempted to continue an explanation, flashing his mischievous grin. Both of my brothers had become accustomed to their natural charisma getting them off the hook, but not this time. We were going to face our parents, the King and Queen, and no toothy grin was going to stop that.

I huffed, deciding to take charge and move this along. No use fussing around with the inevitable, but I needed to say something to establish Kalen's presence here. "Calliope. I respect you as our caretaker, and I value your input. However, this is my mate, and you'll address him as such. I don't care if he's human." My wolf yipped in my head as I spoke, pleased I'd used my Alpha voice. High praise rarely came from that she-wolf of mine, but I hadn't meant to speak to Calliope in such a tone—it had slipped out of my mouth. Kalen's presence provoked a protective response, and my feral side demanded I acknowledge it.

Calliope bowed her head as she addressed me. "Of course, Athena. I meant no disrespect. You know that, dearest."

I frowned. I didn't enjoy using my Alpha nature on her.

Kalen took a gentlemanly approach and grasped Calliope's hand, shaking up and down it a little too fast. He wanted to impress her; I could feel it. His eagerness and interest in my people comforted me, and I let a small smile spread across my lips.

"It's a pleasure to meet you, Calliope. Kalen Ryan." Kalen's hulking frame dwarfed Calliope's. Though small, Calliope held her own.

Calliope tilted her head, taking in Kalen's honest face, and gave him a warm smile. She placed her other hand on his, giving him a gentle squeeze. How had he won over Calliope so quickly? Maybe I wasn't the only one with a magic touch.

"Now then, it's an utter delight to meet you as well, Kalen. I apologize for appearing rude. It's just, well, we aren't used to having humans around. Let's make our way to the King and Queen, shall we? I expect they have an idea about you already." Her voice trailed as she headed for the house, opening the grand sandstone-colored door into the foyer. Calliope had one pace: brisk.

"Here we go." Atlas's eyes rolled.

Lifting my head high and holding Kalen's hand in mine, we walked in. Our footsteps made soft sounds against the swirled marble flooring. I looked to the balcony above our two enormous staircases, taking center stage in our open vestibule. A high textured ceiling with a single quartz chandelier illuminated the great room. The warm lighting made our skin look golden, matching us to the opulent aesthetic of the manor. Tables with ornate crystal vases filled with various floral arrangements sat in each corner. Our manor was home to many varieties of flora picked from our greenhouses and gardens.

I watched as Kalen took in every bit of the room. His mouth opening, then closing and his eyes moving over each statue and pillar, taking in his surroundings.

Voices carried from above as my parents raced towards the balcony. Glancing up again, saw them atop the stairs, observing us from above. Mother gazed down over the staircase railing; her face placid with hints of a smile at the corners of her mouth. She already knew. She always knew.

My father was less amused. His hands gripped the hand-crafted wrought metal banister. I knew he was holding onto the railing to keep himself from launching down the stairs and tearing into our hides. I'd deliberately disobeyed him, and I didn't regret it.

"What is the meaning of this?" Cyrus roared. He was red-faced, eyes bloodshot with fury.

Not wanting to escalate the situation, I remained calm. "Good evening, Father. This is Kalen Ryan," I started, moving my hand to Kalen, who took a place at my side.

Cyrus continued, his booming tone loud with wrath. "'Good evening,' Athena? I don't think so. First, you leave without a guard, then you bring home... a human. How was it even possible?"

"Father, it was unavoidable." I pursed my lips in agitation.

"Unavoidable? Somehow, I highly doubt that. You've always been headstrong, Athena, and we've allowed it because you will be the Alpha, but this—"

My mother put up her hand. "Cyrus, enough." Tact and intuition were *her* finer traits—not my father's. Cyrus ruled with brains and sheer will. The other leaders feared him, feared the King who'd fulfilled a prophecy and brought forth the Triad. "Look at them. Can't you see what's happened here?" She always sensed things, smelled them faster. It was in her nature to know what we were up to, even as children.

Cyrus lifted his nose to the air, and his eyes went wide. "But it cannot be. This is impossible. We don't have human mates."

"Impossible? Really? To an entire world, *we're* impossible, and this union seems outlandish?" She scoffed, then mocked his lower tone. "Wolves don't take human mates." Her brown eyes shimmered as she stared down her nose at my father. "That's an archaic belief for even you, Cyrus. Athena, Anders, and Atlas prove to us every day nothing is impossible." Illiana paused, letting her words sink in for her husband. A less than subtle "*tsk*" left her lips.

Kalen used this opportunity to speak for himself. A room full of wolves, and he didn't flinch. "Excuse me? If I may, sir. From my small understanding, I know I'm not supposed to be here. *Hell*, I really know why I'm here. This is—honestly, I think —well, I know I feel something for your daughter. I'm not sure what it is or it happened so fast, but tonight, has been some-thing out of the books I read as a kid, but ...Athena is real. She's as real as the heart that beats in my chest. So—"

I cut Kalen off, though his words made me feel ten feet tall.

"He's more than right. I went past the Barrier tonight for observation, to safeguard us. I met Kalen. I know he's human, and it's unknown and unpredictable. But... I've felt more scared and alive in these few hours than I ever have. I'll give my life to defend him if that's what you require." I meant every word as it flowed from my heart out of my mouth.

Kalen's head jerked back to look at me as his mouth went slack. "No."

"What do you mean?" I asked, "Do you not want to stay?" My stomach flipped and twisted as I searched his face.

"First, you might need to work on not interrupting, Athena." Kalen appeared to be glowering at me as he spoke. "Second, as perceptive as you are, you've missed the point." I side-stepped, letting my tongue drag on my teeth before I closed my mouth. Kalen hadn't hesitated to correct me.

Odd. Mate or not, most humans avoided altercation. Kalen invited it. I could hear Atlas and Anders snickering in the background. I shifted my head to growl in their direction. The snickering stopped.

"No, Athena. I don't want to leave. And no—you don't get to go giving your life for me in any capacity. I don't exactly know what this wolf of yours is, and I don't fully know what's going on. For all I know, this is a dream." Kalen lifted both his brows and straightened his back. I wasn't sure who he was trying to convince more, himself or me. I swallowed the heat pooling in my mouth, letting it take refuge in my stomach.

My parents and brothers watched this exchange with fascination. It wasn't every day I was told "no," and more than once.

"I didn't realize it came off that way. I'd never expected you to hide. You got a preview with the bouncer. Don't worry, you'll meet my wolf—sooner than I'd like, I'm sure." I covered my mouth, realizing we hadn't discussed my other being. Best to do that now. Just throw another curve ball at him while we were on a roll. "While we're on the subject of my wolf... Remember how I told you I'm different from the others?" I confessed to him as if he were the only person in the room, visions of my family fading away in the background. The nervousness returned, flooding me.

Say it. Just say it.

"Yeah, the Triad," he responded. "You shift into wolves and have abilities."

"I can transform into more than a wolf. Another entity shares our space—a dragon." I examined his pools of blue under his furrowing brow, awaiting his response.

"A dragon? *Wow*...okay. I see," Kalen said, hesitating. "And what does *she* think of me?" He rocked back on his heels, away from me. This time, the fear I sensed from him was different.

I sniffed out a breath, almost letting out a chuckle. It worried Kalen my dragon might not approve—that *we* might reject *him*. Kalen didn't fear my beasts. He feared not being worthy of us.

My heart fluttered again. "Kalen... you needn't worry about that. We—I...care about you." And as I held his hands in mine, gazing into his ever-changing cobalt eyes, I realized I meant it.

"There's nothing more we need to discuss tonight. We must all rest," my mother said. She kept a warm smile on her face as she beamed down at Kalen and me. The creases by her eyes from joy reached her deep brown irises, and I knew she understood.

"Goodnight. Kalen, pleasure to meet you. But, not a word of this leaves this room. I don't want anyone knowing about Kalen yet. And, Athena, I'd like to speak to you in private sometime soon," my father said. His tone was far less menacing than before, but a warning lurked beneath his words. He waved his hand and nodded in our direction, a faint grin at the corner of his mouth. My mother smiled again, blowing a kiss towards Kalen and me. They turned, arm in arm, conversing with each other as they headed down the corridor back to their bedroom. Something was up, and a pinch in my chest gave me an ominous shiver. Why did he want me to keep Kalen's presence a secret?

As usual, Atlas dragged me from my thoughts. "Thank the Goddess. I was about to fall asleep here." He added a theatrical yawn and stretched.

"Yes, big bad wolfy sister has kept us up past our bedtime." Anders winked at me as he added another too-big-to-be-real yawn. I smirked and shook my head.

Don't stay up too late, T. And don't break him! Atlas's laugh echoed in our link.

Yeah, try not to ruin him the first night. I kinda like this one. Anders joined Atlas in his taunting.

I didn't have it in me to grumble at them because, in all honesty, I didn't know what to do now. I'd never let another man—wolf or otherwise—in my room, let alone in my bed. All of my previous dalliances were short-lived, and I'd had no intention or desire to bring them home.

Relationships involving prolonged effort or anything beyond physicality weren't important. Until tonight, most males were an unwanted distraction, like pests I was all too happy to avoid. Here was Kalen, mouthwatering and right in front of me. What was I to do with him, or rather *what couldn't I do?* My face and chest flushed as if Kalen could hear my inner musings.

My brothers continued to laugh down the corridors off to their rooms, knowing it bothered, and in more ways than one. *Assholes,* I thought, and more laughter plagued my mind. Soon, there was silence, both of them tuning me out...

They left Kalen and me alone together for the very first time tonight. I couldn't help but believe it was no coincidence.

CHAPTER 5

"Off to bed, is it?" Kalen grabbed for my hand, gently tugging it. "Funny thing... I'm not the least bit tired." A full-on grin spread across his face. "I guess you're taking me to your room?" he said, looking down at the glossy marble floor. He stroked his thumb across my knuckles, waiting for me to respond.

I wasn't sure what to say. I didn't know how to do this—be alone with him. But I knew I wanted him alone, more than I cared to admit. The Goddess must have an odd sense of humor to put this man in my path, and I wondered if she'd done so to humble me because Kalen was doing just that—correcting me in front of my parents, telling me no. He pushed back, rather than let me run the show. This all reminded me of a sappy human in a teenage chick-flick. The uncertainty, the hormones, my power taking a back seat to how my body buzzed around him.

"Yeah, seems I am." I licked my lips, searching for a sliver of composure.

My room was up two flights of stairs at the highest level in the house. Kalen didn't complain about the hike, quietly admiring the artwork hanging on the walls. He stroked the metal banister and took deep breaths.

"Does your house always smell like peonies?" he asked, stepping around me to walk beside me rather than behind.

Our house did always smell of fresh-cut flowers. My mother insisted on it. She tended beautiful gardens and greenhouses and brought in flowers daily to replace the old ones, which we put out for compost. That compost then fed new life into the next batch of greenery—a beautiful life cycle. I found it strange Kalen even noticed. In my experience, most males ignored floral scents or found them too feminine, except my brothers. They'd been taught to find the beauty in nature and all its splendors.

I paused on the stairs next to this eccentric man, who became more intriguing by the second.

"You know your flowers," I smirked.

"My parents have them planted outside their house, so don't give me too much credit. It's a comforting scent, is all." He chuckled, and we both kept walking up the few remaining stairs.

Reaching the top of the staircase, my door only inches away —I stopped short. A wave of uncertainty and something else bloomed in my stomach. Images of Kalen flashed through my mind, none of which were polite. My legs, previously begging me to run, were now quivering at the thought of him sliding between them.

"May I come in?" Kalen asked me, almost shy as he took a step back, giving me space to decline.

"Of course," I replied, feeling heat rise in my throat. Kalen walked in, slipping his shoes off by the door to keep them off my plush white rugs. Light walls made my room look immense and airy. The décor was lavish and equally elegant, with greenery and medium-sized geometric shelving on one wall, holding some of my favorite books. I kept my closet doors neatly shut, concealing my sizable wardrobe. Leaving things out of place wasn't my style; I preferred a sense of order and found comfort in the organization of my personal space.

I slipped my shoes off as well, leaving them by the dresser. I glanced up to see Kalen admiring the tasteful, pastel indigo curtains hung above my French balcony doors, the moonlight bright enough to shine through the thin fabric and shimmer on the floor.

"Wait! Is that...a balcony? With a view?" Kalen made his way to the doors.

"It's my favorite part of the house. I sit out there to clear my head," I told him as I gazed at the starlight peering through the curtains. He opened the French doors, and the night air hit us both, pushing his pleasant citrusy scent up my nostrils.

Oh, my. Prickling sensations bathed me in warmth and I couldn't tear my eyes off him. The harder I tried; the more gasoline Kalen added to the fire igniting inside me. A distraction, that's what I needed. Anything would do.

"Hey, Google, play 'Reading playlist,'" I said to the little gadget which beeped to life.

"Okay, now playing your 'Reading playlist' via Spotify." Her monotone voice responded. 'Lung' by Vancouver Sleep Clinic played.

"I thought something to ease the quiet. Is that okay?" I watched him regard the light-speckled blackness of the night with admiration. Even motionless, Kalen captured my senses.

"Absolutely. I live for music. It's my passion. Guess I didn't get a chance to mention it earlier, I'm in a band." He looked at me from the balcony. The moon cast shadows on his face, highlighting his cheekbones. "Not a lot of time for small talk tonight."

"*Mm*, seems not, but a musician. Why am I not surprised? Maybe we're meant to be in more than one way. I love music. It soothes my mind, connecting to the lyrics and sounds..." I sighed, taking in a quick breath. "I'm sorry this is so much. I never thought I'd meet someone like you. Well, I never thought I'd meet anyone who I wanted to... make small talk with. Until you..."

"Hit ya like a ton of bricks, as the saying goes," Kalen completed my sentence, his hand rubbing the back of his neck. I couldn't help but watch his black V-neck shirt as it lifted a little, revealing part of his torso.

Kalen strolled back into my room from the balcony. His movements were fluid, almost like he drifted across the floor. There he stood—broad shoulders, lean form, a solid chest, with muscles corded around each limb. He had deep brown, almost black hair that fell skillfully over his sea-colored eyes and glasses.

Focus, I tried telling myself. Then again, there was also something to be said about his mouth, full lips covering straight teeth. Did he have braces as a boy, or was he born flawless? I didn't know. What I knew was I'd stopped speaking, my mind wandering in multiple directions. Rolling my shoulders, I managed to half-assed collect myself.

I cleared my throat. "Exactly, but I'll get to know you as well as you'll let me." And I meant it. I wanted to know all there was about him—his love for music, his family, his life... Everything.

"I'll tell you anything, as long as you extend me the same courtesy," he chuckled, letting his hand drag down his arm. Such a beautiful sound, resonating through his wide chest. It made me feel lighter, like a drug. The grin slid off his face into a pensive stare directed at me, his eyes holding mine without release.

Halsey sang in the background, something about a beautiful stranger. I admired Kalen as her melodic voice sang on. The light in my bedroom created a halo around him. "It was a long drive; did you wanna shower? I can have Calliope bring in fresh clothes," I offered. Mind links came in handy most of the time.

Kalen strode over, stopping to stand in front of me, his taller form looking down on mine. His eyes searched my face as if debating what he should say. "A shower would be great. But better if you joined me?" Kalen extended his hand to me. His brows pulled together, calculating if he had overstepped some invisible boundary between us. I took his hand, doing my best to stifle my curious interest. My heart pulsed harder in response.

"Yes." Parts of me I wasn't aware of flamed to life as I answered. Other less impulsive parts of me said it should embarrass me. I'd never been naked in front of a human before. Humans seemed to sexualize all nudity, but in the Unseen, it was a simple necessity—a skin used to house us until we shed it for another. I'd shifted so many times, not giving a care who saw what, but this felt different, raw even, with a fresh edge I couldn't place.

This wasn't my first time, not even close. I'd dabbled in light petting, kissing a robust wolf now and again. On infrequent occasions, I'd blow off some steam and take a lover for several days at most, careful to be clear about my expectations. All my previous rendezvouses had set expiration dates, and the sex, while gratifying, always lacked in a lasting thrill, leaving me bored. So, I put my energy into becoming a better Alpha, honing my skills.

It didn't help that I'd met no one who provoked me enough to want or try for more. Kalen had achieved that in seconds, pulling me to him like a magnet. His thick, dark hair, his crystal blue-clear eyes, even his glasses made him appealing, drawing more attention to his baby blues. The build of his chest and his muscles flexing beneath his clothes drew my wistful gaze down once more...

I shivered, thinking about his long fingers touching me.

How his powerful hands might feel on my body, my breasts. Kalen opened the glass door and reached to turn on the faucets. Tension knotted in the pit of my stomach, seeing his back flex further. Water rained down, hitting the ivory tiles, and swirled down the drain. The muscles in his arms adjusted to his movements. An image of his arms around me flashed...

"Athena? The water's ready." Kalen's voice broke my train of thought. A blush hit my cheeks. *Did I no longer possess any modesty around this man?* I felt what had to be a snicker from my wolf, who wagged her tail as if to mock my pitiful self-control. His eyes moved cautiously from me back to the cascading water.

From his light tremble, I suspected he was holding back, trying to gauge my feelings, and he was right to. I wavered between throwing myself at him and hating that I desired something sensuous from him. Taking an unsteady step back, I hoped space would give me mental clarity. Again, I looked at the man before me, tall and kind, presenting himself without fear of what I was. After tonight's intensity—what he'd endured coming with me—he deserved nothing less than all of me, and I intended to give it to him. To hell with consequences. To hell with rules. If the Goddess saw fit to deem him my mate, then why shouldn't I be able to be with him in any way I damn well pleased?

I gave Kalen a last once over and sauntered to him. As I placed my hand on the side of his face, his light stubble tickled my fingers. I watched his neck pulse with his fluttering heartbeat. I licked my lips, making them shine, and placed a soft kiss on his thrumming skin. Kalen groaned, and I let my lips graze his jaw, leaving a tentative kiss on the corner of his mouth. Our bodies shuddered, absorbing the shock of each other's touch.

I stepped away from him, putting my fingers on the hem of my flowy top, lifting it above my head. Kalen sucked in air, his heart beating faster and faster. I roused him, as he did me. My mouth lifted into a smirk as I reached for the button of my black pants.

Kalen watched my hands with increased attention. He bit his sweet lower lip as the button popped and I slid pants slowly to the floor and stepped out of them. Leaving myself in nothing but pale lace undergarments, I returned to his inviting embrace.

He rested one of his hands behind my head, curling his fingers into the dusky black hair that cascaded down my bare back in long waves. Tucking my hands beneath his shirt, I tugged up, feeling along the muscled planes of his torso. Kalen obliged, pulling it the rest of the way off. I let my eyes gaze down his sculpted upper body, stopping at his rib cage. On his left side, he had a tattoo of a well-drawn Celtic knot, an endless loop signifying unity and family. Legends said the knot warded off bad luck and invited in good. It had been more than lucky for me so far.

I outlined the winding black lines with my fingertip, dragging my fingernail on his bare skin. Kalen shivered, lifting his chin up and closing his eyes. *Interesting.* The triquetra meant three phases, in reference to females marked by the moon. Three. *Triad.* Was it a coincidence? I wondered if he had more tattoos. My hand sank to the waist of his pants, and I circled Kalen like a wolf did when sizing up prey. His back lay bare and defined as I brushed my hand up his spine to more black lines and circles. Kalen had phases of the moon, planets, and mind's eye inked into his skin, dappled with black stars and spheres. The tattoos etched into his skin were appealing, provoking my interest. My jade eyes flickered, enjoying what they saw. I touched each line, moving my fingers over the designs. Kalen didn't move, letting me observe him. How had he selected such art? Moons and stars?

"Why a mind's eye?" I asked, still mapping the dark lines.

Kalen quaked at the light touches, and his breath hitched. "For guidance. To see what others cannot."

"*Hm.*" I moved my fingers up to the moons near his shoulder blades, marveling at his delicate skin. "And the moons?"

"You already know that. Change, magic, mystery. Take your pick." This time, he turned, taking my hand and placing it over his thumping heart.

I lifted myself up to kiss his partially open lips, soaking in all the sensations. And my, how many there were. He felt good beyond comparison. Kalen's softer moans fueled me on, and I reminded myself to be careful.

He's human and not designed for the likes of my strength.

The song changed, "Mesmerize," a voice from STROM crooned, the ballad's lyrics accurate on too many levels.

My body struggled to listen. Strange stirs and shakes rattled my insides with sparks. With trembling fingers, I reached for the button of his jeans. His exhilaration was so close. My breath caught, and he opened his eyes, darkened with haze, and want.

"I asked you to shower, but I want to be clear. We don't have to do this. We don't have to do anything." Kalen grabbed my hands, pulling them away from his jeans, and pressed his forehead to mine.

Breathless, I answered him. "I know, but I want to. If you do." Lost, beguiled, and full of need, I couldn't avoid my instincts anymore. There was no turning back for me now. If Kalen was the sun, I was hurling towards him like Icarus, flying on a high that knew no equal.

"I just want this to be right. I don't want you feeling rushed like this is something we have to do. Because we don't have to have sex tonight or even in the near future. We can wait if that's what you want. Everything has been a race to the finish. This..."

Kalen gestured to him and me. "Doesn't have to be." He settled his hands on nearly naked hips, only a thin lace separating us.

I exhaled, contented even more by his words. "And that's why I want to. You expect nothing from me. You're full of surprises, Kalen Ryan."

He pulled his naked torso back from me, raising his eyebrows. "Of course, I don't expect anything from you." He shook his head and put his mouth in a firm line.

Then he softened, stroking my arms. The way he touched me, like his hands, would withdraw any second if I asked him to. Just another thing between us I'd never experienced before. Kalen didn't act entitled to my body simply because I was naked. Instead, he caressed my skin like I was delicate, precious... like my choice to share my body with him was something he'd treasure forever.

"Are you sure?" he asked again.

I nodded, biting at my lip. "I'm sure..." His words had blazed from my head down my spine and to my toes. I shivered in his hands, captivated by his touch. "Kalen, you're going to be my undoing." I continued to work at his button.

"I look forward to it. And call me Kale," he said, his mouth twitching into a grin. He took his glasses off, setting them on the bathroom vanity near the white porcelain sink.

My hands moved back to the button on his jeans, and this time he didn't stop me from undoing it. He sprung free. I looked down. Were humans normally this large? I didn't know, nor did I care. I put my hand gently on the outside of his briefs. Kale shuddered under my touch. His pupils dilated, collecting with need.

Working my hand in an upward motion, I looked at him. "You can't hear what I'm thinking, so I'm going to tell you." I held him tighter, watching him quiver in my hands. His eyes drifted closed again, then shot open. "I've never wanted to be near anyone as much as I want to be near you."

He kissed my hair, then rocked away from me, ready to put this moment on simmer, making me want him more.

I made one last attempt at sanity, taking a long breath and holding it while I concentrated on my words. "Tell me if I hurt you."

He shook his head sideways. "You could never." His voice was low, lustful, as he taunted me, pulling down the lace fabric, nice and slow.

Groaning, I pulled us into the shower, Kale's chest tucked firmly against mine. The water hit my back, flowing down, warming me further. I grabbed body wash, pouring it into my hands, and washed Kale, massaging along the way. The smell of gardenias filled the shower along with steam. His muscles flexed and twitched beneath my soapy hands. He peppered feather-light kisses along my jaw as I worked. I gazed up at him, drinking in as much of him as possible. He was beautiful, too beautiful.

His arms wrapped around me, fingers digging into the flesh of my back. With the water rinsing away the suds, I was free to roam and explore his body. Lacing my fingers around his neck, holding him close to me, I brought his mouth down to mine and kissed him until he pulled away, panting. His hair tickled me as he supported his forehead against mine while catching his breath.

"I'm sorry," I whispered. I closed my eyes, the water raining down on both our faces.

"Don't be." He stroked his thumb across my lip, setting ablaze in me flames I was wrestling to cool down. "What did I do to get this lucky?"

I answered him with my mouth to his lips. Kissing him was erotic in ways I didn't understand, and I couldn't get enough of him. He tasted of fresh air and sunlight—if such things had a flavor—and if he was the sun; I was blossoming in his capable hands.

The water continued firing down on us, stimulating our skin. I lost time and myself in the steam, not knowing how long we kissed and caressed, both of us trying to commit every curve, inch, and touch to memory. I could live in this moment for eternity.

Out of breath, Kale placed a kiss on my temple. "I think we're clean enough." He held our hands to his formidable chest, kissing them.

As he released me from our tangled embrace, I replied, "I believe we are." I turned the faucets off as Kale grabbed for the towels. Water skimmed down my body, falling to my feet and dampened the shagged rug. All at once, Kale encapsulated me in fluffy, dry warmth, his hands working over my body to towel me off. Even with the thick fabric barrier, his touch seared me. Satisfied I was dry enough, he took my hand, leading us to my king-size canopy bed, his towel slung low on his hips as if to showcase his body further.

Music and blood filled my ears, along with pulsing desire. I pushed him to my bed, the duvet sinking around him, and let my towel fall to the floor. Kale's eyes worked up and down my body as he moved up the bed, closer to the soft gray euro pillows. Taking a place next to him, I nibbled at the mark I'd made earlier. My ears perked up, listening to him hiss and groan in pleasure. The wolf hummed and my dragon let out a low rumble, both of them creeping below my thin-skinned surface, every one of us caught up in these unfamiliar, corporeal emotions.

I rolled to sit atop him. Kale's hands flew to my hips, matching my pace. Losing my poise, I knew what was about to happen.

Condom. We needed a condom.

Leaning forward to get one from the drawer, Kale used this opportunity to skim my breasts, leaving silky, sensual kisses. I handed it to him, and his teeth tore through the blue foil. He nudged me back slightly. Watching him roll it over his length, I stroked my chest in anticipation. He was impressive, and the thought of him inside me sent a thunderous quake up and down my spine.

"You. Are. So. Perfect." Kale's hand moved from my face down, cupping my full chest. My peaks hardened under his dexterous fingers as he kneaded and gently pulled. I ground my hips against his pelvis, feeling his length against my core. I knew I was ready for him. I lifted myself up, positioning him at my wet entrance. Inch by inch, I lowered myself down on him, until he pushed away the only space left between us. A sated fullness washed over me, and I let my head drop back.

Kale held me on to me as if I were glass, absolutely still, waiting for me. "Are you okay?" he breathed, his crystal eyes genuine and kind. I knew he'd stop right now if I asked, but that was the opposite of what I needed.

"I'm more than okay," I heaved out, reveling in the sight and touch of his almost glowing body beneath me.

Feeling my insides coiling around him, I gradually moved. I'd never done this with a human before. My hips adjusted to his potential frailty. Swiveling myself rhythmically slow above him, carnality overcame me. I arched and moaned. Kale brought his hand to his mouth, then moved his thumb to the apex between my legs, tracing soft circles on my arousal.

Calling out his name, I became delirious with pleasure, gyrating my hips over him again and again. My breasts grazed his chest as I leaned down, placing my hands to his rock-hard shoulders. I wasn't out of breath, but I could hardly breathe as I kissed his lips and neck with as much softness as I could gather.

Kale's throat bobbed up and down, trying to speak. "Y—yes. Athena. Please... Don't stop. Don't fuckin' stop." Kale's panting tone struggled to compose words, his face knotted in between gratification and indulgence.

I writhed quicker, driving myself into a frenzied decadence. In a hurried movement, Kale was on top of me, still tucked between my thighs. He grasped my hands, tugging them above my head, and pinned them to the bed, brushing kisses on my lips and cheeks.

Picking my head up from the bed, I murmured his name. I nuzzled his neck and caressed his mark. I knew my eyes were glowing bold emerald green. With my control spent, my canines slipped down an increment.

"Mark. Me." Kale thrust hard with each word, knowing I'd comply. I tensed, spiraling towards a climax that was unfamiliar in its intensity. My body felt like a live wire, emitting electric sparks with each movement.

He released my hands, dragged a finger down my cheek, and thumbed my bottom lip, revealing my longer canines. Instincts took over and I turned his head to the side, licking his sweet, briny skin, and feeling all his glorious motions inside me. It took little to flip him beneath me one last time. I twisted above him with a newfound satisfaction. I craved his pleasure as much as my own.

"Thea," Kale moaned, holding my hips as he did. "Mark me. Please." He looked at me with breathless passion, sliding his hands up my torso and holding my neck for a moment. He dragged his hand back down between the breasts swaying on my chest. "Do. It."

My wolf pushed my teeth down farther. I leaned down to him, angling my hips. Opening my mouth, I sucked on his neck then bit down as I had before. My vision blurred with starry ecstasy. It shook me to my very center, and an explosion of white-hot light radiated off me. I felt as if vivid colors clouded around me, almost encased in fire, and all I could do was hope Kale didn't burn.

I reared back, taking my mouth from his neck. We both panted, as I watched his eyes glaze, an ever-changing deep blue. His jerked movements let me know he found his own finish. I felt complete. New confidence and power flowed, vibrating underneath my skin like the wildness that lived there.

Kale's words pulled me from my trance. "That was... fucking amazing. Is everything with you going to be like this? I don't even... How are you feeling?" Kale went to assist me in lifting off of him, aware enough to keep his movements slow and measured. We'd both started out with the intentions of being gentle, but that slid beyond our control as soon as we reached the bed. His lips trembled as he tried to conceal his nervousness over my potential soreness, but his delicate hold gave him away. I found it strange for him to worry about hurting me when I could kill him all too easily.

"It was remarkable," I panted out. "It's the best thing I've ever experienced. You were..." A small frown formed on my face as the thought developed in my mind.

Kale propped himself up on his elbow to face me. He furrowed his brows and brushed his hair from his eyes. And as he did, the scent of lavender from the bedding and from him wafted over me. I looked away from his curious gaze.

"Athena. I can see you thinking already. Tell me what's going on in that pretty head of yours." He mapped patterns on my shoulder, his finger tracing swirling lines over my skin.

"Are you alright? I mean, has it always been like that for you? When you were with other human women, was it always... this?" I asked. My brows bunched together. I looked more severe than I should, but I'd always had the luxury of knowing what someone else thought about me, and it wasn't that way with Kale. He left me guessing. From the moment I met him, I was constantly thrown into a state of emotional exposure I was unaccustomed to. With other males, I understood our exchange had been satisfactory and mutually enjoyed, but Kale was human. Had I been too rough? Or...

Kale blew a hard breath out and stretched, causing the down duvet to shift.

"No." He shook his head slowly, the hair moving around his forehead. "Not even close. Never. I wish I could explain it better, but when I'm with you, it heightens everything. Sex with you, it's... like touching fire without the pain. It's an experience out of this world. Then again, you're kinda out of this world." Kale smirked at his corny joke. I couldn't help it; I smiled too, and he kissed my nose. Sitting up and slipping from next to me, he walked to the bathroom to clean himself up. I rolled on the bed, admiring his physique as he stood before the mirror. The broadness of his shoulders, the corded muscle on his back, his eyes glinting with light as he stared at me in the reflection.

His face wrinkled as he washed his hands in my sink. "What's that sound?" Kale's head tilted ever so slightly.

I reared up, glaring out the window, my naked body startling to attention. Had I missed something, distracted by Kale?

"No, it's not outside," he said, looking at the balcony as he came closer to me. "It's like a rhythmic thumping." I perked my ears, moving my head up and sniffing. Rousing my wolf's attention, she yipped. We couldn't hear anything but the music and heartbeats. *Our* beating hearts, thumping along.

My mouth went dry. "Can you hear my heart?"

Kale smiled wide, his head angling to my torso. "Ha, yeah, is that what that is? What a delightful sound. *Hm.* Weird. Never heard it before." Sitting down next to me, he kissed my lips again. I froze, panic and fear crushing me.

"No, you didn't, and you shouldn't. You shouldn't be able to hear it with human ears..." I went cold.

What had I done?

CHAPTER 6

"Get dressed. I'm calling for my brothers," I instructed Kale. Digging into my drawers, I grabbed the first pair of sweatpants and a hoodie I saw. I slipped them on too fast, almost tripping. This is what I got for being impulsive. My teeth clenched together.

"Your brothers? Why? What's wrong? Because I can hear your heart?" Kale quirked his head and pulled on the sweatpants he'd found. When did Calliope slip in to drop these? I suppose that didn't matter.

Atlas! Anders! I heard their fumbled movements before they responded, both of them stumbling out of bed.

What's wrong? What happened? Anders asked.

Dammit, you killed him, didn't you, Thea? Atlas groaned in my head.

No. She didn't kill me, Kale answered. *But I sure as shit feel as if I've died and gone to heaven.* Kale let out a brief, deep chuckle. My jaw dropped. Kale answered Atlas, but he couldn't have heard. It was a mind link—something only wolves had. And Kale was human. Kale was *human.*

Well—he had been.

My blood pressure shot up, racing to catch up to my heart,

which pounded blood into my ears loud enough I almost couldn't hear. My ideas spun in my head like a hurricane, each one sucked up in the twisting confusion of my mind.

"Kale? How'd you hear that?" I asked him. Shock moved over my face, making my mouth droop open.

"I really dunno. You seemed distressed, so I guess I tried paying attention, and I heard one of your brothers' remarks." Kale's face went white, and his mouth fell open. The gravity of what he said hit him.

"Oh shit...oh shit, oh shit. I heard your brothers, but they're not here. I heard your mind! That link thingy you told me about. This is bad, isn't it?" Kale shouted, his hands shaking along with his epiphany.

"Yes. You heard inside my mind."

"Is this some sort of mate thing?" Kale fidgeted, my nervousness leeching off me and clawing into his head, our bond demanding he feel my inner chaos.

"It would be if you were—"

I paused, the severity of my actions weighing me down like cement blocks on my shoulders. I'd wanted Kale too much; I'd ignored potential consequences. But wolves couldn't create other wolves with a bite—that was a cinematic myth. Our limited population in the future was one of the many reasons pairing with a human versus a supernatural was frowned upon, and now I wasn't sure of anything. Doubt racked me, making my body shake.

Atlas bulldozed in first, nearly taking my door off the hinges. Anders crashing into my room behind him. Both were clad in loose shirts and pajama bottoms with their hair sticking up. "Oh, goodnight, it stinks in here, T. We knew it would happen, but it doesn't mean we wanted physical proof." Horrified, Atlas, rolled his eyes and pulled his shirt over his face, continuing to gripe in aggravated groans.

"This is disgusting. Completely natural but nauseating from

this point of view. Way past normal sharing, Thea." Anders grimaced in agony as well, his hands covering his face.

I scowled. I really didn't need this from these two right now. *Hypocrites.* The nights I spent suffering through their various flings and watching them escort out females the next morning, or the times I covered for them when they disappeared all evening...

I didn't give my face a chance to show the mortification hovering inside me. "Grow up, both of you." I sneered at them, not having the time to scold them further for their childish behavior. "Kale can hear my heartbeat. He can also hear our mind link."

"Um... that's..." Atlas took a step back, his brows shooting up in alarm. His brown eyes darkened as he looked from me to Kale.

"Not supposed to be possible," Anders finished the sentence, his manner and tone more level than Atlas's. I watched Anders swallow hard. He took a black hair tie from his wrist and pulled his long blond hair out of his face, twisting it into a low knot. Anders seldom lost his cool, ever the middle child. But this time, his nervousness reached me like an unspoken warning.

A numbness crept up my limbs and into my chest, tempting to carry me away. "Thanks for stating the obvious. Pretty sure we had a similar discussion earlier this evening. What I need to know is why."

"Nothing around here is gonna be easy, is it?" Kale let out an anxious chuckle, his body reflecting my tension with his rigid posture and trembling hands. His fingers pushed through his drooping dark hair. "I like a challenge," he said, trying his hardest to look unphased for me. I watched him chew at his bottom lip and saw the rapid rise and fall of his bare chest. He told me what I wanted to hear and tried to hide the fear I knew spread beneath his skin like a sickness, but I felt it regardless.

His growing uncertainty cut at me with a deadly edge. Kale gave me a soft, fleeting grin. Unfamiliar with the history of lycanthropy and lingering in a sex haze, Kale couldn't fully comprehend the importance this development carried, and his desire to calm me outweighed his panic.

Foolish. This bond was bound to get one of us killed.

I rubbed my temple. "I suppose it's not. Still think you made the right choice coming with me?" I stared at Kale's striking face, wanting him to say yes. His high cheekbones, his jawline hinting at stubble—exquisite. He distracted my thoughts too easily and drew me in.

"Without a doubt. Yes," he said, and I didn't know if he spoke a truth or a lie. As if to hear my doubt, he brushed his lips against my knuckles again, causing me to stiffen to stifle the shiver. Hmm... that response wasn't wearing off. My attraction to Kale understood no limits and had absconded with Kale's sense of self-preservation.

Anders and Atlas remained silent, both of them examining each movement of mine and Kale's. They nodded, engaged in a conversation they didn't care to share. I glared at them, then shifted my eyes.

Kale's mouth went slack. "I'm actually exhausted. You keep talking. If I pass out, promise me you won't let your brothers draw anything on my face." Kale attempted a joke to soothe me, but his body couldn't hide its quick descent into fatigue.

I noticed Kale looked weary suddenly, and very pale. Goddess, he looked awful. Redness rimmed his dark circled eyes, and his skin became pallid and damp. Light sheens of sweat coated his brow and limbs.

A tang of terror coated my tongue like bile. *Puta merda. What had I done?*

Atlas interrupted my internal panic with a fake laugh. "Come on, man. That's half the fun of having a brother. Pranking." Atlas was still chuckling as he clapped Kale on the back, then snapped his hand back like he touched something hot.

Anders smirked. "Felt something funny, did you?" He quirked his eyebrows and directed his comment to Atlas. "Kind of like a spark?"

Atlas turned his hand, examining his palm, then rubbed his fingers together. "Yeah." His dark brows knit together, and his lips tightened.

"Settle down. It's because they're fully connected now. When we make contact with Kale, it'll feel...different." Anders winked at Atlas, giving him an elbow to the ribs.

Kale opened his drooping eyes, trying to focus his vision. "Wait. So, when one of you touches me, you feel... bonded to me, like Athena?" He dropped his head back against the pillows and pulled it back up.

"Yes, and no. It's not to that extreme—" Anders said before Atlas interrupted.

"Basically, when I touch you, it's like touching a cute fucking panda. Like, oh, I just wanna pet this sweet little guy." Atlas laughed again, attempting to eliminate Kale's concern and mock him at the same time. I glared at Atlas, cocking my eyebrow to signal enough was enough. Kale was fading fast, and they were all joking as if this matter wasn't dire.

Kale's eyes dimmed. "Am I still..." He gave a sleepy, half-concerned expression. His mouth sagged, and he slumped forward, exhaustion consuming him. I dodged towards him, bracing my hands on his chest and ignoring the heat spreading up my palms. I pushed Kale back against the pillows. He passed out cold, his body unable to resist the pull of sleep any longer.

Kale hadn't gotten to finish asking his question, but I knew what he intended to ask.

Am I still human?

Afraid not...

"Well, shit. That's one way to fall asleep," Atlas said, his shoulders shaking up and down along with his joking tone.

I snapped my head to Atlas, aggravated by his cavalier attitude. My mind was racing.

What have I done to him? Goddess, what have I done to him? My wolf entered, far less concerned than I. She weaved through my jumbled thoughts, reminding me of Kale's strong, pumping heart, how well he was breathing. I ran my hand along his forehead, brushing his hair from his face. His skin felt hotter—not arousal hot, but heat seemed to pour from him. Kale felt like my hands when I manifested fire. How strange. His body was fighting something.

Something I caused.

"So, is this a bad time to say, 'way to wear a guy out with sex?'" Atlas smirked and lifted his hand to high five me.

I glowered at him, a wild snarl moving past my lips. Atlas held up in his hands, essentially waving a white flag.

"Bad timing. Definitely a bad time." Anders wrinkled up his nose and shook his head, correcting Atlas before I could. Lucky for him.

"Okay. No high five then." Atlas shrugged.

Ignoring Atlas's poor taste, Anders moved forward, touching my shoulder. "We need to go to the library, back to the old books. There must be something that can tell us what might happen to Kale." I looked at my two brothers.

"We've read those books a thousand times. We're a prophecy, and the bad news is no one ever really knew what we could do. Just the same old End of Days bullshit," Atlas said, making a face.

"Unprecedented powers..." Atlas added, wiggling his fingers in the air.

A lump formed in my throat. "You're right. That's it. No one has ever known what we were capable of. But... do you think? No. No. That can't be. Or can it?"

"What?" Atlas asked, looking at me with a furrowed expression. Anders just stared at me, confused right along with Atlas.

"Do you think it could be possible for me to... to make him... a wolf?" I asked, looking at their faces. The idea itself fell over me. If he turned, what would he turn into? What fallout would there be?

"No one's ever done it, or rather, it wasn't achievable. Then again, this whole thing has been a barrel of fucking surprises. Why not add a little more shit to the shit show we have, shall we?" Anders blurted as he rubbed his forehead and leaned against the canopy post.

This wasn't something Kale had agreed to if it was the case. He'd hate me for sure. Regret and guilt bubbled inside me. I paced, my bare feet getting cold from the gray wood panel flooring, and I tugged at the pocket of my red hoodie. I looked back at my bed. Kale slumped against the pillows. I felt like a criminal who'd stolen Kale's humanity.

What a shit show, indeed—one I was fully responsible for. Sure, my brothers had asked to come along to Zephyr, but they didn't ask for this. Kale didn't ask for this. This was the comeuppance I deserved for wanting a bit of *fun*. I rubbed my hands on my face.

Six hours ago, I went out looking for a blood demon and came back with a new mate instead. I'd broken him past the magic Barrier, and, hey, maybe turned him into a supernatural.

This impulsivity Kale set off in me was more treacherous than I'd originally thought. I'd never dealt with anyone was turned. We were all born wolves and innately understood our world and the animal inside. Kale lacked that advantage.

Atlas sighed, padding over to me, and rubbed my shoulder. "Much as I'd like it to be, this really isn't your fault, T. This isn't something you choose—it happens."

"He's right. We went out tonight to kick some blood demon ass. Instead, we got a new brother. Well, *we* got a new brother.

Ha, because if he was your brother, wouldn't that be awkward!" Anders put his hand on my other shoulder, both of them trying to dissipate the storm growing within me.

I drew in a breath and closed my eyes, trying to collect my scattered thoughts. This lack of control I kept experiencing tonight bordered on overwhelming. "Here's the thing. Knowing how this all feels—I'd choose it. I'd choose *him*. Over and over, at almost any cost. I'd sacrifice so many things to get to know him, to keep him safe." I reached up to squeeze both of my brothers' hands on my shoulders. "I jeopardized you both, bringing Kale through the Barrier. What's worse, I don't regret it. I think... I think even without our bond, I'd want to love him. I shouldn't, but I do. You two deserve a better Alpha than what I am right now."

Anders scoffed and crossed his arms on his chest. "I don't accept that." His tone was deep and raised.

"I don't either. Wanting to be with someone you care about isn't a shortcoming. Dammit, Thea! I know we give you a hard time, but you've always been exactly the Alpha we need. You think about everyone. You try so hard to do what's right," Atlas said. He walked away from me, opening the doors to the balcony, and looked out into the starry midnight sky. We all needed a breath of fresh air.

The wind blew, shaking the tops of the trees, and I heard an owl hooting in the distance. The wafting air carried a faint moisture. Rain was coming. I loved the rain. The way it sounded, how it nourished the earth. Rain could wash things clean, make a fresh start, and I desperately wanted to be cleansed of this mess.

Atlas turned and sniffed. He walked back into the room and closed the balcony doors. "You know what, you took a risk at the Barrier. You did it, though. Something no one else has ever pulled off—no one. So, let's cut this pity party short. We're going to the library. We're gonna read those crusty fucking books again until we find something that says our new panda friend is going to be fine!" Atlas huffed and stalked out of the room.

Anders sighed hard and turned on his heels to follow him out.

I sat down on the bed, running my hand down Kale's sleeping cheek. Heat still covered Kale's body and his heartbeat fluttered erratically. He grimaced and exhaled as I took my hand away, making a noise that was somewhere in between a moan and sob. He was dreaming.

"Athena. No. No... Don't..." Kale's words were a quiet sleeping plea for me not to do something to him. I lifted a lock of hair from his clammy face and made *shh* sounds. His face relaxed. He was beautiful, human or not. Even if I hadn't bonded with Kale, he was something to behold. His jawline was kissable and divinely defined. Dimples appeared each time he smiled that hundred-watt grin. His hair was nearly black, but not—more like dark chocolate, decadent, and rich. His lashes were coal-colored and full. A pert nose fit perfectly against his chiseled features. I got lost looking at him. My body jerked, coursing with desire. I didn't even understand how he could have such an effect on me and not even be awake.

How curious. I wondered if it would always be this way—the wanting.

I placed a gentle kiss on his forehead and whispered, "I'll be back." Touching my lips, I felt them tingle from that brief contact. I slipped on my fuzzy house shoes and tiptoed to my door, closing it behind me without a sound. Kale was going to need all the rest he could get.

The library was on my level of the house. An immense room dedicated to a vast collection of books, scrolls, maps, blueprints, and every other artifact our parents had amassed over the years. The library door was security coded with a fingerprint scanner on the doorway, requiring a family member's print before the impenetrable see-through doors would open. The library had a high-pitched ceiling, with large, curtain-free windows. Outside the windows was a hidden set of security alarms, further protecting these artifacts and treasures.

During the daytime hours, light streamed through the windows, illuminating the glass display cases and curios. Lavish rugs with glittering elven threads sat underneath large, plush sofas. Several hand-carved wooden desks with matching chairs sat in the corners for studying.

At night, like now, the moon shone full. It cast candlelight-like shadows on the bookcases and beamed streaks on the framed pictures that lined the walls. I scanned my finger, walked past the giant cases, and found my brothers sitting on the sofas in the room's corner. There were piles of books scattered, open to various pages on the tables and teal cushions around them. They'd dug into the shelves quicker than I expected. The smell of old paper and ink mixed with vanilla and almonds filled the room. Antiquated books had a comforting way of smelling sweet as their compounds changed and aged. I adored the smell, found solace in the aroma of knowledge and books. This time the scent did little to offer me that same relief. I groaned.

"About time you walked in. Taking your sweet time while we do all the work," Anders chuckled, teasing me. I could always count on my brothers for verbal banter, even when I didn't want it. I tucked my hair behind my ears, trying to ignore my unease.

"You weren't molesting a sleeping man, by chance—were you, dear sister?" Atlas laughed deeper, not bothering to look up from the handbound book in his hands, while he joined in taunting me.

I scoffed, my mouth cocking to the side. "You really are a prick, Atlas." I couldn't help but let out a laugh myself, closing my eyes in humored disbelief. Maybe I needed the distraction of the teasing.

Across from Anders, I plopped down on a stone-colored sofa, grabbing the closest open book. It was of Scandinavian origin, and Old Norse text covered the pages. I had taken many courses in old languages, and I could read most. This book chronicled the cycles of lycanthropy—the standard jargon. It talked of our connection to the moon, et cetera. All things I knew. I flipped pages. Nothing. At least nothing new.

Casting that one aside, I picked up another book. This one was more worn, the pages yellowed and tattered. The cover didn't even have a title—it almost looked like a journal. It was handwritten, the ink fading in spots. I rubbed my hands over the pages. This one felt different. I scanned the discolored pages. Lots of symbols. It was written in all different texts and hands. I squinted, trying to will the text to come to life. It didn't.

It did, however, mention the first wolves. Now that was something different.

"Guys. I think I found something," I shouted, my excitement getting the better of me.

Atlas and Anders snapped their heads at me, moving to the couch beside me at record speed. The sofa gave way a bit, sliding back from their weight. Their eyes trained on where my finger pointed. I read aloud, piecing it together the best I could.

"It says the first wolves could create a wolf with a bite. Not so much like a vampire bite, this was more of a transference of life force." I paused, thinking to myself. *Transference...* meaning I might create a wolf, but at a cost. I read further. "The gene and ability dwindled as our lineage branched out." I stopped, letting the book rest on my lap as the magnitude of my actions sunk in.

The gene was gone or was it? But I wasn't just any wolf. *Lupin Dragona, one of the Triad...* The words of the prophecy rang in my ear. My brothers kept reading, their noses almost touching the pages. It seemed my bite potentially contained the power to transform Kale—his biology and maybe even his personality. And what was the cost to me? Would I transform him into something new and not live to see it? Questions riddled me—questions and raw *guilt*. My shoulders sagged under the invisible weight of my discovery.

I blinked in what felt like slow motion, dragging my head up from the book. "When I bit Kale, I took away his free will." My head dropped back down with realization. More guilt accumulated like a puddle at my feet, and I ached. This is why I couldn't be impulsive. This is why there were rules and Barriers. *Consequences.*

"Silver lining, T. He won't be as breakable anymore if he's a wolf." Leave it to Atlas to turn this around. I admired his determination.

"Besides, better a wolf than a cuddly panda." Anders pursed his mouth in a tight-lipped grin and attempted to break the silence again with humor.

I let out a fatigued breath. "Well, I guess when he wakes up, I'll drop another bomb on him, and we'll go from there."

Atlas patted my shoulder, giving it a light squeeze. "Try and get some sleep. You're no good to anyone as a zombie. You look almost as bad as Kale. What's done is done. The way he looks at you... you could tell the guy you infected him with malaria or a biological, life-altering disease. Oh, wait! That's *exactly* what you did. Damn! But, seriously, he won't care. He's one of us now, just a more similar version." Atlas let out a roar of laughter.

I chuckled nervously. "Again, you're an asshole. I think he might prefer malaria. And Just so you know, you'll pay for that joke when I'm less tired and can enjoy it more." A yawn slipped out past my lips, as did my pretend anger.

"'Night, Thea. Try not to kill him with anything else, yeah?" Anders tossed over his shoulder as I walked out of the library. I raised my middle finger to both of them.

Jerks. And I loved them for it.

I crept to my door, opening it with extra care. There was Kale, sleeping, his body relaxed and sprawled out. I stared at Kale's large frame in my bed, most of his body covered by the soft, white duvet. As beautiful as he was, he remained almost a stranger to me in so many ways, and now I'd bound us together for life. I titled my head, admiring him through a soft gaze. I'd make time to learn everything about him, I promised myself again. He deserved my attention and so much more for all he was going to give up.

I crawled into bed—stealth mode activated. As I reached a pillow, Kale jerked towards me. His eyes shot open. His pools of blue I'd already grown fond of—*gone*. His eyes smoldered with a brilliant amber-flecked gold. They glowed at me, illuminated by something I'd set off in him.

"Athena," Kale called out and threw his arms around my waist. "I dreamed you sent me away, and he took you. I forgot— I forgot...And you were gone, and I was stuck as a—it felt so real. But you're here." His heart pounded so hard, I felt it against me.

"Of course, I'm here. It was only a dream. I wouldn't send you away." I kissed his head as it laid on my chest, ignoring what I saw in his eyes for a moment until he calmed. I kissed his hair again as he shook gently against me. "Whatever you dreamed wasn't real. I'm here. I'm here," I hushed, stroking his chaotic hair. "Kale. Look at me." I beckoned him in a subdued tone.

He lifted his head. A fresh tear stained his cheek. My stomach knotted and my heart leaped into my throat. Kale was such a large, strong man, and here he was crumpled up in my arms, our bond running thick in his veins.

"Are you hurt? Please don't...."

He interrupted my concern with a searing kiss, crushing his lips against mine. Kale's fervor was clear in his fast pace, as was his arousal nearing me. I fell into his kiss, his tongue claiming my mouth. A delicious sizzling grew, pooling low in my stomach. Kale's eyes... it took every ounce of self-restraint I had to draw back from him.

"Kale, give me..."

He bored into me with his shining eyes, his hands on both sides of my face, rubbing his thumb along my bottom lip.

"I'm sorry," he said, his tone low and deflated. "I don't mean to push you. I didn't even ask you if you wanted this right now. I... this is a lot. All of it. I'm probably not even human somehow, and I just wanna erase the thoughts of it—be close to you, like this." He shook his head as he whispered, no longer looking at me.

This man was always going to test my self-discipline. I'd always thought I was an expert at remaining composed, but it seemed I was wrong. "I didn't stop you because I don't want this." I put my hand to his chest. "Or you, because I do. You don't know how much." I held the gaze of his now amber eyes, longing for the less complicated blue ones. "But before this goes any further, in any aspect. Your eyes, they're... flaring gold and amber. I'm sure... I turned you. It's not something that most if anyone else can do. I thought it to be a dead gene. This isn't supposed to be possible. If you need time to process or even want some space from me, I understand." Instead of backing away, he pressed his face close enough I felt his breath hit my face.

I closed my eyes.

"So, I'm really not human anymore, am I?" he asked, his words carrying a hint of sadness. I opened my eyes to face him. I owed him that much.

"No." It's all I could do to keep from getting teary over what he'd lost—what I'd taken.

Kale looked away and got up, walking to the mirror. Maybe this is it, I thought. Maybe this will drive him away. I made him into something he never asked for. My wolf yelped in disagreement. She was certain Kale was ready to be one of us.

I watched Kale put on his glasses, blink fast, then take them back off to pull at his eyelids, trying to see past the radiating amber. His mouth dropped open, and I stilled, waiting.

"*Hmm.* No more glasses either, huh? This is so fucking crazy," he hesitated, pushing a deep breath through his lips. "I preferred blue, but if this is permanent..." another exhausted huff emanated from his chest. "I'll take it."

Kale continued fiddling with his face, back muscles rippling as he moved. He turned on the faucets and splashed his face with water. His body still trembled.

This situation kept getting more complicated, and I thought, I should have run, saving us both the trouble.

He licked his lips, eyeing his reflection. "Every fiber in my being told me I should leave, but I wouldn't, and I still won't, but—"

"Kale, I—"

He shook his head, casting his darkening eyes downward and then back up to the oval mirror. "She's right, you know."

"Who's right?"

"Your wolf? You can't drive me away." He pulled a half-hearted smile onto his lips, and I couldn't tell if he understood the seriousness of the situation. "I'm the *Bella* to your *Edward.*"

I half-smirked. "You watch too much TV, and I'm not sure that's the best comparison."

Kale shrugged and wiped his face. "Maybe but turns out tv might be right. So, if I'm becoming a wolf, then that's what I'll be. Looks like you're stuck with me now." He turned towards me. A wicked grin crept across his face. I didn't understand his calm—how he willingly accepted such a fate. He parted his mouth as if to glean my innermost wishes. Those lips were going to get me every time.

A lump formed and I stammered, words alluding me. "I... I

forgot you're hearing inside my head. The connection must be getting stronger." I swallowed, doing my best to digest what he had said and to ignore his torso braided with lean muscle. My eyes ran up and down his form, drinking in each feature. The way his sweatpants hung and hit below his cut 'v' was enough to stop me in my tracks. I felt a blush creep up my now heavy chest, to my throat. My wolf roamed my head, pleading and whining in praise of what we both saw.

"*Hmm*. There's something else. I know you want me right now. You're trying to restrain yourself. Don't. Don't ever hold back with me." Kale's smile faded, replaced with palpable lust that crackled between us. I wanted to let go, give in. I needed to.

She's fucking perfect. I'd give my eyes. The beating heart from my chest if she asked. Anything to have her... Kale's lips didn't move, but I heard him loud and clear, his mind speaking volumes. I could feel our link, more solid now. His thoughts were transparent to me. He didn't know how to shield me from them yet. I threw out the last of my hesitation. I didn't need sleep, just him—amber eyes and everything else.

I let the wholeness of being near him take over my senses. It was like letting my body float in water, weightless and free.

Kale crossed the room faster than normal, his bare feet padding on the floor. My playlist hummed low in the background; I could hear the melody of Arizona's "Let Me Touch Your Fire" urging us on.

He reached me, pushing me down to the soft bed, and settled between my legs, hitching my thighs to his hips. My body was all too happy to oblige, coiled around him, pinning him to me.

I'll never get enough, Kale's mind hummed as he blazed a trail of kisses down my cheek and ear. He stopped at the dip between my neck and shoulders, inhaling the scent of my skin and nipping at my throat.

His thoughts were uncontrolled, sliding into my head and sticking in my ears. *Someday I'll mark her. God, she smells amazing.*

I moaned in his ear, taking in his breath on my skin, his mind quieted.

Kale lifted away from me, pulling me up with him into a sitting position, my legs remained snug around his waist. He went to grab my shirt. I beat him to it, shredding the fleece fabric in my hands as I jerked too hard, excitement and demand flowing through my veins.

"Let me get the sweats. No need to ruin a good pair of pants." He smirked, tugging at the waistband, and taking them down slow enough to make me twist. His patience was more intact than mine, allowing him to take his time and savor each movement.

Damn him for having this effect on me.

Kale pushed me back down, taking my hands in his and placing them above my head, holding them to the mattress. He brushed kisses across my mouth. His lips were too damn soft yet capable of destruction I knew I'd ask for. Each kiss was laced with passion and sweltering with need. Each touch burned in a way I couldn't articulate, and I wanted more.

He held my two hands with his one, grinding his erection into me. I whimpered into Kale's mouth as he held my face, squeezing my chin. I'd never given up so much control, and I loved it—craved it even.

Kale's skin sizzled, like fire crackling against me. His free hand roamed to my breast, cupping the soft, heavy tissue, kneading it. His fingers tweaked at my fully erect nipples atop my breasts, making me arch my back further into him. A groan escaped Kale's parted lips. He looked down at me, eyes alight, flickering along with mine.

Mmm. I think I've found what I've been missing. Kale's mind was lurid as he roamed down the planes of my body, never rushing. He released my hands, and I twisted them in his hair. Kale caressed my breasts again, running and cupping his hands along each sensuous curve. When I shuddered, he took a hardened peak in his between his lips in response, lapping with a skillful, delicious intent.

He traveled further down my body, stopping to dip his tongue in my navel. He looked up at me again, his hair falling over his hooded eyes. Grinning, he nipped my hip. He kissed his way over to my other side and nipped at that hip. This was something new. Tremors racked my limbs, Kale's fear from moments before replaced with a feral determination.

"I'm going to kiss every inch of your body until you can't take it. I promise you this—you will scream my name," his voice rasped with fresh authority.

What was this savage gaze in his eyes? A primal desire I didn't know, but I was beyond sure I wanted it and my body immodestly begged for it.

"Yes." I nodded, breathless and damp in anticipation, the tension behind my eyes telling me they erupted in an even more vivid green.

Kale parted my thighs wider, raising up to put his lips on my knee. He drew himself down at a devastating pace, covering my thighs in purposeful kisses. He opened me a bit farther and put his mouth to my sweet spot, making focused circles. He pushed my legs apart, ravaging me like a starving man to feast. My body bucked upward as I lay helpless to control its involuntary motions. Prepared for this, Kale held my thighs, letting his fingers dig into my soft flesh. He kept on, dipping inside me. He was ruining me from the inside out in more ways than one.

I called his name over and over, and I didn't care if the entire Unseen heard me. He had no right to feel this good, yet it didn't stop him from rolling wave after wave of pleasure through me.

Thea, Kale's mind called, hard and brash. I consumed his

thoughts. Tangled images, words, and hints of songs. He kept working, moving along my arousal and entrance with focused attention. Kale's hand moved from my thigh, and all at once, I felt his finger sheathed inside me. I curled my fingers into his hair, tugging him closer as if I could bring him farther into me.

Her smell and taste are—she's exquisite...

I lost it—Kale's unspoken words, my undoing. My legs trembled around him, and I saw colors, so bright and vibrant. Blues and purples erupted beneath my eyelids and onto him. Spasms rippled over my body. I was floating and tethered to Kale simultaneously. My less than delicate groans pleaded to be locked in this colorful bliss. Kale's eyes glowed; he wasn't nearly done with me, though I didn't know how to move any of my limbs at the moment.

Kale placed himself at my entrance, little self-control left. He reached above me, opening my nightstand with too much force. The drawer and all its contents tumbled to the floor with a loud *crack.*

Neither of us bothered to pay any attention to the noise. He sheathed himself with another condom; the wrapper flying Goddess knew where. This time he didn't ease himself in. In one thrust, I had him fully, my body molding to his. I wrapped my legs around his back, jolting at the sensation.

Kissing me with unreserved passion, Kale moved in and out faster. He reared back, leaving me on the bed, and grasped my calves, pulling them farther apart, pumping in a downward motion. I felt that deep, pulling sensation building again. I reached my hands to his muscled chest, moaning beneath him.

Was it possible to... Surely not?

Kale stared down, eyes fierce with golden passion. He'd heard my thoughts.

In one movement, he turned me over, my stomach now flat against the bed. He drew my hips up to his, pulling them until they reached him. One thrust and he went inside me. With one hand, he gripped my hip, and the other, he twined my hair around his fist like a rope.

"It. Is. And... You... Will..." He pushed deeper into me with every word he uttered. No one had ever commanded me to do anything, and this I'd have done without being told. I turned my head to gaze at his face when I could open my eyes. Kale touched my mouth, rubbing his thumb along my lips while working his hips against me. I was coming undone in so many ways, swimming deep in sensations. He moved back down, his chest almost touching my back, and nipped the hollow spot between my neck and shoulder. My skin sizzled where his lips kissed and lapped at my too sensitive skin. A chill blasted down my spine from his cool breath. My mind was thrown elsewhere, lost and, somehow, found all at once. I cried out for him again, calling his name like he was the answer to every question I'd ever had.

Kale lifted my almost limp body to face me as he finished. His eyes flashed bright and filled with a primitive sharpness. A few more movements and his body jolted to a halt. I clung to his back, my nails clawing into his hot skin. I couldn't bear to let him move away from me, not yet. He pressed his forehead to mine, panting. *Gods, what was this buzz?*

Kale broke our breathy silence first, his tone tamer this time. "I don't understand. How? How are you real? You make everything better than anything I've experienced in my life. How?" He laid us down, resting himself on top of me.

Enjoying how his weight felt on my chest, I grinned and sighed with delightful satisfaction. "I don't have any answers for that or the words to tell you what this feels like." I gestured to us, and the lack of space between us as our bodies laid tangled together, bound by more than physicality.

Music filled the quiet for a moment, the notes dancing in my head. Kale closed his eyes, still amber and glimmering with the new golden power he possessed. He took a harsh breath.

"I'm afraid I'm going to wake up and realize this was all a dream. That you aren't real. And I'll be left alone with this longing and space in my heart that no one can ever fill because of a woman from a dream. A woman I followed down a rabbit hole." His confession hit me in the chest like a bullet.

I shifted our position, allowing me to lie on top of him. My skin glided across his, and I reveled in how he felt. Smooth, but firm, and somehow hot and cool. He was a glorious combination of all opposing sensations.

"I'm afraid too. That I'm going to make a mistake. Because for the first time in my life, I have no idea what I'm doing. I grew up believing I had one purpose. To rule, to fight. All these noble and bureaucratic ideals." Kale listened, his breath slow and steady, his eyes boring into a hidden part of myself I had kept hidden away. My head rested on his chest, and I breathed in his incomparable, sweet marine scent. "Now, I'd be happy to never leave this bed and let the world sort itself out if it means I get to stay here with you—that you'd be safe."

I kept my ear to his chest. My new favorite sound beat in my ears. Kale's heart was a song I'd put on repeat and never turn off. I hadn't wanted this, believed I hadn't needed him, but his presence had gone straight to my head and, more so, my heart. I'd closed myself off to the idea of feeling this closeness to anyone, and Kale was the key to unlocking the fortified border around my heart.

"*Hm.* We can be afraid together then. At least we won't be alone." Kale hugged me closer for a second, then reached for nearby tissues. He shuffled a bit, then dropped them in the small gray trash bin, and rolled back to me, tugging the down-filled duvet up around us.

"I dunno if it's the mark, the excitement, the sex, or you, but I can't keep my damn eyes..." His voice slipped away. Sleep took him as fast as it did before. He was changing, no denying that. Changing because of what I'd done to him. And yet, the guilt

I'd felt waned. In my heart, I knew, if given the choice, I'd abscond with his humanity over and over to have him.

I closed my eyes, letting my thoughts wander further before sleep inevitably took me. Nothing I'd read knew how much Kale would change or how fast he'd progress. What had transpired between us indicated a rapid pace. He'd been more aggressive and assertive with me this time—a giant tell. The growing unknowns ate at me, but my mind hazed. The uncertainty tired me. My body felt sore, in a good way. None of it made any sense to me. I'd never been tired or sore from anything before.

The exhaustion proved to be too much, and I drifted into a heavy sleep with Kale's heated body wrapped around me. His icy exhaling lulled me into a dreamless rest, and each time we awoke—we made love again. Every time, it felt more incredible than the last, and for the first time, my body understood unleashed pleasure.

CHAPTER 7

Sun poured in through my balcony doors. It felt good on my skin, but I had no spare time to bask in its warmth. Today I'd jump back into research. I'd find any scrap I could. Even with this irrational situation unfolding, I couldn't forget why I had gone to Zephyr. I'd need to go back as soon as possible. Xercarus was no minor threat. He was an end to the Unseen and humanity if he was, in fact, planning a comeback.

No good demons could just stay dead.

I stretched, feeling a few twinges, and rolled over to look at Kale. He looked serene locked in a sound sleep. His chest moved up and down in a rhythmic motion, and his hair laid on his forehead. I hugged myself a bit, smiling, and tiptoed out of bed, forgoing using the bathroom to avoid making any noise. I picked my sweatpants off the floor and pulled them back on. I pursed my lips, remembering my hoodie was unusable. I took Kale's black t-shirt off the floor instead, tugging it over my head.

I'd grab some breakfast and check back in on him. I lumbered down the marbled stairs and padded to the kitchen, which I found empty. Everyone had already eaten. This was the first time I'd slept past seven in... I wasn't sure how long. The kitchen smelled of eggs and fresh blueberries. They left a basket out on the copper granite counter, and I helped myself to several of Calliope's muffins. Opening the fridge, I took out a bowl of ripe strawberries and cranberry juice. I broke Calliope's rule and drank directly from the bottle. I tossed the empty container in the recyclable bin, took several bottles of water from the drawer, and let the heavy stainless-steel door close.

I bit into a strawberry, juice collecting on my bottom lip. I closed my eyes, savoring the natural sweetness and tartness.

"Someone's hungry." Anders popped his head into the kitchen, startling me so much I dropped my strawberry on the ceramic tile.

"Indeed. Get an early workout in, Thea, or just a late one?" Atlas sniggered, plopping at the island on the stool closest to me. I bent down, my hair falling in my face while I picked up the strawberry.

"You two are simply too funny for words." I stood back up, tossing the berry into the garbage disposal, and opened my palm to whiz a minor fireball toward Anders.

Nothing.

My palm lay empty. It didn't manifest. I stared at my hand, my eyes going wide and my brows arching. I'd never been unable to harness fire. That was peculiar.

I shook my hand as if trying to wake it up. As I did, dread filled me, making me sweat, my mind zipping through the events of last night: the library, the book... *'an exchange of life force.'*

Oh, no. I lost my... *No. Gods, no.*

I called my dragon. Nothing—only a deafening silence. I covered my mouth with a trembling hand. I took a deep breath and held it, trying not to expose myself and the worry attempting to roll off me and onto my brothers.

My wolf, whose presence felt groggy, faded in and out throughout my sprinting thoughts. Saddened and unnerved by her lack of usual spunk, she left me alone in my mind with a quietness I wasn't used to. I darted my eyes to Atlas and Anders, who were both standing nearby and trying to hear my internal battle. My emotions were at risk of boiling over. I clenched my teeth together so hard my jaw popped.

The word '*rest*' echoed in my mind. The only piece of information my wolf shared. They needed rest. Okay. But what did that mean?

This was the cost we read about—the price I had to pay. I couldn't shift, and for how long, I didn't know. Would my dragon come back at all? I tugged the ends of my hair, looping them around my fingers. I couldn't rush their need to recuperate. If a situation arose calling for either of them, I was out of luck.

I reminded myself I'd trained for years in hand-to-hand combat in my human form. I wielded most weapons with ease and possessed a jaw-cracking punch, but I relied on the strength, the *fire* of my wolf and dragon. We'd always been together. I felt a touch of loss and more guilt. This mindset was becoming an annoying and unwanted habit, and I was in no mood for bad habits.

Pull yourself together Athena, this must be temporary. Just temporary.

"So... are you human now?" Atlas looked at me. Worry creased his face. I knew he couldn't hear my mind anymore, no matter how hard he reached for it.

"No, I'm not, but I can't manifest fire or shift," I replied, feeling defeated. Bitter bile burned my throat, and I swallowed it down. I was lucky. My price was something I could pay. Others before me had lost more.

Anders grabbed an apple, trying to busy his mouth, and bit into it more voraciously than necessary. His attempt at keeping a cool exterior wasn't entirely working as I watched his eyes dart from me to Atlas.

"Don't worry. I can still take you both." I tried to drag them from their troubled thoughts. With my wolf asleep, trying to use mind links seemed a bad idea. Adding strain on my unstable counterparts was a poor idea. "I'm still me." I stuffed down my own concerns to ease theirs.

I'm still me.

I took a huge bite of my blueberry muffin—anything to take my mind off my lack of powers. The tangy berries burst on my tongue. I hadn't realized how hungry I was, beyond famished. My muffin disappeared.

"What'd that muffin ever do to you?" Atlas shook his head at me. I looked down to see my shirt covered in crumbs. Hmph. I shook my shirt, dusting them off.

Calliope bustled into the kitchen. "I knew I would find you all by the food again. Some things never change," she said, reminiscing of our younger days. We used to come in the kitchen for repeated snacks but always ended up racing around the large island counter, seeing who could get the last cookie or whatever there was only one of. We always loved a good row. I often won. To be honest, I'd have won every time, but it meant a lot to my brothers to keep up with me. I knew their feelings even then. Atlas and Anders didn't want to be baggage. They needed to show me they were strong enough to defend me. I couldn't fault them for that. It was honorable.

One time, during one of our famous races, I launched a fireball and hit the cabinets. Blasted one right off the wall. Calliope and my mother weren't nearly as thrilled with my skills as I was that day.

Fire. My fire.

Goddess, I hope it returned.

Calliope interrupted my thoughts. "You'll all need to get dressed and get moving. Chop-chop." She waved her hand, shooing us away.

I groaned, knowing she was right. The mountain of things I needed to get in order grew by the second.

⁂

Several weeks passed. No one questioned Kale's presence. And why would they? He smelled like us now, and the guard didn't often pay attention to all our comings and goings. Kale and I used this time to tie up loose ends. He'd taken care of most things over the phone, but some needed to be done in person, requiring him to leave the Unseen. I went with him to LA a couple times to check out his penthouse. He found a renter to take over the lease and hired movers to pack up his things. It made sense for him to stay at the manor where we'd monitor his changes, and frankly, get to know each other better. It was like dating in reverse.

I wanted Kale's company more and more, and not just physically. He made me laugh despite the circumstances, and his dimples made me melt. Even Anders and Atlas enjoyed him, taking turns picking at him. He fit right in, except with my father. He took little interest in Kale at first, but if we ate together in the evenings, he'd ask him questions in cordial attempts to get to know him.

Kale avoided his family's phone calls but occasionally returned a text. His parents remained worried, and if they knew exactly what Kale had gotten into, they'd freak like most humans did.

I played out a monologue in my head: *Hi, I'm Athena. I'm from a world you didn't know existed, and I've turned your son into a supernatural being who can shift into a wolf. Pleasure to make your acquaintance.*

Yeah, I'm sure that'd go over really well.

Kale possessed a unique disposition for taking things well. Nobody reacted to us like Kale, which still struck me as odd.

Then again, we were mates. Bonded together. That had to account for something.

As Kale and I navigated our new bond, my brothers dug deeper into Zephyr, and my parents stayed on their phones or in conferences. They'd wanted to conceal Kale's existence and how I'd created him, but this afternoon that was ending. My father insisted we all attend today's council meeting and tell them about Kale.

At first, the secrecy bothered me, but telling the council about Kale made me uncomfortable and sweaty. It's not that I enjoyed attending meetings to begin with or liked answering to anyone, but something was off. Not just Xercarus, whose potential presence was bad enough, but something deeper. Something my parents didn't care to share, and I couldn't put my finger on what.

I still hadn't heard a peep from my wolf or dragon. Fire eluded me, and mind links were impossible. The silence was painful and made me restless. I'd complained about the beings within, whined about my wolf's interference, and now I wanted nothing more than to hear snarling. I didn't realize I'd unknowingly become ungrateful of the gifts given to me. If I didn't have other pressing matters to occupy my time, I might've lost my mind, but I hated to admit Kale kept me busy in more ways than one. He filled the quiet and opened me up to possibilities. The possibility of danger was one of them, but the more time we spent together, the more his closeness comforted me.

I got up early, letting Kale sleep in again. Little things often tired him, his body struggling to keep with the changes. Not to mention he'd had nightmares almost every night, waking in a frantic, ice-cold sweat.

The spicy aroma of coffee guided me downstairs to the kitchen. As usual, Anders and Atlas lingered at the island, chatting among themselves. They gave me a nod and kept talking.

"Meetings. My favorite," Anders sulked, knowing full well

we'd be under the council's microscope, especially me. None of us were fond of administrative jargon. My father had always indulged us in that way. He never required us to handle business at the investment company we owned, even though we were all board members. And on more than one occasion, he let us avoid the council, especially over the past several weeks. Supernatural red tape wasn't my style.

Atlas gave me a sidelong glance. "Can't imagine who they might be so curious about."

I scoffed at them. "Can we dial down the sarcasm a notch, boys? I just got up. And whose side are you on anyway?" I flattened my palms on the countertop, acknowledging my lack of patience for some of their anecdotes this morning.

Atlas ignored my posturing as usual. "Yours and panda's, of course. We're just giving you a hard time." Atlas smirked at me.

I grabbed another muffin, wrapped it in a napkin, and snatched the waters. I trotted off back toward my room. I'd seen and heard enough of them already today. As I reached the grand staircase, my mother called for me.

"Athena?"

"Yes?" I turned to her, flashing a good-morning smile.

"We've had little time together these past weeks. I imagine you're struggling with all the emotions of having a mate." Her voice was serene, seeking to soothe me. Even as an adult, my mother possessed the ability to reduce my stress and quiet my inner voices.

"I am. It's very alien to me. I love you, Father, and my brothers. This is just different and intense."

Illiana put a hand to her chest, twirling a crystal necklace between her fingers. Not much caught her off guard. "*Ah*, I completely understand. The whole bonding occurrence is rare. Not all of us are lucky enough to find our true companion."

I swallowed. "Right, but you can be happy without a mate. I didn't feel something was missing until I met Kale."

"*Mm*, yes. You don't know the sensation until it hits you. It'll get easier." She tugged the blue gem harder. Something troubled her, though, she masked it better than most.

I examined my mother's face, trying to see past her well-built facade. I observed her eyes glazing over a bit, water brimming on her lower eyelid.

"Oh, *meu amor*." She moved a short distance to embrace me, knocking the muffin from my hand. "How is Kalen doing anyway?" she asked, holding me.

I wanted to give my mother a straight answer, reassure her. I couldn't. Sure, we'd taken care of his affairs. His family knew he was safe and moving somewhere. His brother, Brody, kept calling to check in. He didn't trust Kale's actions or the idea of a new girlfriend. But my mother wasn't asking about the trivial stuff. She was referring to his changing.

"That's the thing, I don't really know. Kale's transformation appears to be progressing at an unprecedented rate. Anders, Atlas, and I go to the library every night to search for anything." I felt a drop of relief, but unease washed over her face, consuming her soft, tan features.

"You go to Kalen, check on him. I need to speak to Father. Just be ready by noon for our first meeting in the conference room. Bring Kalen, if he's able." My mother's voice wavered as she took me into her arms once again and placed a chaste kiss on my cheek. What was this about? She knew my wolf and dragon were gone. She'd known for weeks. But again, something else pained her. That much I gathered.

As if sensing my doubt, she stopped and spun to me again. "Don't worry. Kalen is your destiny. He found his way to you, and this is your path. Faith, my sweet. Nature makes no mistakes." Her smile mildly comforted me, like her words.

I bent to retrieve the muffin and jogged up the stairs. The salty, fresh scent of the ocean waved over to me again. It was delightful. I knew what waited behind my door: Kale. I opened it with the caution a mother used when trying to avoid waking a child.

Tangled in covers, I found him sound asleep. Good, he needed the rest. I set the muffin and waters on the wide dresser, then moved to my double-doored closet to retrieve a suitable outfit for meetings. I grabbed a pair of white, wide-legged trousers and a fitted navy top. Kale stirred from the bed, groaning out a yawn as he shuffled the pale duvet and pillows around him.

"Good morning, lovely." Kale's voice was husky from sleep. "Did you know you smell like fresh lavender and watermelon?

"Watermelon?" I chortled. His senses changed daily, evolving into something more fine-tuned. His eyes, though, stayed dazzling sapphire blue. Thank the Goddess. One thing was moving in the right direction, at least.

Kale beamed at me with his illustrious smile. "It's my favorite fruit and lavender is just soothing. My mom used to put it beneath my pillow as a kid to help me sleep. Come to think of it, I was prone to nightmares then, too." Kale shrugged, turning his mouth in a slight frown.

I thought of Kale as a child, imagining those same striking eyes on a small version of himself, his wild hair going every-where. He must've been a beautiful little boy. "I suppose I could smell like worse things to you."

"To me?" he asked, rubbing the sleep from his eyes. His hair remained a tousled mess, but in the most appealing way. Even waking up, he looked amazing. I inhaled, taking in the crisp, woodsy fragrance he gave off. I loved the changing notes of his scent. It was enough to distract me.

"*Mm-hm.* As mates, we smell unique or, rather, significant to one another. To me, you're like a fresh ocean breeze, kindling pine logs, wildflowers, or a hint of citrus. It changes. And to you, I smell like a squishy fruit," I said, smirking, then bit my lip.

"Squishy fruit? How dare you insult watermelon! That's blasphemy, and I'll not stand for it." Kale threw his hand to his bare chest with exaggerated insult.

I very much wanted to banter with him, to sit and relish in his company, but duty called. I needed to get dressed and presentable. Goddess. What would Kale wear? Not those gray sweats.

Definitely not. Those were an obvious distraction and unacceptable attire to meet pack council leaders, no matter how much he made those sweats look good. We'd brought several boxes of his clothes over, but nothing quite suitable for a meeting of this caliber.

Okay, Thea. Get. It. Together. My thoughts took a turn down a more improper path. Shaking my head, I moved to my vanity. Someone had draped clothes over the chair. Calliope. How did she do that? She was a wonder. I smiled to myself.

I sauntered in Kale's direction and sat at the end of the bed.

"On the bed. Just where I want you." Kale reached for me, his mood and hazy eyes displaying an overt seduction.

I used all my willpower to dodge Kale's advance. If I gave into that, I'd never get ready. Plus, we needed to have a conversation. "*Uh-uh*, none of that right now. We have things to discuss." I cleared my throat and swallowed my desires.

Kale let out a snort of disagreement. "Does it have anything to do with the nice clothes on that chair?" He cocked his head towards the mirrored vanity and plush gray chair.

"My, aren't we perceptive today?" I teased him, putting a light kiss on his cheek. "And yes, it does."

"*Ah*, who could forget a thing like that," Kale said, his mood as chipper as the smirk residing on his face. That was apt to change.

I rubbed Kale's shoulder. My news had bothered me, and I suspected it would do the same to him. "We have a meeting to attend this afternoon. I've told you about the council. Well, they finally got wind of the situation, and they have some questions. Mostly for me."

Alarm took over Kale's features as he sat up straight, his face distorting. I didn't need a link to tell me that. "But you did nothing wrong." His voice got louder and his tone sharper. "You helped me, and now you're being punished? First your wolf, now... this is bullshit, Thea. You don't deserve it!" The blue in his eyes faded, and if I wasn't mistaken, his canines elongated.

More than anything, I wanted to erase Kale's guilt. That was about as likely as eliminating my own. "I know, but this isn't about what I deserve. There has to be balance. You didn't sign up for any of this. I'm sure you went out for a good time and went home with me instead." I pressed my fingers to my temples, wanting my dragon and wolf back as much as, if not more than, him. "Right now, I need you to get dressed. There's time to shower if you want to—"

Kale shot up off the bed. The light sheet that'd been covering him hit the floor. He reached for the bedpost, holding on to steady himself. "Shower? That's the least of my concerns. You—you're my concern. Not some meeting where they tell you how you can't possibly be with me, which by the way I've heard just about fucking enough of!"

Kale's body tensed, and his chest flushed with anger. He was losing control. I knew all too well what this was. Kale was going to shift if I couldn't relax him. This wasn't the place, nor the time to release a new wolf. The wood of the bedpost creaked, giving way from the pressure of Kale's grip.

"Kale, it's just you and me right now. Come here. Let me help you calm down." His body was uneven, his muscles tense, fingers extending with sharp claws forming, and the hair on his arms longer. He grimaced under the discomfort, not able to govern his movements. Kale leaned his head to me, rubbing his forehead against mine.

"Athena." His face rippled with change, reverting back to

his human features. I saw his fingers retracting, less claw- and paw-like. His long fingers looked more like the ones I'd come to know and feel so well. "I'm sorry. I dunno what's wrong with me. I'm worried about you, and then a voice urged me to be more defensive. I got more frantic, and so did the influence. I'm sorry. You know I'd never do anything to hurt you." Kale moved his eyes away from me, looking out the balcony as he sat back down on the bed.

I sat down next to him, put my hand on Kale's knee in reassurance, and then moved to massage his thigh. Not necessarily a wise decision, as I knew all too well us touching would lead to more. As usual, my body hummed at the contact. "I understand—more than you know. Don't apologize for this. I'll help you as much as I can. Since this transformation keeps leaping forward, we must work on calming techniques."

Kale closed his eyes, blowing out a breath. "Calm. Got it."

"I'm going to get dressed. I know it seems I'm always asking something of you. I don't mean to. This is my life, though. I'm one of the Triad and royalty here. You're part of all this now. Our people just need to be assured you aren't a threat—that we can still keep the Unseen and its peoples safe."

"Safe," Kale said, rolling his eyes. His jerked movements remained restless. The wolf was vying for control. "It seems as if things are always being asked of you, too. You aren't free to make a decision without permission or a huge discussion. You make a choice and then have to explain yourself. If you're an Alpha, why don't you do as you please?"

He was, in most ways, correct. I heaved a sigh, patting his knee again and moving off the bed. I knew you couldn't argue with a determined wolf, but you could distract or even appease one. "I brought you one of Calliope's famous blueberry muffins. Eat it. You'll feel better."

Kale got up and shuffled to the dresser, retrieving the baked good. He bit into the muffin, devouring it in a few bites. His voracity made me chuckle.

"What?" he asked, crumbs covering his chin. I set my shirt down and went over to him to wipe the leftovers from his chin. He wrapped an arm around my waist. "Thank you. I apologize for my—"

"Please don't apologize anymore today. I mean it. You've experienced too much, and so have I. You're allowed to lose it here and there. I swear, anyone else would've gone running for the hills. Hell, *I* wanted to run. But you didn't, and I'm so thankful for that. Let's just get through today minute by minute. We have each other, and right now, that's all I need." I put my head on Kale's chest, and he rested his chin on top. Both of us sought a moment of solace in one another's embrace.

Kale sighed, knitting his eyebrows together and letting go of the last of his reserve. "I'll get dressed. I'll go with you and say whatever they need to hear. You know you said before you felt like you were putting me in harm's way. I don't think that's true. I put you in harm's way. I make you question your destiny. I took your... Christ, I took your wolf." He let out a frustrated groan. "I'm making you doubt your strength. All of that... then I try to fight you on looking presentable and going to meetings. Where you'll have your judgment questioned again." Kale's hand wiped down his face in exasperation. "My nightmares are gonna end up coming true. You're gonna wake up and realize this isn't worth the hassle."

Hassle. I scoffed at the word, folding my arms across my chest. How could he believe he was a hassle? If anything, I was the one who'd uprooted his entire life, not to mention changing him into a supernatural. I wasn't sure if I wanted to shake him silly or adore him more for his honesty and his desire to not lose me, as misguided as he might be.

"First of all, you took nothing from me. Second, I'll deal with you being upset. It's justified. What I'm not gonna tolerate

—and I mean I *refuse* to hear it—is you telling me you're not worth it. Because it's not true." I shook my head, pursing my lips. "If they never came back to me, if the leaders questioned me for days, weeks, forever even, it wouldn't matter—any of it. It wouldn't change my mind about you, and I wouldn't want it to. So, go ahead. Get pissed. But don't tell me you're not worth it." This was the first I'd yelled at Kale, my Alpha nature barreling through. I might not have my wolf, but I retained her flare for dominance.

Kale was quiet for a moment, tousling his hair, then gave an unexpected hearty chuckle. It was a splendid sound that almost pulled me from my irritation.

"I hear you loud and clear." He gave me a nod and slipped the fitted, dark-wash denim pants on. Then he pulled a light gray knit sweater over his head, smoothing it down and pushing up the sleeves until they hit right below his elbows. I couldn't decide if this looked better than the sweatpants or not. Kale looked good either way—delectable even. Calliope had a gift. This ensemble fit as if it were tailor-made.

As Kale bent to tie his shoes, I dragged my gaze away to finish putting on my top and slip into my heels. Getting ready used to be such a simple task. It was less so when I followed all someone else's movements. I smiled to myself, biting my bottom lip, while Kale strolled in the bathroom and grabbed a toothbrush.

I positioned myself in front of the mirror, pulling my long, raven waves into a sleek, high ponytail. I twisted the tail-like rope of hair, pinning it up, and paused to take myself in. My reflection was the same as it had always been, yet I felt different. The physical intimacy I'd continued to experience with Kale had been remarkable, and somehow, it showed, like a soft peach glow on my skin.

Out of the corner of my eye, I spotted Kale, admiring me. He walked over, wrapping his arms around me as I placed the last pin in. His touch engulfed my senses. I inhaled deeply. Even in three-inch heels, I wasn't quite his height. Was he taller than before? For a woman, standing six feet, myself, I had an imposing height, intimidating most individuals. Not Kale. He was anything but daunted by me. His current emotion pressed hot against my backside.

He leaned further into me, letting his breath brush my ear. "I know the answer's yes, but do we have to go?" His question was more of an appeal to my other inclinations, in hopes he might sway me.

"Mm, yes, we do," I said, drawing away from his tightening grip. He was much sturdier than when he first came here.

My heels ticked on the tiled bathroom floor as I crossed the room to the bedroom door. Kale followed, grumbling to himself along the way until we reached the sweeping staircase.

Kale stroked his hand down the polished wrought metal banister while we walked. At the bottom of the stairs, I lead him to the right, passing through a corridor. The great skylights above us allowed the sun's rays to beam through and warm the tops of our heads as we passed under them. Sensing Kale's eyes watching me, I purposefully swished my hips. The fabric of my trousers tugged tight, emphasizing my curves. I calculated each step of my cobalt blue Christian Louboutin heels, every click echoing on the marbled floor.

Unsure of what possessed me into taunting Kale, I soon found out the price of my mischievousness. Kale inhaled, rushing up fast, spinning my body with ease between his able hands. Moving with precision in his newfound agility, Kale pinned me to the wall. His eyes flickered gold before he buried his face in my neck, giving me a small kiss, then nipping at me. A muted gasp passed from my open lips, and my eyes rolled up into my fluttering eyelids.

"Perhaps..." Kale said, pausing to drag his nose up my neck to my cheek, a growl rumbling between his words. "It's best," he hesitated again to place a light kiss to the corner of my mouth, making us both shudder, "if you don't *tease* me."

Shocked into silence, I stared at Kale, both of us energized by his display. I nodded at him, a wicked grin playing on my lips. Kale raised one brow, tilting his head to observe my features. Fast as he'd pinned us to the wall, he released me, leaving an empty space between us.

"Your brothers are coming." Kale's eyes flashed. The heat between us cooled like they doused with ice water. I unruffled my shirt, putting myself back together, annoyed I had not heard my brothers coming. I walked to the doors of the conference room, again with Kale a pace behind me, only this time with a smirk I knew was on his face.

CHAPTER 8

*A*nders and Atlas met us from the other direction, jogging past me to the opaque conference room doors, and pushed a button to let us in. My parents were already sitting inside in their usual seats at the giant glass table, which took up most of the room. Most of this conference would take place via Zoom, thus avoiding the leaders leaving their posts for such an impromptu meeting. We set several computers and large screens up in the room's front and waited for the calls to connect.

I took a seat next to my brothers opposite our parents. Shifting down, Anders and Atlas emptied a chair, making room for Kale to sit beside me. I nodded in appreciation of their gesture. It appeared they must have their adult pants on today. Kale sat down, letting out a brief huff. His disgruntled and aroused attitude hadn't dissipated.

Our father spoke, addressing me first. "Your mother tells me your dragon and wolf still aren't with you?"

"No. Seems they're not," I answered, crossing my legs at the ankle to be casual.

Our father scrutinized Kale, sniffing the air. "And it seems his transformation is near completion."

"I suspect so. His wolf attempted to present himself this morning," I added, keeping transparency.

Atlas and Anders, who'd been discreet and quiet, looked up from their phones and joined the conversation.

"His wolf is already calling shots?" Atlas asked, but he wasn't looking at me. His eyes zeroed in on Kale.

Anders swiveled his chair to look at me then Kale. "That's dangerous. He could hurt you, Thea, and you have no way to protect yourself." He trained his sights on Kale as well. Both were now bearing down on him. Wolves' instincts to protect their own ran deep, but I wouldn't let this exchange continue.

"I'd never hurt Athena. That's not an option." Kale's voice trembled, and he was on the verge of losing command of his actions.

Atlas and Anders knew what they were provoking. "Oh, yeah, because you're an expert on wolves? Which you had no idea existed until what, a month ago?" Atlas sneered, pressing Kale further, waiting for detonation.

Kale's nostrils flared, the corner of his mouth twitching.

"Enough," I stood up as I shouted, flinging my chair backward. "You're trying to piss him off into shifting! You wanna help me? You wanna protect me? Then respect Kale. Wolf or no wolf, I'm your Alpha, and I'm far from fucking helpless."

My insides burned with fury. How dare they try to sabotage him, and worse, treat me like a delicate kitten? They both knew better. I gritted my teeth. Anders and Atlas were behaving as if I was incapable of handling myself, which irked me even more. My dear brothers also seemed to have forgotten my proclivity for spells, which didn't require a wolf or dragon. I thought about snapping my fingers and making their tongues numb to remind them, but now wasn't the time for a temper tantrum— much as I wanted to throw one.

Anders hung his head a bit. "We apologize, Athena. Upsetting you was not our intent."

"We only wanted to see what we were dealing with... if he's a normal shifter or something else. We stayed up reading again. You're a hybrid, Thea, and your Alpha blood runs deep. You could've created anything... Kale's likely a wolf of standard size and ability, but maybe not. He has the potential to be the size of an Alpha, like you—or like you were."

Anders took over without missing a beat. "And if that's the case, we'd both need to be around to maneuver him, with you in your current state—"

"—of not being able to shift," I finished the sentence, saying what Anders had intended to.

Someone from behind us let out a gasp. My father cleared his throat, drawing our attention. It was then we noticed the monitors and screens were all on. The council heard at least part of what transpired. Kale examined my expression, raising his brows as I took my seat again. I tried putting on a fake smile, hoping it appeared far more genuine than it felt right now.

"Good afternoon to you all. We appreciate your time." It was my mother, Illiana, addressing the faces on the screens. Their expressions ranged from disgust to amusement.

"This meeting is quite necessary, I see." It was Oriel Reed, head of the East Coast packs. He managed affairs there as an extended hand of my parents. All the leaders in North and South America answered to our family. European and Asian packs created their own set of rules and conducted affairs of their own accord, often resulting in a clash on how to handle situations. But here, the packs—while operating with independence—all honored the same code of ethics.

"So, it's true. Princess Athena can't shift? For how long?" another member inquired.

"Is it permanent?" More voices and chatter. My eyelids fluttered, annoyance seeping out.

"How is the Triad supposed to guard the Unseen if their Alpha's wolf and the mighty dragon have gone dark?" probed another leader, Alder Rivers. This question stung. "There are no other dragons left besides Athena."

The voices grew more urgent, each one clamoring into my head louder than the last. I wanted to put my palms over my ears and scream. Instead, I folded my hands in my lap, knotting them together.

"A human? We don't bond with humans—it's not done. It is beneath us. Besides, humans aren't capable of the amount of loyalty it takes to form a bond with a wolf." This comment got my attention, making my head snap to his screen. It was Clay Baywood, a council member from Alaska. I'd never cared for his attitude prior to this. Now, his stance on humans cemented my opinion. I ground my teeth, wishing I could set him on fire.

"Mr. Baywood, while it's unknown to have occurred before this, I assure you, my mate is very much bonded to me, and I to him. You'd do well to remember who you speak to." My lips curled up, and my tone bordered on vicious. The audacity of Baywood's remarks irked me further from control.

I heard a chair creak and glanced to my side.

Kale's expression was dour, sweat beading at his hairline. I watched him clutch his knees again to reign in his response. "Pardon my interrupting these condemnations because that's exactly what they are. A biased viewpoint about a species you clearly know very little about. Humans possess plenty of loyalty, more than you're showing Athena. She's an individual, you know, not a damn guard dog. You all appear to see the Triad as a tool, to use them, yet never letting them show their genuine power. I care about Athena. For who I know she is and will learn to be, not for what she can or can't do for me. Maybe humans aren't the ones who are beneath you." The timbre of Kale's voice was deep, fueled by anger.

His energy matched mine, emboldening me and giving me a noticeable aura of satisfaction. I summoned my concentration, trying my hardest to not look as impressed and proud of

Kale as I was. We'd had little time together, though it appeared to make no difference. He kept showing me the man he was and the wolf he would be—dominant, like me. I'd created another Alpha, or rather, given his spirit the opportunity to be one.

Clay Baywood's narrow face pinched up, and he sputtered. "King Cyrus. Surely, you don't intend to let Athena and that mongrel human speak to me in such a manner? He is nothing more than a pet," he simpered to my father. His manner repulsed me, and I snarled at the screen.

"Mongrel?" I repeated. Venom filled my mouth, and I was full-on sneering. "That mongrel will be your King one day."

My father stood up from his chair, pointing his finger at the screen. "Clay, unfortunately for you, it is exactly what I intend to do. This meeting is for discussion, not for you to hurl offenses at my daughter, who, if you recall, dropped everything and came to your pack's assistance when ice ogres blundered in and were destroying your towns. Athena didn't hesitate to march herself and her brothers into a bloody skirmish. As for her mate, you *will* consider Kalen Ryan part of our family and refer to him with the same respect given to us. Do you understand me, Baywood?" No one ignored a command from my father. As the reigning Alpha, all deferred to him. His word was law, binding by invisible ties.

I nodded, regarding my father with gratitude. I examined his features like so many times before. His royal blue eyes were the only part of his face that carried his age. Mature worry lines creased around them, making him look tired.

Wolves aged much slower than humans, our metabolism allowing us to live for hundreds of years in the right circumstances. My father's face looked almost the same as when I was a child, like when he'd read to me at his desk. It didn't matter how busy he was or what kingly duties beckoned to be done when I trotted in with my little storybooks; he always let me cuddle up on his lap. He read them all while making funny voices.

Father, I thought. *Thank you.*

"Excuse me, Your Majesties." It was Williamina Cedargrove from the Midwest Packs who pulled me from my reverie. If I heard correctly, and it's fair to assume we all did, your.... mate. He was human, but no longer is? At least in some part?" Williamina was younger, with a deep brown complexion that matched her determined eyes. An accent lingered in her words, and I'd always admired how she carried herself with poise when others lost their heads. She possessed a more docile disposition than the other leaders, always seeking peaceful solutions to any disagreements. Her outward placidity masked the fact that Williamina earned her place as leader by killing a band of orcs, who'd been hunting humans in the wooded terrain of northern Minnesota. A silly thing like a Sasquatch might not be real, but nasty blue-skinned orcs absolutely were.

I oscillated my body to take in the full view of all the screens and their impertinent questions, though some were more like accusations. "That's correct. Kale was human. During an unplanned exchange of blood and marking, it altered him. We're unsure of the extent of the transformation or his capabilities as a new wolf. We plan to run several tests."

My brothers got up and straightened their postures, taking stances next to me. Kale flashed a grin, eating up my resentful tone and confident manner.

"Your bite did this? Humans have been bitten before. How can you be sure this was the cause?" Williamina posed, her curiosity cresting as she leaned forward in her chair.

"I can assure you, Ms. Cedargrove, Kale had no contact with anyone else. We witnessed the initial exchange, and he began changing soon after," Atlas submitted his testament, folding his arms across his broad chest.

"I see. Another gift from the Goddess, no doubt. Blessed be

the Triad." Williamina bowed her head in reverence to us. "Welcome, Kalen."

At least one member accepted him. Not that it mattered. I'd battle all of them if I had to. For Kale, I'd do anything. No unjustified prejudices were going to hinder our relationship.

Oriel Reed spoke again. "I was under the impression we'd move forward with a union between Princess Athena and Regent Prince Henri Pelletier, uniting us with the European packs and ushering in a new Alliance. We would be..."

My face went white with rage and disappointment. I snapped my head back in my father's direction. "Union? To Henri Pelletier? When was I to be told about this? On the day you all planned to ship me off as if I were a pawn? Tell me, did he offer you a dowry for me too? How much was I worth? You don't have the right!" My temper flared as I clenched my fists. I felt a burning in my soul, my eyes flickering like matches being struck. The very idea of being with another after finding Kale was intrusive to my mind and body. That wasn't even the worst part. The council believed they could barter a union to me as some kind of peace offering, like I held no more value than a mail-order mate.

"Athena... It's not like that. It was an idea. Something I'd planned to discuss with you. Besides, last time you attended an event with the Pelletiers, you seemed to get on well with Henri." My father paused, looking at me with a tenderness in his eyes, his lips softening as he tried to reason with me.

I did the opposite, shooting him an iron-clad scowl. He was correct about me getting along with Henri. If only he'd known how well we'd got on... but a union behind my back was unacceptable. I opened my mouth again, only to be interrupted.

"Tsk," my father clicked his tongue. "Athena, this was all before you met Kalen. We were unsure if you were capable of a bond. I presumed that with your powers, you might never find a true match. Your dragon has never responded to anyone outside you and your brothers. I was looking toward a future for you." Even though my father was King at present, he knew he'd crossed a line regardless of my undisclosed brief interlude with Henri.

Cringing at his words, I shook my head low; the betrayal cutting into me.

No—Alphas didn't bow their heads under pressure. I whipped my head back up, staring my father down, refusing to accept such terms.

I locked eyes with my father, challenging him. "So, if I couldn't find a mate on my own, you thought my best option was to pair with someone who could or would find one? And then what? We'd rule together as he bedded someone else at night. A princess by day, babysitter by evening. How despicable. I am Athena Whiteridge, Alpha of the Triad, born of fire and wolf under a blue moon. I belong to no one unless I choose to. *I* choose. My future doesn't get to be decided for me."

The room stilled, no one daring to take a breath. No one spoke to the King in that manner, and I'd done so without batting an eyelash. I'd have set the room on fire to get my point across. My father had cast a blow to my heart and ego, but my dignity wouldn't allow me to suffer in silence.

Stepping back from the table, Anders eyed our father through narrowed eyes. "You weren't actually considering that, were you, Dad?"

Atlas shook his head in silence while turning his back to our father and pacing.

"Cyrus! How could you even think such a thing?" My mother looked at my father, displeasure filling her widened brown eyes. She hadn't been privy to this arrangement either.

"All these years, you encouraged us to trust in our bond, telling us that together we could bring unity. Yet, you didn't believe we could bring unity without coupling Athena to that pompous French..." Atlas couldn't finish, his lips pulling into a harsh sneer. Backing away, he shook his head and paced.

Crash!

Kale's chair flew back, slamming into the drywall. Pieces of chair splintered into the air. "You could've stolen our chance at finding one another. She's everything. Despite that, you thought to give her away?" She's m—" His eyes were back to that fiery, golden amber, canines sharper than before.

Snap.

I heard a bone crack in contortion. And then another.

No, not now.

Kale needed to calm down. He dropped to the floor, his body shaking and twisting.

"Hey, hey," I said, kneeling to stroke Kale's arm. "I know you're upset. I am too. Kale, you need to relax."

Kale's bones continued cracking to readjust. It was too late. No choice but to let this run its course, whatever that was going to be. Kale's body lay twisting and contorting on the dark carpeted floor. Pushing his face into the fabric, Kale labored to muffle his screams, and saliva pooled at the corners of his mouth. I stood by, my heart warring between wanting to meet his wolf and worrying for the safety of others.

My brothers stepped in front of me, tucking me behind them. Atlas released his shield. A thin veil of silver surrounded us. I held firmly to Anders's arm. He was tense, flinching now and again. Shoving my shoulder into Anders, I pushed out in front of him to see Kale. I wanted to hear his mind. I strained, trying to pick up anything, but I couldn't.

Dammit.

Atlas's and Anders's eyes never left Kale's form, watching him writhe in agony. The first shift was wicked. It was a terrible shock to your system and an unfamiliar group of sensations, none of which felt very good. Anders and Atlas absorbed a dulled version of Kale's pain, but Atlas didn't drop his shield, never faltering as he pushed aside his connected discomfort.

Gasps and whispers came from the screens. Kale created quite the captivated audience as he transformed. I couldn't spare the time to focus on what they were saying. It hurt to watch Kale struggling on the ground. His wolf fought hard, changing and manipulating Kale's body until he gained control. His frame took its new shape.

Kale raised himself up, shaking his new body. A low growl rumbling from his deep chest. He was glorious—a large, brown wolf. Not any brown, but the same chocolate, almost-black hue of Kale's hair. His pointed ears flattened as he observed the screens, and he rumbled more growls, baring his large white teeth. Kale lunged forward toward the screen Baywood's weasel-like face was on. He knocked several chairs over in his speed.

The spectacle stunned the entire council into a strange, soundless awe. Even my parents didn't speak, letting Kale flex his enormous new body.

I called him. "Kale. Come to me." I knew I was the only way to keep him from tearing apart the electronic presence of Baywood. I moved around Atlas and Anders. Anders's hand bolted to reach for my arm.

"You know he won't hurt me," I said, brushing off his hand and pushing past Atlas's shield. "Kale."

Kale turned, and his amber eyes met mine. He moved on all fours to me, tilting his massive head from side to side. I put my hand out, palm up. His wet muzzle sniffed, then licked my outstretched hand. He leaned his head into me, moving down to rub his giant furred body along my arm.

"Hello, my wolf. Keep him safe," I cooed at the hulking animal. He whined, a high-pitched playful noise, then straightened and stood tall beside me. His legs were long and spindle-like until he reached his shoulders, where the muscles were thick and sturdy under glossy fur. Of course, he would stun in any form.

A loud laugh startled the room, and I looked back to the screens. "*Ha!* This is the only wonderful news! Look at him. Superb. With the ability to create more wolves, we can expand our numbers. We can make a move into elven territories, maybe even take on the water nymphs. Their lands hold the greatest riches. With more capital, we can bend the human government to our will." Baywood's tone was as sinister as his proposal, and his beady eyes blurred black. He was more diabolical than I'd ever imagined. We needed to remove Baywood from his place and take him into custody. I thought an arranged union was the worst thing I heard today, but this was far more appalling. Baywood continued laughing like he was in a state of mania. His tone carried overt maliciousness, and a malicious wolf was dangerous.

Our mother, Illiana, reared up out of her chair, her eyes glaring daggers at the screen Baywood's laughing face was on. "Elven territory? That's out of the question. The elves have done nothing but help us. They lost as many in the Great War against Xercarus as we did. Why would we ever launch such an attack on peaceful people? And the nymphs—we'd all drown in such a foolish endeavor. Elves and faeries are endowments of nature. It's a disgrace to even suggest such atrocious ideas. And to think of enslaving humans... You're out of line, and I won't hear any more of this acrimonious talk. *Já chega!*"

And with that, my mother slammed her hands onto the table, making it shake.

I'd never seen her so enraged. Her dainty index finger pointed at the screen, and her posture was taut. She cursed Baywood in elven under her breath. I knew my mother's people had a long and entwined relationship with elves. She'd told us many stories of her adventures through the jungle with elves and wild cats.

As children, Mother taught us to respect and practice the elven ways with nature. Treat nature as an equal, and in return, it would grace us with all its splendor. Our mother made sure to teach us her native language. She wanted us to have more than just her blood in our veins. She wanted us to have her culture, and we did. Nature was part of us, and we found balance in it. It was also why the Solstice Festivals were essential in transitioning seasons. Elves and faeries encompassed an almost heavenly balance. An attack on them was an attack on nature itself. I couldn't imagine the consequences of such an action.

"You will see our guards shortly, Baywood. What you speak of is a punishable offense. I hereby strip you of your title. You are no longer a leader or member of this council." Cyrus doled out his orders. The council remained silent for a few moments, each of them likely shocked by Baywood's behavior and how quickly their King removed Baywood from his place.

I pushed the intercom button with too much force, jarring the device. "Logan, please take your best to Baywood's area. We have removed him from leadership and stripped his title."

Oriel Reed cleared his throat, trying to gather our attention. I looked up, nodding at him to speak. His voice was quieter this time. "I meant no disrespect, Your Majesties. I merely wanted what was best for our Alliance. I shouldn't have been so careless. I will not forget my place in the future. Many blessings to you and your new mate, Princess. I wish to continue to serve the crown and Triad." Oriel's face was kind, and his broad features were open. He did his best to backpedal and put himself back in our good graces. His words carried an air of sincerity, and up until this meeting, I'd liked Oriel a great deal more than some council leaders. I was sure he'd meant no harm, nevertheless, I didn't appreciate his participation in trying to pair me up.

Lifting my head higher, I focused myself on Oriel. "I won't say you're forgiven, though I admire your admission and appreciate your honesty. I look forward to establishing a more truthful line of communication with you in the future. Thank you, Mr. Reed. You're dismissed." I clicked off his monitor. The screen went black. Kale shook his fur and howled in agreement. It was the first time I had ever dismissed a leader from a meeting. My parents and brothers didn't speak, all of them eyeing me in anticipation of my next move.

"Thank you all for joining us today. I apologize for this not going as it should have. I'd like you all to know we appreciate your continued support, and I will be able to shift in the future. The Triad will remain protectors of this Alliance and the Unseen. As of now, we adjourn until we can sort out Baywood's treachery. We shall reconvene soon. Thank you again."

All the leaders nodded in approval and disconnected. Before I could get another word in, I heard my father.

"Athena, if I could speak to you in private for a moment." My father motioned for me to sit next to him.

I snorted, shaking my head, far too angry at the hidden proposal. I didn't have the patience to sit. "Father." I left my formal tone behind. "Not now. I'll talk with you, just not now. I can't. I need to have a clear head to hear you. I just don't have it in me. Kale was tested to a limit. Now that he's finally shifted, I have to get him to the lab. Not to mention, I've put off investigating what's going on at Zephyr for far too long."

A heavy sigh came from my father. "I understand. I betrayed your trust. But you must know I did what I thought was right and best for all of us," he offered. He stroked his ash-blonde beard and leaned back in the chair like he knew I had something else to say.

An unladylike laugh tumbled from my mouth. "Yes, you did what you believed was right for everyone else but me." That was all I said—anything else was far ruder. I turned my back to my father.

I touched Kale's pointed ear. "Let's go." I started to leave the conference room. My footsteps hit the floor hard in the best attempt at stomping I could manage in heels.

I heard a chair roll. "Wait, Athena, there is one more thing—about Zephyr. I'd planned to meet with you and your brothers before, but it got lost in the chaos." Cyrus wrung his hands. Was my father, the Alpha, overwhelmed? This was an emotional state I'd never witnessed from him, the smell of anxiety wafting off him. My father was always the epitome of composure and something had him shaken.

I walked back toward him, putting a hand to my hip and glaring. Curiosity and confusion piqued my interest. "What is it?" I asked.

"You're right. Humans have been disappearing, but not just humans. Wolves, vampires, elves. We've been monitoring the situation, and it's reached a critical point. Xercarus is back, and if we are correct, he is creating an army of supernatural beings just like all those years ago."

I scoffed. My blood boiled. He'd blown off every hunch I had about Xercarus, ignored my requests, and now the demon was creating a new horde. "This is exactly what I feared. You told me to leave it alone, called me overzealous and stubborn, and you knew. You knew! Now we have an army of supernaturals. That's fucking brilliant! What about the humans? What's he doing with them?" I tried keeping my voice down, but it was futile. I couldn't believe what I was hearing. *The lies.* How could he?

He'd known all along my intuition was right, and he'd gone out of his way to dissuade me, and for what?

"We believe they're being used to..." Cyrus stopped, swallowing. "Feed them." His voice trailed off.

Kale snarled, his body hunched to the ground, ready to pounce. I touched his side for reassurance. Our worst nightmares and fears were being realized, but this is what I was meant for—what the Triad was meant for.

The prophecy.

Prophecy had fated my brothers and I to fight that beast back to the hell. I had to believe we'd fare better than the fire people.

Anders paced. "How long has this been going on?" His voice hinted at hostility through his clenched teeth, and he cracked his knuckles to busy his hands.

"How many died while you waited, Father? Dozens? Hundreds? We could've been looking for him, extending our search, digging deeper!" Atlas was no less indignant, throwing his arms in the air with agitation and pacing the small space.

"We wanted to safeguard you. We thought if we could locate his lair..." Our mother crossed the room to the three of us as she tried reasoning.

"You can't justify this, Mother. It doesn't matter if you meant well. We're here to protect you. If you never let us try, we can never succeed. You said to have faith, but where's your faith in us?" I needed her to understand. We all did. "In order to fulfill the prophecy, we need to fight him."

Anders went to wrap his arms around our mother as tears fell from her dark eyes. "This isn't something you can prevent or beg the Goddess to make it go away. This is our purpose."

Hugging on to Anders, she looked at Atlas and me. "You're my children. We love you. To sacrifice your children for the greater good is much harder than you can understand. I begged your father to hold off. To give me more time. It was me who didn't want you to know. I did this. I'm sorry, my loves." She muttered in Portuguese, holding on to Anders as if it were the last time she'd ever hug him.

"We're sorry, Athena, but it's true. We wanted to spare you a fight. It's clear we cannot, but you can't blame us for trying to keep you safe a little longer." Our father took my face in his hands, letting his thumb stroke my cheek. My anger still flared. What they'd both done was selfish, but part of me understood.

I understood the desire to protect someone you loved. I'd do anything for them, my brothers and Kalen. I sighed into his hand.

"I thought if I sent you to France, away from this, I could protect you. It was never about an Alliance. It was always to keep you and your brothers safe. Athena, when I held you the first time, almost twenty-five years ago, you were so strong. I knew then I'd do everything I could to spare you from harm, whether or not it's your destiny." He pulled me into a tight embrace, and I held him back. His familiar fresh rain smell calmed my nerves. It consoled me, knowing he wasn't willing to pawn me off for business. He came from a place of love. It all made sense, but it didn't change how much danger he'd put us all in.

Our mother opened her arms to us. I tucked myself into her, Atlas and Anders embracing us both.

I wanted to be madder, but I no longer had it in me. "I know you both meant well, I do. We love you, too, but this was inexcusable." I kissed each one of my mother's cheeks then looked her in the eyes. "Now, if you'll both excuse us, we have a lot to get done and less time to do it." My mother gave a quick nod, her eyes still glistened with fresh tears.

"Right, then. Take whatever forces you need. I have to accompany Logan to Baywood's. I need to see for myself how deep his madness goes, and I want to know every detail you uncover at Zephyr. This time, no secrets." Our father gave each of us a hug before straightening his overcoat. It was strange, but not because he wasn't affectionate with us. His posture was rigid, radiating the same anxiousness I'd never felt from him before. He took our mother's hand, their conversation wordless, and they both left the office. I knew they had many things to discuss before my father departed, so it was best to let us all get on with this hectic day.

I returned my attention to the boys, including Kale in all his wolfed-out glory. "We need to prepare to locate this den as soon as possible. We're going back to Zephyr tonight. I shouldn't have let it go this long. I know it's related to this." I could feel a surge of determination in my voice and something on the back of my neck tingled.

"You feel that too, huh?" Anders leaned on the glass table, typing something into an iPad.

"Maybe this time we can get something done, without you losing your mind over panda over there." Atlas rolled up his sleeves and jerked his thumb in Kale's direction.

With a yap, Kale pounced on Atlas. They hit the ground with a loud thud. "Oh, come on, now. You know I was only kidding," chuckled Atlas. Kale backed off him, snapping at Atlas's pant leg.

"Time to shift back, bro," said Anders, raising his eyebrow at the two of them. "Playtime is over."

Kale cocked his magnificent head to me, the amber in his eyes swirled with flecks of gold. I nodded. Without my abilities, we couldn't communicate. I sighed.

Kale braced his posture, trying to figure out what he needed to do. I heard the familiar snapping and popping, his body once again moving to the carpeted floor. He was in less pain this time, more accustomed to the change. After a few more cracks, there stood Kale, a man again with his face coated in light perspiration.

Anders and Atlas wasted no time hooting.

"So, that's the appeal. Not bad for a human." Atlas laughed harder, blatantly mocking Kale.

Kale leaned over and repositioned his hands to cover himself the best he could.

"Again, I find myself telling you two to grow up. I know there are other things far more useful you could do with your time right now, like getting the lab ready. I'd like to take samples from Kale while the shifting energy is still fresh." I found it hard to be irritated when the sight of Kale was hilarious.

"Haven't you taken enough samples from the poor guy?" Atlas joked, never one to let an opportunity pass by.

Kale smirked; his humor more intact than his clothing.

"You think this is funny too, eh?" I shook my head. All three were like teenagers.

"As a matter of fact, I do. I'm naked. Give a guy a break." Kale shrugged, letting another laugh out.

"Glad you see so much amusement in these situations. It's like we haven't been told a demon is back and eating his way through humanity." I eyed the three of them, trying to get them back on track.

"Alright. Point taken. Meet you in the lab. Bring pants." Anders and Atlas headed to the basement, cackling the entire time.

"Pants. Right." Kale's famous grin was in full effect but sagged when he looked at the grim expression on mine. He mouthed the word *sorry*.

I waved it off. "The first couple times shifting always leaves you kinda a loopy and keyed up. It's the extra adrenaline." I glanced down. "I, uh—I'll save you the walk of shame. I'll run upstairs and get you some clothes." I did my best to avoid staring.

The doors opened behind us. "No need, lovey. Here you are. Hurry up before you catch a chill." Calliope for the save again. A miracle worker.

Kale one-handedly accepted the clothing and started moving to the back of the room to put them on. "Thank you, Calliope. I apologize for my, uh, nudity."

"Needn't apologize for the skin you were born in. As a wolf, you'll find yourself in these situations often. Best to not be a prude, I always say." With that, Calliope straightened the hem of her white shirt and rushed off through the doors, her cinnamon-colored hair bouncing as she went.

"Thank you again, Cal," I called to her, appreciating her saint-like ability to know exactly what we needed. Calliope possessed an uncanny sense of showing up at the right time to save one of our asses.

"My pleasure," Calliope said, her voice muffled due to her already being halfway down the hall, on to her next task, no doubt.

CHAPTER 9

Kale, clothed again, came swooping up behind me, taking me up in his muggy arms. The powerful sensation of happiness whenever I was near him startled me, engulfing me, body, and mind.

"You were outstanding in there," he said, kissing my cheeks with a sweet eagerness.

"And you were exceptional, as well. You handled your wolf like a pro."

"High praise. Why, thank you, Princess, but I'm not gonna lie. I don't love this new aggressive streak. The lack of control—it's not me." Kale rubbed his arm as the grin dropped off his lips. I understood what he meant. Control over your wolf took time. Even I couldn't always reign in that wild nature.

I moved a hair from his face. "You'll get there. I'm just surprised you haven't freaked and run off yet."

Kale gave me a wink. "Thought about it."

It was good to see him like this, making jokes. I knew once things settled down, we'd never run out of things to banter about.

"*Mm*, funny. Ready?"

"Not sure if I've ever been ready since I met you. It's been one hell of a ride, but worth every second," he answered. "You actually have a lab in your basement? Can't say I'm surprised. This place legit has everything. What else do you have down there?"

"Besides a lab? We have a big pool. More like a grotto," I said, leading him down the hallway by a loop on his jeans. "As for the lab, our parents built it a long time ago, when we were kids. Gives us a place to log information or examine any creature not capable of healing. As a shifter, you'll heal at an accelerated rate, and you already know Anders can cure or repair most injuries."

"I'd like to check out that grotto, but another time, as usual. So, abilities? You mentioned it a couple times. Let me see if I've got this. Anders can heal, Atlas has shielding, and you...?" Kale paused.

"And I..." I let my words die off. I didn't have any of my abilities right now. An emptiness crept in my chest.

"Can create," Kale filled in the dead air and stopped my heart from sinking.

"I guess that's accurate, except we didn't know I could do that until you." I frowned a bit, letting the weight of what Kale said settle in. I hadn't thought of it that way before. I looked at turning Kale as a mistake—an unwanted outcome—but he looked at it as a gift.

"Well, that and fire. It doesn't get much hotter than a woman who can make her own fire." Kale picked up my odd mood and pushed me gently into the elevator as he talked, his voice deepening as his eyes darkened. "Then again, being with you is like *playing with fire*. Seductive... erotic... a little dangerous. Promise you won't burn me, Thea?" He backed me against the wall of the elevator, catching my lips with a kiss that made me hazy, his hands framing the sides of my face. As always, my body melded to his, swept away in his every movement.

The elevator dinged. Kale released his hold and my mouth,

backing away from me with a sly smirk. "To be continued," he promised, dragging his hand down my contour.

I flushed and fiddled with my hair, trying to get rid of any evidence of his effect on me before heading out of the elevator. He'd almost made me forget I didn't possess fire at the moment. Clever boy.

We walked down a short cement corridor to the lab. The opaque glass door slid open, letting us both in the room.

Atlas and Anders had laid out what we needed for a blood draw. We had the lab furnished with the latest tech. Computers, diagnostic machines, rolling chairs, and cabinets full of tools, gloves, and other equipment lined the light walls. Several plush gray chairs and an examination table took up the center of the room. The room was clinical but not off-putting. There were old, framed yellowed photos on the walls—medicine people from before my time. The room smelled hygienic like a doctor's office, but the aroma of peonies swirled about from the vase of fuchsia-colored flowers sitting on the concrete slab counter under a shelf of medical books. My mother left no room flower-free.

"Take a seat, my man." Atlas gestured to an oversized chair. "Hope you aren't scared of needles."

"I know this is going to disappoint you, Atlas, but I'm not. Been donating blood regularly. O-negative. Ha, look at that! I'm special, too." Kale winked at me and plopped down in the chair, rolling his sleeve up.

Atlas tied off Kale's arm, and his veins bulged. A quick poke, and Atlas had the three vials he needed, plus two extras for later labs.

I put droplets of Kale's blood on several glass slides to check out under the microscope. Not entirely sure what I was looking for, I left them and made sure Kale's arm was no longer bleeding. The puncture had healed and faded away. I patted the crook of his arm. "All better."

Kale rubbed his arm, observing his new skill.

Atlas pushed back out of his chair, walking around Kale and me to put a vial in the centrifuge. Atlas always had a knack for sciences. As a kid, he had too many chemistry sets. When Atlas wasn't teasing Anders and me, his nose was in a book. His love of knowledge and skillful mind often took a backseat to his smart-ass commentary. Atlas looked over the slides, adjusting the scope to magnify whatever caught his attention.

"Well, that's disappointing," Kale broke the silence with a small puff.

"What is?" I asked, shifting my stance and angling closer to Kale

"If I heal fast, that means no more band-aids. Half the reward of getting poked is the cool band-aid," Kale chuckled and rolled his sleeve back down to three-quarter length.

Anders clicked away at the computer, typing in more notes. "Does the little boy want a lollipop, too?" Anders mocked him. Kale opened his mouth to respond.

"Dammit!" Atlas said, slamming his hand down on the counter.

Our heads all snapped in Atlas's direction, his exclamation jarring us. Atlas's plastered his face to the microscope as he continued to mutter.

"What's wrong?" My heart skipped a beat, wishing I could see into Atlas's head.

"Lemme guess, I'm half wolf." The smile faded from Kale's face when Atlas didn't take the bait.

Swiveling his chair in my direction, Atlas put his hands in his lap.

Oh, no. Whatever it was, it wasn't good news.

"I can't be one hundred percent sure about most of this, but from what I can decipher, Kale's body is working in overdrive. His cells obviously aren't human anymore, yet they aren't what we see in a wolf, like us. Nothing looks right."

I hunched over to look into the microscope. "What do you mean *'not a wolf'*? That doesn't make any sense. Let me see." Sure enough, something was off. I didn't know half as much as Atlas; however, I could see whose blood Kale's samples resembled, but still, something wasn't right.

Atlas looked from Kale to me. "Best guess? Your bite created a wolf. But you didn't just bite Kale, did you? You gave him your blood. I think your blood is the key to making a new... dragon." His dark eyes connected with each one of us before he carried on.

"If your blood can create dragons, that's phenomenal and hazardous as fuck, to you and everyone else. With Xercarus taking supernaturals, you'd be a prime target. If he had you, he could make his own personal fire-breathing hell-horde." Atlas's words jumbled in my head all at once, giving me a sharp pain in the temples. I winced and rubbed the side of my head with my fingers.

An army of supernaturals with the power to control fire and potentially shift into dragons. This had just gone from bad to worse. I had as much chance to stop Xercarus as I did to help him destroy our worlds. *Great.* The good news kept pouring in. I wanted to scream or claw someone's face off. None of this was anything I wanted to hear.

"Are you sure?" I asked Atlas, knowing he had no more information available.

"No, not really. His blood is off, like he's... never mind." Atlas shrugged in annoyance, turning his attention back to Kale's samples. He moved the slide around and the microscope up and down.

Kale sputtered. "Not 'never mind.' What is it?" He struggled daily, trying to adjust to his new life with me and as a supernatural, but this development shook him.

Atlas sucked in his lips, then chewed the inside of his cheek. "You sure you were entirely human?"

Kale's brows creased together, and he shook his head in disbelief. "Yeah, I'm human. Or *was*, whatever."

"Maybe not." Anders pointed out. "I mean, how many humans know their lineage six or seven generations back? Who's to say you don't have a supernatural ancestor."

Kale shook his head in disbelief. "Wait, slow down. You're saying I was never fully human to begin with?"

"Exactly. Might explain why you never feared us like you should and why Thea's abilities took such a hit. That's a pretty powerful exchange. If one blood exchange was enough to bring out your gifts, what would trying to make more supernaturals do to you?" Atlas didn't look up as he scowled while flipping through files, tossing them aside when he didn't find what he was looking for.

Anders looked from me to Kale. "It's a fair guess to say it'd kill Thea, especially if she wasn't given time to recover."

Kale hadn't said another word yet. A deep frown formed on his face as he sat chewing at his nail. His skin looked sticky and pale, like he was going to be sick. "So, what am I, or was I? You said you could hear them both, right? I only hear the wolf. There's nothing else in there." Kale's tone was rough. "What if there's no dragon, and Thea's blood isn't capable of making one? Xercarus wouldn't have an interest in her then."

I took Kale's hand. "Hey, we'll figure it out. We always do. And a dragon isn't like a wolf. They're discreet, for lack of a better word, and only speak to you when it's necessary. You'd never know it was there until it showed itself."

That was the truth. We had no way of knowing what Kale had inside him and why his body had reacted this way. He was too new, his senses too raw and full of emotion to say with any real accuracy. The idea of Kale being a descendant of a supernatural made sense. He was becoming so powerful, and faster than anyone expected.

Atlas huffed and scratched his head. He understood there

wasn't time to sugarcoat the situation for Kale, much as we all might have wanted to. "Xercarus would still have a hard-on to get Thea. Even making more wolves would him an advantage."

Kale blew out a breath, dragging his hand through his hair. "Thea? Maybe it wouldn't be a bad idea if you stayed by Atlas and Anders for tonight. I don't know what's lying dormant in here. What if I lose my shit again, and I can't control it?"

Kale's blue eyes flickered to amber. I could see him fighting his want to be near me with his need to keep me safe.

"Hey, Kale, we got you. I'll run your blood again, and until then, we won't let you turn Thea to ashes. No worries, bro," Atlas said, lifting his head from the iPad screen. Atlas had meant to lighten the mood—it had the opposite effect.

He looked back down at the iPad, swiping a few more times. "Just like we won't let Xercarus take her to bring on a damn Armageddon."

"Wait—I could set Thea on fire? Why the hell would you say that? Is that honestly a risk? This is—" Kale's eyes darted around. He put his hands to his hips and dug into himself.

"No, it's not. You're not gonna set me on fire. Fire doesn't burn me, and Xercarus can't try it if he doesn't know about my blood." I strove to comfort Kale. It made my skin itch, watching him struggle. It also didn't feel good thinking about being used as a mobile host to create a mindless dragon army, either.

"Very low possibility you'd barbecue Thea. She's fire resistant, at least she was, but if you did, I'd heal her. Problem solved," Anders said, giving a brief nod.

I glared at both my brothers. They scurried off to fiddle with lab equipment, giving Kale and me a moment.

Touching Kale's arm, the tension I felt radiating off him leached into my hand. He averted his eyes and stepped away from me, my hand dropping into empty space. His movement surprised me. He'd never intentionally repositioned away from me before. I felt a prickle in my chest.

"Thea, I need some time to clear my mind. I just gotta get outta here for a bit. Away from— " Kale's jaw twitched as if he was trying to choose his words with the utmost care.

"Away from me. I understand." I shifted farther away, offering Kale more space. I did understand. It didn't lessen the sting.

"Don't read more into this than there is. Okay? I just need a few minutes. Gets so hard to focus my thoughts when I'm around you and all this. It's a lot of shit to take in." For the first time, Kale's voice was flat and emotionless, not giving anything away.

A throb in my chest crept in, trying to choke me up. I swallowed, hoping to hush my internal pressure. Kale asked for space, which was more than reasonable. I knew all too well the effects our proximity had on the mind.

Wanting to give him what he needed, I gave him a quick smile and hoped it was enough to fake casual.

"I get it. I do. I... You go on ahead. I'll catch up with you later. We'll get things ready for tonight. We leave at seven if you want to come. If not, that's fine too." I smiled at him again, doing my best to mask my discomfort. Kale's eyes were dark, full of what must be regret. He turned, walking back to the elevator without looking back. I wondered if the regret was for walking away from me now or not walking away soon enough.

Dammit. I wanted my wolf. She was my connection inside his mind, but Kale deserved his privacy. His thoughts belonged to him. I had no right to them unless he wanted to share. I worked my jaw and tapped my shoe.

Atlas got up from his chair, rubbing my back. I heaved a discontented sighed. "Athena, hey. Get out of your head. I promise you. Kale's just going to collect his thoughts. That's all." I glanced up at Atlas and twisted my mouth off to the side. Could one thing go right today?

"He's right. It's a lot. We're a lot. He wants to be more in control of himself. Can't blame him. We told him he probably wasn't fully human and that he's hiding a boogeyman in there with him." Anders eyed me. Sympathy was something I wasn't used to. An Alpha without her wolf, getting sympathy. I was killing it today. I felt in too deep, way over my head. This is why I'd never wanted a mate. I had no clue how to shoulder someone else's mental pressures.

Realization hit me in the face, making my mouth pop open. "You mind linked him, didn't you?"

"Yeah, sort of. He linked us." Atlas's brown eyes dodged away from my glare. "He wanted us to make sure you understood his feelings for you haven't changed."

A laugh that surprised even me erupted from my throat. "*Ha.* So, this is how it feels? How fucking obnoxious. Always having someone talking around you," I complained, the delirious laughter ending. Another feeling I didn't enjoy —exclusion.

Come back already. I hollered inside my head, wishing either of them would respond.

Nothing.

"Guess so. Sorry, Thea. We want you back to normal, too. It's boring not hearing you growl constantly." Anders patted my shoulder. I placed my hand on top of his, giving it a gentle squeeze.

"And don't worry. Xercarus won't touch you." Atlas crossed his arms, then dropped to his sides and walked back over to me.

"No, he won't. I'll die first before we'd let him." Anders's harsh tone matched Atlas's determination.

I stood for a moment, shaking my head, taking in their declarations. This was too much. "Alright. Enough moping. Meet you at the training course to grab some gear before we go." I proceeded to the door, then stopped short, taking a long, deep breath in through my nose and exhaling from my mouth.

Whining about what I couldn't change wouldn't help me. Preparing for tonight, however, would.

Turning back around, I looked at my brothers, who'd gone back to their screens, but looked up when they felt my gaze on their faces. I took a second to really see them for once, and Anders's words hit me again.

"I'll die first."

Despite all our bickering, all our taunting, they were loyal to a fault. A tear fell. I didn't know if I'd survive a world where they didn't exist.

I wiped the waterworks away with the back of my hand and closed the distance between them and me. "I love you. Thank you." I hugged them both, squeezing them tight. I didn't need to do everything on my own. I had Anders and Atlas.

I let them go, sighing. *Responsibility awaits*, I reminded myself. "Get the guard ready. Logan's gone, so make Gage run point. He's more than competent. I have a feeling we're going to need them nearby."

Stopping the elevator door with his large hand, Atlas bounced inside. "I'm going to get a sandwich. Cal picked up some pastrami and ham the other day. It's calling my name from here." Just like that, Atlas's seriousness had vanished, replaced by hunger.

As the doors closed, I thought about Zephyr, about how I'd let it go too long. I'd let Kalen take priority and put my responsibility to the Unseen on the back burner. Now, who knew how many would pay the price for my mistake and my parent's delay?

Atlas piped up again, distracting me. "You hungry? I'll even make you one."

"No. Thank you, though. I'm good." My appetite had vanished. The elevator opened, and I headed upstairs, leaving Atlas to destroy the kitchen. Poor Calliope. Atlas's precision in the lab did not extend to the kitchen. There was likely to be mustard on the backsplash and cabinets when he finished.

Not sure where Kale had gotten to, I went upstairs to my room. Queuing up some music, I opened the balcony doors wide, fresh air hitting my cheeks. With this view, I hoped to forget as many of my duties as I could. I tried focusing on the crisp breeze coming off the water. I couldn't. My worry for Kale consumed me and I wondered if he could adjust to what the labs discovered. It weighed on me, knowing I'd passed even more onto Kale, but what was he? If he was prone to becoming a dragon, what were the odds he had some kind of way back great ancestor who was from the Fire people—or even Fae? Fae and Nymphs dallied with humans all the time. Could anything with him be easy?

Not a chance.

I took a deep breath in, trying to let it go, but I became more concerned about Xercarus by the second. My body vibrated with nervous energy. I refused to be part of a scenario where I was his puppet. That was not an option for me.

Closing my eyes, I sat on the cushioned chaise, taking in the fresh pine scent and sun on my skin. Khalid's melodious crooning resonated from the small speakers, weaving around my thoughts. The longer I held still, breathing in and out, the more rejuvenated I felt. Nature and music always had a tranquil effect on me, allowing me to straighten my mind. Inhaling another soft breeze that came rolling in off the lake, I got up, feeling serene and more collected. Faith, my mother told me. One must have faith that this would pan out, someway, somehow.

Best to ready myself for tonight. My plan was to up my attire game. I wanted the VIPs to notice me. Odds were, they'd have some inclinations as to what was happening at Zephyr. That'd been my goal several weeks ago, but it didn't go as planned. This time I'd have no distractions. I'd have Kale with me and, while he had an alluring hold over me, I'd be able to resist it more now that we'd been together in more ways than one.

Walking to my closet, I opened the doors and moved hangers back and forth, searching for the right outfit. It needed ample sex appeal. I pushed more clothing around in my closet; the hangers scrapping on the bar that held them.

Ah, this would do.

A floor-length ruby red cocktail dress, backless, with slits on both sides, baring more of my thigh to make my legs look even longer. I slipped on my garter—not one for holding up stockings. It was custom made to fit like a glove and hold my blades. Just because I couldn't wolf out didn't mean I was less lethal. Claws and teeth were not my only defenses. I went to the other side of the closet, looking at my shoes, pulling a pair out, then putting them back in their slot. Hm, a pair of strappy black three-inch heels caught my eye, and I pulled them out.

I went to the mirror, putting on mascara and a bit of blush. I pinned my hair up on one side, letting the rest fall down my bare back. I scanned my reflection again, deciding my lips should be as crimson as my dress. I lined my lips, watching the red color spread. There.

Perfect.

This ought to do the trick. I looked sexy, and I knew it. I gave my reflection a cocky grin.

A small click behind me let me know Kale was back. *Mm, Kale*, I inhaled. Such a short time, yet I had missed his presence. Kale smelled divine, refreshing and clean.

"Athena? I'm sorry about earlier. I need time to—" He came into my view. From the confounded, wide-eyed look on his face, the dress was getting the exact response I wanted.

"You look..." Kale shook his head back and forth as if to shake away his lustful thoughts. He could shake his head all he wanted. The effect my appearance had on him kept hold of his attention, drawing him to me like a moth to a flame.

"I look?" I paused, prompting Kale into speaking again, and flashed a demure smile in his direction.

"Gorgeous. Though that doesn't describe you well enough." Kale was next to me quicker than I'd anticipated, letting his hands roam down my torso, then curving around to my back until he reached the roundness of my bottom. He squeezed it, licking his lips, and leaned in. His icy breath hit my cheek.

"I had every intention of coming in here and having a conversation with you, but, uh, I seem to have forgotten what I wanted to say." Kale surveyed me again, his hand brushing the hair from my shoulder.

"Mind the lipstick, please." I smiled again, purring in his ear. I couldn't have cared less if he marred my lipstick, colored me with crimson, but I pretended to carry some semblance of sound mind. We needed to have a conversation, but I'd done enough talking today.

"It's official. This is a dream. You're a fantasy. Too bad I might shred the first person who touches you." Kale kept his grip on me, his breathing quickening.

I inhaled him, drinking him into my senses. Kale possessed an air about him that was fresh and crisp, like a day on the beach—an intoxicating mix. "I don't think that'll be necessary but can't say I'd react any better. Jenny didn't know how close she came to losing her hand."

As I spoke, Kale squeezed tighter on my backside, hoisting me around his waist, then set me on the white granite counter with a light thud. "Oh," I mumbled, his maneuver catching me off guard. I let my one leg twine around him, my heel touching the back of his thigh, drawing him nearer. His presence lifted me out of time and brought me to a place of peace that did not exist anywhere but in his arms.

"Let's not talk about her right now. So, you said mind your

lipstick. You said nothing about anything else?" Lowering his hand, Kale trailed his fingertip down my chest between my breasts, stopping to let his fingers brush between my legs. My head fell back. I knew I'd never stop wanting to feel him this way. I gasped, moving my thighs farther apart, giving him the access he and I both desired. Kale shifted himself even closer, panting, his finger tangling around the silky material of my undergarments.

"I like where you're going with this…" My voice was breathy and needful. I pulled my focus, best I could. "And it saddens me to say we can't. If we start now, neither of us will stop."

"Mm." Kale bent his head, letting out a displeased groan into my shoulder. "Right. It's not like humanity is depending on you or anything."

I moved my hands through his hair, holding his face to mine. "I promise I'll make it up to you later."

"I look forward to you keeping that promise." Kale pressed a kiss to my cheek, resting his hands on my hips. "Nothing with you is ever simple, is it?"

He helped me ease off the marbled bathroom counter. My heels made a soft click as they hit the tile. "No, seems not. You might've mentioned that before." I cocked my brow, placing my hand on my jutted hip.

"Yeah, it's just all starting to really hit me, but earlier, when I asked for some space, I—it was stupid. But for a moment, I thought things might settle down. I was just getting the hang of this wolf thing. Now, I feel like a beast who could snap, and that's not me." Kale picked at a frayed string from one of the woven bands on his wrist, then kept on going. "And I have this nagging thought in my mind I can't shake. I thought if I took a walk, I could reason with myself it wasn't real. You know the dreams I keep having?"

"Hard to forget." A heat rose to my cheeks, matching my

dress, remembering his nightmares and what we'd often do after. I grabbed Kale's hand. His palm was sweaty.

"Mm, yeah, but what if they aren't just bad dreams? Hear me out. Each time, you send me away as this man is taking you. Thing is, he's not a man. His shape's kind of like one, but he's something else. His skin was like this blistering red, eyes completely black, like empty pits. When he opened his mouth, a gross black ooze spewed out, and it sounded like screams from so many people." Kale's cheeks lost their color and his brows knit together while he searched my face for answers.

I felt my face going pale with unease and nausea. I swallowed the saliva pooling in my mouth. "Wait, did you say black eyes?"

"Yeah, these hollow, soulless-looking fucking craters."

I'd read the book a hundred times over the past months. It was in the library. Our history of the Great War... Kale's dreams were about Xercarus. But he'd never seen him or the book. My mind raced. Kale couldn't possibly have seen the illustrations. He was asleep each time we researched in the library.

"Tell me. Tell me what you're thinking?" Kale lightly shook my shoulders, trying to grab my attention again.

"Your dreams. I think you're dreaming of Xercarus, but you've never seen him. You couldn't know that." I was uncertain of what all this meant, but I had a few ideas.

Kale shuddered. "No. That can't be right." His denial would not change what I knew to be true.

"We'll go to the library. I'll show you the books, the illustrations. What you described is Xercarus, I know it. Call Atlas and Anders, have them meet us in the library. We'll figure this out."

Kale did as I asked him, summoning my brothers.

For the first time, I was glad neither Kale nor my brothers could hear my mind because I did not know what Kale's dreams meant for us, and that terrified me.

CHAPTER 10

nders and Atlas sprinted into the library as I was pulling *Great War: Volume I* off a tall brown shelf. I slammed the oversized book down on the table, dust from the pages flying into the air. I opened the book, flipping pages too fast.

"Here. Look," I said, pointing to Xercarus's menacing portrait, blackness streaming from his twisted mouth, claw-like hands ravaging a human body. "Xercarus. Deep red skin, black eyes. It was said when he opened his mouth the souls of those he devoured cried out a deafening scream."

Xercarus—a beast of nightmares, foraged from the nefarious black depths of a hell the human world could not fathom. And here, he played among Kale's nightmares, seeping into his head like the dark plague he was.

"What's this all about? We know what Xercarus looks like, Thea." Atlas took the book, reading several paragraphs and thumbing through more pages.

"Kale's nightmares. He's dreaming of Xercarus."

"What? No way." Atlas shook his head. "Kale's never looked in these books until now. How could he know how he looks?

How does that even work?" Atlas's mouth twisted into a grimace, and he sneered at the mention of Xercarus.

I eyed Atlas as I tapped the gruesome illustration. "That's my point."

"It means we have more issues." Anders had a different book in his hands, his eyes not lifting from the page. It was the tattered, old, journal-looking one we'd looked at before. "Life-force exchange. Maybe after all this, you gave Kale a little of your *Triadness*—know what I mean?" Anders ran his finger along the pages of the book, reading fast and flipping more pages.

"*Triadness*? Anders, you're not making any fucking sense." Atlas wrinkled his face and narrowed his eyes, staring at Anders, who still hadn't looked up from squinting at the book.

Anders put the book down on the table in front of us. "Okay, hear me out." He stood up straight and shook his hands, trying to gain his equanimity back to explain himself. "You, me, and Athena have abilities—ones others don't possess, right? Athena gave Kale her blood. Who's to say she didn't ignite a small ability in him?" Anders raced on, putting his hand to his brows, then pinching the bridge of his nose. "The gift of sight, or premonition. Ever notice how dulled Thea's senses are? I don't think that's just her wolf and dragon going AWOL. Her awareness is lower. She's not feeling us or even Kale half the time. Didn't she get startled earlier? I mean, no one sneaks up on Thea."

"Dude... you're right. We had to tell her what Kale was thinking. Even if she couldn't link him." Atlas gaped at me, taking in what Anders said. "You should've been able to sense Kale's intensity toward you, and you've always been able to feel us..."

My mind dashed to catch up to Anders's breakthrough, and I had to push down my annoyance of being talked around like I wasn't in the room. I rolled my shoulders, attempting to relax.

Fat chance.

I could've smacked myself. It hadn't dawned on me how I wasn't sensing people. Even Kale had sensed my emotions, and I couldn't sort his out. I took in a deep breath, then blew it out. I was finding frustration to be my new normal. I clicked my heel on the floor.

"I've been so wrapped up in this," I motioned between Kale and me, "I wasn't paying attention to everything I was missing. Dammit. Okay, so, premonition. I gave Kale the ability to see the future?" The words tumbled from my mouth. "Seems like a sick joke in more ways than one. This doesn't bode well for us, because if that's true, it means Xercarus... captures me."

"Shit," Atlas muttered, his face paler. He dropped down to the sofa, taking a seat.

"No. No. No!" Kale yelled, both hands fisting in his hair, pacing like a predator in a cage.

"We all need to calm down. We know nothing for sure. This is all guesses and hunches at this point. To be safe, we'll operate as if all things could be possible. We'll also assume I'm going to regain my abilities. If there's one thing I know, we can change the future. I placed my hand on my brothers' shoulders. I didn't know who I was reassuring more.

This was far from over. I had no intention of letting Xercarus use me for anything. No one lorded over me. I planned to take his head off and breathe fire down his neck. That's the only future I'd get on board with.

Kale trembled, his own predator lingering beneath the surface, ready to leap out and hold guard. I gathered Kale's tall figure in my arms. "This isn't what you bargained for. Not what I had in mind either, but everything is going to be fine. We can change what you saw."

Kale stepped back out of my embrace, bending at the waist like he was going to be sick. Instead, he took deep breaths through his nose, expanding his lungs. I didn't touch him while he collected himself. The faint smell of fear and sweat melted off him. Hands on his knees, Kale looked up at me. As fast as he'd bent over, he was standing in front of me, amber dancing in his eyes.

Kale laid his hands on my face. "How'd you do that?" he asked me, searching my expression. His eyes falling to my red lips then moving back up again.

"Do what?" I asked, looking into his warring eyes.

"Make it all go away. You crashed into my life. Blew everything I thought I knew to pieces, but—" Kale kissed my forehead, releasing me from his grasp to look at my face. "I know I'm where I'm supposed to be, and I'll stand with you through anything."

Energy surged through me, buzzing about. Having Kale gave me a greater purpose.

I gave him a knowing grin. "First, we need gear. Atlas, show Kale to our weapons vault. Fill the Jeep with silver cuffs, stakes, tasers, anything you can fit. And Kale, take whatever you feel comfortable handling and can conceal. If nothing else, if something goes wrong, shift."

Kale whipped his head in my direction at what I said. "Shift? I thought one of the key points was to keep knowledge supernaturals obscured?"

"It is. But we have plans in place for containment. We'll have our media group say there's been a large gas leak causing hallucinations, hysteria, and the effects will wear off soon. If they feel the need, seek care from the local ER. Everyone will go home, thinking they inhaled fumes. Safe and sound, none the wiser." I crossed the room, replacing the books in their proper place on the shelves.

Kale rubbed his arm, tightening his jaw. "Seems kinda underhanded."

It was dishonest, but as long as we kept as many as we could from harm, it was a necessary evil.

Kale sucked in his lips, taking in what I'd said. I replaced more books on the shelf. I almost forgot how much Kale still didn't know about the Unseen, the precautions we took to keep ourselves hidden from humanity. Most humans weren't ready for our existence yet. Too many would hunt us for trophies or pick us apart, looking to capitalize on our corpses. He may not be human anymore, but Kale made me want to shed a light on our kind. He gave me hope maybe we could coexist in an acknowledged and respected capacity. Today was not that day, though, and our secrecy remained of the utmost importance. I wouldn't adjust our Alliance to suit Kale's whims.

"Come on, Kale." Atlas clapped his palm on Kale's back, moving him along.

Atlas persisted, using his notorious habit of aggravating me. "You'll learn Athena is a whole lot of business and a lot less pleasure most of the time." He laughed, leaving with Kale. Kale shook his head and threw a toothy, comical expression over his shoulder, putting his fist to his mouth.

"You're really lucky, Atlas!" I hollered after him. I thought of using a spell to trip him, but I closed my mouth, thinking better of it.

He chuckled again. "Yeah, I know. By the time you get your fire back, I'll have pissed you off about something else."

I heard what had to be Kale elbowing Atlas, then more laughter as they headed down the corridor.

# CHAPTER 11

The car ride breezed by, the Barrier no longer an issue. Kale spent his time attempting to use his so-called sight, but he couldn't glean much. The harder he tried, the more frustrated he became.

"I can only see someone. Can't make out who or what outside of it being a male, I think."

Premonitions and visions were a fickle magic. Not unreliable, but not something you could time. They required intense focus and practice to hone the ability—or, in Kale's case, falling asleep. I thought of the tattoos on his back, the seeing eye. That didn't seem like a coincidence. I'd known no wolf to possess the gift of premonition. Sight was magic that came from fae and certain high-ranking elves.

Kale groaned, stealing my attention from my musings.

"Hey. That's better than nothing. Means we get at least one step closer." I gave Kale's sweating hand a squeeze. "You need to give yourself way more credit. You're doing great—better than most. Think of it this way: you met a girl you thought was human; she turned you into a shifter. Then for kicks, we're up against a demon who wants to kill us, and you see the future.

That's not overwhelming at all." I chuckled. "You're the champion of handling the unexpected."

As we walked to Zephyr's entrance, I noticed the same wolf from the last time standing at the ropes. He bowed his head as he let us in. Anders's power had worked like a charm; the bouncer clearly didn't remember a thing. The line behind us jeered in complaints as he let us in ahead of them.

The club remained dimly lit, the same as before. The boys flanked my sides, trailing behind me. Alcohol, wolves, and the faint scent of blood swirled up my nose. I hadn't noticed blood last time. Blood meant vampires. Music pounded loud in my ears. Thirty Seconds to Mars's "Love Is Madness" boomed through the many overhead speakers. I took Kale's hand, leading him to the lit up, smokey dance floor. Dancing seemed as good an idea as any to gain attention from the VIP area—not to mention how much I'd enjoy provoking Kale.

Biting my bottom lip, I bowed my body into Kale. Swirling my hips on him, he took my waist in his hands. He held on steadily but didn't stop me from moving against him, only rocking with me. He had a natural, seductive rhythm, matching mine with ease.

"What. Are. You. Doing?" Kale's pitch was rough, full of gravel, and his eyes darkened to a royal blue shadowed under the moving lights.

Angling my torso against his chest, I leaned my head farther back, putting my red lips to his ear, and whispered. "Getting attention... from you and everyone else. Do you like it?" I kept my tone demure, unlike my feline motions. I ground against him with delicate diligence, paying attention to his every breath. I savored each moment as I worked my body on him. Even before he'd turned, Kale's physique was admirable. Everything about him was built to draw attention. How many hearts must he have broken with a simple smile?

And now, I had *his* heart.

"You know I do." Kale's brazen excitement pushed high and rigid against me. I continued to rock my hips, swaying to the music while my arms lifted around Kale's head. His body responding and moving fluidly with mine. Turning myself to face him, I trailed my cleavage along his firm chest, a tantalizing move that stirred us both.

Kale inhaled sharply, drawing his tongue along his longer teeth. "Continue moving like that... I'll take you to the bathroom, and I guarantee you we won't be doing what we came here for." This wasn't a threat; it was a flirtatious promise, one intended to push him over the edge.

"*Mm*. True." Wrapping my hands around Kale's neck, I played with his loose hair. "You'd be doing me..."

Just as I was pressing upwards to his neck, someone interrupted us, clearing their throat. I turned my head to face our unwanted intruder, a small, ruddy featured man. His eyes, dark and beady.

It hadn't taken long to grab someone's interest. My smile faded, and I felt almost disappointed at how fast my plan had worked. I wasn't sure which of us was more enchanted by the dancing, me or Kale.

Anyone who tried picking up a woman while she was with someone else wasn't likely to follow a moral code. "Excuse me, Miss. My employer, Mr. David Alexi, has invited you to join him in lounge eight."

I raised my eyebrows, puffed my lips into a mock pout, and tried making my tone aloof. "You can tell Mr. Alexi I don't enjoy being interrupted. But I'll join him." I headed to the staircase, wagging my hips as I walked. The shiny fabric of my dress stretching over my ample curves.

Kale grasped my lower arm. "I'm coming with you."

Kale needed to behave. This could be our lead, and a possessive wolf tantrum was a setback we couldn't afford.

I leaned into his ear. "You're going to need to remain in

control. We know this David isn't calling me up to say hello." I did my best to use my Alpha temperament on him.

Kale pulled his eyes away from me, nodding to Atlas and Anders, who were sitting with a group of attractive young women. I watched the women vying for their attention with their flirtations and touchy gestures, each of them hoping to gain a new love interest or tryst with one of my brothers. I couldn't blame them. Anders and Atlas were good-looking and every bit as charming when they wanted to be; Anders with his signature crooked grin and enticing soft blue eyes that invited you in; and Atlas, bolder, the confident bad boy some women craved. He drew them in, using his golden-flecked shade of dark brown eyes to smolder, and if that didn't work, he had this sly habit of biting his bottom lip to seal the deal.

I almost felt bad for the women, who I watched, toss their hair back, angling themselves closer to my two brothers. They didn't stand a chance. Neither of my brothers often, if ever, bed human women. They preferred the less delicate company of elves, half-blooded fae, wolves, even vampires, and they avoided nymphs entirely. Anders caught my gaze, narrowing his eyes on me, showing me his alertness while he continued talking. Atlas threw back his drink with a laugh, raising his hand to order another round for the group, and winked at me from a distance.

The weasel-like short man with unblinking dark eyes offered his hand to me. "If you're finished, you may follow me."

I rejected his touch, opting for the railing instead. "Lead the way."

We headed up the black staircase, the scent of blood getting stronger. We reached another rope. The gentleman nodded and let us pass—all except Kale. The giant bouncer put his hand on Kale's chest, shaking his head in disapproval as if to say, *"Not you."*

Was this going to be a reoccurring scenario? Last time, I'd

been the one who handled a bouncer situation without tact, and I was a seasoned supernatural. Kale's newness made him far less predictable. I started to say something when Kale's chest rumbled, causing the man to jerk back his hand. Kale's eyes glinted gold, a warning of what lurked beneath his surface.

"Seems you've brought a pet with you, my sweet little morsel." It was the voice of a man.

Hm. Not a man.

I sniffed again—a vampire. The smell was a dead giveaway; they had a cloudy whiff of blood around them. My head followed the voice. It landed on a vampire with an expensive-looking, all-black suit. His coiffured bright blonde hair framed his pale, narrow face. Severe brows and sharp features gave him an animalistic appearance. He wasn't altogether unattractive, though that didn't change my blatant disinterest outside of the information I might obtain from him.

"Let him through," the vampire continued. "Our lady in red has him on a short leash." The black-suited vampire's tone was full of mirth. He gave me a long-toothed smirk, gazing at my body from top to bottom.

Ah, this was a smug bastard.

I stifled the impulse to roll my eyes. Vampires weren't all bad. In fact, most were decent. But this one... I couldn't detect even an ounce of decency from him.

Kale frowned and used his shoulder to push past the bouncer. The larger man stumbled back from the shoulder check, sure to keep his eyes down. Kale took a place nearby, leaning on the railing, his back to the crowd down below. He made sure his eyes could see me from any angle as he looked on.

"For a wolf, I find you quite appealing. I often avoid rabid dogs; however, I've never been one to pass up beauty. And you, my dear, are a rare, quite exquisite gem." He trailed his finger down my cheek. Without warning, my skin crawled, and I turned my cheek away. My nose wrinkled from the scent of blood, and goosebumps covered my arms. It wasn't from the chill of his bony touch, but more from the fact that his hands didn't belong on me.

I was missing most of my extra senses, but one thing stayed evident: something depraved this vampire, and that made him dangerous. I felt it in the way my bones groaned from his touch, my body warning me to avoid his hands. He stank of more than blood. He carried a distinct and poisonous air of death with him. His pressed suit was covered in the dank smell that not even his potent cologne masked. It burned my nostrils. Goddess, how much blood was on his hands? How many suffered under his wrath? Perhaps I didn't want to know. I stifled the urge to choke him on the spot, to rid the world of his presence.

I heard a distinct, muted growl. Kale's lip twitched, trying to avoid curling into a full-on snarl. He didn't appreciate the vampire touching me any more than I did, and he wasn't shy about displaying his lack of enthusiasm. But Kale didn't feel the ugly darkness of murder cloaking this vampire.

The vampire grinned again, showing his pointed teeth and looking down his slender nose.

"Pity. You wolves. Always so quick to settle. How can you limit yourself when there are so many flavors to sample? I've been around for centuries, my treat; I promise I can show you things a *dog* cannot." Chuckling, he rested his cool hand on my open lower back. I shivered with abhorrence; he was much too arrogant. "David Alexi. Whose company do I have the pleasure of having tonight?" He attempted to make a stroke up my spine.

My lip quivered, and I moved away from his touch. If he didn't know my identity already, I would not give it all away up front. I gave him the first name that came to mind.

"Lena." My hand went to my hip. "Is there a reason you requested me, in particular? You seem to have an aversion to wolves. I can't understand why I'd fit your fancy as I'm very wolf-like myself." David's entire manner repulsed me. He was repellent. There was no way women submitted to him without a trance. His attitude appalled me, and the way he referred to women was enough to turn my stomach—or make me want to rip out his throat.

"*Mm*, dearest, your dress is my favorite color. Blood red, naturally. A bit cliché, I admit, but I'm a fierce traditionalist if nothing else."

David swished a drink around in his glass. I knew by scent and color what it was. Blood. I scanned the lounge for the human source.

"The color suits you. It was made for your luscious skin." He licked his lips. "You look utterly delicious."

Kale's growls grew louder; soon, human ears would hear him. His posture was severe, unbending as he leaned forward off the balcony railing, clutching the metal banister as it bent beneath his fingers.

The cold vampire laughed. "Calm down, pup. I'm not here to steal your toy. I only want to borrow it." David's amusement radiated on his face as he reached to grasp my rounded bottom.

Leaning in closer to David, grasping the lapel of his over-coat firmer than necessary, "I'm...no...one's...toy..." I murmured in a hushed tone. David pulled out of my grip, straightening his jacket and staggering back.

"What's the matter? Don't like snacks who fight back?" I stared him down, daring him to try to outrun me. Atlas and Anders dispatched the bouncer and were at my side, Kale behind me to cover my back. "I'm going to need to know where —or rather whom—that blood came from."

David snorted, disgusted at our advance. "You don't know who I am. I'll make you regret this." David's words were threatening, but no one without preternatural senses could hear over the human chatter and pounding music.

"David," I said, wagging my finger at him. "It seems you don't know who we are. We're the Triad."

"The... no... it can't be. Of all the wolves, I had to..." Faltering on his words, David took a step back from me, bumping a high-top table behind him.

I wagged my finger at him again. "Tsk, tsk. Seems red isn't your lucky color tonight. Now, where did the blood come from?" I wasn't backing down, my eyes boring into his.

"He'll kill me, you know," David whined, his eyes bulged from his pale head.

I chuckled. "And we'll kill you if you don't tell us exactly what we wanna know. At least this way, I might be inclined to let you walk out of here." I pulled a silver dagger from my garter, tapping it to his chest. "Your choice." This time it was me who smirked.

"I'd just tell her, man, she's no fun when she's angry." Atlas grinned, letting his canines slip down. He put a hand on David's shoulder, squeezing hard enough to break any human man's clavicle.

"Hands off me, mutt," David spluttered. "I'll tell you. This place, Zephyr, it's a blood house. Downstairs they keep all kinds of individuals for..."

"Blood, like some kind of fucked up Starbucks." Kale's voice held fury, harsh and deep. His eyes flickered blue to amber, rage intent on David.

"*Oh*, haha," David cackled, his eyes darkening. "Not just blood. Some don't even make it out from downstairs whole again. And all right under the mighty Triad's nose."

Anders and Atlas growled this time. I didn't have time to feed into David's baiting me. "You said all kinds of individuals, like what?"

"Oh, you really don't know, do you?" David's sneer was ever-present. "Folks from the Unseen go missing, but where do they go? They go down below. Their blood drained to feed the rest, or maybe he turns them if they're powerful enough."

"Who? Who turns them?" I asked, straining on David's shirt. Didn't matter. I knew the answer.

Xercarus.

This whole fucking place was like a Venus flytrap. Inviting you in, and some never got out again. Disgust soured in my mouth. To be served up as a blood bag or, worse, turned into a mutated corpse for a vile horde.

"The original boogeyman himself, Xercarus," David proudly announced, a taunting grin playing on his thin-lipped mouth.

I heard snarling from my brothers and Kale again. A few more words, and David's blood would run along the floor for all the humans to see. I could so easily end David right here, impale him, and remove his head. A shiver of excitement ticked up my back; we needed to get to the basement before I lost my restraint. The lights and sounds in Zephyr moved around us, music pulsing through the dark floor and into my limbs. I couldn't help but look down, wondering what lay beneath our feet.

"Looks like we are going to take a tour." I pushed David toward the stairs, dagger at his back. "After you. Run—they'll kill you. Piss me off—*I'll* kill you. Are we clear?" David nodded.

Not so sure of yourself now, are you? Disgusting deviant.

All of us walked down the stairs, navigating the gyrating crowd and shuffling closer to a hall with a red exit sign above it. Didn't take long to arrive at a hallway I obviously hadn't noticed the other night. Off to the left, there was an unmarked elevator requiring a key card for access. I pushed the dagger farther into David's spine, knowing if the silver pierced his skin, he would be in severe discomfort. David snarled but complied, removing a key from his pocket and swiping it across the sensor.

The doors opened with a ding. Swiping his key again on the keypad inside the elevator, he pushed button "B."

Basement. *Of course.*

Where else would you keep human and supernatural meals? I chewed on the inside of my mouth. My agitation grew by the second.

"Anders, call Agent Connor. We'll need his team here," I ordered.

Agent Connor was our human contact for any situation involving supernatural and human altercations, safety, or press. Before us, Connor had worked alongside our father for twenty plus years, sifting through everything from average lawbreakers to more delicate issues. Connor, having been around our father so long, watched us grow up.

Once we were of a "responsible" age, as our father had put it, Agent Connor kind of inherited us. He was the standard 'good guy.' Late-forties, graying hair, medium build, and always in street clothes. Connor didn't believe in the formality of law enforcement and government. *"How are people ever supposed to trust you if you're wearing a cheap suit?"* He once told us. Had to hand it to the guy—Connor was good at pretending to be mundane when he was anything but. Lethally accurate with his gun, he carried silver cuffs and wolf tranquilizers, and he didn't get squeamish about us shifting. We liked the guy, and I considered him a mentor of sorts. His experience and the thoughtful way about him made him easy to get on with.

Connor was head of a facility and department that kept their eye out for illicit supernatural events and tasked a glorified cleanup crew. In the past, we often required their assistance for media coverage and anything dealing with the human condition.

Ding.

The elevator came to a halt, doors opening to a huge room. The smell hit us hard before what laid before us sunk in. The cleanliness of the area did nothing to mask the odor, a rancid combination of filth and decay. The scent of death loomed over us, inducing a revulsion, which was doing its best to overtake my logic. This was what I'd gotten a whiff of weeks ago—the darkness I couldn't shake.

The room was a sterile, makeshift clinic with an old asylum feel. Glass containment units stood in front of us in rows.

Not containers.

Cages.

These were cages, at least thirty of them. Inside the units, I could see strung up people, and not all were humans. Crudely improvised IVs dangled from their motionless bodies. We were too late for most of them. The stink made sense. No one had bothered to remove the corpses who were bled dry—no more to give. An enraged helplessness pushed in around me as I kept looking, walking faster, searching for anyone still alive.

Anders was on the phone with Agent Connor.

"Connor, we're looking at an underground blood house. Around thirty containment units. I'll find a back-access route for your entry. Yeah... yeah. If you could have your guys detain everyone from the VIP lounges for questioning. Use Protocol..." He looked at me, unsure.

"C," I interjected, surveying inside the nearest container. "And the staff—have him hold back the staff, too. One of them is bound to have something we can use."

Anders nodded at me in acknowledgment. "Right, C. Thea said detain the staff as well. Uh-huh. Yes. Thanks." Anders tucked his phone back into his jean pocket. "He's about twenty minutes out."

"What? What is this?" Kale covered his nose and mouth, trying to stop the stench from further invading his nostrils. I could see Kale wanted to wretch, his stomach fighting to push up its contents. He was still getting used to his preternatural sense of smell, and this rot made it worse.

"Looks like a buffet for vampires. You know, the Starbucks you mentioned." Atlas curled his lip, making no attempt to disguise his contempt. He shoved David to the ground. His body hit the cement with a hard thump. "You're fucking deplorable. Feeding off... this." Atlas pointed towards the rows of glass. "They're fucking helpless. You can use trance—this shit is unnecessary."

David, not knowing well enough to quit, barked a goading laugh towards Atlas. "Stupid wolf. Killing them slowly is more fun. What you see here is the first. Won't be the last either. When Xercarus is back to full power, we will dictate who lives and dies. Humans will be at the bottom of the food chain, where they belong. Sniveling, fragile bags of blood and flesh. As for their supernatural sympathizers, you'll die with them. I'll drink your—"

Snap. A bone crunching sound of ripping muscles filled the room.

Atlas had moved in a blur, without warning. No one had time to stop him. His brown eyes flashed with harsh anger. David's bloody, decapitated head hung from his hand, and the vampire's twitching corpse lay in a spreading pool of dark, thick liquid on the floor.

"Shut. Up," was all that came from Atlas's snarling mouth. His chest heaved up and down, body coursing with adrenaline.

My eyes went wide, and my eyebrows shot up. "Atlas! Dammit! We needed him." My voice rose in shock. The rational side of me tried to be pissed at Atlas, but I couldn't find it in myself to hold Atlas accountable for killing him. Deep down, I applauded Atlas, and I stifled a proud smile.

I guess it wasn't as deep down as I thought.

I didn't condone rash behavior, but David was a monster beyond all reason—no remorse, no respect for life. It was all too clear David had lost every tangible thread of humanity in his years on this Earth. We'd never have let David go out into the world, knowing he would commit violent atrocities on people who had no knowledge or defense against him. David had to be cut loose; he was a liability and a Xercarus follower.

Caving to his Beta nature, Atlas knelt at my side, bowing his head to ask my forgiveness. "I'm sorry, Thea. I am. Not for killing him, for making it harder for us to find Xercarus."

"Don't apologize. He would never make it through the night anyway. You did us a favor. Now we don't have to listen to his poisonous rhetoric." I patted Atlas's shoulder, pulling him closer to my waist. "Stand up. Get rid of that head and find someplace to wash your hands." Atlas picked himself up from his knees. He dropped the bloody, dripping mass, and it rolled unceremoniously across the cement floor.

I watched Atlas scan the room for anything usable to clean his hands of vampire blood. There was a large stainless-steel sink in the very back of the room. After rinsing his hands, Atlas wiped his wet hands on his dark-wash pants. He quickened his pace, returning to his place at my side. Atlas kept his head down, his eyes averting mine. Guilt hovered over his usual playful features. I wanted to reach Atlas's mind, let him know everything was going to be fine, but I couldn't. I clenched my teeth together. I knew he was rebuking himself for killing David, and I wasn't able to help him shake it.

Kale came over, a sullen look on his face. He sighed and gave Atlas a knowing squeeze on the shoulder, nodding in support.

Walking to the closest row of temporary cages, I peered inside the first one. A girl. She couldn't have been more than our age. Her head sagged over a metal fixing across her neck. Her once flashy clothes were ripped, blood-stained, shoes missing. Her frail body slouched, forced to stand while strapped to a concrete block. I put my hand to the box and closed my eyes. She was alive.

"Ignis Incedium," I whispered, both hands on the glass now.

The wall melted, evaporating beneath my hands. I could've broken the bullet-proof glass by hurling my fist through it but didn't want to waste valuable energy or create the unneeded mess. "Anders, hurry. There's time to heal her wounds, and for the love of the Goddess, keep her unconscious."

Shaking his head in disbelief, Kale came closer to me. Touching my palms, he traced down each of my fingers. "I know they said you were good with spells. Seeing you do one is a whole other experience. You're fucking magic."

"I am. Then again, you are too." As much as I wanted to linger in Kale's uplifting atmosphere, I returned my attention to the containment units, peering into the next one. The longer I looked at these poor individuals, the darker my mood turned. My body ached, making me stiff, like part of me broke for them.

I held up my palms. "Ignis Incedium." Again, melting away the wall of glass until I left nothing. A young-looking male vampire, his skin sallow and cold, with a purplish tint. His appearance suggested he was younger than David in both human and vampire years. I regarded the fledgling vampire with caution. I touched his face, lifting his chin. My heart pinched along with my face. Kale gasped behind me, taking in the malnourished boy along with me.

Reviving the vampire without a proper feeding source on hand was dangerous for him. No one here wanted to revive the vampire, only to kill him moments later in a different fashion for simply being starved. I decided since he wasn't in as dire a condition, I'd leave him strapped down until we could get blood bags from Connor. I would not feed him one of his cell-mates—that seemed additionally cruel. Damn me for not thinking of raiding the lab for blood bags—rookie mistake. Connor should be here any minute. Then we could get this vamp in talking condition.

I carried on down the line. One dead, two dead, three dead... death overwhelming the room, and the helpless corpses piling up. A mixture of rage and misery washed over me. Human lives brought to an unnecessary, grotesque end. And the disemboweling and feeding on inhabitants from the Unseen... It was unacceptable. I could sense my eyes darkening, the anger pooling in them.

I looked down at my trembling hands.

"Right under the mighty Triad's nose."

David had been all too correct about that. The disappointment in myself was thick and hard to swallow as I looked around at all the hanging heads of those I'd never save.

Anders reappeared with Agent Connor hot behind him. "Blood house, eh? Athena, I'm not gonna sugarcoat this for you. It's bad. I counted seventeen dead. Hm... Make that twenty-four. Completely drained. Several are missing organs." Connor's voice was gruff as he walked the room.

A huff snuck out from between my lips. "I know. This entire club is a front for a blood demon, Xercarus. Last time he was loose, humans suffered the *plague*. We're going to do everything we can to track him down." I marched to the containment unit holding the vampire. My strappy heels clicked with each step on the cement. "We need several blood bags before Anders heals this one up."

Connor took a step into the unit, tapping his shiny brown Oxford on the vampire's bare foot. "Jason. Grab four bags of blood from the van. Wait—make it six. This one looks hungry." Agent Connor radioed, then regarded me. "Do you have any other leads you can follow?"

"We had a lead. He met a hasty exit," I shrugged, retaining eye contact with Connor.

"Hmm." Connor stroked his chin, examining each of us through his deep-set eyes. "So, which one of you killed him? The new guy?"

Kale gave a scoff, letting his mouth fall open. "Are you talking about me?" he asked, pointing a finger to his own chest, while his eyebrows shot up into his hairline. If the situation wasn't so severe, I might have smirked at the surprised expression taking over Kale's face.

I tightened my jaw, regaining my composure. "As Alpha, I take full responsibility for the circumstances leading to his death."

"That answers that—Atlas. If it wasn't the new kid, it's gotta be him. Far more impulsive than Anders ever was. Told that boy a hundred times..." Connor almost chuckled, walking to stand next to me. "I always knew you were gonna make a great leader, Athena. Your dad has always been so proud of you—of all of you. This is a solid find. We had no idea this shit was going on in Zephyr. We'll be looking into any suspicious activity at any newer clubs. These places are like cockroaches— where there's one, there's more."

I nodded at his compliment. "Thanks, Connor. We appreciate you collaborating with us, as usual. Anders is going to wipe the survivors' memories for the last seventy-two hours. We can't risk questioning them."

Connor stroked his stubbled chin, narrowing his eyes into slits. "You realize you'll be giving up valuable information by forgoing their questioning? And your vampire here is the only supernatural survivor," Connor said. It was more of a statement than a question.

I folded my arms across my chest. "I'm aware. They've been through enough. I won't subject the humans to more trauma. It's unfair enough to expect this one to answer questions." I eyed the slumped, pitiful form of a vampire.

"Sir." A younger agent who must have been Jason handed over several sloshing, dark red bags to Connor.

Walking in next to the limp vampire, I touched the bruise-colored cheek, feeling an ache of sorrow in my chest for him again. I left him strapped; I couldn't have him lashing out at Anders while he was waking him.

"We're ready, Anders. Work your magic." I called to my brother, who was double-checking corpses.

He stood, leaving behind another lifeless body. Anders raised his hands to the confined vampire. Closing his eyes, he moved his hand to touch the brittle chest. The vampire's eyes flew open, the whites of his eyes red with frenzy. He thrashed violently, attempting to kick and hiss in fear.

"Shh, it's okay, now. Here, drink." I put the torn bag to his dried, peeling lips. He took deep gulps, a few scarlet drops running down his chin. Dropping the empty bag, I offered him another. "There. We're going to help you. I can't unstrap you until I know you're lucid and calm. Okay?"

The vampire's bloodshot eyes darted, and he nodded fast in understanding as he emptied the second bag. Tearing another open, I moved a dingy hair from his dirty, blood-crusted face. He flinched, his eyes reflexively closing at the contact. He might look young, but I wouldn't know how old he was until he told us. What I could gather was that his move into the supernatural world has been anything but pleasant.

After giving the vampire the last bag of blood, I looked to my brother. "Anders, I think we can unfasten him now." Anders turned his head, no doubt mind linking Atlas and Kale to take a closer, more defensive position.

I undid the leather binding around his midsection first since it seemed safest. Then his legs. Last but not least, I released his hands and neck.

Rubbing his throat, he stared at me. His eyes were still too discolored and dark to see what his natural shade was.

"Thank you." His voice came out as a rasped croak.

"You're welcome. I'm Athena. What's your name?"

"Lin...Lincoln. Lincoln Harper." Fidgeting with his wrists, his eyes darted around. He appeared to be reading the room or looking for a way to escape. Likely both.

I extended my hand. He didn't take it. "Hello, Lincoln. Do

you know how you got here?" I kept my tone delicate to keep from startling him. I reached for Lincoln's arm, and he snatched it from my grasp. "Shh. I'm sorry, I didn't mean to frighten you." Kale moved in closer behind me, his posture rigid, not trusting Lincoln's unpredictable movements.

"What... what happened to him?" Lincoln questioned, lifting a feeble finger to point at David's headless body.

"Unfortunately, he wasn't a very good individual. He hurt people, including the ones in here." I tilted my head, trying to answer him the best way I could without risk of him distrusting us further. "Do you know him? Is he the one who brought you here?"

"Yes," Lincoln uttered, his voice still hoarse. His posture straightened; he wasn't as small as I'd thought. "He brought us all here."

"Do you know why?" I pressed Lincoln, trying to maintain eye contact.

"He said he could help me."

"Help you how?"

"I guess he turned me. I didn't know how or where to..." Lincoln's posture drooped again, alarm and shame both rippling off him. He stared down, unable to make eye contact with any of us.

"Eat. It's okay, you can say it. There's nothing wrong with what you are." I did my best to give Lincoln a reassuring nod. I wanted to hug him and hold him to me, but I knew better. "You said he recently turned you. That's strange. Vampires don't create a new one just to abandon them. How old are you anyway?"

"Seventeen." Lincoln's demeanor shifted, his brows pulling in and his jaw tensing. He looked back up at me with ice in his gray eyes. "People have abandoned me all my life. Why should this be any different?" Lincoln spat his retort with viciousness. His mouth reddened with the deep garnet color of the blood. "I was a foster kid. In and out of shitty, abusive homes. No one wanted me, until... well, you see how this worked out." He picked at his frayed clothing.

I felt a pang in my heart. Poor kid. I was right. He was young, in more ways than one. Lincoln wasn't much younger than me, but I'd lived a different life—one of love and luxury.

Connor strolled up, keeping his hands in Lincoln's view. "Why don't we take him to a supernatural safe house. Let him rest. Tomorrow we can start fresh."

Lincoln moved back, shrinking back into the container. "Another foster home, great. Some things never change. Even after death." Lincoln rolled his eyes, trying to make himself smaller. I examined his features. For a vampire, his color was poor, too purple and pale, his skin papery from lack of hydration. He was, in all senses, a teenager—one who didn't ask for what he got. I pursed my lips, making my decision.

"You can come with us. You'll find our home more comfortable than a safe house. Then, when you're ready, we can talk more about what happened here."

"Us?" Lincoln's eyes widened, his hands tugging at his torn, filthy blue shirt.

"Yes, me, my brothers Atlas and Anders, and my mate, Kale." I smiled, pleased Lincoln appeared intrigued by my offer. The closer he was, the easier it would be to gain his trust and learn more. Plus, I wanted to help him.

A sharp growl brought me from my thoughts.

"Kale?" I snapped my head to catch sight of Kale's face, his mouth turned down and his eyes whirling with amber and gold.

"Thea. May I speak to you in private for a minute?" Kale's stiff manner and firm tone showed off his discontent as much as his growl had. I raised my eyebrow.

I glanced over at Atlas, whose brows went up, listening to

whatever Kale said that I couldn't decipher. Anders's gaze toward Lincoln narrowed with focus.

"Of course," I said to Kale through tight lips. Kale was lucky he couldn't hear my mind.

Now, now, wolf boy. Better watch who you're growling at.

I gave Connor the go-ahead to approach Lincoln while I excused myself to have a discussion with Kale. We walked to an empty corner of this dismal room, both of us eyeing one another.

"What's the matter?" I asked, folding my arms over my chest. I knew it would amplify my cleavage, but I didn't care if Kale got an eyeful. He was about to get an earful anyway.

Kale did his best to divert his eyes away from my chest, shaking his head to maintain his focus. "You're just going to invite a stranger into your home. Doesn't that seem dangerous to you?" Kale's tone was stern as he stared me down. I wanted to tell him this was not his best idea. To stare down an Alpha was perceived as a challenge. I thought it best to be sarcastic versus dominating.

"Well, it seems having strangers in my home is becoming a habit. Worked out fine last time, didn't it?" I put my hands to my hips, giving him a cocky stare.

Kale huffed in defiance, squaring his jaw. "Athena. That's unfair. You know this is different. I wasn't a starved vampire."

"You're right. It is different." I kept my eyes set on Kale, not willing to budge on my stance with Lincoln.

The space between us rippled with a chill as if an icy electric current had charged the air. Goosebumps crawled up my arms, prickling my exposed skin. Kale folded his arms across his chest, and the icy surges pulled back as if being drawn back into his body.

"You're stubborn," he said, his teeth clicked together as he squared his jaw. The stiffness moved along his face.

I cocked my eyebrow. "So are you."

Something untamed flowed beneath Kale's golden skin. Whether it was lupine or wyvern origin, I couldn't decipher. "I'm not comfortable with it. It doesn't feel right. I said we'd meet someone tonight, but I didn't know who. What if it's him?"

"And what if it was David?" I countered. "We know he won't be following us home." I jutted my chin high, unwilling to give away control of the conversation, but my eyes softened the longer they locked with Kale's. I wanted to hear him out. He was going to be my partner from now on, and I needed to learn to listen.

Kale rubbed at the starting scruff on his jaw. "No, I suppose he won't. Glad he's dead. Not gonna miss that piece of—"

"I'd like to go with you. I don't wanna be with people who can't help me with what I am." Lincoln's low rasp intruded on Kale's sentence.

I gave Kale a last glance. He puffed out a breath. "Whatever. Fine. Let's bring him."

I grinned. Victory. "Settled then. You'll come with us. I'll have one of our guards help you to a car. We'll be leaving in a while after we wrap up details with Agent Connor."

The room, once full of rotting bodies, was empty. Connor's team categorized everything and loaded it into vans for proper examination, then burials. Anders had healed those he could and rid them of any painful memories from this experience, leaving them in a sleeping state. They'd take the survivors to St. Luke's Hospital, conveniently staffed by government officials aware of our existence. Doctors would offer them the best care, though, after Anders assistance, they'd require none.

Anders's ability was the most useful. He had the gift of giving someone a second chance if he got to them in time. Tonight, he'd saved six lives, including Lincoln's. I knew Anders would feel it wasn't enough. Not because he suffered from a hero complex, but because, like our mother, Anders hated loss of life. Each time he couldn't bring someone back, it ate at him.

But in this upcoming war, any life saved was a small battle won.

We were getting ready to head back up, out the front entrance, ensuring no one was aware of what transpired beneath their feet when Connor hollered to me.

"You call me tomorrow, as soon as he spills anything."

"Absolutely." I agreed with a curt nod.

In the elevator, we all were quiet, the mood somber and heavy. Each of us processed what had taken place. The bodies, the death loomed around me, sinking into Atlas and Anders. Their eyes were darker and narrowed, trying to fight off the morbidity of the night.

Kale's hand found my back. After such a gruesome discovery, his touch was a wanted relief, filling me with a small sensation of warmth. The doors slid open; the hallway empty except for an amorous couple making out. Music roared like before. The four of us made our way to the dance floor, heading towards the exit.

As I walked, something jolted Kale's hand from mine. I twisted my entire body in his direction to ascertain the threat. What I found left me grinding my teeth and balling my hands into fists at my sides.

It was Jenny. Again, she pawed at Kale. This girl was like a bad penny. It was enough to make my blood boil. Luckily for her, shifting was not an option. My wolf would've had something to say about Jenny trying our patience a second time.

Jenny jabbed her finger at Kale. "You said you didn't want a relationship, Kalen. Now you're here again, with her!" Jenny staggered, more intoxicated than the first time I'd seen her. We didn't have time for drunken ranting, and I lacked the tolerance. It'd been a trying evening, and this didn't help matters. I huffed again, biting my tongue until it bled. A metallic, earthy taste touched my tongue. I hoped my silence gave Kale a chance to sort this out for the last time.

"Don't make a scene, Jenny. We've been over this. I said I didn't want a relationship with you, not that I didn't want one. And that was months ago. Why don't you get an Uber and sleep this off?" Kale side-stepped away from her, scoffing as he did.

"I'll tell you what. I'll sleep with your friend Troy. Cheated with him the entire time we dated anyway," Jenny slurred, stumbling side to side. Her cheating on Kale was more offensive than her having dated him. I wished I could snarl at her, tear into her like an Alpha should. But I noted her flushed pink cheeks from the alcohol, and her fake lashes on one side were coming loose. She had a dark stain on her cream top, indicating a drink was spilled or sloshed onto her. Her unkempt appearance matched her slurring, catty tone.

"Good for you. Sleep with whoever you like. You always did. Hell, we both did. Just remember, you're not hurting me. You're hurting yourself. You get that Uber, okay, Jenny? Bye," he said, his face hard, showing no emotion outside his eyes, which hinted at pity.

Kale felt bad for Jenny. Maybe he was right to. I'd been jealous, but of what? A woman who'd been in an unhealthy relationship, then got dumped? Hardly seemed worth it, and, truth be told, Jenny didn't warrant my jealousy or wrath. In her, I saw a glimpse of the old Kale and the life he'd walked away from. My shoulders relaxed, and I released my lips.

I looked at Anders and Atlas, both of them angling toward the exit and rolling their eyes. We needed to wrap this up and get out of here. Lincoln waited for us in one of the cars, and my conversation with him was far more pressing than anything Jenny had to say.

With my possessive streak dulled, and empathy taking its place, I touched Kale's arm. "We have to go." I reminded him.

Jenny narrowed her eyes into angry slits. "Hmph. You...you let this trash in a slutty red dress tell you what to do now? She's nothing but another stupid fucking groupie. She'll get her picture in TMZ and bail." Jenny hollered and swayed.

Red crossed my vision. I'd wanted to let this go, be the bigger person, but this woman tempted me to remove her limbs or seal her mouth shut with magic. My fingertips itched, and my lips tingled, asking me to spell her.

I took a deep breath through my nose. *Be the bigger person, Athena*, I repeated to myself. I held that breath, hoping by the time I released it, Jenny would be out of my sight.

Atlas stepped forward, moving past Kale and me. "Jenny, I don't know you. And, I'm happy not to. I'm gonna need you to not say another word about my sister." His warning came with a hint of a growl, and Jenny took a shaky step back.

Atlas glared at Jenny; his brown eyes set as if trying to bore holes right in her head. He'd never been one to tolerate someone giving me a hard time, outside him and Anders.

Anders raised his eyebrow, pulling out his phone. "Let's help you call that Uber, shall we?" The screen lit up as he opened the Uber app, but Jenny sloppily shoved his hand away.

Kale's body went stiff, then trembled. His eyes gleamed amber, and his teeth were longer. "Never call Athena trash."

Jenny sneered first at me, then at Kale. She braced her hand on the tabletop to steady herself. "Why? What are you gonna do about it, Kalen?" She threw her head back and laughed. "Does she know her time is limited? That you'll be on to the next one soon? It's already been, what? Almost a month? Come on, Kale, tell her! Tell her she'll be replaced!"

I watched Kale's expression go icy. His mouth trembled. "Jenny. Don't." He'd never looked so severe, and Jenny was in no condition to heed his warning.

"What? You don't want her to hear how you couldn't deal with being famous, so you changed women like you do your clothes? Show her that, Kale! Come on!" She continued to antagonize Kale. My hands twitched. I wanted to burn her alive, and I could. One spell and she'd be nothing more than smoke and ash, but I knew better. We could not afford a huge supernatural scene.

I swallowed, summoning all my self-control. I stepped in front of Kale, wrapping my arms around his waist. The music throbbed louder, like the volume went up with his fury. Yelling at Jenny was useless. You couldn't reason with the irrational, and that making sure Kale didn't release the beast I saw pushing to come out took precedence.

"Hey. Look at me," I said, his body quivering against mine, but did as I asked him. His eyes locked on mine. "It's just you and me. Doesn't matter what she said." I touched his cheek. His body slowed its shake to a dull tremor as I continued stroking his face, my fingers craving the feel of his strong jaw and light stubble. I saw Atlas inch closer from my peripheral vision. He readied himself to take Kale down if this continued to escalate.

"Whatever," Jenny sniped. "You'll come back when you realize she doesn't give a shit!"

Kale moved around me too quick, standing inches away from Jenny. "You wanna insult me, fine, go ahead. But you're not gonna stand here and talk shit about her." Kale pointed to me, who still stood not quite behind him. He shook his head. "You have no idea—" Kale was losing his grip, shaking harder. He glanced down, clenching his fists at his sides. Centering him became more important than teaching Jenny a lesson about respect.

Jenny wobbled, finally silent, though her mouth gaped like a stunned fish. She stomped her foot like a child having a tantrum and snatched Anders's phone to order her ride.

I touched Kale's arm. "I'm fine." And he started backing away from Jenny. "I have it under control."

I gave him a gentle nod but didn't fully trust the animal in him. I focused my attention on the very intoxicated woman before us. I raised my voice to talk over the music. "Jenny, I wanna give you some advice because I think you need to hear it. Respect yourself. You're better than this. And have a good rest of the night." Turning on my heels, we left Jenny to collect her thoughts and her Uber. The small crowd watching our little tiff dispersed when they realized they'd be no fight to witness.

Vultures.

I couldn't wait to get out of here.

Reaching the exit, I seized my opportunity to question Kale. "Groupie, huh?" I asked Kale as I grasped the door handle, my legs exposing with each step. My heels clicked on the cement.

"You caught that?" Kale scratched the back of his neck in anxiousness and tried to change the subject. "I wouldn't have hurt her, you know. The wolf—he wanted to be sure we didn't let anyone treat you like that."

"Mm-hmm. I know you wouldn't have, and I don't miss much." I gave him a sly smile, nudging him with my elbow. "So, groupie?" I wasn't about to let this go. Kale had told me about his previous relationships, his life on the road, but never in too much detail. His bad-boy past embarrassed him, and until tonight, I didn't push the issue.

"She definitely caught that, bro. Females of all species have radar for that kinda stuff." Atlas grinned, jabbing Kale in the ribs as we walked to cars. The bouncers at the door nodded to us on the way out, nothing to say about Kale's humanity tonight, or lack thereof.

Anders's raised the key to the car, pressing the remote start. Shoving Atlas forward, Anders offered us a bit of privacy. I heard Atlas cuss at Anders for the unexpected push.

"Okay, remember, I told you I'm a musician? I'm in this band, The River. We're pretty good. Opened for Coldplay in 2017. Went on tours. So yeah, you could say there were parties and groupies. But let the record show, I find that term vulgar."

My jaw dropped. "Coldplay? You're kidding? You never mentioned that. Wait—The River? I've heard your music, Kale.

I have some of your songs... That's amazing. Why didn't you tell me? You always seemed so secretive about it, and I didn't want to push you after—well, your voice is... Explains the women. I imagine there were *many* of them." A ping of possessiveness reared its head again, but I tried stuffing that away. I felt sad he hadn't shared this with me before. I looked at the ground, staring too hard at the cracks as we walked. We'd both had other partners, other lives, and I couldn't change the past or who Kale or I had been with before. Why should it matter if I had him now?

Kale stopped walking, taking my upper arms into his hands, bringing me closer to him. He glanced down, blew out a breath, then brought his gaze back up to mine. "Maybe you need to hear this, maybe you don't. But that's exactly why I left for a while. I had everything, but I'd become someone I didn't know— someone I didn't like. Nothing had meaning. I felt empty. None of it mattered. The success, parties, drugs, women... It's a lonely fucking existence. To be surrounded by so many people, no one listening. Because I knew none of them really cared—" He hesitated, glancing away again, an expression of shame tainting his downcast eyes. "The meaningless sex... it was something to do. One of those things you do when trying to run away from yourself. The fact is, I left that guy behind a long time ago, and I didn't want my past to affect our future. This is hard enough as it is. But you helped bring out a part of me I thought might be gone. I know it's complicated, and I don't care. Because of all the things I've had, places I've been. I want you most." Kale's tone was level and serious but softer than before, like he was speaking from his soul.

He didn't take his eyes off me. He let them roam over my face, taking in my changing expression. I blinked fast. My lips trembled ever so slightly. His admission took me off guard. I imagined him lonely but not alone after a show. Women flocking to him, and the fake smile he must've worn and the drinks he downed to get through the nights. The pills he took to wake himself up.

Kale didn't smile. His face kept that strained grimace. "Giving up all my bad habits was easier than all this. This is gonna sound first-worldly, but I never thought I'd long for the simplicity of a camera being shoved in my face again or deciding what I'd wear out to party."

I made a small laughing noise. I didn't know what to say to him. I understood where he was coming from. I wasn't famous in the way he was. No one tried snapping my picture, finding out if I was dating. No, you didn't see my face on the cover of magazines or in blogs. Kalen was the opposite. He'd spent the past six years in the spotlight. Every move watched, published, and judged.

We had more in common than I originally understood. Monitored by the world in different ways, with expectations thrust upon us at every turn. Kale told me he wanted out, couldn't deal with the fame. Could he handle this? Another life of expectations and uncertainty?

Kale stopped us again, and my thoughts halted with us. "I dreamed of you, your green eyes. They called me. Those dreams, they pulled me from that darkness, from the nothingness I felt. You walked in Zephyr, and those eyes—your eyes—I dreamt of them for so long. Then I saw you, and they shined like a breath of new life. You were like a vision realized. Scared the absolute shit out of me. Because I was so sure you couldn't be real. I panicked, but I knew I'd come with you. I knew I wanted to be someone you could love." His hand dragged through his falling hair, and he looked up to the sky. "Do you see them?"

I lifted my chin, hoping a tear didn't escape, and let my eyes follow his. "See what?" As I gazed at the moonlit sky, the clouds moved to let the stars peek through. I felt his eyes on me, an intense stare that heated my cheeks to match the red hue of my dress.

"The stars, Athena. You belong among those stars. They were made for you."

I shivered, and that tear rolled down my cheek. I wiped my face with the back of my hand before more drops could fall. I exhaled the breath I'd been holding. Kale bore no resentment towards how I changed him or my previous flings, yet I was trying to hold onto and criticize situations that occurred long before I'd stumbled into his life.

I heaved a sigh, feeling petulant for letting such a thing get to me. His confession left me raw. I searched for words, a response to his honesty. I guess I needed to take a lesson from Kale—or more than one. My soul had never felt more comforted and whole. I watched Kalen look at my brothers and give them a sly smile while shaking his head. And then it hit me, like a blow I'd didn't see coming. My ears buzzed. The realization set in, and the echoes in my mind got louder. It didn't matter the short time we were together—I loved him. I'd never get enough time with him. I'd never tire of him.

The weight of *"us"* barreled down on me, and I tried my best to articulate. "I don't know what I expected you to say or what I wanted to hear. I'm sorry you were alone. You won't feel that way again—I want you most, too. And if the stars were made for me, they were made for you, too." I side-hugged Kale, squeezing his comforting warmth to me. He tilted his head, placing a kiss on my hair, inhaling me. My emotions hadn't settled, and I clung to him, squeezing him even closer. The gut-wrenching thoughts of a different Kale, one unhappy and lonesome, hounded me. I winced. He rose to fame and lived in a glasshouse where all the world saw his faults, and most did nothing to stop his descent.

"Lavender," he murmured, breathing in my hair as it blew against his shoulder. His voice hauled me away from the rabbit hole I was about to tumble down. I inhaled slow. In and out. *Saltwater. Plumeria.* Fresh and splendid.

I'd calmed by the time we reached the cars. They lined all the vehicles up, ready to go. Dropping Kale's arm, I wandered to one of three blacked out Tahoes. I knew which one Lincoln was in, so I opened his door. Lincoln hissed, drawing back in surprise.

"I apologize for startling you. I wanted to let you know, I'm happy we found you." I smiled warmly at Lincoln. His face was so youthful, almost familiar, yet child-like in certain ways and now frozen in time. He needed a family. A home and people to love him. Maybe we could give him what he deserved, teach him to be a moral vampire. At this moment, without my wolf, I felt I was more level-headed. I missed her, all her spunk. After all, it was she who helped draw me to Kale. I'd forever be thankful for her call. But learning to be a leader who held more compassion and less possession couldn't be a bad thing.

Lincoln's face twitched with residual apprehension. Dipping his head to stare at his knees, I took my cue to leave him to his thoughts. "See you in a few hours, Lincoln." I looked up at the front seats. "Gage, you take good care of him now." Gage turned his bearded face, nodding in my direction. I shut the door and headed to my car.

I hopped into the warm Jeep, my dress opening high on my thigh when I sat. Kale put his hand atop my leg, taking the rest of the chill off my skin. I looked up front, Atlas at the wheel again, quite sure he was enjoying getting to drive again.

"I need to sleep." Anders's face was pale, with dark circles under his blue, red-rimmed eyes. Healing that many, keeping them sedated, took a lot out of him. He also wasn't fond of memory wiping. Anders believed it took away their free will, and I wasn't in disagreement. Then again, did anyone *need* to remember being brutalized, used as a food source? If we could give them peace of mind, to me, that appeared a better solution.

Anders slouched over, snoring lightly by the time Atlas pulled off.

"What's the plan, Thea?" Atlas glanced at me in the rearview mirror, hands tight on the steering wheel, tension in his tone. It wasn't hard to guess that Atlas didn't want Lincoln around either.

"We're going to settle Lincoln in for the rest of the night. I'll brief Mother when we get home and try to call Father. Tomorrow, see what he's willing to share with us. Definitely gonna have to ease in with him. He's just a kid. I'm under no illusions of what he's capable of if left unchecked."

Kale gawked at me, his hand gripping my thigh in surprise. "Back there, you made it seem like he wasn't something to worry about. I even told you I didn't trust the idea of bringing him along."

"*Ooh*, damn Kale." Atlas put his fist to his mouth, keeping his eyes on the road.

I angled my torso to Kale, raising an eyebrow. "A vampire, newly turned or not, is always treated with caution. I want him where we can see him, get him to trust us. We need the information in his head." For the second time tonight, I refused to back down from the decision to bring Lincoln with us, putting my mouth in a hard line as I stared back at Kale.

Exhaling, Kale shrugged his shoulders. "I still think it's a bad idea, but you know more than I do about supernaturals."

I patted his hand. "Kale. I trust your intuition. I do. Right now, Lincoln is our only connection to Xercarus. I'm willing to take a risk if it means stopping Xercarus for good."

The car was quiet again. Kale put his arm around my shoulders as I pulled my phone out of my garter, the shuffling breaking the stillness. I messaged Calliope and Mother, letting them know we were bringing an unexpected guest and what I thought he might need to make his stay comfortable.

Calliope messaged back in record time, three dots

appearing before I could finish the second message. She was on a mission now. I smiled down at my phone, envisioning Calliope setting up an unused bedroom, her cheerful disposition wandering from room to room collecting what she needed and having what we didn't have brought over. She lived for a project. With no young children in the manor anymore, Calliope jumped at the chance to have any kind of youth around. She was designed to care for someone, and her need to provide that care was sorely neglected as we aged. Lincoln could give her fresh purpose.

My mother was no less excited, only mentioning she'd tried calling our father but hadn't gotten through to him yet. That seemed odd, but he was likely busy removing Baywood from the council.

Kale stroked my arm while I put my head to his shoulder, his fingers leaving an invisible line on my skin. Blinking my eyes, I let myself drift into silence, contemplating our next move, while part of me mourned the ones we lost.

"Thea. Tell me something." Kale broke the quietness in the car.

"What would you like me to tell you?" I answered him, my lips perking up in a partial smile.

"Anything. I just don't want you stuck in your head again, not letting me in."

"Yeah, sorry. I analyze what I could've done better. How about you tell me more about you instead? We've got a few hours ahead of us. And I'd love to know more about what you do. *Besides groupies.*" I snickered a bit, going for a lighter tone. I knew Kale would take my joke in stride. I needed something to cheer up the mood. The heaviness of Zephyr, Lincoln, Kale's profession—it all weighed me down, putting a block of tension between my shoulders. I rolled my neck, willing it away.

"Ouch." Atlas gave a small laugh, tapping the steering wheel along to the new song by Stellar.

Kale's famous smile pulled at the corners of his mouth, revealing those pearly whites. "Well, what else would you like to know? Kalen Ryan is an open book."

I thought for a second, tapping my lips. "Tell me about your family. I know you have a brother, but what are they like?"

A glimmer of fondness twinkled in Kale's big blue eyes. I could see him contemplating before he replied. "I know I've told you they're really great. My mom, Linda, she can bake like you wouldn't believe. And man, does that woman have patience. She tolerated all of our nonsense as kids, read to us every night. She reminded me what it was to be a good man—to be accountable, you could say." Kale's eyes brightened. "My dad, Jonathon, he's a lawyer, like I said. He had this crazy work schedule. Made it hard for him to be around as much as he wanted. But when he was, he made the most of it for us. Took us camping, out fishing, hockey games. I'm a huge Black-hawks fan, be aware of that. You're looking at a season-pass holder." He tugged at his shirt, letting it fall back to his chest, clearly proud of his statement.

"And your brother?" I asked, shifting closer towards him, eager to learn more.

Kale smiled wide. "Oh, yeah. Brody. He's three years older. Don't ever tell him I said this, but he's the best brother I could've asked for. He taught me how to play baseball, football, how to ride a bike. Really everything. He's also the one who suggested I take a leave from the band. He saw what I was doing to myself." Kale's brows furrowed, then raised up as he shook his head. "He's overprotective nowadays and pretty pissed I've ignored his calls."

I took his hand, giving it a gentle squeeze. "So, stop ignoring his calls. I mean, you don't have to avoid him because of me." Kale smiled a bit, and I nudged him. "Maybe just don't tell him I turned you into a supernatural being. He'll definitely hate me then."

Atlas chuckled from the driver's seat, bobbing his head along to the quiet music playing.

"I don't think he'd hate you, but I don't think he'd believe me either."

I shrugged casually. "Most humans can't understand, but we don't have to worry about that now. What else does Brody do? Besides worry about you?"

"He's in his third year of residency at UCLA Medical Center. The neurology department. He always wanted to be a neuro-surgeon. My mom lucked out with Brody. He's our family over-achiever. I, on the other hand, asked for piano and guitar lessons. Come to think of it, you remind me of Brody."

"Me? How so?" I asked, raising my brows. "Because neurol-ogy, that's impressive. And since when do you use self-depre-cating humor? You're an amazing musician. You opened for Coldplay and made it up to number one the Billboard one hundred."

Kale rubbed his neck, looking away before he replied. It was an obvious nervous habit of his. "Yeah, yeah... But ever since we were kids, Brody had this 'goodness' about him. You know? He was constantly concerned about other people and wanted to help—like you. Sometimes..." Kale hesitated, tilting his head to the side. "Sometimes, I worried Brody tried so hard all the time because he was afraid of not being enough. Brody's gay. I always knew. I didn't care. He's my brother, and our parents are super supportive. But some of Brody's so-called friends... weren't." Kale's brows furrowed, and his frown deep-ened as he recalled the memory.

"Especially a few of the football guys. They were in love with my brother when he was just their quarterback, throwing passes and taking them to state championships, but several turned their backs on him when he came out. Started talking shit about him. I didn't care that I was a freshman. I picked a fight with one prick in the hall. Brody was so pissed, but at the same time, he wasn't." Kale's fist clenched. "He told me that dick wasn't worth getting suspended over. I disagreed—totally worth it." He let out a laugh, his eyes crinkling in the corners.

"Dad high-fived me when he came home that weekend. It wasn't until his second year away at college Brody admitted to me what it meant that I defended him—to know I had his back through anything. He told me I gave him the courage to be himself. I've never felt prouder."

Atlas slapped the steering wheel, amused. "I'm gonna have to disagree with your brother on that one too. That dude definitely needed to be punched in the face. You made the right choice."

I watched Kale clap his hand on Atlas's shoulder, praising his comment. I admired their jovial behavior. After such wretched findings at Zephyr, it brought cheer to my heart, seeing Kale and Atlas getting on so well. It was disappointing. Anders was too exhausted to hear Kale's story. I hoped we'd have more than enough time to share more of these moments.

I rubbed Kale's leg. "It's amazing you have a solid relationship with your brother. Family is so important. I'm sorry we haven't made the time to talk more about your family sooner."

"I can't believe we haven't talked much about my family before. It's crazy—being so caught up in a supernatural world. Caught up in you, really." Kale paused again, mulling over what he wanted to say. "I know this is new, but I want you to meet them. Is that possible? I don't know all the logistics yet, and I just know they'd love you. Oh, god—" Kale stopped short, his face dropped, and his eyes widened with panic.

"What? What is it?"

"I'm different now. The wolf—I'm a wolf. Can I even be around them anymore?"

Atlas swooped in as if he was trying to prevent something bad from happening. "Whoa. Kale, man. Slow down."

I wasn't sure what to tell Kale. I wanted to meet his family;

the thought gave me butterflies. There wasn't exactly a rule we had to follow regarding humans knowing about us. It was more of a *"do no harm policy."* Most humans couldn't handle our existence—this we knew. Meaning, we didn't disclose our reality to any human. "Kale, hey. Yes, you can see your family anytime you want. And I'd love to meet them if that's what you want." I let out a breath to continue. "We can work out our slowed aging later, maybe figure out how to tell them about us. I'll do whatever it takes to make this work for you and them."

Atlas looked back. "Right, if they freak, we can have Anders wipe their memory of it. Start fresh, try again."

Kale jerked his head up, his eyes gaping wide at Atlas. "Wow, okay. This is big. I dunno how I feel about wiping their memories. I won't hurt my family, but this is my life now. And I'm not willing to let them go either." Kale put his hand on my exposed knee, squeezing it for reassurance, his eyes bright and large as he gazed from me to the window.

"I'd never ask you to trade them for me." And that was the truth. Just because he'd inherited a new family didn't mean he had to give up the one he was born into. I leaned over, turning Kale's face to mine. I place a light kiss on Kale's lips.

Kale took my face into his hands, his thumbs stroking my cheeks, and he kissed me again, parting my lips ever so slightly to touch my tongue with his. He pulled back from the kiss, staring at me with reverence. Atlas picked up on the mood and skipped the opportunity to grumble this time.

"See, there's that thing you do again. I wanna panic, and you make me feel better. The doubt, the anxiety, and fear. God, Thea—where the hell have you been all my life?"

CHAPTER 12

The Jeep came to a slow stop, parking in our usual location. One of the Tahoes pulled in beside us, and the other two drove straight into the garage. When I got out, I searched for Lincoln's shape first. He emerged from the car behind us, shoulders hunched, with his head low. I noticed how tall he would be if he didn't hold his head down so far, as if he was trying to curl into himself. Watching him take in our home, I saw his mouth drop open then snap shut. Just like with Kale, I'm sure it seemed very grandiose to our adolescent newcomer.

I waved my hand, gesturing for him to follow me. "Lincoln. Welcome to Whiteridge Manor. I'll take you to where you will be staying. Please, don't hesitate to ask for anything. Treat this as your home."

Kale stayed close, within arm's reach, while Anders could only wipe his eyes and mumble, "Goodnight," before ambling off toward his bedroom.

Atlas eyed Lincoln with as much suspicion as Kale did, both of them sniffing the cool air. They remained tight-lipped, likely maintaining an inner conversation in reference to our minor guest. I did my best to ignore them, moving on with my tour. It's not that I wasn't skeptical of Lincoln too, but I had a feeling about him I couldn't pinpoint.

I filled the quiet as we walked through the halls. "I've had some blood bags put aside in a small fridge in your room. Drink what you need. If you run out, we can get you more. You must be starving." I did my best to give off an unintimidating vibe and smile at him. Atlas and Kale did nothing of the sort, standing behind me like sentries on patrol.

Lincoln put his dirty hands into his ripped pockets as we made our way to his room. His appearance was very much in disarray—filthy clothes, ill-fitting and torn in multiple places, shoes scuffed and worn. Under grit and grease, I could see the bright blonde of his hair, dark circles under his almost gray eyes. Even as a vampire, he had a feebleness about him, from the lack of feeding and draining himself. I hoped, for his sake, he'd be refreshed tomorrow morning.

Movies never really got much correct about vampires. Daylight didn't kill them—it merely slowed them down and exhausted their energy. Crucifixes did as much to deter a vampire as it did to wolves—nothing. Vampires didn't sleep in coffins, or at all. Their bodies didn't require the rest other creatures did because they weren't fully alive anymore. This fact also relieved them of the necessity to eat every day. A vampire could go days without feeding unless exposed to trauma, wounds, or, in Lincoln's case, both. Taking larger quantities of blood from a vampire would kill them like it would anyone else. Cinema *had* gotten one thing right. Silver burned vampires in a debilitating way, something Lincoln had already experienced in that slaughterhouse below Zephyr. I shivered at the thought of all of them, caged, terrified. I vowed I wouldn't let anything like that happen to him again.

"There's a shower and fresh clothes waiting for you as well." I opened the white wooden door to the room I'd had Calliope ready for Lincoln. His mouth popped open again.

"I'm staying here?"

"Yes. You should have everything you need to get you through the night. The tv works, with Netflix, there's a Bluetooth speaker, books. There's a phone with our numbers programmed in if you should want or need something. We had a gaming system put in with the newest games." I offered a warm smile. "I don't know anything about them, but I suspect you might." I attempted to make Lincoln feel welcomed but stifled the urge to pat his back. I didn't want to risk startling him again.

"Thanks. This is…is really all for me?" It was the first time I saw what looked to be a smile creeping onto Lincoln's tired face.

"Of course. We want you to relax. There will be guards outside your door for safety precautions. They won't bother you." I motioned to Gage and Pierce, who were both standing ramrod straight nearby.

"You already know Gage. He's not so bad." I winked.

"Okay. This is super nice." Lincoln held onto the door as he finally looked me in the eyes. They were just as I thought, a pastel heather gray. Vampires were stunning creatures, designed to suppress your senses and lure you in—the perfect predators. Lincoln was no exception. Once cleaned up, I had no doubt he'd be a handsome and powerful young vampire.

"You're welcome. Well, we'll leave you to it then. Goodnight, Lincoln."

The door clicked closed, Lincoln disappearing behind it. I heard a hushed, *"Wow,"* from behind it.

"You're really good with him." Kale leaned on the wall, his arms folded across his chest, observing me. His previous distrust faded into smiling admiration.

"I'm trying to treat him with the kindness I'd want to be given if I were in his situation." I made my way through the hallway, nodding at both Pierce and Gage. Kale and Atlas followed.

Once in the kitchen, I saw my mother waiting at the island counter for us.

"Children. My loves. Where's Anders?" Our mother questioned, hurrying towards us.

"He's asleep already," I answered, perching on a chair and taking my heels off. I let them fall to the floor, clattering as they hit the light ceramic tiles.

Kale rubbed my shoulder as he walked by, heading for the fridge and opening it. "I don't know about you, but I need a drink."

"There's beer is in there, or the good stuff is in the bar." I pointed across the kitchen to our hidden, built-in bar. Kale let the extra-large fridge door close, heading over to the white marbled countertop. "Press the silver button."

Kale furrowed his brows and looked down, pressing the button. I heard a mechanical clicking, and a tall drawer lined with various expensive bottles of whiskey, bourbon, vodkas, and gins rose up from inside the counter.

"You've got to be kidding. This kitchen has a hidden liquor bar? You could've mentioned this before."

"You didn't ask," I laughed. "It's keeping them temperature-controlled, like the wine cellar."

Kale whipped his head to look at me. "There's a wine cellar too? I don't think I ever need to leave here."

I smiled at his amusement. It felt good not to always keep up my serious exterior around him.

Bottles clinked as Kale moved them about, searching for one he wanted. "Old Fitzgerald Bourbon. Perfect." Taking a tumbler from the shelf, he poured a heavy shot, downing it all at once.

"Atlas, you want one man?"

Atlas said nothing for a moment, but his silence spoke

volumes. Kale poured another drink and strode over to Atlas, who leaned on the granite counter.

Illiana flourished her arms, her purple night robe sleeves swishing. "I'm glad you're all home safe and sound. I wished Anders was up, but healing always took a lot out of him." My mother turned her attention to the still quiet Atlas, her face softening. "And you, my son?"

Atlas took the glass Kale offered, slamming down its contents. I knew killing David weighed on him. The events from the entire day ate at him, chipping away at his well-manicured *"I don't give a shit"* exterior.

"Atlas. What's wrong?" Illiana took my brother's face into her tan hands, stroking his cheeks like she always did, and Atlas buckled. His soundless facade crumbled.

"I overreacted and killed this vampire. He was a fucking monstrosity, Mom. But we needed him." Atlas's beaten tone washed over me. He was harder on himself than he deserved. I didn't like seeing him like this. My stomach twisted in pain, matching Atlas's emotion.

Our mother clicked her tongue. "If you killed him, then it was the right thing to do." She hugged her hulking son, her arms barely able to wrap around him.

I tried to reason with him first, knowing it was likely useless.

"Atlas, we went over this. We had to eliminate David. You did what needed to be done. We still have Lincoln. I'm sure he'll be able to tell us something."

Kale grimaced in disgust, pouring himself another bourbon. "If you didn't take his head off, I was going to." He shook his head, feeling the burn of the bourbon down his throat.

"Yeah, but what about you, Thea? What about what Kale saw? What if we lose you because I killed him?" Atlas's brown eyes threatened to water, pooling with doubt.

"You won't lose me," I said, rising from my chair to take

Atlas into a tight embrace. His huge body trembled in my hands, making me want to hold him closer. "Atlas. Shh." I stroked his hair. His anxiety rolled on to me, but I held him steadfast, giving him whatever strength, I could.

"You're the Alpha, Thea. If I fail to protect you…"

Releasing Atlas enough to see his face, I grasped his chin between my fingers. "Stop. You've failed at nothing. You need some sleep."

Our mother, who'd been eyeing Kale with a curious look on her face, placed her hand to his forehead.

"*Nossa*," she whispered, jerking her hand away. She darted her gaze to me. "He has the power of sight. When did this happen?" She waved her hands, her bracelets sliding down her arms made a tiny clinking sound.

I shook my head. "Right away, I guess, after I marked him weeks ago. We just didn't realize," I continued, "The night-mares… turns out he's dreaming of Xercarus. Anders figures I might've awakened an ability in him."

Grabbing the bottle of Fitzgerald bourbon from Kale, my mother took an unexpected swig, brown liquor swishing down her throat. We gawked at her. "You need to call your father."

"Alright." I took my phone out, opening my contacts. It started ringing. More ringing. I heard my father's familiar baritone voice on the other end.

You've reached Cyrus Whiteridge. I'm currently unavailable. You may try my office for inquiries. I will do my best to return your call in a timely manner. Thank you. Voicemail. He should've been off the plane by now. Perhaps he was in a meeting, trying to appoint a new official for the area.

"Father, it's Athena. We have some updates on Xercarus and Kale's condition. Call me when you can. I love you." I touched the red end button on my screen and glanced up at my mother. "No answer. Should we wait up for his call?"

Our mother shook her hands at us. "No. No. You've had a

rough day. Go rest. You all earned it. You'll need your wits about you tomorrow for talking to Lincoln." She had always been insistent about our rest. That habit hadn't changed as we aged.

"Goodnight, my darlings. I love you. All three of you." She put her hand to her mouth, kissing her fingertips and blowing kisses to me, Kale, and Atlas.

"Love you, too," the three of us said in unison. There wasn't a time I could remember when my mother didn't exude this one-of-a-kind tenderness. It drew you in like the warmth from a favorite blanket. She rarely compelled anyone around her with orders or commands. You *wanted* to be around my mother, wanted to make her happy, and in return, she gave out sincere affection none of us could get enough of.

I put my hand on Atlas's back. If I had our link, I'd have reassured him again. Instead, I stayed quiet, tugging him toward me. He knew what I wanted to say to him.

"Love you too, T."

I leaned into him, causing him to go off balance a bit. We both laughed. Felt good to have a moment of laughter after the chaos of the day.

CHAPTER 13

I flipped the light switch, and my bedroom lit up. I walked through the white archway to the connected bathroom, fumbling with the pins in my hair. The rest of my black hair tumbled down my back. Pulling open a drawer, I took out a container of makeup wipes and cleansed my face. My lips were less red and back to their bare state.

Kale took this chance to come up behind me, locking me in his grip and nuzzling my neck. I sank into his embrace. Calm and delight washed over every inch of me. Tension moved from my shoulders, finding refuge low in my belly. My body was continually receptive to Kale's.

"This is inappropriate after this evening's affairs, but I've wanted you in my hands since I saw you in that red dress. If you're not too tired." He paused behind me to kiss my shoulder, sliding the strap of my dress lower.

A petite gasp snuck out past my lips. Gauging my enthusiasm, Kale pressed on, moving the other strap down. I let my head fall against Kale's chest. Spinning me around, Kale gathered my dress to my hips and placed me on the counter, as he did before. The fabric stretched, pressing farther up my thighs. Reaching behind his back, he lifted his soft knit shirt off, exposing his stomach. He showered me with kisses, placing them across my collar bones. I felt cold air between us as Kale snapped himself away from me. He squeezed his eyes too tight, making them water. Surveying him warily, I put my fingertips to his heaving chest.

"Kale, is something—" My nerves bundled, and I felt a fresh unease that traveled to each of my limbs.

Kale didn't waver as he held me in place. "Your dad, Thea. It's your dad. Something's gonna go very wrong. I saw it... He's..." During the time it took Kale to tell me, I felt a blistering agony blow out from my rib cage like my chest was going to burst.

My head was burning. I thought I heard my father's voice calling to me. *Athena... I, Cyrus Whiteridge...*

I clawed at my throat, willing myself to take in another breath, then I heard it—a scream of pure misery. It was my mother. Oh, Goddess, what was happening? It felt like something was being torn away from me and pushed inside at the same time. I felt my knees giving way. Kale looped his arms beneath me.

"Atlas! Anders!" Kale shrieked. They didn't come. Kale panicked as my vision fuzzed in and out. Carrying me out of my bedroom, he searched for my brothers or the source of the scream. I couldn't tell; my head hurt. Racing us downstairs, we came upon my mother crumpled in a heap on the floor of the foyer.

Cries poured from her. "He's gone! Oh, dear Goddess, he's gone!" Calliope rushed to her, sobbing alongside her.

"Illiana. Please, what is it? What's happened?" Calliope pulled my mother into her arms, patting her head as she wept. Atlas and Anders clutched themselves, limping down the stairs.

"Why does it hurt so bad? What is this?" Atlas seized his

chest again, crumpling over the banister, but doing his best to get to me. Anders was faster.

"Please, just give her to me." Anders held his arms open to Kale. He was asking him for me. "Let me fix whatever's wrong with her," he sputtered, almost unable to hold himself up.

Kale shook his head low. "Anders, you can't heal broken hearts." Kale hesitated, holding me to his chest, but, in good judgment, let my brother take me. Anders held me close as I molded myself to his chest. I knew what had happened. I felt it rip through me when Kale touched me. My father was dead. Pain and something else scorched me inside again as my mother continued to weep and rock herself on the cool floor.

Kale's hands were in his hair, and his voice cracked. He used all his strength to not be overcome by our anguish barreling down on him. "What good is this ability if I can't even use it to help you? You can't shift, and for what? So I can watch your heart break with no way of stopping or repairing it?" His dark hair fell into his face as he bent his head, putting his hands on his bare hips. Kale's fury bubbled, wanting to provoke him further into shifting.

My eyes burned as I looked at Anders's flushed face. "Father is gone. I feel him, though." My voice was no more than a hoarse whisper. Kale dropped his head, the sorrow swallowing up the room.

I heard my mother's bracelets scrape the floor as she moved to pick herself up. She wiped tears from her reddened cheeks. A fresh purpose flared in her bloodshot eyes. "Athena." Her voice didn't waver. I met her savage stare, a look of determination in my mother's eyes I'd not witnessed until this moment. "I, Luna Queen Illiana Whiteridge, hereby submit my reign and obligations to Athena Whiteridge. I pledge to her my obedience and loyalty, as she is the rightful Alpha."

Confusion collided with my pain, and I winced, then closed my eyes to concentrate. *What had my mother just done?* When my father died, she would be the active ruler. Instead, she offered submission to me, abdicating her claim to being Alpha.

Intense heat grew in my chest, diffusing to my limbs. I felt my body bristling with scalding light. My eyes flashed open with a surge, one I recognized, but this was bigger.

"Thea's eyes. Her eyes are back." Atlas rubbed his face, regaining some balance, and had enough the sense to back away from me. Anders grabbed on to Kale, tugging him backward as well.

Feeling like an explosion occurred inside my chest, I ran. I smashed through the front doors, splintering them off the hinges. I kept running. My skin cracked, seeping out light, rupturing open across planes of my shaking body, revealing iridescent white scales. Long talons replaced my fingers, and horns sprouted from my head. My dragon was back, and she was angrier than she'd ever been. I dropped to the ground by the forest edge, in an open clearing, surrendering to the transformation. Voices flowed like babbling streams in my ears, a whisper above echoes. The family had followed me out, watching from a distance as I morphed into something new.

My body parts continued their contortions, twisting, manipulating into a much larger figure. As my mass took up more space, unrestrained power seemed to ooze from my scales. My transformation came to its end, and my back swelled, bowing upwards. Giant wings erupted from beneath the surface. This was an unexpected addition. Testing them, I flapped the colossal, lustrous spans once, twice, three times, observing myself lifting from the dewy ground. I drove myself up higher and higher, reaching the clouds. Straightening my neck, I turned loose a fiery breath. Fire poured from my sharp-toothed mouth, lighting the sky brighter than the stars.

The fiery voice bellowed in our shared mind. Sharing space and time with her like this was extraordinary. The power we commanded was like no other. Our thoughts intertwined, fitting together like puzzle pieces. Another blaze of fire tore up my throat, flaming the air.

Turning my attention to the ground below, I boomed a glorious roar, calling to my family and pack. Atlas and Anders dropped down, completing their transformation first. Their familiar white, fur-covered heads bowed down, honoring the significance of this moment. Kale followed suit, shedding the rest of his clothing, releasing his dark brown wolf. I roared another call, and Calliope and my mother knelt in reverence.

I am the Alpha Queen.

Our guard crowded around, taking in my snowy-winged form. Many of them gazed upon me in awe. One by one, they kneeled freely, providing their allegiance and acknowledgment. This bestowal of respect denoted my transition to reigning Alpha.

My family accepted me.

High as I was in the clouded night sky, I saw a small figure almost hidden in the background—Lincoln. His face was wrinkled and pale with terror and suspicion. If I drew attention to Lincoln, they'd execute him on sight. It was crucial that I hurry before his scent rose to them. I lowered myself until my claws could touch the soil beneath me, digging into the soft earth. Releasing my dragon, my human form returned, shrinking back to size. I sensed my mother approaching me, her arms open. She'd removed her shawl, wrapping me up tightly to keep the cool night air from hitting my very exposed skin.

"The night you were born, your father knew how magnificent you were. You were born to lead, my love. This was his last gift to you. I sensed him submitting his Alpha to you before he —" She stopped speaking and wiped a tear away before she kissed my cheeks. Calliope clasped her hands, weeping behind us.

"*Ah*, my sweet babe. Your mother is right. Your father would be so proud." I turned, taking Calliope into a half embrace, holding the shawl to my shoulders. I wanted to soak up their warmth longer, cry on my mother's shoulder, but more pressing matters pulled my attention elsewhere. Twinges of hurt tugged at me, the loss simmering around the edges of my mind. This was not how I imagined taking my place as Alpha. I'd wanted to rule, but not like this. I bit my cheek and took a deep breath. This was not the time to feel sorry for myself. I shook my head, ridding myself of the bitter thoughts, and looked at my family.

I nodded to my brothers and Kale. *Stay as Wolves. Lincoln is out here. Do not let him escape.* Mind linking. I missed this the most.

My wolf gave an enthusiastic yip and marched around my mind with pride. She was happy to be back, but even her presence wasn't enough to make me rejoice.

"Lincoln," I called for him, knowing he'd hear me. Kale bristled at my left side, shaking his thick shaggy coat. Anders took footing at my right, and Atlas was close behind. I looked around. *Covered on all flanks.* "Lincoln, don't be afraid. Come out." Trees swished, bending the breeze and movement. Kale's ears erected fully and twitched, trying to locate the direction of the sound. Anders nosed the ground, sniffing and pawing anxiously.

He's here. I can smell him, Anders announced.

If it's a game of hide and seek he wants, I'll give him one. But the winner takes the loser's limb, Atlas growled.

"*Shh.* I *do not* intend to hurt him, Atlas," I scolded.

Bushes whooshed again from a suddenness moving within. "Athena?" The voice was minuscule, as if he was trying to make himself as small and unnoticeable.

"Come out, Lincoln. We won't hurt you," I promised him, giving Anders and Atlas a hard glare.

Lincoln emerged from the shrubbery, twigs sticking in his cleaner hair. His face was almost angelic now that it was free from grime. "I'm so sorry, Athena—I didn't know. He said you were all bad..."

I clutched the shawl taut to me to keep from revealing anything indecent to Lincoln. "Who said we were bad? What did you do, Lincoln?"

"I—I'm, " Lincoln stuttered uncontrollably, his nerves getting the best of him. "David. He said you hated all vampires after he turned me. He promised, if I just did what he said, I'd be free. He said the Triad would kill me..."

"It's alright, Lincoln. You didn't know." I inched closer to him when I heard Atlas and Anders shouting in my mind.

The hell, he didn't know. We need to get rid of him! Atlas's white head shook with fury, heartache fueling his anger.

Thea, we need to kill him! Anders sounded off. Even as in his animal form, woe rung clear as a bell in his exclamation.

"No," I said outwardly. I wasn't going to kill him, and neither were they. Anders and Atlas snarled at the ground. Kale remained unmoving by their commotion, his golden-amber eyes watching and his ears listening.

"Tell me what happened, Lincoln."

"David lied, I think... but I saw him dead, and I panicked. I thought when you put me in the car, you were taking me off to kill me too. So, I used my phone to text a number David gave me. He said just tell him where I was being taken, and I did. Then when we went got here, you didn't kill me. You gave me a room, acted like you cared." Lincoln hesitated, his voice breaking, unable to stay level.

Rushing to take in all this information, I narrowed my eyes to stare at Lincoln. A shell of a boy everyone had cast aside, abused, and abandoned. I believed he hadn't intentionally caused damage. "You told a man? Do you know who?"

"Um... Bay... Baywood." Lincoln sunk to the ground as if waiting for his death sentence to pass. Atlas and Anders were too happy to oblige, advancing on Lincoln's cowering form, teeth bared, saliva dripping from their tense jaws. "I deserve to die... I ruined it... I'm just so sorry." No tears fell from his eyes. Vampires couldn't shed tears, but that didn't stop physical sobs from shattering through Lincoln.

Anders howled, ready to attack. Atlas dipped down on his hunches, preparing for his ambush. Without a second thought, I angled myself between Lincoln and my insistent brothers.

Move, Thea. You heard him! He deserves this! Atlas raged forward in my head.

"No. He doesn't. We will not perpetuate the cruelty he's endured. We are better than that. He deserves better. We are the Triad, and we honor the laws and our father—we do not harm innocents."

Innocents? Our father is dead because of him. And what, we just let him live for his treason? Anders was less angry and more perplexed, his ears flattened.

"We let him live because he didn't know any better, and our father is dead because of Xercarus and Baywood. Lincoln isn't even an adult. I don't kill children, do you?" I posed the question to my brothers.

Kale, who'd remained soundless until now, monitored the exchange with fascination, tilting his scruffy head. *Thea. Let me get closer to him. I won't hurt him. You have my word on our bond. I can see something. It's vague and blurry, but definitely there.*

I nodded, condoning Kale's request. I trusted his word. "Lincoln, Kale is going to move closer to you. He won't harm you." Lincoln scarcely batted his eyes, remaining stationary.

A breeze blew, wafting Lincoln's scent around. Our guards and other pack members had gathered nearby, ready to launch an assault on the unknown intruder. Kale hulked his large wolf figure to the cringing shape, laying down in front of Lincoln. Sniffing, Kale put his nose directly on Lincoln, inhaling and practically snorting. I opened my mind, finding my way to Kale's. He let me in through our bond, and I saw...

Lincoln laughing, his face pulled in a beautiful grin. His arms wrapped around... Atlas and Anders. He was between them. Smiles on their faces. A navy graduation cap atop Lincoln's head. Atlas pulled Lincoln into a massive hug. Anders patted his back, pride beaming from his face.

Leaning on a white Tahoe was Kale and me, Kale's arm casually draped at my waist. Lincoln released Atlas and Anders, running to me. He picked me up, swinging me around. I heard myself speak.

"You did it! We're so proud of you." I placed a kiss on his almost white-blonde hair. Tears pricked my eyes. My Lincoln.

"I did. It's all because you believed in me, Thea." Lincoln set me down, his gray eyes bright. Lincoln leaned into me. The sun on his face made his skin even more flawless and beautiful—a vampire in the body of a young man.

"Job well done, Linc! You didn't forget our deal, did you?" Kale's pleased smile was full on his face. His hand went to his pocket, pulling out a key fob. Gage drove up in a new Jeep Wrangler.

"Oh, my god! Yes! Kale, you're the best!"

Darkness. Kale's mind went blank, his vision dissipating. Touching Lincoln let him see a premonition. A future together if we kept this course. Bigger than that, Xercarus was nowhere to be found in Kale's premonition. I was so caught up in the vision, I hadn't noticed Atlas and Anders had linked into my thoughts. They viewed Kale's vision along with me. Their snarls faded, heads cocking in my direction.

"Lincoln becomes part of our family. We grow to love him. We all bore witness to Kale's premonition." I spoke not only to my brothers but to the pack and our guards, now surrounding us. "Lincoln is part of our family. If anyone is unkind to him, you'll answer to me."

"Yes, Alpha!" The crowd resonated their response to me. Their loyalty to me was unquestionable.

We lost our father but gained another brother. The Triad—our real power was our family, our bond. This is how we would create unity—by offering understanding. But, when I got the chance, I'd roast Xercarus to ashes. We'd put an end to his demonic plague of an existence, or I'd die trying.

Kale gave a sloppy wet lick up Lincoln's cheek. Lincoln jolted with shock as if a bomb had dropped near him. I knelt down, holding onto Kale and looking directly into Lincoln's soft, gray eyes. "You made a mistake, but you're welcome to stay. If that's something you want."

Lincoln's eyes were wide, looking from me to Kale. "After what I did, you're offering to let me stay?"

"Yes. Lincoln, you deserve a family. We can be that for you. I got a glimpse into your future. You're going to do good things. Now, let's get inside. I'm freezing, and I'd like to get dressed." I shoved away my sadness, compartmentalizing it, and gave Lincoln a smile, extending my hand to help him off the ground.

Losing my father hadn't rescinded from my mind. A large piece of me remained haunted by the knowledge he was very much gone, but my father had left a portion of himself with me. With Kale's vision, one thing shined harder than the grief. *Hope.* Hope would be exactly how we got through this.

Walking in the house, everyone was somber. The boys, still in wolf form, went bounding up the stairs, their claws clicking on the hard surface. I heard each of them head off to their rooms to retrieve clothes. I hugged my mother's shawl to my nose, inhaling her scent. Lilacs and honey swirled in my sinuses. Kale's insistent prodding with his wet muzzle on my hind end brought me back into the moment.

"Kalen," I rebuked him. He knew his nose was entirely too close to my nearly exposed bottom. "Alright, upstairs!" I pointed to the staircase.

We both jogged up the steps, Kale taking three at a time. Reaching my bedroom, I closed the white door behind the giant brown figure. Immediately I heard cracking, snapping, and readjusting of bone and tissue. Kale shifted back. I grabbed the first things from my drawers: black leggings and a loose Stranger Things graphic tee.

Kale stood before me, fully nude. There was nothing to not enjoy about what I saw. There wasn't time to spare for that undertaking, but being under him seemed like the quickest way to bury some of the pain, which lingered and made my bones ache.

"You like Stranger Things?" Kale's tone carried a hint of surprise along with his tilted head. I knew he wanted to distract me from the hurt and from his body. He put on the infamous gray sweatpants I enjoyed so much, along with a relaxed black t-shirt.

"I do like Stranger Things. You believe Hopper is gone?" I asked, already heading to the doorway. Conversation with him, despite the crippling events of the night, eased my mind. I'd need all the mental clarity I could muster—we had to discuss and review so many things. My thoughts shifted back to Lincoln, a seventeen-year-old new vampire holding valuable information we'd need to ensure a future for us all.

"Definitely not. I'm a traditional optimist." Kale's long legs caught up swiftly to me as both of us made our way back down the stairs.

Optimism. I could use a healthy dose of that, I told myself.

You could use it. Take whatever you need from me. That memorable voice of Kale's moved through my thoughts. I looked up at him with a startled expression. I hadn't realized how forceful my contemplations would be after my ascension to Alpha. My father had never let out internal opinions he didn't care to share. He'd had this expert control I never understood until this moment. Bereavement struck me all over again, leaking in around me like waves threatening to flood a small rowboat lost at sea. There was so much I'd have to learn on my own. I'd have to relearn how to contain my thoughts and not shoot them down my link to Kale. As Queen, I'd also possess the ability to communicate with my immediate pack members over great distances.

My head snapped up in realization. "Wait. Long distances. That's it! I'll try reaching Logan's mind. Maybe he's alive," I blurted out.

Kale's brows shot up, and he watched me with care, presumably concerned I had lost my mind. "What are you talking about?"

Logan... Logan... If you can hear me, come back to us. Come back.

Nothing but dead air. My shoulders sagged. I knew it was a longshot to assume Logan didn't meet the same fate as my father. They were inseparable. Logan was nothing if not a loyal friend and Beta.

"Nothing," I said, only because I didn't want to share the added disappointment. I took Kale's hand instead. The connection eased and frazzled me at the same time.

We walked into a full kitchen. Clanking pots and shutting cabinets, my mother was flitting about, bringing out food from the pantry. Appetizers and snacks covered our island counter. We all needed to eat. Shifting required energy. If possible, it was preferable to eat soon after and replenish that spent vigor.

Calliope busied herself over the stove, making some of our childhood favorites, moqueca and acarajé, a taste of comfort from our mother's Brazilian heritage. The smell of the peppers, garlic, and black-eyed peas on the stove did little to alleviate the dull ache in my heart. Kale and I took seats at the counter, diagonal from Lincoln, who sat quietly, fidgeting with his nails.

"Lincoln, *meu filho*. There's no need to be reserved." My mother addressed Lincoln with benevolence. She could've been hateful and callous, but that was not the way of our mother. It was obvious she intended to adopt Lincoln into her heart, disregarding the circumstances of his arrival and affirming Kale's premonition. She curtly set down some cutlery, then graciously strolled to the stool where Lincoln was perched, taking his hands into hers.

"Now, you listen to me—dreadful things happen in this life. How you respond is what makes you. Cyrus is no longer with us, and I'll long for him every single day until my time comes, but destiny has thought to provide us with you. A kindness indeed."

Illiana dabbed at a single tear, taking his hand again, and continued on. "You chose to be honest at the expense of your life. That's no small feat." She lifted her arm slowly, stroking Lincoln's cheek softly with the back of her hand. He flinched slightly at her unexpected touch, then closed his eyes, taking in her gentleness. She patted his knee before returning to her ingredients.

My mother peered up again from her chopping, her delicate hands barely showing any signs of age. Her skin lacked wrinkles, with nimble fingers and her nails simply manicured. It was those same fine hands that held me as a child when I'd wake from a nightmare. Hands that braided my hair before training. I didn't understand how she could move right now, let alone cook. My mother had a strength I couldn't understand. She had lost her mate, and yet she soldiered on. I wondered if I'd be half the Queen my mother was. Her kind voice brought me back to the moment.

"Athena, while you dressed, I was able to get in contact with some of our people that accompanied your father. They're on their way back as we speak, with several followers from Baywood's. It seems he wasn't alone in his descent into madness. They believe we've also lost Logan. There was an explosion, and they haven't found either body. Don't worry, loves, a few of our members are staying behind to keep searching. If you approve, of course?"

"Absolutely, mother, thank you. I may be the new Alpha, but I trust your judgment and decisions. It's just strange to talk…" I replied, losing the words to finish. My mother gave me a knowing nod and closed her eyes as if to let me know I didn't have to finish.

I grabbed the box Cheez-Its. Starving, I tipped its crispy contents, filling my hand. I popped half a dozen into my mouth, savoring the salty crunch. I wasn't sure how I was eating, but my stomach was growling so loud I had no other choice.

Between chews, I took the opening to talk to Lincoln. "I think you can help us. Baywood wouldn't have believed we let you live. Odds are, he told Xercarus you'd be long dead. We can catch them by surprise if you can tell us whatever you remember…" As I was about to proceed, Atlas and Anders ambled into the kitchen, taking bags of pita chips, hummus, and several pints of blueberries. They took up the remaining seats, spreading their food all over.

Lincoln wasted no time answering me, eager to redeem himself. "I'll tell you everything I know, Athena." Lincoln took in a deep breath out of habit. "I'd been sneaking out of my current foster home. I'd heard there were jobs you could get at Zephyr, even if you were underage. I wanted to make a little money to get the hell out of there. That's where I met David."

This information didn't make me any happier. David was helping Xercarus by recruiting kids for human food bags. Atlas growled; I could tell this didn't sit any better with him.

"You know what? I'm glad I took his head off, fucking deranged—"

"Atlas," my mother chided his use of language at the table. "Watch your mouth while you eat, love."

"Go on, Lincoln," I pressed between eating another handful of Cheez-its, still surprised at how ravenous I was at a time like this.

Lincoln looked at each of our faces, swallowing one more time. "Well, he told me I was different. That I was what he was looking for. Before I knew it, he bit me. Fuckin' hurt. I must've passed out, though, and woke up starving. My stomach was killing me. David tried explaining how I was better than human. That I was a vampire now, and these wolves called the Triad would kill me. He said you tortured vampires for fun, and if I helped him get rid of you, I could have anything I wanted."

"We torture vampires. Isn't that a fucking joke?" Anders sneered, unable to contain his revulsion.

Our mother clicked her tongue, shaking her finger. "Anders, I just told your brother. Please watch your mouth at the table. Manners." She was ladylike to a fault, never even looking up from the cutting board as she spoke. I knew she was busying her hands as much as her mind.

I leaned in, giving Lincoln my undivided attention. "Did David say why he thought you were different, or was that part of his charade to lure you in?"

"He said I look like them." Lincoln pointed to Atlas and Anders, who sat dumping berries into their mouths. "David rambled on about how you'd pity me because of those two."

This statement threw me off, and I observed Lincoln's features closer. He was tall when he wasn't slouching, with shaggy light blonde hair, and, like my brothers, his face possessed an innocence that bordered on mischief. The more I examined Lincoln's qualities, I realized it was true. He carried strong resemblances to Atlas and Anders. More so Anders, with his lighter eyes. How had I not noticed it before? Maybe that's why I felt so compelled to bring Lincoln with me, to protect him. David had acted as if he didn't know us, but he was a dirty liar. David knew plenty about the Triad.

"That's why David risked inviting me to VIP even though he saw me with Kale. Our dead vampire had a plan as well."

"You mean David was setting us up?" Atlas jolted straighter in the chair.

Lincoln nodded slowly. "Yeah, he was. He told me he'd lead you guys to me downstairs. David gave me a phone, with his and that Baywood guy's numbers. Told me to ping my location and send it if I got close to your place. Said he'd make sure to not drain me."

Lincoln fidgeted on the stool, bouncing his leg up and down, but he pressed on. "I passed out on and off after he hooked me up. I was down there for days, maybe a week. I dunno. Watching the others die. David would come down now and again with another body over his shoulder, taking out the dead ones like they were some kind of garbage. Sometimes he'd fill up bottles, taking them back upstairs. I know, deep down, if you guys never showed, he'd have left me down there to die with the rest." Lincoln's voice cracked, but he was hell-bent on keeping his promise of full disclosure to us.

"Hey. Lincoln, take a break. You've been through a lot, and that's an understatement. I have some calls I need to make. The rest of the leaders in the Alliance need to know what's happened to my father. I should be the one to tell them their King is..."

This time it was my voice that broke. How did anyone prepare to talk to people about a loved one's unexpected passing? But I didn't have a choice. They needed to know. They deserved to know.

My mother dropped her utensils. They hit the floor with a clinking clash. "Athena. You're in no condition to speak—"

I held up my hand. "Mother. Please. I understand your concerns. It's my responsibility to our Alliance, the one you and father worked so long to grow and maintain. And if we are to stay united against Xercarus, I must show them I can lead. That even in times of great sorrow, I'm strong enough..."

A loud scoff came from my right. Kale's face was tight with a frown. "You don't have to prove anything to anyone. You are strong enough. I know you are. You've done enough. Everyone here has been through too damn much. Don't you think you deserve a minute to mourn, Athena? A few fucking seconds even?" Kale threw his words at me through gnashing teeth. His anger wasn't aimed at me, but that hadn't stopped his words from hitting the target anyway.

I looked away, sighing. It was difficult not to agree with Kale. All he wanted to do was shield me from more discomfort, but his goal was shortsighted. He was only seeing me, and this was much bigger than any of us.

I wished for my father to be here, or Logan. Logan could guide me through this. He'd been with my father even before my mother.

"Kale. Don't you think I want that? But that's not how it works here. I have a responsibility—" My phone suddenly vibrated hard against the marble counter. Unknown number. I stared at it for a moment, a blank expression on my face.

"Who would call you this late?" Atlas asked, moving closer out of curiosity.

Anders stopped chewing, eyeing the skittering phone on the counter.

My hand shook as I picked up the phone, swiping to answer. "Hello."

The line was quiet for a moment, but then I heard fatigued breathing. "My Queen, I apologize... it took me so... long. I couldn't reach you... I couldn't find... a... phone." His words rasped out between jagged, labored breaths.

I wanted to scream. My body pulsed, consumed with anxious exhilaration. "Logan!" I shrieked in his ear. My mother and Calliope froze, dropping everything. A plate smashed to the floor. Anders jumped up so fast his chair flew backward into the cabinets.

"Logan! Holy shit, it's really Logan?" Atlas rushed to me, causing my hair to whoosh around my face.

I pulled the phone from my ear, my hands trembling. I pressed the speaker button so all of us could hear him. "Logan. Goddess, it's so good to hear your voice. Are you okay? Where are you? When can we get you home?" I realized I was firing questions at Logan faster than I knew he could answer. The kitchen was downright silent, all for Logan's labored breaths over the speaker.

"It's really good to hear you too, Athena. I'm pretty beat up, but I'll be alright. My healing is slow. Your father—" Logan hesitated, sniffing. "He... Baywood had himself rigged with explosives to ensure we didn't capture him. He detonated himself. Cyrus—he knocked me out of the way. I couldn't stop him. Goddess, I tried. I'm so sorry."

Tears rolled down my mother's cheeks again. Without a word, Kale got up from his seat next to me, wrapping my mother up in his large arms. "I'm sorry." He whispered into her hair. "I'm sorry I couldn't see faster." My heart nearly fell from my chest, watching him console my mother like that. A lump formed in my throat, making it tight. She embraced Kale back, throwing her arms around him, wearing a small, warm smile. She wiped the tears from her face. Kale released her from his grip and stood quietly again to listen to Logan.

I drew my gaze back to my lit-up phone screen. "Logan, we know you did all you could."

"I need to tell you something important, but first—do you have a vampire with you? Kill him, Athena. He's their pawn. Baywood was a supporter of Xercarus." Logan ran out of breath for a moment, but not long enough to let me tell him about Lincoln. "He's after the Triad—he's after you, Athena. He knows you can create new wolves. Baywood told him every-thing from the meeting. He knew your plans to go back to Zephyr. It was a trap."

Logan's pitch was reaching a manic point. His concern for our safety outweighed his body's need to recover.

"Logan, slow down. We met a vampire. He's not what you think. Lincoln is no follower of Xercarus or Baywood. It's a long story, but I need you to get back to us first."

"I will." Logan's voice faltered, showing his exhaustion. "Don't you worry about me, I'll be fine. You be safe. Don't trust that vampire. This thing with Baywood runs deep. And Athena, you need to be the one to tell them. It has to be you. Your father... at the end, he submitted his Alpha to you. He believed in you. Show them all—you can lead."

Tears pricked my eyes. The lump lodged in my throat grew, making it ache and feel dry all at once. "I know, and I will. Thank you. Be safe and see you soon. You keep this phone, okay? Until you get back here." My face hurt from trying not to cry.

Logan took a deep breath. "Yes, Alpha."

The call ended. The screen on my phone darkened. My hand covered my trembling mouth, attempting to take in what I knew. As I did, I let loose a sob. It racked through my body and into my soul. My vision went fuzzy and black around the edges, threatening to knock me down. Atlas, who was closest to me, pulled me into him. His big arms wrapped hard around me. I squeezed onto my brother, his warm touch engulfing all of me as I bawled, feeling the loss of my father all over again.

"Thea, it's going to be alright. Cry as much as you need. I'm here." Atlas kept steady, holding me. I could feel everyone's eyes on me. The room was solemn and quiet, my sadness fogging the air. I sniffed again, hiding my face in Atlas's shoulder for another moment.

Be strong, I told myself.

I leaned away from Atlas and looked up into his glossy brown eyes. I watched the worry flicker in them. "Thank you. I'll be alright," I pushed up on my tiptoes to hug him again. *I love you.* "I'm going to head up to the conference room, declare an emergency meeting, and tell them about father. Why don't you all try and get some rest?"

"Not a chance." Atlas's tone was soft as he spoke.

Anders's blue eyes bore into me. "We'll sleep when you sleep."

I nodded, appreciating the solidarity. There were very few things I was certain of, but several burned crystal-clear in my thoughts.

One, Logan was alive.

Two, Xercarus was most definitely after me.

"Alright." I took a deep breath, attempting to declutter my racing head. "I'll see you all in the morning. After the announcement conferences, I think I'll rest for the night." I turned, grabbed my phone off the counter, and headed out of the kitchen, leaving my family to their own devices.

"Wait up." It was Kale, jogging to catch up. "Did you think you were gonna do this alone?"

"I suppose I kinda did." Heartache was eating at me, weakening my reserve and begging me to find a corner and weep.

"That's your first mistake. I'm with you every step of the way. I won't say a thing if that's what you want. Let me support you." Kale didn't reach out to touch me like he often did. Instead, he stared at me, wanting me to decide based on what I wanted rather than what his touch could sway me to do.

I took in his offer, knowing most of me wanted him nearby. His presence was consoling, the only thing making any of this bearable. "Of course, I want you with me." We walked hand in hand the rest of the way to the conference room. Neither of us spoke. Thoughts of what to say consumed my brain. How did I tell everyone their leader, their King, was killed, and they've inherited me? Which, as of this morning, few of them were all too keen on.

I pushed open the double doors, my fingers searching to press the lights icon on the iPad mounted on the wall as I walked in. The room flared to life. I moved to switch on the monitors. I swiped my fingers through the various screens, searching for the right contacts. I bypassed their office lines and went straight for direct phone numbers. I'd start with Oriel Reed and Williamina Cedargrove since they'd been the most accepting earlier. I dialed their numbers, putting them both on the large conference-room speakerphone. The phones simultaneously rang. On the third ring, they both picked up.

"Hello, Oriel Reed speaking, what can I do for you at this hour, Your Majesty?"

"Williamina Cedargrove, here as well, sir. How may I assist you?"

Their voices were groggy and slow. I'd clearly woken them both. "I'm sorry to wake you like this. However, it's imperative I speak with you both."

"Princess Athena. Heavens, what's the matter?" Williamina answered me first, her voice a soft soprano pitch.

My words stuck; saying it out loud made it real.

Come on, you can do this, Athena. Tell them.

"My father... he's—he's dead."

Gasps from both lines showed their intense shock. "But—he—we just had that meeting this afternoon; what has happened?" Oriel asked. Williamina lightly sob.

"He accompanied Logan to Baywood's region. Baywood was a follower of Xercarus. I guess he'd strapped himself in explosives to avoid being taken into custody and blew himself and my father up." I swallowed, though my mouth was completely dry, and kept my composure.

Control. I told myself. *Don't let your emotions get the better of you.*

"Athena, I am truly sorry for this tremendous loss. Cyrus was a great Alpha and King. He earned every bit of our loyalty and trust. I will pledge my continued loyalty to your mother as our new leader." Oriel offered his allegiance to my mother, but would he extend the same to me? I was about to find out.

I took another deep breath. "Thank you, however, that's something else I need to discuss with you. My father submitted his Alpha position to me right before he... he passed. My mother also submitted her title. I'm the Queen. I intend to do my best to honor my father and his sacrifice. The Winter Solstice is nearly a month away. I'd appreciate it if you'd attend as we celebrate my father's life and achievements. "

Oriel responded to me first. "It would be my divine honor to join you at the Winter Solstice, my Queen. Your father would be proud. One small concern, if I may, Your Majesty. Are you any closer to finding out when you'll be able to transform again?"

Williamina spoke up, clearing her throat in distaste over Oriel's questions. "A personal invitation from you to attend Winter Solstice is a true honor. I shall be there, Your Grace." Her angelic voice rang through the speaker.

I lifted my head high, not that either of them could see me. "You needn't worry yourselves over me or the Triad. I'm fully capable of reaching my wolf and dragon. In fact, I've developed the ability to fly."

"Why, that is an incredible advance!" Oriel did very little to cover his astonishment over the news.

"This must be an honor from the Goddess. She sees fit to bestow another gift onto the Triad. My pack and I are humbled to serve under Your Majesty's reign. I'm saddened for losing our honorable King Cyrus, may he rest in peace with the Goddess and elves, but perhaps this is our silver lining. A new gift for the Triad and a stronger bond with humans, with our soon-to-be King at your side." Williamina's declaration sprung new hope and brought forth subdued courage in me. I was thankful for her open arms and kind words. I'd remember her unwavering faith and well wishes in the future.

Oriel sighed, likely processing what I had shared with him. "There isn't much that we can do tonight. I appreciate you taking the time to connect with me on such delicate matters, especially after this morning. This means a great deal to me, and I'll not forget it. I shall spread the news of our great King's passing with nearby members. I know I speak for myself and Williamina when I say we look forward to ushering in the Winter Solstice with a new Queen and King. We will be by your side if the time comes to battle Xercarus. You can count on that."

"Absolutely. You have my word and support as leader of the Midwest. Let us bid you a good night, to rest and mourn. We owe you that much."

I covered my mouth, overwhelmed by their genuineness, though it energized me to carry on with my calls. "Thank you. I appreciate your compassion and dedication. I look forward to seeing you both at the Winter Solstice, as well. Goodnight."

"Goodnight, Majesty," they said in unison, both ending our call.

Kale got up from his chair and marched toward me. He put his warm hand on my back, rubbing up and down my spine. "You did great, and they seemed to take the news well."

"Yeah, they did. Only a dozen more calls of repeating myself..."

Kale exhaled, pursing his lips. He didn't bother trying to persuade me into waiting until tomorrow. He understood the significance of these phone exchanges and took a seat again while I dialed up the next contact. This was going to be a long night...

Three hours later, I had finished my last call. I went over the details as best I could each time. And each time, they met with sorrow and condolences. The lack of hesitation I received over announcing my status change surprised me. On each call, the council members had all been accepting, offering loyalty and blessings, but talking was tiring. My throat burned, telling me I needed a drink. Kale sensed my thirst, hopping up and grabbing a bottle of water from the mini-fridge.

"Here, drink." He unscrewed the cap and placed the water

in front of me as I stood, leaning over the glass table with my palms spread out.

I lifted my head to catch Kale's gaze, taking the bottle. "Thank you." Drinking large gulps, I took in his eyes. They were soft, the blue as striking as ever. My stomach did a flip. My mind skipped, a shattered mess of ideas and fears. I wanted release from the sorrow, even for a moment, to feel no dull ache of pain. I knew Kale could give me that freeing relief. I set the empty bottle on the table, rolling away the chair between Kale and me.

"Kiss me." I linked my arms around his neck.

"Thea... " Kale held back, hesitation filling his lack of movement as much as his tone.

I put my hand to Kale's cheek, rubbing my thumb across his mouth, then placed a kiss on his lips. A hushed groan slipped from Kale's parted mouth. I leaned up to kiss him again, more insistently this time. Putting my hands on his chest, I pushed him toward the wall behind us. Kale moved his legs with mine, matching my steps until I had him flush against the wall. I heard the drywall crunch a bit from the impact when we hit it harder than I anticipated. I was in no mood to check the damage, and neither was Kale.

I continued kissing him while his hands caressed my back. Passion burning up my veins, I put my hands in his thick hair, wrapping it around my fingers. I reached my hands down to lift his shirt, and it tore off. Kale pulled away from me, his eyes flickering back and forth from blue to golden amber. I didn't care that we were in the conference room. I wanted him now. I put my hand on the waistband of his sweats, attempting to free him from them. That's when I felt Kale's hand grasp my wrist, stopping me.

"What's wrong?" I asked him, huffing, out of breath.

"Not here."

"What? Why? Don't you want to?" I cocked my head a bit.

"It's not that. I want you, trust me. I always want you. But you're not thinking clearly. You're upset. We don't have a condom with us, and I'm not risking getting you pregnant because we're careless."

My eyes widened, and I covered my mouth. Kale was absolutely right. I'd wanted to make the grief go away so much I'd set aside my better judgment. My cheeks felt hot, flushed from embarrassment, and I angled away from him. I wouldn't deny I wanted to bury the pain of my father's death any way possible, but I couldn't believe I'd forgotten about the necessity of protection. I'd had no need for consistent birth control before Kale. I didn't engage in sex often enough to concern myself with it, but now my needs had changed. I should've taken care of this weeks ago. My jaw twitched, and I put going to our pack physician toward the top of my growing to-do list. We'd have no accidents.

"You're right. I'd like to say I don't know what came over me, but I know exactly what did. I just wanna forget..."

Any lingering hope I had of thwarting my grief vanished, making my lungs gasp for bits of air. My shoulders slouched, feeling too heavy, and my mind spun around fragmented memories of my father in my head like a never-ending carousel. I needed to get out of here, out of this room where I could try to breathe again.

Kale kissed my forehead, sighing again. "Athena, you and me, we're partners now. None of this has been easy. I wanna make you feel better in any way I can. Don't think it's an easy feat getting a hold of myself. I want you all the time. It feels inappropriate how often I think of making love to you, but at the moment, it's not my body you need." Kale paused, dragging his hand through his hair as he always did while blowing a breath out. He touched my cheek. "Listen, there's a nice, big bathtub in that bathroom of yours upstairs. How about I run you a bath? Help you relax."

I took another shallow breath, nodding yes. His kindness never ceased to amaze me. Kale continued to be a beacon, like an ever-burning lighthouse pulling me back in from the storm.

Kale chuckled softly as he bent to retrieve the fabric shreds from the floor. "Good thing I wasn't attached to this shirt."

I bit my lower lip in embarrassment as we made our way out of the conference room, upstairs to my bedroom. Exhaustion hit me like a train.

As we reached the staircase, I heard faint laughter coming from the kitchen, my family still awake. That sound ignited a tiny spark of joy in my chest. I tilted my head, my mouth perking up into a closed-mouth grin. I guess nobody wanted to be alone after tonight.

CHAPTER 14

The water gushed into the oval-shaped tub with a splash. Kale sat on the stone edge of the bath, sifting through bottles. I watched him read over each one with care. Choosing his selections, he poured capfuls into the steaming water, swishing it about with his hand.

"There, that should do it." Kale stood up, wiping his wet hand on his sweats, a pleased expression on his face. The aromas swirled around me, dampening my nerves. Rose hips, lavender oil, and jasmine bubble bath. Hmm, of course, he would choose lavender. It was a calming combination; lavender was every bit as soothing for me, too.

"Come here," he said, offering his hand to me.

I did as Kale requested, lingering in front of him. He undressed me, taking care to not tug my ears up with my shirt and never touching me more than necessary. His eyes trailed up and down my naked body, not making a sound. Reaching for the basket on the sink, he grabbed one of my black hair ties and gathered my hair into his hands. To my surprise, he managed a presentable, messy bun atop my head.

I gave a tight-lipped smile, appraising his handy work. He held my hand, easing me down into the large soaking tub. The water was balmy, cloaking me in snug warmth. I leaned until I rested against the back of the tub and closed my eyes, letting the fragrances and heat consume me. I heard Kale shuffling and then kneel near the bath.

His hands found their way to my exposed shoulders, kneading my muscles. "Just relax. Let me take care of you," he whispered, his sweet, cool breath brushed my ear. "I don't need to be a massage therapist to feel how far this tension goes. Before you, I would've said I can't imagine what you're going through. And yet, now, I feel it. I feel it like it's my own. Your sorrow, the heartache you keep trying to hide and avoid. You can't do that to yourself."

He moved on the floor, leaning over to kiss the top of my head. "In the conference room, I know you wanted to bury the pain. I used to do that. I think you did, too. Looking for something to bide our time, to forget." Kale continued kneading my shoulders, moving his long fingers up to massage up my neck. "And, Athena, I'll do whatever you want, but you can't bury this. You have to grieve for your father. It'll eat you from the inside out if you don't."

Kale removed his hands, turning his body to see my face. Placing one hand beneath my chin, he wiped away my tears. I hadn't even realized they'd been slipping down my cheeks. I squeezed my eyes shut tighter, attempting to will away the sadness, but more tears flowed down. I couldn't block out the void my father had left anymore, so I let go, letting soundless sobs splinter throughout my body. I curled my knees to my chest, hugging them tightly to me. The pain ebbed and flowed, washing over me and clinging to my skin. I felt Kale get up, and suddenly the water sloshed all around me. Kale's arms enveloped me, pulling my naked body to his chest. He'd climbed in the tub behind me, sweatpants and all.

"It's going to be okay. We'll get through this. Shh..." He kissed my temple, rocking me as I sniffled. I put my hands to his arms, clinging to him. He was not only a lighthouse guiding me back home, but an anchor to keep the sadness from dragging me away. I let my head fall against him while the tears streamed down my face. It had been years since I gave myself permission to cry, and with each droplet, I let myself feel.

The tears came slower until I felt as if they'd run out. I wasn't sure how long it had taken me to cry myself out, but there was Kale, solid behind me, humming a soft melody in my ear—letting me feel exactly how I needed to.

"You're soaked." My voice came out hoarse and thick. Dipping my hand in the water, I touched his clothed thigh and let my body settle further into him.

"I'll dry. I've noticed this habit of yours. You're always trying to take care of everyone. You forget about yourself." Kale kissed my hair, breathing in my scent and letting his hands wander down my arms to wrap around my waist.

I sighed, huffing through the last of my sobs. "I don't know any other way to be."

Kale turned me a bit to see his face. "I'm not asking you to change, Thea, only to think of yourself too. Let's get you out of here. The water is catching a chill." Kale got up from behind me, dripping onto the white rug. He pulled my robe off a hook from near the shower, wrapping me in the downy softness. After making sure I was comfortable, he tugged off his sopping sweatpants, wringing them into the draining tub. I left the bathroom, my still-damp feet leaving prints on the floor as I walked to the dresser. I opened a drawer, taking out a fresh pair of pants for Kale. We needed to get more of his clothes. I put another mental note on my lengthy to-do list.

Kale took the pants, slipping them on without too much trouble. "I'm going to put these on the balcony, so they'll dry quicker," he said, opening the door. Right as the door opened, a breeze brought in a strange, foul odor. I turned my head, but I felt like I was moving in slow motion. "Don't!"

"What's that smell?"

No sooner had the words left his mouth than I saw a slimy, blackened, and disfigured hand grab Kale's throat. Kale gurgled a bit, his body being lifted from the ground by the figure.

Snarling, I lunged forward. "No!"

I saw its full form now. It was hideous, with a face full of scars and gnarled features. Part of its nose was gone—ripped off. No hair, just pointed, bent ears. The whites of its eyes were hollow, shrouded in blackness. Xercarus wasted no time before sending in one from his legion to launch an assault. The beast sneered at Kale, chomping its broken, decaying teeth.

My eyes burned and flamed green, fire pushing to my exterior. "Put him down," I demanded, lifting my hand and letting an orb of fire grow in my palm. The deformed creature stared me down, a malevolent grin pulling at the jagged mouth.

Opening my mind, I called to Kale and my brothers. *Shift, Kale! Anders! Atlas! Get up here!*

The mutant creature eyed me with disturbing interest.

"Athena..." The voice dragged out my name with spite on its breath. "You want us to put him down? This one smells good. Maybe we eat him... You have something we want." I watched its blistered tongue flick toward Kale's sputtering face.

"Shift!" I hollered at Kale, and he thrashed harder.

"*Nuh-uh*, Princess. You want this one back? You come with us." The clawed fingers dug into Kale's neck, his blood running down from the punctures.

Anders and Atlas burst through the door, neither in wolf form. Lincoln was close behind them. I watched his face contort, and his eyes grow wide as he took in the monstrous creature.

"*Ah*, the brothers. Master would like a healer. We want that one." A grimy finger extended to Anders. I snarled at the thought.

Over my dead body.

"Like hell, you'll get either of them!" Atlas shouted, his wolf-life features pushing forward.

"You will do as the Master wants, or he dies." The cruelty in its shrill tone heightened.

Kale lifted his hands, placing them on the fiend's arm, attempting to free himself from the deathly grip. Kale struggled, gritting his teeth while amber took over the blues of his eyes. Thank Goddess, he was going to shift. Kale squashed the mutant's arm, the bones splintering between his hands.

A horrid screech rang through the air, and it tried swiping at Kale with its other claws.

"What is this?" it shrieked at us. The arm Kale crushed beneath his hands turned a frosted blue as if it was freezing. I squinted my eyes. It *was* freezing. The clawed hand released Kale but remained in the air.

"What's happening?" Anders asked.

Kale picked himself up off the ground, ferocity booming in all his expression as his chest heaved up and down. He put his hands on the creature's chest. Its deranged squawks continued while blue spread across its body. I couldn't believe what I was seeing. Kale stepped back, leaving the mutant to clutch at its icy chest with one usable talon as it crumpled to the ground.

Lincoln burst past Atlas and Anders in a blur, using his vampire speed, and charged into the room. He ducked under Kale's arm and out of his path, diving onto the writhing figure laying on the ground. Lincoln raised his hand high, then brought it down with a smash, shattering the mutant's chest, sending icy black splinters into the air. The shrieking and movement stopped.

Lincoln lifted his hand, blackened with a mucus-like substance from the heart he'd seized. The heart juddered with a few more dying pulses. Lincoln examined the organ, his face wrinkled and mouth twisted, filling with repulsion. He compressed the darkened heart until it oozed out of his hand.

The fire in my palms extinguished, and I rushed to Kale's side with Anders hot behind me.

"Are you okay? If... if I'd thrown a fireball, I might've hit you. Let me see your hands!" I turned Kale's hands around, staring at them. They felt much cooler than normal, like ice. I held onto Kale tighter, taking as much of him into my arms as possible. He was alive. I looked down at Lincoln by my feet. "Lincoln! My Goddess, what were you thinking? It could've killed you!"

Lincoln's expression broadened. "I'm not even sure. I didn't think. It's dead now, right?" Lincoln was staring at his slippery hand, unable to look away. I wondered if he was going into shock.

"Definitely dead," Anders answered, staring at the mess on my floor.

"Good." Lincoln gave me a vacant expression. I worried he was in shock.

Atlas stood in the doorway, shaking his head with amusement. I had no clue what he found funny. "Kale's a damn ice dragon." He rubbed his chin, keeping his eyes on Kale. My mouth popped open along with Kale's.

Our mother made her way into my room, interrupting our discovery. A gasp tumbled from her lips. "Children! Lincoln! Are you all alright? Let me see you." Illiana made her way to Lincoln first, holding his face in her hands. "Ah, my boy." She clicked her tongue. "You can't go running into the melee with these four." Her concern bubbled over, making her brown eyes crease in the corners.

"Mother, why don't you take Lincoln to clean up? And could you have Calliope gather us a team to get this mess down to the lab?" Giving my mother someone to nurture was the fastest way to calm her nerves.

"Of course, love. Anything you need. Lincoln, my dear, come with me. Let's get you some fresh clothes." Lincoln, whose mouth remained agape, got up and followed Illiana out of the room. Good. With Lincoln out of the way, that eliminated one distraction.

"Kale, I hate to tear you away from my sister, but I need to see your throat." Anders moved past me, putting his hand to Kale, helping his regeneration along. "There. He's all yours, Thea. Good as new."

Kale touched his throat, blood and blackness coating his fingers. "Ugh." He stalked off to the bathroom, turning on the sink faucet and scrubbing at his neck with vigor.

"My powers heal, Kale, not clean. That's on you," Anders said, mocking Kale's groan.

Several of our guard staff entered the room, carrying totes of the supplies required to clean and sanitize my balcony.

I nodded to them. "Thank you both. I appreciate you doing this at such a late hour. We'll get out of your way."

"No problem, Alpha. We'll get this downstairs and off your floor right away. You'll never know it was here." They bowed their heads at me in agreement, setting off to work on the messy corpse. Appeared I'd need to double the patrols around the manor. No one should've gotten this close.

Kale emerged from the bathroom, grumbling. "Can we have one night go as fucking planned? Or even an hour?" Kale's patience was depleted, his hands pinned at his hips.

"Iceman, chill out. You knew things were fast-paced around here." Atlas nudged Kale, aiming to relax the mood as always. "We knew this was coming, but anybody else wanna talk about what I wanna talk about?"

I rubbed Kale's back as we walked to the library. He threw a look back to Atlas. "Yeah, I can freeze things now?"

"Exactly! How cool is that? Ha, I made another pun." Atlas chuckled, hopping into a gray recliner. "Ha. 'Cool.'" He laughed again to himself.

Anders went to the bookshelves, plucking a book from its

place. "Real funny, Atlas, ya idiot," he said as he opened it, reading to himself.

"So, what did it feel like? Freezing that thing?" Atlas continued his inquisition.

Kale sighed, putting his hands to his hips. "Honestly, cold, but like I could do anything. I wanted to kill it. Just reach in and freeze its heart. This family is going to turn me into some kind Jeffery Dahmer-type murderer."

"You're no murderer. What came on my balcony isn't alive anymore, not like we are. Xercarus uses demonic sorcery to keep them animated after he disfigures them. You can kill them—or rather disrupt their connection to Xercarus—by ripping out their hearts or decapitating them. At least that's what we've read. Seems Lincoln did a fine job of it," Anders said, without looking up as he thumbed through pages.

"Kale, you realize you're more of a Ted Bundy type, right? Smooth with the ladies." Atlas laughed at his own joke while Anders covered his mouth, trying to suppress a smirk. His jests made me feel almost normal again. "And Lincoln. Holy shit. Didn't see that coming. Little vamp man has quite the spirit. I think your vision is right Kale, I'm fixin' to like that kid a lot."

"Lincoln's reaction was rather impressive, but it seemed too easy. That beast could've fought more, and it didn't." I paused, knowing, in my gut, I was correct. I shook my head, pinching the bridge of my nose. "Something isn't right. That creature acted like it was toying with us more than anything. It was after something else besides me."

I walked to the wall where we had an iPad mounted. The screen lit up to life, and I clicked on our home monitoring system. Nothing stood out until camera C. A hooded shape stood outside the lab. I watched as the shadowy figure sniffed the room and touched where Kale had been sitting earlier. I felt Kale behind me, watching the screen with me. The cloaked figure didn't look like a mutant. Its movement was too fluid and calculated.

"See, there? I knew it. It was looking for something in the lab and downloaded files from the computer. I'm willing to stake my life that it was after the tests we ran on Kale. Xercarus is going to know about Kale and me..." My voice trailed off, seeing the look of horror on Kale's frowning face.

"How did it even get access? Damn it. Baywood! Fucker's lucky he's dead!" Atlas shouted; his fists clenched.

I shook my head, trying not to smash the iPad. "They took our samples."Anders, who'd been reading, piped up. "Things just went from bad to worse."

The fact that anyone had gotten into the manor shook me to the core. A chill moved down my spine, and I hugged myself. This was no coincidence.

"Someone let them into the manor," I said. Anders shot me a worried look while Atlas fumed around the room. We had a traitor in our pack, in our home, and we'd have to find out who without tipping them off.

We spend the next hour compiling a list of staff and guards to check out. Anders watched the security footage over and over, looking for any clue to indicate who was in our lab, but whoever it was had kept their face hidden from the security cameras. That fact alone pointed to an inside job. I decided it was best to keep our suspicions between us until we had more concrete information. We couldn't risk questioning them outright.

More secrets. Just what this family needed.

I rubbed my eyes. My eyelids were still heavy from crying and made heavier by fatigue. Kale looked up from the tablet screen he'd been staring at with Anders.

Kale's face relaxed, and he got up to come sit by me. "Alright, can everybody please give us a minute?"

"Sure, man. No problem. We could all use a little rest. Thea, we'll deal with the lab. Anything crazy comes up; we know where to find you." Anders patted my shoulder.

"Thanks, guys. I know this has been…" I heaved out a breath. "Well, honestly, tonight was without a doubt the most horrible night of our lives. I don't know what to do next. I just— I can't lose anyone else. I can't lose either of you." I stood up and reached for Anders, who took me into his arms, squeezing me hard. Atlas joined our somber embrace.

"Triad," I heard Anders whisper.

"Triad," Atlas repeated.

I lifted my head to admire them, blue and brown eyes meeting mine.

"*Triad.*"

For the first time, I watched their eyes light up. Green shuffled around their irises. Our connection had never been stronger. Atlas placed a quick kiss on my forehead. Anders did the same before they headed downstairs to clean up yet another mess.

Kale touched my back. "Thea, I'm sorry. That was rude of me…"

"*Shh.* I get it. I didn't wanna talk about it anymore, anyway," I said softly as I turned to face him.

Kale clutched onto me, a familiar glossy expression taking over his eyes. "I'm not scared for myself. I'm terrified I'm going to lose you, and I don't know how to manage it or overcome it."

"I understand. More than you know. Here, come with me." I put my hand out, willing Kale to follow me.

I took him to a long glass case. Inside were artifacts collected over generations. I opened the case, taking out a pendant. The chain was from the early 1900s and made of white gold. On it hung a silver-veined leaf. Elves made it as a protection totem, said to ward off those who would harm you.

The pendant dangled from my hands as I lifted it above Kale's head, draping it with care around his neck. It laid against his chest, right above his heart. I put the leaf in my hands, bringing it to my lips.

"Praesidium Amare," I whispered to the chain. It glowed a soft green.

Kale looked at me in wide-eyed wonder. "What—what did you do?"

"It'll protect you. When someone seeks to harm you, it'll turn red. And if we are apart, you can speak my name to it. It will turn green like it is now if I'm okay. I know it's not much, but it's the only peace of mind I can offer you."

Kale touched the pendant, holding the leaf. "This is— Athena, you're more brilliant than I ever could've imagined." He rushed his words, in a hurry to kiss me. His lips crashed into my mine, and, for a moment, we were tongues and teeth. I let my body curve against him, melding into his hands.

His kiss was ardent, full of everything we felt tonight— sadness, terror, relief, *love*. Kale lifted me gently around him. He carried me as he walked us to one of the oversized plush sofas. He laid me down, never breaking our connection as he propped himself above me. His lips picked up the pace while a hand dashed to my waist to untie my robe. It fell open to him, giving Kale full access to my body. He stroked his hand down my supple chest to rest on my hip, letting his hand knead my soft skin.

Kale exhaled. "I'm not sure I have the restraint to stop this time. I need you to tell me no." His breath weakened; his earlier resolve gone. "Just tell me we can't." Closing his eyes, Kale pressed his head to mine, his hair tickling my cheeks. "You know I'd never force myself on you. Never." His voice was a fraction above a murmur in my ear. His breath brought me to life.

I took his hand and placed his palm to my breast. "No," I said, panting as I laid beneath him. Kale inhaled and shifted off me, but I pulled him down to my chest. "I said no because I don't want to stop you." I reached into my fallen robe pocket, producing a foil package.

"Where did you get that?" Kale's voice was high, full of amusement and longing.

"After last time, I wasn't getting caught off guard again. I snagged some before we left." I bit my lower lip.

Kale's irises ignited, amber flecks staring down at me. He kissed my lips, tracing his fingers on my neck as he tucked a lock of my hair around his finger. He moved down my neck, to my collarbone, at a taunting tempo, leaving dainty kisses and licks as he went. I arched my hips into him, feeling his hardness through his pants. I could sense the wetness pooling above my thighs. Our many starts and stops today had left me with exhausted anticipation, and I wanted Kale inside me—to share our closeness. Guilt skulked around my thoughts, but I didn't want to hear anymore. All I wanted to hear was Kale's muffled moans and our hearts.

With tenderness guiding his actions rather than insecurity, Kale paused. He sensed my slight hesitation and gazed softly down at me. I nodded at him, signaling my readiness. Kale reared up, nothing on his chest except for the delicate chain laying on his skin above his thrumming heart. I watched the power in his movements, steady and calculated. His hunger for me tethered inside. He put his muscular hands to the band of his pants, lowering them until his mass was displayed fully to me. I handed him the foil package. His advances were rapid, and I found him between my legs. The cool metal of his illuminated chain suspended above me, casting dancing reflections in my eyes.

Kale touched my lips, letting his thumb linger on my bottom lip. "I wanna watch you. Hold you in my arms as you thrash beneath me, knowing it's me fulfilling all your cravings. Let me give you that release, and when you flush and cry out, I'll know I've done it right."

Pulling Kale to my chest, I wrapped as much of him into my arms as I could. Books surrounded us, yet the only words I thought about were his. I felt him push into my depths—the depths of my body and then my soul. While we made love on the sofa, I let go, melding into Kale. Our bodies turned loose of our hearts, allowing the essences of our beings to collide and possess one another. To have Kale was not only to give away my heart but to have his soul within me and freely give away my own.

You are the light in my dark. I pushed my words into Kale's mind as I came undone beneath him, losing myself in our feelings.

CHAPTER 15

I awoke, my eyelids fluttering in protest of the light streaming in. My naked body felt overheated from being swathed in Kale's hot embrace and a throw from the sofa for so long. The boiling temperature begged me to wiggle away. Instead, I kept quiet, taking pleasure in listening to Kale's soft breathing. Our serenity didn't last long. There was a polite knock on the archway, and I heard my name.

"Athena. Are you in here? Atlas told me to come get you and Kale. He said there's a truck here for Kale."

I scrambled up, looking for my robe. "One second, Lincoln, we're just…"

Lincoln rounded a bookshelf. "Shit! I'm sorry! Oh, God, um —" A mortified expression covered his face. He turned around in a blur to face away from me, putting his hand up to shield his eyes. How did he even get in here? You needed a fingerprint. Damn Atlas, he must have programmed it in.

I kept myself covered with the throw. "Lincoln, it's fine. I was about to get up anyway." I did my best to keep my tone good-humored and less embarrassed than I was.

"I should've known something was up when Atlas started

laughing before he asked me to come get you. What a dick-head." Lincoln let out a small chuckle, loosening up.

"We'll be right down. And, Lincoln, you need to learn that Atlas can be a jerk."

Kale groaned. "Ahh, no. Atlas is definitely a dick."

Lincoln headed out. "Alright, see you downstairs." His tone was almost cheerful, as if he wasn't rescued from a hellhole or ripped out a heart last night.

Sitting up, Kale put his pants back on as I slipped into my robe. "What's this about a truck?"

"Not sure, guess we'll find out. I'm gonna put something else on besides my robe. Be right back." I hurried out of the library as I hollered back to Kale, who still sat on the edge of the sofa rubbing his eyes.

My room was spotless, like nothing had even transpired last night. The smell of sanitizers and bleach was strong but dulling with the aromas of several soy candles. The linens were fresh, my bed crisply made.

Calliope, I mused.

Rummaging in drawers, I took out dark pants and a light knit sweater. Good enough. I looked in the mirror and saw my hair unkempt, strands sticking in the air. I ran my fingers through it with little effect. I reached for a brush on the vanity, tugging my hair in an attempt to tame the waves. Giving up in a huff, I set the brush down and left the bathroom.

Kale met me at the stairs, and my heart skipped a beat from seeing him. "Ladies first," he said. His hand touched my lower back, guiding us down.

The front door was open, letting the sun pool on the floor, warming the panels. I heard my mother's melodic voice talking and someone outside. Whose voice was that? I listened closer. It was Ben Browning, my father's assistant. Though Browning was a human moniker. His given name was Bennion Valna.

My lips pulled up into a smile when I saw the young elf's face. He was only a little older than I and from the elven territories in the Midwest, somewhere near Michigan. He touched my mother's shoulder; his eyes twinkled with sadness as he spoke to her. He was shorter than Kale and my brothers but had a broad chest and shoulders. Ben was pristine in appearance; most elves were. Styled light brown hair covered his pointed ears, giving him a studious vibe, and he was professionally dressed in business casual attire. Tailored navy slacks and a pale blue button-down shirt with the sleeves rolled in crisp lines to three-quarters length. I noticed he kept touching the shiny Chopard moon watch strapped to his wrist. A gift my father had custom made for him last year.

Ben was more than an assistant; he was like family. He'd worked for my father for five years, moving up in the ranks of the investment company, and was highly capable, often running the firm in our absence—like now.

We walked farther outside. The sun shined bright in my eyes, making me squint, but I saw the large, yellow moving truck that was parked in front. Ben caught sight of me over my mother's shoulder and bowed his head low.

"Queen Athena, there's nothing I can say to lessen your loss. Please know I am forever at your service for anything."

My heart clenched. "Thank you, Ben, but just Athena, please. You know me better than that." Ben nodded, giving me a closed mouth grin of appreciation.

"What's all this?" I asked.

Kale scratched his hands through his hair, he'd never seen an elf yet, and Ben's sparkling eyes and pointed ears grabbed his attention. *What is he?*

An elf. It was hard to remember how foreign this still was to Kale.

And he looks like that all the time? he asked, referring to Ben's less human features.

I glanced at Ben again, admiring the hint of iridescence his skin gave off and his feline-like pupils. *Yes. Elves glamour their appearance to humans, so they look fully mortal. You're not human anymore, so you see his true form.*

I've been missing all this. Kale continued to observe each effortless movement of Ben's. Elves carried a grace about them most other supernaturals couldn't attain, but they were immortal. I imagined anyone gained a great deal of poise when they had years to perfect it.

I touched his arm. *Afraid so.*

To avoid gawking at Ben any longer, Kale peered into the back of the open truck past the movers. "That looks like some of my stuff."

"*Oh*, this must be him. Pleasure to finally meet you, Kalen. The King ..." Ben's tuneful voice broke, sadness creeping into his words, but he cleared his throat and persisted. "Cyrus briefed me all about you. It seems this was his last wish. He tasked me to have your things brought here. He—well, he wanted you to feel welcome here, sir. Cyrus felt terrible about the union proposal. He got this idea in his head to make it right with you both. He'd want you to know he was proud to have you join the family, Kalen, so very proud."

Kale stepped forward. "Sorry for staring. I've just never—"

"Seen an elf before. It's the ears. You'll get used to them. Soon this will all be normal for you." Ben gave a reassuring nod.

"Do you mind?" he asked. Opening his arms to Ben, Kale took him into a giant bear hug. "Thank you for this. Thank you," Kale said as he released Ben from his grasp.

Ben offered a kind smile in return. "As I said, it's my pleasure, Majesty. I'm happy to serve the Whiteridges."

My mother squeezed my shoulders, stifling her urge to cry. "See, darling, your father wanted nothing but happiness for you and Kalen. Have his things put in whichever rooms you two see fit. I'm going to lie down for a bit."

"Mother, wait." I observed her. Her face creased between her brows, and her eyes looked tired and slightly bloodshot, showing the stress of yesterday's events and her grief. I couldn't put my head around her willpower to keep going.

"Don't worry, Athena. I'm only tired." She blew me an air kiss. "You children keep me young, but you wear me out. Come get me if you need anything, anything at all," she said, continuing to walk away. "Oh, and there's something special on the truck. Your father arranged it before he left."

Ben watched his former Queen leave, bowing his head. Then I found his eyes on me again. "I should go too. If you don't mind, I'm happy to clear and adjust schedules for you at your father's office. I can take charge of preparations for the Winter Solstice as well. I'll only need to bother you for final decisions, and you can take this time to spend with your family and hunt that bastard down." Ben's eyes hardened at the mention of Xercarus, and I saw the hairs on his arm stand up. He wanted that demon dead as much as the rest of us.

"Ben, that's more helpful than you know. Thank you again for this, but more than that, thank you for being a loyal friend to our family and my father. I know how much he cared for you."

He dipped his head and put a hand up to wave goodbye. A forlorn expression still marred his handsome features as he tried to smile. Ben hopped in his sleek silver Audi sedan that he'd parked behind the moving truck and drove off down our curvy driveway.

Kale came up behind me, hugging me. "I can't believe your dad arranged this. Thea,

I..." he wavered his voice a mixture of contentment and sorrow. " He really wanted to include me in your life. It means so much, and I can't even tell him thank you."

I turned myself to face Kale. His eyes glistened in the sun.

He appeared younger today, or maybe it was the way the light reflected off his high cheekbones. "I wish you could've gotten to know him better. He really was a wonderful father and inspiring leader."

"Me too. But, Thea, I already knew that. Look at you, your brothers. They dick around a lot, but you three, are like superheroes. The only person who might be cooler than you is Iron Man. And I stand by Robert Downey Jr.'s performance." Kale hugged me tighter as he tried to make me laugh.

I couldn't help but smile at this child-like comparison. "You do realize, by those standards—you're a superhero too. I don't know many individuals who can make ice out of thin air."

Kale shook his head, his shaggy hair covering his eyes. Eyes I loved so much. "True. Maybe I'm Iron Man then."

"You wish!" I said, giving him a small shove. The carefree laughter felt pleasant. As the smile poured over my entire body, I realized I shouldn't be this content, not with all these horrible happenings. Yet, here I was. Laughing already with someone I loved. It was true, whether or not I had wanted it. I was in love with Kale. Perhaps this moment was an offering from my father. I soaked in the sunshine and fresh air as Kale hopped onto the back of the open truck, moving past boxes and digging through his things.

"*Oh* my God. No way! Thea, your dad. No way. Holy shit!" Kale shouted. His hands ran through his hair.

I wandered closer to the truck, hoping to see what had gotten him all riled up. "What is it?" I asked, glancing up at Kale while he lifted off packing blankets revealing several guitars.

"It's—it's a Fender Telecaster Thinline Black. But it's a signed one from EDEN. I mean, I idolize this guy's music."

There was a folded note beneath a white bow on the guitar. Kale tugged it off and read it aloud.

Kalen,

I know our initial meetings didn't paint me in a great light. I have a lot to make up for with you and Athena. You're a good man, one of profound character. Athena will need that strength someday. She deserves someone she can be herself with and loves her for it. In the short time of seeing you—I knew. You're the one for my daughter. We both know Athena is no child, but understand it's hard for a father to let go of protecting his children. I hope in the future you'll know exactly what that means. Until then, accept this token of apology and welcome to our family, son.
Cyrus

Kale clutched the note tighter. Both of us had tears in our eyes. The "something special." Here I thought he and my mother had gone to talk about Baywood. I'd been so wrong, they'd arranged a gift, or at least my father had.

Kale hopped off the truck and took me in his arms, holding me to him with almost too much force.

"How did he know? How could he find that out?"

I shrugged. "He had his ways."

"I'll love you enough for the two of us. I can promise you that," he said, tucking the note in his pocket.

"I've no doubt in my mind you will." I kissed Kale's chin, feeling an ache in my chest. As I leaned further into our embrace, I felt a vibration coming from Kale's pocket.

Reaching down, Kale retrieved his phone. "Ugh, shit. It's Brody. I've gotta answer this time."

"Of course." I stepped back, giving Kale room.

"Hey, Brody, what's up?" Kale answered with as casual of a tone as he could. I heard muffled yelling from the other end.

"Brody, whoa. Calm down. No. It's fine. I'm fine. Hey, just... would you wait a damn minute?" Kale hesitated in the conversation, waiting for the other voice to relax. Kale raised his voice at Brody. "No. No. It's not like that at all. I moved out. It's not a big deal. The lease was up anyway. Watch your mouth, Brody! You know what? I'm sorry..."

Kale turned away, pacing some as he kept talking into the phone. "No. Yes, it's because of her. Yeah. I do. When? Well, that's too bad because you're gonna love her. We can't, now's not the best time." His tone softened. The sweet smile on his lips turned down into a frown.

The conversation between the two continued as I gave directions to the movers where to unload the boxes.

"It's crazy. I know. Never felt this way before in my life. Yeah. Uh, a few months. She's—haha, no, she's incredible... you wouldn't believe me if I told you. Beautiful. Athena, yes. Athena Whiteridge. Three brothers. Anders, Atlas, and Lincoln. Tonight? I can't. Maybe in a few weeks." Kale's eyes met mine.

"What's he want?" I already knew Brody must be angling to see Kalen. It'd been weeks, and I knew Brody must be itching to see what Kale was up to.

Kale covered the phone. "He wants to have dinner, but I said it's not a good time."

I shook my head no. "You should go. He needs to see you."

"*Umm*, sure. I'll be there. I'll make it work. Yeah, I'll ask her, but it's just bad timing. No, it's not an excuse. Okay, bye. Okay, tell mom I'm sorry. Mm, K, bye." Kale pressed "end" on his call, looking at me with a renewed happiness in his eyes and lips.

Kale opened his mouth. I could tell he was already about to apologize. "Don't you dare. He's worried about you, and you can't blame him. You've been MIA for what for weeks?" I said, my eyes flashing at him. I knew how important familial ties were and felt a bit sheepish for not putting forth more effort to keep Kale connected to his family.

"Yeah, he was. I guess my mom told him someone was moving my stuff. Not sure how she even found out. Photographers hang out at my house from time to time, but since I've been lying low, there's no reason. Whatever, it doesn't matter. I agreed to meet him for dinner tonight at Napolita's downtown. It's his only night off this week. He's dying to meet the woman who snatched up Kalen Ryan." He put air quotes around his name.

"*Ahh*, the famous Kale Ryan. What a lucky lady she must be," I chuckled.

Kale smiled, then bit his lower lip. "You'll come then?"

I couldn't help but bat my eyelashes and return his grin. "Ah, I really need to focus on who got into the manor last night." Kale furrowed his brow and frowned, giving me a pouty face. "Fine. Fine. I'll see if Gage can deal with it. I wanna meet Brody, but you need to take this more seriously." And I meant it. Most of me was curious to know the people closest to Kale, but I chewed my cheek, thinking of how wrong meeting another family member might go.

"I do take it seriously, but everything with this place is serious. I mean, when are we allowed to just live? Either way, this is gonna be amazing." Kale planted a chaste kiss on my temple. I gave a stiff grin, tucking away my concerns. Kale deserved this moment of joy.

"You say amazing now until we tell Anders and Atlas. Those two are going to tag along. They go where I go."

"Right. Yes, the goon squad. You know, I'm looking forward to it. I think Brody and I can take them." Another beaming smile prevailed over Kale's ecstatic expression. "This might be the best day ever—the woman I love meeting my favorite person, a guitar from... shit, Thea. I'm so sorry. That was fucking callous."

"No, it wasn't. My father, he wouldn't want us wallowing over him. You're right. We need to live. We'll meet your brother and, eventually, avenge my father's death. But tonight? Tonight, we'll have pizza."

I had an appointment with our physician Dr. Samantha Birch mid-morning. I left Kale and Calliope to tackle the movers. Dr. Birch's office was a few miles away, on our family estate.

Our consultation was brief. She knew what I needed, and provided a physical exam and commented on how she admired our "responsible behavior." I decided there was no need to alert her to our close call in the conference room and how I had little to no responsible behavior in that scenario.

An ample smile never left Dr. Birch's face. She bounced with each step, and her gray eyes gleamed. She bordered on too happy and maybe a tad overzealous to have a patient in her office. Which looked less like a traditional doctor's office and more like a brightly painted, sanitized library with a paper-covered examination table in the center. She'd covered the pale-yellow walls with bones from various supernaturals. The bookshelves reached from floor to ceiling, and she had books and magazines ranging from human medical sciences to sea nymph anatomy and treatments for demonic bites. I shuddered and wrinkled my nose at the word demonic.

As a pack doctor, she was often unnecessary and spent most of her days reading medical studies versus treating anyone. Regeneration made her services often unneeded, and with Anders available even less so, nevertheless, we kept on her retainer and paid her a large sum to stay.

After a chat, she provided me with the medication I needed. Letting me know that since my cycle fell right, I could have the hormonal shot right now. It'd be effective right away. And thank goodness for that. There was an elixir made by Sprites that could halt cycles, but it was harder to come by with sprites not willing to make many appearances anymore after their disagreement over the Alliance. Fickle little things.

I thanked Dr. Birch for her time, turning to head out the front door, but not before she stuffed a full bag of contraceptives in my palm. "Always good to keep these on hand, but you already know that. Don't you, Alpha?" She gave me a pleasant, toothy smile and walked me outside.

A curt nod was my only response. I didn't particularly enjoy being reminded of my past trips to her office. My previous trysts didn't feel real anymore—like they were distant memories I couldn't quite make out, all except for Henri-fucking-Pelletier. I shuddered, trying to shake off the image and the chill it gave me.

Dr. Birch patted my shoulder and bowed her head while offering to be available for anything I might need. I nodded again, giving her a proper thank you, and shut my Jeep door.

She made a tight turn on her black kitten heels, adjusting her white coat, and headed back inside the stone and log lodge while I pulled out of the gravel driveway.

Several hours later, Kale's things were unloaded and unpacked due to Calliope's professional-level organizational skills. Kale took another room near my own for all his instruments and music equipment. Calliope even had a new dresser delivered within an hour to the house, making sure all Kale's clothing fit, and my closet now hosted half of his attire.

Kale went to the walk-in closet, looking over his things hanging next to mine. He touched one of my dresses, a small smile pulling at his lips.

"This is such an odd sensation. My things... here with yours. Makes it feel more real, you know." Kale pulled a sports coat from the rack. "This isn't mine, though. Come to think of it, this isn't either," he said as he plucked another jacket from the line before hanging them back up and laying out what he intended to wear tonight on the bed.

"That's Calliope. She's added to your wardrobe, no doubt. Making sure you have more formal pieces for events and appearances we'll eventually make."

"*Ah*, like the Winter Solstice." He cocked his eyebrow up at me, pulling on his navy, slim-fit chinos.

I tilted my head, admiring his coy nature and the way his pants fit. "Yes, like the Solstice. That's a very important tradition here. You'll meet the winter faeries and—"

Kale cut in with interest. "Faeries? You have faeries here. I thought Atlas made that up. How come I haven't met any other supernaturals?"

"We kind of have separate territories. Don't worry. At Solstice, you'll meet plenty of elves and fae. I gotta say, we have wolves, you and I are dragons, and you're engrossed with faeries?" I asked him, pretending his words wounded me.

"Oh, come on. All kids are obsessed with the tooth faerie." He tapped his teeth to emphasize his point, then finished buttoning his white J. Crew shirt.

I bit my lip, doing my best to respond in a timely manner. "Hm, the tooth faerie. Hate to disappoint, but that one is a myth. You'll be pleased to know that what you call mermaids exist as well. Though they prefer the term sea nymphs."

Kale's mouth dropped open, and his eyes looked as if they might pop out of his head, "Stop it. You're just now telling me mermaids are real, too. That's... Disney really knows everything."

We both chuckled. "Yeah. Did you think humans did all their animation? At this rate, I'm thinking you'd have been more impressed if I'd have told you I was a mermaid rather than a shifter."

Kale grabbed me in his arms, a smirk still dancing on his lips. "No way. My girl makes fire, and that's as hot as you can get."

He placed a quick kiss on my cheek, then sat on the bed. "This is like the time my mom told me Santa wasn't real. Guess she was wrong." Kale laughed, then composed himself again.

I loved his humor, the way his lips curved up when he laughed so blithely.

"Thea." Kale interrupted my musings, his tone drifting upwards. "The Solstice—when you talked to Oriel before, he mentioned a king. Was he referring to me?"

"Who else?"

"So, I get to be King, just like that?" He bent down to tie his white Nikes.

"Pretty much. At the Solstice, we'll formally introduce you as my mate. If and when we decide, there will be a bonding ceremony, and you'd become King." I felt my cheeks burn with a rosy flush. Kale looked up at me, examining my hot cheeks, and smiled again.

I continued, trying to ignore my wandering mind. "And together, we'll keep the Unseen and the human world safe. I know things move at a blistering pace here. Had you been born into this; it might be less overwhelming."

Tilting his head and softening his eyes, the smile slowly disappeared off Kale's face, morphing into a calm focus. "Nothing like a little pressure to get the blood flowing. Not sure I'm cut out to lead anyone, but you misunderstand my motivations. I wanna be all those things to you and more. I just have one issue—" he paused and ran his fingers through his hair. I raised my eyebrows, curious for him to go on. "I want to marry you at some point. In the traditional human way. Is that even possible? To get married in front of my family and friends?"

My mouth dropped open a bit. Kale never ceased to amaze me. My heart perked up, beating faster at his questions, and the smell of the fresh sea intensified. "We can make it possible."

"Good." Kale got up, swooping me up into a kiss and carrying me back to the bed, kissing me. "I want the world to know you're mine, and I'm yours. I wanna say my vows, giving myself to you in every way humanly possible, even if I'm not one anymore."

I brushed his hair back with my hands. "I love you. Beyond reason."

Kissing my forehead, he rolled back off me, his signature grin locked in place. "Same. Now, let's get that fine ass of yours dressed. I'm ready to smash some pizza."

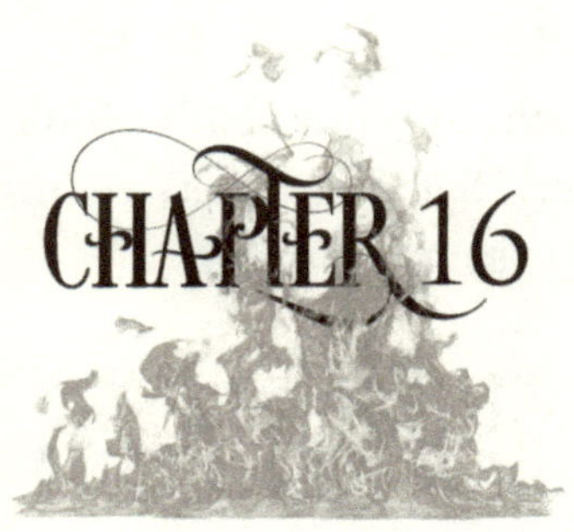

CHAPTER 16

Turns out telling my brothers about our unplanned trip to downtown LA tonight was easier than expected. Both of them were unusually accommodating. Anders arranged our added transportation and hotel stay, booking us two suites at the Ritz Carlton. Atlas got extra security on the house, pack members patrolling every fifteen minutes. We opted to leave our lead, Gage, behind. He was Logan's first in command and most skilled to handle any situation. Besides that, I trusted Gage. If we had a traitor around, it wasn't him.

An unforeseen issue came in the form of Lincoln, who objected. First, he begged, pleaded for us not to go. When that didn't work, he changed tactics.

"Athena, please. I can feed again before I go. I won't get in the way. Just let me come along." Lincoln's insistent request didn't land on deaf ears. I didn't enjoy watching him so worked up, and his upset made me fidget, shifting my weight from one leg to another.

Anders reached my mind. *Thea. He's a kid.*

He's a teenager and a vampire. You remember cutie over there tearing into a chest, right? Atlas interjected into our thoughts.

Anders, I hear you. But, would you rather leave him here—alone? I knew Anders was trying to look out for everyone, and Atlas was looking to stir the pot like usual.

Lincoln frowned harder. "Come on, guys, don't do that thing you do. Don't talk around me." Even in a frown, Lincoln's youthful face and sweet gray eyes didn't look malicious. If I hadn't witnessed him tearing the heart out myself, I'd safely assumed Lincoln wasn't capable of hurting a fly, but Atlas made a fair point. Lincoln was a vampire with speed and agility on his side, and he was downright deadly when it came down to it. Plus, as much as I wanted to, I didn't fully trust Lincoln. The fact remained that none of us knew him well enough to cross him off as a threat.

Kale frowned and gave a heavy sigh. "Thea, coming from a person who was left out of your conversations, it fucking sucks. My vote is, bring Lincoln."

"Same," Atlas announced.

Anders huffed, "It's nothing personal, Lincoln. I just wanna avoid any unnecessary predicaments. I vote he stays behind."

I looked at all these men in my life, all of them bearing firm looks on their faces. Not wanting to disappoint any of them, I gave them all a good-natured smile but eyed Anders in particular. "Majority rules. Lincoln can come along."

"Yes!" Lincoln fist pumped, his mouth turning up in a smile.

"Don't go getting ahead of yourself. Put some bags of blood in a cooler, in case you need them. I mean it, Lincoln; stay away from any trouble if it arises. I have a feeling my mother might be more upset if something happens to you than one of these two." I pointed my thumb at Atlas and Anders, smirking at my taunt.

"Let's not play 'Who's Mom's Favorite' game, shall we?" Atlas scolded mockingly and ran his hands through his fluffy blonde hair. "Because I'm gonna win. I'm the baby."

Anders shoved Atlas in jest. "You're a damn baby, alright."

"Atlas, man. Don't take this the wrong way. I'm one-hundred percent sure Linc here is our baby now." Kale gave Atlas an impish grin and pulled Lincoln into a side hug. Lincoln's face lit up at being included in their razzing.

Finally, making our way into the garage, the automatic lights powered on. I hollered, "Hey Kale, which one? I might even let you drive."

Kale stopped laughing, his jaw dropping, "Holy. Shit. I was wrong. You're definitely Tony Stark. Look at all these!" Like a kid in a candy store, Kale raced over to our vast array of cars, "Thea, you're telling me you guys own all these, and you drive a Jeep?"

"Hey now, don't insult my girl. There's no need to be flashy all the time. Tonight is special, and I'm hoping Brody is a car guy."

"Brody is absolutely a car guy. We both took shop classes, and our dad has this classic, super slick 1969 Dodge Challenger. He'd let us work on it with him—I can still smell the carburation."

Lincoln stroked his hand down the side of our blue Audi R8, "This thing is beautiful. I think I'm in love."

"Careful on the paint, Linc." Anders grinned at Lincoln's fascination.

"If it's a Challenger you're looking for, you're in luck. In back on the left, that black one." I pointed Kale in the right direction, then collected the keys from the wall, tossing them to him. "She's all yours." As the key hit Kale's palm, a recognizable scent wafted in the garage, and I heard a familiar gait.

"Logan!" I turned and ran, catapulting myself into Logan's open arms.

Logan faltered, stepping back, and winced as I entered his heartfelt embrace, "It's good to see you too, Athena." If I wasn't mistaken, I heard him stifle a groan.

"*Oh*, Logan, I'm sorry." I turned him loose from my tight embrace. "You're not fully healed."

Anders was next to Logan, in a moment, accessing his condition, running his hands over Logan's muscles. "Logan. This is bad. How did you even survive that blast? Your ribs are cracked." Anders put his hands to Logan's chest, closing his eyes as he mended Logan from the inside out.

"I really don't know. I thought I was dead. The pain faded away, and then I heard Athena calling my name. I pulled myself through the debris, crawling. I had to get back to all of you. It's what Cyrus would've wanted..." Logan dead-stopped. His wild eyes locked on Lincoln and launched forward. "You—I'll kill you."

Lincoln froze, almost awaiting the assault. "I'm sorry," he mouthed to me.

"Stop! Logan, please. Don't take another step toward him." I looked up to Logan. He was my father's right hand. It was unnerving to command him, but I kept a firm gaze.

Logan held his place, obeying me while eyeing Lincoln. "He's a vampire. The one Baywood said was a trap. He's the reason Cyrus is dead."

"Logan, listen. I understand what he must look like, but it's not like that. Truly, it's not. Let me explain." I tried my hardest to reason with him. My lip twitched, knowing I'd shield Lincoln.

Lincoln stood up straight, clearing his throat. "It's okay, Athena. He's right. This is my fault."

I whipped my head in Lincoln's direction, inhaling. "We aren't doing this again. What's done is done."

In a quick stride, Kale was by Logan, grabbing his shoulder without force. It was a tender grasp. "Let me try something. I think I can make him see." Kale's tone was determined, and his blue eyes set on Logan. The ways Kale continued to step up solidified his place with us. I found my eyes pulled to him.

"How?" I asked.

Logan moved his narrowed, suspicious gaze to Kale. "What's going on?"

"Just shush for a damn second and open your mind." Kale reprimanded as he kept his hold on Logan. Logan complied, overriding his own instincts. Logan was a fighter; taking action was his strong suit, but Logan was loyal and did as Kale said. Unfortunately, in wolf culture, there was no democracy—only hierarchy.

Logan's eyes glazed over, stilling, "What is this? What am I seeing?"

Kale was showing Logan his vision of us. I linked in to watch the premonition all over again. The laughter, the love, but one thing was different this time. Gage wasn't driving the vehicle for Lincoln. It was Logan. Logan made his way back to us, proving the visions could change—for the better or worse.

I hugged Logan again, his stance relaxed. "It's our future."

Atlas interrupted the moment as usual. "Good to have you back, Logan. I won't let Athena bore you with her dumpy story-telling skills. Go shower and be down in twenty. You're riding with us." Atlas smiled; he couldn't contain his content over Logan being home. I felt the well-deserved relief washing over him and me as well. Even Anders's mood was settling into a state of muted joy over Logan's return. Logan's presence was like having a piece of our father back, and I'd take whatever closeness to him I could get.

"Yes, sir." Logan nodded curtly, heading for the doorway.

"Logan, don't do that," I called after him.

Logan managed a weak smile, but I saw the uncertainty lingering in his eyes. He straightened his back and left.

"Do I really look old enough to be a 'sir?'" Atlas laughed out.

Anders tousled Atlas's hair. "Nope. But you're old enough to be an ass."

Atlas flipped Anders off. "Whatever. Haters gonna hate."

"You two are ridiculous. But, on a serious note, did you find out anything new with our mutant friend? I messaged Connor earlier about the attack to keep him updated." I focused my attention on Atlas, our resident medical examiner, and science whiz.

Atlas rubbed his hands together. "It's a vampire or was. There's not much left of its original DNA. It's like Xercarus strips them of their identity in every form, inhabits their bodies, like a hive mind."

"Disgusting. That black goo smells fucking terrible. I think I can still smell that stink on my hand," Lincoln blurted, shaking his hands and wrinkling his face. "Why does he do that?"

Anders offered an explanation, "Control. If he can't sway you to follow him, he destroys them. That's how demons work, Linc."

"It's wrong, what he's doing. I can't wait until you fry his ass, Athena. I'll die before I let anyone use me again. I swear I will," Lincoln huffed, his declaration hitting me square in the chest.

Lincoln's brows furrowed, making him look older. I crossed the garage to him, putting my hand on his back. "Can you drive?" I asked him.

"Yeah, I have my license. Taught myself." Lincoln's jaw tensed as he offered his reply.

"How about I let you pick whichever one you want, and you can drive?" I said, striving to cheer him up.

Lincoln's eyes shot up, a wide smile covering his full-lipped mouth. He really resembled my brothers when he smiled. "Seriously?"

Kale beamed at Lincoln, who looked like a kid in a candy store. *Good call, Thea. He needed that.* Kale divulged into my head.

I made eye contact with Kale, giving a small head bob. *I know.*

Lincoln went straight for the Range Rover Defender. I glanced at Atlas and Anders. "Yup. Get the keys off the wall."

"Linc, whatever you do, don't trash that car. It's one of my favorites," Anders popped off.

Kale and I were laughing as Logan strolled back in, twenty minutes later on the dot. He'd showered and dressed in all black. He wore a button-down, cuffed at his elbows, and pants fitting his muscular frame.

Logan looked exceptional for his age; he was Kale's height with a broader build. His hair showed no gray, only light sandy brown, cut in a modern fade. Logan had the most welcoming fawn-colored eyes, like fresh honey. The only thing setting Logan apart from us, his tattoos. They peeked out of his shirt, just above his collar, and a small one right behind his ear stretching down his neck, reading '*Lupus Intus*.' It meant wolf within.

Born wolves couldn't have regular tattoos; our skin regenerated and rejected the ink. Logan had his tattoos scrawled on him by an elf from my mother's country years ago, before we were born.

Coraia was her name. Logan told us about her once. His eyes glazed when he spoke her name and a suppressed smile twitched on his lips. Logan had fallen in love with the elf priestess on a trip to visit my mother's family. Logan never used the word, but I suspected Coraia had been more than a love interest, from the way Logan's face lit up and fell when he'd told us about her. His reaction told me Coraia was his mate, but when it was time to go, Logan stayed by my father's side as his Beta. And Coraia stayed with her elven people, to guide them. Over the years, he saw her less and less.

With my father gone, Logan would be free to live his own life and perhaps a life with Coraia. It was a pleasant thought, thinking of Logan finally having the love he deserved.

Kale rubbed my back, bringing me to the present.

Logan would easily pass for our youthful uncle. Uncle Logan. It wasn't a stretch; Logan watched us grow up every step of the way. I could only hope Brody bought our story and wasn't suspicious by meeting us all at once.

"Looking good. You clean up well." Atlas put his arm around Logan's strong shoulders. It was the first time I saw Logan offer a smile since he returned. I knew his heart was aching with my loss of my father. *What did losing your Alpha feel like?* I cringed, never wanting my brothers to find out.

Anders pulled his navy sport coat on and adjusted his Apple watch, "Let's get this show on the road. I got another room, just in case."

"Brody is gonna think you're more famous than me or something with this type of entourage," Kale smirked, opening the Challenger door. "Too bad you're better than a celebrity. You're a wolf. My big bad wolf." Kale winked at his words.

A rumble escaped my throat, a wild vibration at Kale's praise.

"Don't do that," Kale said as he squeezed my thigh. "We have plans tonight. It's hard enough to maintain my own self-control without battling the furry spirit in here." He broke off for a moment, thinking. "Is this ever going to stop?" he asked, casting his eyes down for a moment.

I tilted my head. "What?"

"You know, the needing?"

I clenched my thighs together, the pressure behind my irises causing my eyes to flash green. "Not likely." I grabbed his chin between my fingers, kissing his jaw. Goddess, he smelled divine; the Invictus cologne he put on amplified his scent. I'd said not likely, but I knew this connection between Kale and I was next level and not something that faded over time.

Kale turned loose a possessive growl as if reading my mind, and the engine roared to life. Shifting the car into gear, giving it gas, he burned the tires all the way out of the garage. I popped my mirrored aviators on and cranked the radio; Jaymes Young's 'Infinity' pulsed through the surrounding speakers. Kale took my hand in his, bringing it to his mouth, grazing his teeth softly against my knuckles.

Amber glinted in his baby blues as he sang. His voice echoed in my ears like a sleek serenade. Kale was unbelievably talented, hitting notes with precise ease. I imagined him on the stage, captivating a huge screaming and singing audience. He was an obvious natural performer. That much was apparent.

With one hand on the wheel, the other clasping my hand, Kale continued to regale me with his velvety voice.

He's beautiful, my wolf whimpered in agreement.

CHAPTER 17

We pulled up in front of the restaurant, the tinted windows lit up with Edison bulbs. Napolita's was one of those low-key pizzerias, with traditional styles and innovative concoctions landing them 'Best Pizza' awards. I realized I was starving. On the outside, there were red bistro tables for conversation and sharing a drink under their canopy and a few umbrellas for when the California sun got too hot.

Kale insisted on opening my car door. "Thank you. Such a gentleman." I winked at him, flashing him a smile and pulling my long leg out of the car. I'd chosen to wear a similar color palette as Kale, cropped light-wash jeans, and a dark indigo silk tank top paired with my starch-white Nikes. Several woven anklets wrapped around my tan lower leg Kale had no trouble staring at.

"Even your ankle is sexy," he said, raising his eyebrow.

After getting out of the car, I watched Logan emerge with Anders and Atlas. He appeared more relaxed and comfortable than before. Lincoln zipped up behind them, touching Logan's back to get his attention.

"You don't know me, Logan, but I've heard a lot about you and Cyrus. I'm gonna prove to you, I'm a good person, vampire, or whatever," Lincoln announced, standing rod straight and meeting Logan's eyes.

Logan met Lincoln's gaze dead on. It was a wolf tactic. Anyone with little resolve backed off under a wolf's stare, not Lincoln. He might be a teenager and new vampire, but he was full of conviction, enough not to bow under Logan's stare.

"I've got a lot to learn a lot about you, Lincoln." Logan offered his hand to Lincoln to shake as an equal. Lincoln took Logan's hand, vigorously shaking it up and down.

"Game time!" Kale hollered at us. "I think I see Brody inside."

Atlas grabbed Kale's shoulders, chuckling, "No worries, we won't tell your brother we've seen your junk." Kale rolled his eyes, laughing.

Logan stepped forward, opening the door for us. I scoured the dining room, searching each table and settling on a dark-haired man that looked too much like Kale. It had to be Brody. He was looking at his phone, reading something, and not noticing our arrival. My stomach pulled in on itself. Humans had never had this effect on me before. I'd never given a second thought to if I impressed anyone, nor did I particularly care, and now I found myself wanting Brody to like me, seeking his approval. *Ahh, how the mighty had fallen...*

"Reservations, Whiteridge," Anders addressed the young hostess, flashing a sly grin at her. She had an alternative style, light hair, dark lips, and gauges, but couldn't escape Anders's bright smile and charm.

The young woman stared at Anders, likely flustered by the group that stood before her. She checked her list. "Yes, r-right this way," she stammered a bit. I found her whimsical voice charming. I was used to this response—Anders and Atlas were definitely pretty boys. I imagine looking at the men surrounding me, the hostess was struggling to be professional. I couldn't blame her.

We rounded several black and white splatter-painted tables, coming closer to the reading Brody. Kale grabbed onto my hand, squeezing it gently. "He's gonna love you. Trust me," he cooed in my ear. I smirked.

Right.

"Here you are. Your server will be right over to take your drink order." The pretty hostess smiled and rushed off, likely going to alert the server to the table of handsome men she was headed for.

Brody looked up; a huge warm smile spread from his mouth to his eyes when he caught sight of Kale. Brody got up from his cushioned seat, making his way to greet Kale.

"*Ah*, little brother! Good to see you after not answering my calls or texts for weeks." Brody released Kale, clapping his back, and then his eyes settled on me. Brody examined me with a distant unease, but he was sure to never let the bright smile leave his face.

"Wow, you must be Athena. Kale didn't lie, you're lovely! So good to meet you. I've never in all my life had the pleasure of sharing dinner with a girlfriend of Kale's." Though Brody's words had been kind, sarcasm laced his tone.

I beamed at Brody despite his tone, batting my lashes too many times, understanding his quarrel likely didn't lie fully with me. I looked over at Kale, whose eyes shone bright, appraising me with pride, "Pleasure to meet you as well Brody, I've heard a lot about you." I offered my hand to shake Brody's. Brother or not, I didn't fall prey to intimidation.

"Ha, no way, come here." To my surprise, Brody opened his arms instead, asking me to walk into his hug.

I smiled again and happily obliged. Brody was warm, with brawny arms, and smelled similar to Kale, only lacking his allure. He stood an inch taller than Kale, with a leaner, lankier build, undoubtedly from running around a hospital during his long shifts.

Letting me out of his arms, Brody took in the rather large group of men behind me.

"You must be something special, Athena, you've come with quite the entourage. You might just rival Kalen for the spotlight." Brody raised his brows and eyed me warily.

"I said that same thing." Kale raised his eyebrows and smirked as well. "You learn to get used to it, though," he mused, pulling out a dark wooden chair for me and then himself to sit next to Brody. Napolita's atmosphere was comforting and almost vintage, with various Polaroids on the walls and the fragrance of fresh tomato sauce whirling around.

"Since Kale obviously isn't going to, let me introduce you to everyone. Brody, these are my brothers, Atlas, Anders, and Lincoln."

Brody outstretched his hand. "Big family, huh? Great to meet you."

"Yeah, triplets plus one. Pleasure to make your acquaintance as well. I'm Anders, Athena's middle brother," he said, shaking Brody's hand.

"Anders, pleasure as well, man." Brody grinned, showcasing his perfectly white teeth.

"Atlas Whiteridge, former baby brother. Good to meet you, Brody. Kale here is quite smitten with our gal Thea. We'll probably be related soon." He let loose an easy chuckle.

"*Ha*, you think so. If Athena will have him, I'm all for it." Laughing as he spoke, Brody released Atlas's hand to reach for Lincoln.

I laughed light-heartedly as Lincoln stepped forward toward Brody. A smile plastered to his face that reached his gray eyes. Lincoln stood tall, accepting Brody's proffered hand. Watching Lincoln's hurried movements, I knew this was the first time he'd been included in familial introductions, and a sense of pride filled my chest. *I'm so glad we found you.*

"Lincoln, youngest brother." He shook Brody's hand with enthusiasm, then stepped aside.

I gestured for Logan to come forward. "Last, and certainly not least, our uncle, Logan."

Not ready to lower his guard, Logan gave a tight-lipped yet pleasant smile. "Nice to meet you, Brody."

With the greetings out of the way, we all took seats at the large, multicolored rectangular table. I tucked my hand under the table to give Kale's thigh a reassuring pat on the knee.

So far, so good, yeah? I asked as I entered his thoughts. Kale merely locked his eyes on mine, giving me his thousand-watt grin.

Brody surveyed the table of new faces. "What kinda pizzas are we hungry for tonight? I'm a huge fan of their Margherita. It's delicious."

"Sounds perfect. You had me at pizza, though." I met Brody's shrewd gaze. His calculating eyes roamed over my face, trying to get a good read on me.

The other boys were intently checking out the retro menus, flush with choices.

"I have to say, it shocked me when Kale said he moved because of a woman. He's always been so, I dunno, unreachable." Brody glance at Kale, trying poorly to maintain a casual tone, though his statement was anything but.

"Gonna come in with the heavy right away. Nice, Brody." Kale set his menu down, adjusted to look directly at his brother.

"Had to say it," Brody said, his brows going up into his hairline. Before we got here, I'd internally lectured myself on how this dinner was a waste of valuable time in my search for Xercarus, but sitting near Brody, seeing his distrust of me up close—I realized I made the right call. If Kale had any chance of making this work, his family had to get to know me.

Tension crawled down my limbs, making my feet feel like

bricks. My wolf was annoyed by the questioning, pacing around in my mind, while I concerned myself with control. Brody was used to the old Kale, a more easy-going, passive version of this brother. Supernatural Kale may not possess such niceties, and we couldn't risk a public freak out.

But Kale only laughed, rubbing his chin and bristling just a touch while he rolled his shoulders. "Unreachable? Ouch. Seems harsh."

Atlas, as if on cue, decided this was the perfect time to crack a joke. "Trust me when I say, Thea's reached Kale just fine."

I threw a '*shh*' look to Atlas and continued to concentrate on Brody. "You know, Kale and I are both in fresh territory, but I can assure you, Brody, I'm not like the company you're used to Kale keeping."

Brody and I sat silently for a moment staring at one another, both of us waiting for the other to blink. The rest of the table watched the standoff. I understood why Brody was protective of Kale. He'd seen him at his worst, and Brody had no intention of letting me bring Kale back to that place.

Kale stirred, reaching up to touch my cheek. His lips twitched as he tried to subdue his new wolf nature. "Iron Man to the rescue," he whispered in a low voice, grinning at me. The connection of his fingers to my cheek ignited my skin, fanning a flame for him that remained lit. I leaned into his touch. A smile tugging at my cheeks.

Brody broke the moment. "I apologize, Athena. That was forward of me to say. I meant no offense to you. But I needed to see it." Brody's face expressing a shift to a genuine jovial mood.

Kale turned back to his brother; his mouth turned down. "See what?"

"The way you look at one another. It's all I need to know." Brody patted Kale's back.

"Back to the pizza then?" Anders asked.

"Back to pizzas," Logan piped up. "I'll take a pepperoni."

A few moments later, we'd agreed on our selections, and the server ambled over. She was of average height and build, fair skin, and definitely pretty. I could see her taking in the table of men and the only woman with them, me. She stared, and her mouth popped open a bit as she appraised each one of my brothers and Logan. I stifled a laugh. I could relate to the sentiment; I felt the same when I looked at Kale, even for a moment. Part of me felt bad, knowing they wouldn't return her swooning.

Tossing her hair with a less than subtle flip, the server approached the table, standing closest to Brody. "Hi, I'm Jade. What can I get y'all to drink tonight?"

"Why don't you start us off with two pitchers of that new beer you have on tap, Dream State," Kale answered her, raising up two fingers.

"Is there anything else I can interest you in?" she asked, her voice saccharine in pitch.

"I love a good beer, but can I get a gin and tonic as well, Hendricks if possible," Atlas addressed the server with a grin but didn't bother giving her the full attention she'd been hoping for. The look of dissatisfaction clung to her drooping smile for a moment before she carried on collecting the rest of our drink order.

"I'll have water, thank you," Lincoln added. Fortunately, vampires tolerated small amounts of human food. They couldn't subsist on it and took a long time to absorb into their cells, but it wouldn't hurt Lincoln to swallow a few bites to avoid drawing attention to himself.

Conversation flowed as freely as the drinks, but with our rapid metabolism, getting drunk took copious amounts of alcohol consumed in a very short time or a particular faerie brew called Bia Cava that could knock any supernatural flat on their ass. We kept some at home for special occasions or when Atlas felt extra cheeky.

Brody, on the other hand, didn't possess such a luxury. We all watched him reach that happy, tipsy point, which only enhanced his appealing sense of humor. Brody amused us with stories from his and Kale's youth. About how, one time, in particular, Kale got lost looking for their Golden Retriever puppy, Molly, who had been in Kale's bedroom the entire time.

In exchange, we all shared as much of our childhood as we could, careful to leave out anything that could clue Brody into what we really were. It was good to hear the laughter around the table, most of all Logan's. Even Lincoln joined in, talking about school and how, in the future, he wanted to help foster kids like we had helped him. I felt the calm blanket of normality encircle me while we enjoyed each other's company. The noise and anecdotes lessened the harsh reality of my father's death and the attack on our home.

Brody took it all in, adding commentary, with humorous jabs at Kale. He was thoughtful and compassionate, like Kale. Brody possessed a big heart and a will to change the world. I could tell he was and would continue to be an amazing doctor.

At one point, Kale wandered off with Brody to the bathroom. I assumed they wanted a few moments to chat privately. They came back, Brody's arm slung around Kale's shoulders, an enormous grin on Brody's face. Kale put his hand to his mouth, then moved it to touch the chain I'd given him.

"Time to get Dr. Ryan a Lyft home," Kale announced while laughing at his brother's stupor.

"Who's the older, more responsible one here, me or you? *Hm.* Yeah, might be time for me to head out. Thank god I don't start 'til noon tomorrow." Brody leaned on Kale; a tipsy smile covered his face. "Speaking of work, I've meant to ask. What are you planning to do with all your free time, Kalen? Can't live off those good looks forever?"

Kale's brows lifted as if the question surprised him. He puffed out a breath. "I've had some time to think about it. I don't want to go back on tour. I wanna produce. I've got the funds and the time. I'm thinking of starting my own label. Put out the music I wanna hear."

Brody lifted his slightly drooping chin. The beer clearly making him sleepy. "Hey. That's—I'm proud of you, Kale." Brody's voice wavered, but that smile stuck to his lips.

I touched Kale's leg under the table. *Do it. Start your own label. You're too damn talented not to.*

Kale didn't turn his head to look at me, but I felt him touch my thoughts. *I will. I've got most of the information I need. It's something I've always wanted, but I didn't think I could manage. Now—I know I can. And I wanna thank you for that.*

I took a sip of my beer. A music studio. Kale deserved to pursue his dreams. Music made him happy, brought out a light in him I wanted the world to see shine. Brody was right to be proud of him. I certainly was.

I excused myself from the table, finding our waitress near the u-shaped lacquered bar, tending to other patrons. When she had a moment, I asked for our bill. I pulled out my metal Black Amex from the back of my phone, paying the tab before anyone noticed what I was up to.

The young server smiled perkily at her tip and went back to tapping a beer. "Thank you, you all have a goodnight."

"We shall, thank you," I said.

I wandered back to the table, taking my seat next to Kale again. He acknowledged my presence with an admiring smile. Kale leaned back in this wooden chair, grasping my hand to brush a quick kiss on the top.

"That's crazy sweet," Brody said.

"Don't mind me; I'm drunk and damn happy for Kale." Shifting in his chair, Brody side-hugged Kale again with extra force.

Returning his brother's embrace, "Thank you," he whispered low enough, so only Brody and I heard him. "She's everything I never knew existed and so much more," Kale disclosed to him.

Brody pulled away from his little brother, his eyes glazed, fighting to keep a tear from escaping. "I'm proud of you, Kalen, always have been. You did good, kid. She's perfect for you," he said, clapping Kale one more time on the back.

My heart swelled over Brody's sentimental comments. If only he knew how right he was. Maybe one day in the future, Brody would understand.

The rest of my boys started getting up from their chairs, stretching. We exchanged our goodbyes, expressing our enjoyment and desire to go out again soon.

As promised, Kale ordered a Lyft for Brody as we exited Napolita's. We stood near the curb as we waited for a Camry to show up for Brody.

Pressing a button on the key fob twice, the Challenger rumbled to life. Brody's attention whipping toward the sound, "Holy shit! Where'd you get that?" Brody's excitement was palpable.

"It's Athena's. She was kind enough to let me drive." Kale chuckled and side-eyed me but kept his gaze on his brother's similar giddy response to the car.

"Athena, do you mind? Can I see in there?" Brody asked, his eyes glued to the Challenger.

"Go right ahead. Looks like we have a few minutes before your ride gets here." I motioned my hand to the car.

Brody stepped off the curb, heading to the driver's side for a look inside. I glanced at Kale, his necklace all a sudden glowing red. I sniffed the air, searching for a scent of danger.

Nothing.

"Kale," I said, feeling fire bubble up in my chest and into my limbs. He glanced his eyes down, observing his necklace now, too. Atlas and Anders, sensing the change in my mood, moved closer to Kale and me, taking defensive poses. Lincoln froze, but a hiss escaped his lips as if waiting for someone to jump out at him.

"Where is it?" Anders inquired, his blue eyes darkening and darting to find whatever triggered Kale's pendant. Logan walked off to investigate a nearby alley. Logan rolled his shoulders, getting ready to shift and unleash his wolf on anything that dared to move.

Atlas hunched down, wafting more air into his lungs. "I don't know. I can't smell anything supernatural."

Brody emerged from the Challenger, shutting the door behind him, while a huge toothy grin spread from ear to ear. I heard an engine rev, tires screeching forward. Before we could act, a tinted car whizzed by. All we heard was the thumping of Brody's body being hit, then crinkling metal and fiberglass as his body rolled off the back of the car.

Brody's body lay motionless, crumpled on the asphalt.

No...

CHAPTER 18

Kale tore towards his brother, screams ripping from his throat. I felt my heart crushing all over again, trying to suffocate me. I couldn't succumb to the sensation; not this time, I needed to maintain focus.

"No. *Oh* God, *oh* God, Brody, please no. No!" Kale sobbed, clutching his limp brother to his chest. Blood covered Kale's shirt and hands.

"We need to move him. Pick him up now. We can fix this!" I hadn't meant to shout at Kale, but no one could witness what happened besides us. If we could get Brody to the alley, we'd maybe save him and avoid exposure. My mind blazed, sifting through worst-case scenarios and the feeling of Kale's misery.

A cloaking spell should help—it couldn't make things any worse.

"*Indespectus*," I said, flourishing my hand in the air toward Kale. I wasn't sure how much of us I'd shield from the potential prying onlookers, but at the very least, Brody and Kale would be invisible to the human eye for a while.

Atlas shot me a harsh look, his face churning down in concern.

Kale sniffled, tears streaming down his reddened face. But

he did as he was told. Gathering Brody into his arms with ease, Kale got back to the sidewalk. He carried Brody to the mouth of the dark alley. Anders leaped into action, attempting to take Brody from Kale's shaking arms.

I felt Kale in my head, loud enough to ring my ears.

Why couldn't I see it? Why couldn't I see it? Kale's strangled words filled my head.

"Let go, Kale. I can heal him as long as he's alive. Feel his muffled breaths? He's alive, and I can reverse this." Anders remained calm; his voice tranquil as he tried to convince Kale into giving his brother over.

Logan returned from the alley. "Bring him down here."

Anders set Brody down, placing his hands squarely on Brody's barely moving chest. It only took a moment. I examined Brody's body, the damage done to his brittle human form. His hair matted and darkened with blood, the viscous liquid pooling around his head. *Goddess, let him live.*

Coughing and sputtering, Brody jolted upright a bit too fast. "What happened? *Ugh*, I'm filthy."

Brody rubbed his hands down his blood-coated shirt, then touched his face, leaving bloody smudges on his cheek.

"Wait, this is blood. Why am I covered in blood? Was I hit by a car?" Brody's eyes darted wildly in every direction. His mind searching for logic where there was only magic.

Shit. I heard Atlas loudly in my head. Anders caught our gaze.

Anders shrugged. *He was supposed to be down longer.*

Kale wiped his face with his sleeve, hugging Brody to his chest with ferocity. I understood exactly how Kale felt, all too well. The pain, the terror that coursed through me when I lost someone I loved. Melancholy emotions encased my spirit all over again, this time though—we fought off death.

"Kale, Kalen—you're crushing me," Brody breathed out, trying to remove himself from Kale's grip.

"Sorry, I'm just—you're okay. I thought... never mind," Kale said, and his red eyes found Anders. "I—I can't thank you enough." Kale couldn't seem to control what he was saying, his words running together.

Anders worked to ease his expression, softening his mouth. "*Mm-hm*," he said, knowing he hadn't enough time to wipe Brody's memory of the accident.

Don't thank me yet. Anders pursed his lips.

Brody examined us, eyes narrowed and full of mistrust. "Someone answer me. Did I just get hit by a car?"

Atlas stepped back, rubbing his neck in frustration. "Yeah, some asshole hit you, but you're fine."

"I am? I mean—I am," Brody said, taking a physical check of himself. "I've got to get to the hospital. I could have head trauma, a bleed, anything. I need a head CT. Where is the blood from?" Brody's drunkenness was long gone, and he hit us with a barge of questions. The adrenaline was fresh in his veins. A leftover side effect from Anders healing him.

Brody's voice had a fresh edge. "I don't seem to have a scratch on me, yet it's all over my shirt. Christ! It's in my hair. Was anyone else involved in the accident? I need to access their injuries." His eyes were dark and moving around us.

"That won't be necessary. It was a hit and run," Anders said, a guilty expression taking over.

Brody tilted his head and paced. "That can't be right. Kale, what the hell is going on?" Brody asked and looked to his brother for answers. His hands clenched along with his jaw.

Kale stared at me, wordlessly asking permission. *Go ahead. If it goes completely south—Anders will have to wipe his memory.* I replied using our link.

I understand. Kale nodded in acceptance.

Kale put his hands out to Brody. "I'm going to tell you something. It's gonna make me sound insane. But I need you to hear me first. To remember, I'm still your brother."

Brody panted. "What the hell are you talking about, Kalen? You're starting to really fucking worry me," he replied as he pushed himself off the alleyway brick building.

"A while back, I was out with the guys at Zephyr. I ran into Athena. Long story short, there's an entire world you don't know about." Kale paused, trying to let his words sink in.

Brody shook his head. "Come on now. Stop it. This isn't funny."

"Listen to me, Brody. There's this huge supernatural world, the Unseen. Thea and her family are from there. I know how this sounds, but don't have me committed yet; I promise I'm not crazy." Kale let it all tumble out of his mouth, maybe too hastily.

I folded my arms, resigning myself to what we'd likely need to do to Brody. Humans weren't designed to absorb this kind of information. I didn't know how many human memories Anders had wiped over the years to avoid the freakout.

Brody rocked back on his heels, moving away from Kale and putting his fist into his hair. "What you're saying, Kalen is the definition of a delusion. A psychotic break." Brody walked the alley, kicking the bricks of the building in frustration. I stayed quiet; this wasn't my battle, not yet anyway. This was something Kale had to do on his own.

"I know that. Trust me, I do." Kale kept eye contact with Brody and resumed trying to explain.

Brody shook his head more rapidly, biting his lip so hard it looked like he drew blood. "No. No. I don't think you do. And all of you? You're in on this? Letting him go insane?"

Lincoln moved forward and cleared his throat. "He's not insane. Kale's a wolf. But he's more than that—you'll see." His eyes were earnest, the gray color shimmering like they'd collected stars. Was he trying to use his trance on Brody?

Brody snorted and backed up. "Just stay away from me. None of you touch me." He held his hand up to Lincoln, ensuring he didn't come any closer. "They've got you wrapped up in this, too, huh? What are you supposed to be? A *wolf* too?" Brody rolled his eyes and put air quotes on the word "wolf" while he glared at Lincoln.

"No, 'fraid not." Lincoln tapped his mouth with his index finger and didn't say anymore. Now wasn't the time to reveal his true nature.

Kale took a step toward Brody. "I need you to trust me."

"Trust you? I don't even trust myself right now. Kalen, I don't know what they have you on, and I don't care, but let's get you to a hospital. You need help."

I closed my eyes for a moment, then glanced at Logan, who stood rigid with his arms crossed. A vein in his forehead pulsed while he watched the opening of the alley, eyeing each car that drove by and making sure no one walked down to surprise us.

My heart ached for Kale as he kept trying to help his brother understand the truth, but the harder he seemed to try, the more manic Brody became. I couldn't take it anymore. I had to say something. "Brody, I'm sorry. I'm aware how this must sound, but Kale is not high or lying." I took a few calculated steps in Brody's direction, where he was pacing again, and I kept my hands where he could see them.

"You. I don't know what you did to him, but he was doing just fine before you came along! You know what? It doesn't matter. This is probably a delusion brought on by a concussion. I'm gonna close my eyes, and you'll all disappear." Brody rambled, his mind scrambling to make sense of the situation. He grabbed at the sides of his face with shaking hands.

Kale groaned. "You're not fucking delusional, and neither am I. I can prove I'm a shifter. Let me show you," Kale said, reaching his arms out to Brody, pushing forward on his quest to make Brody understand. I wanted Brody to understand, to believe us, if only for Kale's sake.

How much longer are we going to let this go on? Anders looked at me and moved closer, changing his posture. He readied himself to pounce on Brody and erase this unpleasantness.

I shrugged at Anders. *As long as we can.*

Atlas just shook his head and huffed as he went to join Logan at the mouth of the alley. I sensed Atlas didn't care which way this unfolded. He was over the drama.

Lincoln approached me. He put his head down and snaked his hand into mine. I gave him a gentle squeeze, offering the reassurance he sought—or maybe it was me who needed the reassurance.

"It's gonna be alright, you'll see." I rubbed my thumb along Lincoln's boney knuckles, his long fingers dwarfing mine. I tried my mother's method—having faith. I had this gut intuition about Brody. And it stood to reason—if Kale descended from something supernatural, Brody did too. He should possess some inclination to understand the truth, I hoped.

Brody stopped pacing and walked to Kale, looking him directly in the eyes.

"Show me how? Because I wanna understand you, Kale, I do. But what you're saying goes against everything I've studied."

"Use your eyes. Call for your wolf, he'll answer." I nodded slowly, doing my best to convey my confidence to Kale.

"Eyes?" Brody stared, creasing his brow and wrinkling his face at Kale as if trying to see through him.

Kale nodded at me and closed his eyes, asking his wolf to come forward. *I need you. Help me show him, to make him understand.*

Brody braced himself for the unknown, crossing his arms over his chest. Kale's body jolted. A low rolling rumble resounded from his chest and up his throat, causing Brody to jump back. Kale unhurriedly opened his eyelids. The fiery amber embers filled his irises as he met Brody's hard stare. Instead of backing away further, Brody moved closer. He took Kale's face into his hands. He moved Kale's head around, looking at the glowing orbs that belonged to his brother. Brody freed Kale's head from his grip, taking a few steps back. I watched Brody's thoughts spin, trying to put together the world he knew with the magic Kale had shown him.

Kale's head fell, his eyes looking down. This time, he waited for rejection of the truth, like I had before. My insides churned, aching for Kale. I wanted to reach out and console him, tell him it would be okay, but I had no way of knowing that.

We all stilled, giving Brody as much time as we could afford. Brody roughly rubbed his face hard, then wrung his hands. He looked back at Kale, facing his uncertainty over the situation. Brody dropped his hands, walking to Kale, and pulled him into a solid embrace.

"Brody," Kale said, his face stuffed into his brother's shoulder. "Are we good?"

Turning loose of Kale, Brody's face remained neutral and unreadable. He didn't answer right away, only examining his brother further. I watched Kale. His eyes filled with a soundless plea, begging Brody to accept him.

Brody exhaled hard. "We're gonna be. Whatever you are, I'm with you—" he stopped, throwing me a glare. "Doesn't mean I'm not freaked the fuck out and don't have a shit ton of questions for all of you."

"I wouldn't expect anything less," Kale replied. "What do you wanna know?"

I'd wandered down the alley to where Atlas was standing, trying to give them privacy. I rubbed Atlas's back. I knew deep down worrying about Kale and Brody upset him.

Atlas peeked down at me and leaned his head on top of mine.

A moment later, Kale came jogging over to me, a bounce in his step. He lifted me up off the ground and swung me into the air. "It feels so good to have him know the truth—like I can breathe again." His eyes shone with smoldering sparks.

"I completely understand."

Kale set me down, and we walked back over to Brody, who had his hands to his hips.

"So, how the hell am I not dead?" Brody asked, addressing all of us.

"Anders healed you," Kale replied.

Brody raised his brow. "*Mm-hm. Ha!* How?"

Kale struggled with how to word his response. I stepped forward, helping him out. When it came to the practical-minded, seeing was believing.

"Perhaps a demonstration is better," I offered. "Atlas, would you come here, please?"

"I know what you're up to, T," he said, turning his head and rubbing his jaw. But he made his way over to me.

Upon his approach, I lifted my arm. "Slash me. If I do it, it'll close up too fast."

Atlas's eyes went wide. "No way."

I sighed, lifting my arm to him. "Save us time, just do as I ask," I advised him, not ready to go full Alpha in front of Brody.

"Thea, come on, don't." Kale frowned, trying to interrupt. While Brody hung back, narrowing his eyes. He might be open to what Kale was telling him, but I noticed him keeping a fair distance away from my brothers and me.

Atlas took my hand, releasing his claws, he tore into my arm. I winced. It certainly didn't feel good, that was for damn sure, but physical pain was easier to deal with than heartbreak. Blood poured from the wounds down my arm and hit the gritty, wet alley pavement. I watched Kale and Brody's faces go pale, and both their mouths dropped over.

"*Oh*, fucking hell!" Brody exclaimed, stumbling back. His eyes almost protruded from his head.

Anders casually strolled over. This was nothing. He'd healed ghastlier wounds. He touched my upper arm, and I felt the injury closing like it never existed. Kale ripped a piece of his shirt off and wiped away the remaining blood.

"I really wish you wouldn't have done that." Kale rolled his eyes, putting his tongue into his cheek, displeased with my demonstration. "It wasn't necessary."

"Why? Easiest way I could think of to get the point across," I said. "And look—all better."

Brody walked over to me, not taking his eyes off my arm. "May I?" he asked, taking my forearm into his hands and wiping it again with his already stained shirt. He turned my arm over and over, moving his fingers up and down to my wrist. His fingers were delicate, tracing my veins. I imagine being a doctor made this all the more captivating, like a mini science experiment.

"That's remarkable," Brody said. "He can heal anything?" Brody was far more curious than frightened now.

"Pretty much, yeah. As long as you're alive. But if death occurs, I can't reverse that," Anders replied.

Lincoln, who'd taken a spot by Logan, popped back over, a smile on his wide mouth. "They can regenerate too."

Brody gave a signature Kale move, swiping his hand through his thick hair. "Wow, um, okay," was all he said. Brody looked at each of us over, again and again, his doctor and science-based brain still trying to make sense of what he saw and heard.

Logan and Atlas ambled over. Logan fiddled with his phone, seemingly uninterested in our current conversation.

Atlas took his hands from his denim pockets. "See, we're not so bad," he mused, smirking at Brody.

"Are you all wolves then and do that weird eye thing?" Brody asked, studying each of our faces.

"All except for Lincoln here." Kale shuffled Lincoln's blonde hair.

Lincoln balked and adjusted his mussed hair. "Come on, Kale."

Brody squinted his eyes, trying to gain a better look at Lincoln. "Are you human?"

"*Ha*, I used to be." Lincoln checked my face before continuing, "I'm a vampire."

"You've got to be kidding me..." Brody palmed his face, leaving pink marks. "Is everything from the movies real?" He sunk to the ground, leaning back against the brick wall. He rested his head on his knees.

"Essentially, in some form or another." Anders chuckled, amused by Brody. I felt Anders's relief over not having to subdue and wipe Brody's memory.

Brody huffed and pushed himself up off the wall, dusting at his torn, dirty pants. "Nothing personal; I think I'd like to go home now. A car fucking hit me, and I found out everything on the sci-fi channel is real. So, yeah, I already have a headache for tomorrow."

Brody forced a lighthearted smile on his lips. His acceptance of our existence didn't surprise me. He was so much like Kale, trusting and open. Brody loved his little brother, and he was willing to listen to him rather than having him committed. The Ryan brothers were a special breed of their own.

"Want me to go home with you?" Kale offered.

Shaking his head, Brody waved Kale off. "Nah, go on with Athena. We can catch up later."

"No, no. Kale should go with you, make sure you're alright," I interjected my opinion between the two men. Brody had no business going home alone, and I needed time to think.

"Unless you're scared of your little brother?" Kale taunted Brody.

Brody gave a shaky laugh. "Absolutely not. I'm no red riding hood."

"Settled then. Take the car. I'll ride with Lincoln," I said to Kale, trying to keep my tone light. I realized I hadn't been away from him for longer than a few hours at a time. Being without Kale didn't upset me. It was the thought of what might happen to him if I wasn't around nagging at me. But after last night, I knew he could defend himself. The thought brought me little comfort.

I felt Logan tap into my head. *I'll stay behind, out of sight. Keeping our future King safe is of the utmost importance. Someone meant to hurt Kale—I can feel it.*

I agree. Whoever swerved that car meant to hit Kale. But you just got back, and now you wanna go out on another mission?

It eases my mind when I have a task. Let me do this. Logan was asking for my approval.

Nodding at Logan, I walked to the car with Lincoln as Brody and Kale chatted.

"Hey, where do you think you're going?" Kale called after me.

"Home."

Kale raced over to me. "Not without this, you're not." He stopped talking and caught my lips in a blistering kiss that stirred awake my other senses. "Text me when you get home."

I kissed him one last time. "It'll be the first thing I do." Kale turned me loose, watching me over his shoulder as he walked away with Brody.

Anders got on his phone and canceled our reservation. Everyone agreed Whiteridge Manor was the best and safest place for us to be.

I let Lincoln drive, happy to be a passenger while I thought about who tried to hit Kale and why.

Since Kale and I collided, everything had grown more complicated, and I still had no idea who'd gotten into the manor last night or where to find Xercarus. I felt like a failure. I was too distracted, and that pissed me off. I'd never dropped the ball like this before, and each day Xercarus roamed free, the more lives we lost. I had to get my head on straight.

"Athena, can I tell you something?" Lincoln asked, his voice quiet.

I turned my head to face him. "Always," I replied, hearing the turmoil growing in his tone. I gazed at Lincoln. I never wanted him to feel pain again. He'd endured too much. I patted his arm, waiting for him to confide in me.

"I've had some bad nights. But, this...scared me," he said, keeping his eyes on the highway.

His confession took hold of my heart and my breath for a moment. "I was afraid too, for lots of reasons," I admitted to him. Fear was natural, if wholly uncomfortable.

"Really? Because you never seem afraid of anything. You're not weak like me," he uttered, not taking his eyes off the road, but his hands tightened on the wheel, making the leather squeak beneath his fingers.

I shook my head. "I'm scared all the time. When I didn't have my powers, I was terrified, but being afraid isn't a weakness. The bravest people get scared, but we act anyway, like you did last night and tonight. You're anything but weak to survive what you have. Do you understand me?" I patted Lincoln's knee, then gave it a gentle squeeze.

"Thanks, Athena." Lincoln half smiled as he continued to watch the road. "Oh! I almost forgot. I got some numbers off the license plate."

I jerked my head in his direction, my heart galloping in my chest. "From the car that hit Brody?"

"Yeah, 377 JC. That's all I got before Kale startled yelling."

"Lincoln, that's excellent! Why didn't you mention that before?" My voice upped an octave, and I scrambled for my phone.

Lincoln shrugged. "Kinda slipped my mind for a while with

Brody almost dying and all. Sorry," he apologized, clenching his teeth together.

I got on my phone, messaging Anders, then Gage, and Agent Connor. It wouldn't take us long to match those plates. And when we did, someone was going to pay. My wolf reverberated her agreement.

CHAPTER 19

*L*incoln parked the car in the circular driveway. I bid him a quick goodnight, kissing his cheek before I got out. Anders and Atlas hadn't made it back yet; I was sure they weren't far behind. I left the garage, heading straight inside to speak to my mother. I needed her guidance, or maybe to get me out of my head.

I didn't bother shutting the front door. Lincoln's footsteps were trailing behind me. The giant house was quiet. Calliope was a famous night owl, and by the smell wafting around the open foyer, I knew she was in the laundry room.

I went upstairs in search of my mother and found her bedroom door closed. The scent of jasmine floated around me, candles burning. I knocked softly, but there was no answer. I opened the door to find my mother, balled up on her bed, one of my father's wool sweaters tucked in her arms. Hints of an earthy smell before the rain swirled up my nose—my father. He always smelled of the woods before a good rain, fresh and cool. I missed him; a tear pricked the corner of my eye. I listened to her quiet, rhythmic breathing. Inching farther into her master suite, I tip-toed into the walk-in closet. My father's and mother's clothing hung side-by-side. I reached for one of his old sweaters. I took a downy, olive green one, the sleeves tattered from years of wear. I put it beneath my nose, inhaling.

Taking a cue from my mother, I pulled the sweater over my head, surrounding myself with the delicate fabric. I folded my arms around myself, remembering how it felt to be in his arms. I looked around their room. His nightstand still had things, untouched. A newspaper, an old worn brown book, and an ink pen. His journal. My father kept journals for as long as I could remember. He said it helped it leave the day behind and start fresh. I walked over to his side of the bed and stroked the soft leather cover. I put my fingers to my lips, kissing them and putting them back to the book as if to kiss my father goodnight.

I'd talk to my mother tomorrow. She required time to recover, more than anyone else. A pang of heartache searched to occupy my chest; as I admired her resting form, I thought about how much she'd lost and then had given to me. Her strength was extraordinary. I hoped I possessed a fraction of her fortitude.

"*Boa Noite*," I said in a whisper as I closed her door.

I headed up another flight of stairs to my room, knowing I should go down to discuss the evening with my brothers. But I wanted to be done for the day. If anyone needed me, they knew where to find me. Taking my iPhone from my pocket, I swiped up to open contacts, tapping Kale's name.

Made it home all safe and sound.

It didn't take long for three little dots to appear, letting me know Kale was responding. I felt comforted, knowing he was with Brody. Kale's miserable cries were still fresh in my mind. I flinched at the memory. Kale needed to stay the night with his brother, more than he understood. He lost Brody for a moment, but Anders brought him back, something we couldn't do for our own family. There weren't many things I wouldn't give to have one more conversation with my father, to just hear his voice again.

My phone vibrated.

Good. I miss you. Brody is taking this like a champ. I told him everything.

I miss you too. You needed this time together.

Yeah, we did. He's taking the day off tomorrow. He hasn't done that in...EVER.
My only real concern is who hit Brody.

We'll have that answer soon. Lincoln got some of the license plate numbers.

I sent my phone on the bathroom counter, gazing at my reflection. A week ago, life was completely different. I had goals of becoming Queen, being a fierce Alpha. Now I was Queen, and it couldn't have mattered less. The face in the mirror was mine, but so far from the same. I'd experienced true loss and a soul-binding love in such a short time. I imagined Kale if Anders hadn't been able to save Brody. Whoever hit him did it because of me. My union with Kale constantly put him in jeopardy. This time, Brody suffered the consequences of Kale and I being together.

I washed my hands, splashing warm water on my face, then

brushed my teeth more briskly than required. Kale would be safer away from me.

My phone vibrated and chirped, the little noise demanding my attention. Two messages from Kale.

He got the plate?! Startin' to love that kid!
What are the rules on killing? Whoever did this to Brody has it coming.

The rule is no needless killing. Whoever hit Brody meant to hit you.
Your necklace glows when danger is present for you.

Idk if that makes me more or less angry.

Neither makes me less angry. I'll get to the bottom of it, promise.

I know you will. I think we r headed to bed pretty quick anyway. I'll bring the Challenger back tomorrow.
G'night Thea. Love you.

Love you too. More than you know.

Don't worry about the Challenger. Brody can keep it since he almost died for it.

Is that a bribe?

For him not to hate me? Maybe.

He doesn't hate you

Sure. Goodnight.

Night.

I stood by my bed, kneading the sleeves of my father's sweater. I tossed my phone on the white nightstand and leaned on the canopy bedpost. Thoughts of how to keep Kale unharmed from the situation pressing against us assailed my mind, badgering me over and over. It was a close call with Brody tonight. Next time Anders might not be able to resolve it. I wouldn't have Kale suffer the same fate as my father. Kale's visions proved anything could change. I needed to keep Kale away from me for his own good.

My wolf lifted her head, paying close attention.

What other choice do we have? I asked her.

Silence. Figured.

She had no more of an idea how to keep Kale safe than I did. I'd distance myself from Kale, keep him away. His well-being was more important than my selfish desire to be with him and continuing to involve him in a situation he never asked to be in.

Exhausted, I sat down on the bed, letting myself fall back onto the mountain of pillows. I don't know how long I laid there. Time ticked away, each second eating away at my resolve.

I wanted a little more time with Kale, to see his face again, hold him against me and feel his warmth, damned the consequences.

I knew a spell. I'd never tried it, but I was feeling reckless. I wanted Kale, and if I couldn't have him here, I could *conjure* him. The spell would show me Kale as he was, a spirit version of him—in theory. If I got the words right.

I put my palms up in the air. "Tactus Verum Amor. Tactus Verum Amore. Tactus Verum Amor."

Pressure pushed from behind my eyes, and my body shook. Silvery light poured from my hands. Kale's body shimmered and appeared next to me, his sleeping form on my bed. He wasn't really here—only a manifested vision of him. He was shirtless, sleeping in his black fitted briefs. The chain I'd given him lay on his chest. One hand was on his stomach, the other sprawled above his head. I slipped my clothing off, shedding each layer. I grabbed a soft knit throw from the end of my bed and climbed in next to Kale. I covered us both, stroking his hair as I did. His brow furrowed over his closed eyes. His long lashes grazed his cheeks. I kissed his forehead, careful not to wake him.

"Athena," he said, his voice quiet and muffled. His eyes remained closed. I'd be nothing more than a sweet dream to him.

I snuggled in against him, finding that comfortable skin-to-skin nook. I placed another soft kiss under his chin as I wrapped my arm around his chest.

"*Mm*. Thea," he moaned softly, almost inaudible. I held him tighter. It was as if he was really there, next to me, his chest heaving up and down with each breath. I laid my head on his chest, listening to his heart, and nuzzled my nose on his bare skin.

Kale rolled, causing me to look up at him. "Thea," his lake blue eyes opened, gazing into mine.

"Is this a dream?" he asked, sleep clinging to his voice.

I caressed his cheek. "Yes, it is." I lingered in the moment, lost in the way his skin felt exactly the same.

"If it's a dream, I can kiss you then."

Batting my lashes, I held his face to mine. "You can kiss me as much as you'd like."

Kale leaned into me, pressing his lips to mine; it was a gratifying, indulgent kiss. He moved his hand to cup my cheek. His kiss fanned my yearning for him. Sensing my body, he propped himself up on his elbow and rolled until he was on top of me. His hips pushed hard against me, as did his solid length, dipping perfectly at my center. I arched into him, emitting a low groan from my mouth. Our kisses were slow-burning and deep. He was so real, I wanted to keep him like this—sheltered and frozen in time.

"I want you," Kale whispered. "But can I just hold you?" Even in his dreams, he was a gentleman, never needing more from me than I offered. His eyes fluttered closed, and I pressed dainty kisses to each of his eyelids.

I rolled over his stomach and chest right against my back. "Hold me for as long as you can."

"We need our blanket," he murmured into my ear. Right after he spoke, he rolled again, pulling the duvet up and around us.

"I love you," he said, drowsy and on his way back to sleep.

"*Você ilumina minha vida.*" I grazed my lips on the top of his hand that lie around me.

Almost out, he mumbled. "What's that mean?" He let out a long sigh, his breathing slowing into rhythm.

"It means you light up my life."

I felt his lips curve up as he smiled into my hair. "*Mmm,* I'm gonna need to learn Portuguese." Kale was sound asleep moments later, his nose nestled into my hair. His breath lulled me into a sleepy haze while his heartbeat right along with mine.

"Sleep and have the most wondrous dreams." I cooed at him before my eyes shut a final time.

I woke up early, my bed empty and cold on one side. I stroked my hand against the pillow where Kale's head had laid. My spell had long worn off. It was time to get up and face the world. Rolling off the side of the bed, I pulled my hair into a crude, messy bun, a few black strands falling into my face. Getting dressed, I put on a high-impact sports bra and cropped leggings. As my hand went to grab a fresh shirt from my dresser, I changed direction, picking up my father's sweater and shrugging it back on.

I needed to go for a run. Tension had already plugged up my limbs, making me feel cagey and cornered. My phone chirped; it would be Kale. Of course, he would wake at the same time. Picking up my phone, I opened his message.

Good morning beautiful! I had the strangest dream last night. So weird. It was like I was with you.

I tapped the screen, deliberating, not answering. I didn't want to be cruel to Kale, only push him away, keep him at a distance long enough for me to solve this. The idea compressed my ribcage, leaving my sternum tight, hindered my breathing. I swallowed a hard breath down; the pain would be worth it. I would take anything my traitorous body threw at me. I checked my emails first, giving myself a moment to chill and welcoming a distraction.

I understand you're busy.

I knew Kale was perceptive, and beyond that, even at a distance, he could pick up on some emotional changes. That was the thing about mates—Kale possessed an innate ability to understand me without trying, matching me in ways I wasn't aware of. That didn't mean we wouldn't fight or disagree, especially right now. Kale wouldn't appreciate me avoiding him, but I would not ask his permission to keep him safe. As Alpha, it was my given right to protect my own.

I fumbled with my phone and the idea that keeping him away was the right way to handle this, or maybe it wasn't. Within a minute, Kale was swaying me. I shook my head, getting off the bed to wash my face, hoping that would clean away my doubts. I stared in the mirror; dark circles rimmed my eyes. I was more tired than I'd ever been, exhausted from my own thoughts.

I walked back into my room, opening the balcony doors and taking a seat on the powder blue chaise out there. A breeze blew strands of my hair off my face and swirled the changing air around me.

More chirping, I picked up my phone, another message from Kale.

I'm runnin errands with Brody. Gonna catch some breakfast at this place downtown. Breakwave.
Best pancakes you'll ever have, def wanna take you there.
Talk to you in a bit.

I squeezed my phone, the screen turning black. I looked at

my reflection, the screen becoming a mirror I had no desire to see.

My phone chirped again, lighting up and hiding my image. Kale's name on the screen I opened it.

Miss me yet?

My impulse was to smile, but that would only make letting him go harder. *Stop it, Athena.* I thought, biting down on my lip so hard it bled. The metallic, earthy taste of my blood hitting my tongue made me shiver.

I set my phone down and left it at that. Reading anymore would have me asking him to drive here right now so I could confess my insecurities, and I had no intentions of doing that. Logan was near Kale, and that was enough assurance.

Getting off the chaise, I walked back to the bathroom to brush my teeth. Then, out of habit, I went back and grabbed my phone, tucking it in the mesh pocket of my leggings.

Downstairs, everyone piled into the kitchen, eating. Calliope had set out an array of fresh fruits, cut-up papayas, oranges, bananas. The aroma of her dark, strong coffee charged my senses. Caffeine, maybe that would help me focus.

My mother looked more herself today, her chestnut curls pinned loosely atop her head, her eyes were bright and clear. I watched her buzz about the kitchen, her and Calliope in perfect sync, never battling for space.

From the range oven, my mother took out 'Pao Frances,' a French bread recipe from home that she'd kept with her over the years. She set the piping hot bread in the center of the table, along with fresh pads of rolled butter in a dish next to it.

Lincoln was the first to acknowledge my presence, "Morning Athena," his tone was high and cheerful, chocked full of his exuberant youth.

A familiar rusty scent filling my nose right as I got a whiff of the tumbler—blood. The muted smell didn't bother me, and it gave the illusion he was drinking nothing more than water or juice. He was sitting between Anders and Atlas. I noticed how well he fit in and how easily my brothers had accepted him. Lincoln looked like he belonged. I smiled to myself for a moment.

"About time you got up. You'd think with Kale gone last night, you would've gotten some sleep," Atlas smirked, picking at me right off the bat. His mischievous brown eyes trying to egg me on.

I didn't bother responding, instead looking out the bay window. His comment didn't aggravate me like it normally did. I lacked the desire to engage in his antics. Atlas put down his ceramic coffee mug, examining me through wide eyes. Me not giving into verbal combat was a big enough 'red flag' for him to take notice. He picked a red apple from the wooden bowl, chucking it in my direction. Without looking at him, I raised my hand, giving my wrist a flick, and disintegrated the apple to ashes that disappeared before hitting the floor.

I flashed my green eyes at him, in no mood for his shit. Atlas took his mug back into his hands, sipping his coffee and going out of his way to not look at Anders. I knew Atlas was linking Anders when I saw his head bob up and down and narrow his eyes to observe me with the critical fascination he often reserved for books.

My mother smiled, missing the entire exchange. "Athena, come sit, come sit." She gestured to the open stool at the island. Not wanting to tip her off to my mood, I took a seat.

"Coffee?" she offered.

"Sure."

She poured the steamy brown liquid into the mug she set in front of me and winked.

I sipped at the coffee. It warmed me all the way down, the bitterness biting at my tastebuds.

Lincoln chattered to my mother and Calliope, both of them enjoying his energetic nature.

Over the past several days, Lincoln had blossomed. He stood taller with confidence, no longer hunching his shoulders and dulling his height. His appearance aligned with current trends, and he was now the proud owner of a new collection of Vans. Calliope had taken it upon herself to get Lincoln on a computer, and together they ordered a new wardrobe. She also had him in the enrollment process to the elite private school for supernaturals, Park Haven. Yesterday, the headteacher gave Lincoln online courses to test his affinities and academic levels. Turned out, Lincoln breezed through his tests this morning, passing with some of the highest scores the faculty had ever seen.

Lincoln opened his MacBook, reading the emails aloud to Calliope, a satisfied grin on his lips. I was happy for Lincoln, but I zoned out in and out as he talked.

Anders got up from his stool, taking a spot right next to me. "Thea, tell me?"

"Tell you what?" I looked up from my mug, a vague expression taking over my features.

"You know what. You're in your head. I don't wanna go digging in there, but—" Anders hesitated, gauging whether he should urge me farther. I wasn't mad at him; I just had no desire to talk about it, and I didn't want or need the intrusions.

"I actually have a few emails I need to send. Gotta get back to Ben about the Solstice arrangements. This year is going to be... different. Besides, don't you and Atlas have more tests to run on that thing in the lab anyway?" I grabbed the coffee craft, refilling my coffee mug, and left the kitchen, not saying another word.

I walked through the corridor and up the stairs to the second floor of the house until I reached the office. I felt Atlas trying to say something, but I put my hand to my head as if to physically push him out of it.

Not now, please. I linked while opening the door to my father's office. I guess it was my office now. I grimaced, looking around the room that didn't belong to me. This didn't sit well. Then again, not much did this morning.

"Ouch," I hissed, looking down at my arm, wondering what stung.

It wasn't until a drop of hot coffee splashed on my wrist, leaving a burn. How did I not notice I'd made my cup of coffee boil...?

Get a hold of yourself, Athena, I grumbled.

CHAPTER 20

The office lay untouched. Pens and a few papers sat on his desk alongside his computer. Bookcases lined his walls from ceiling to floor. My father believed literature could save the world and that a well-read leader could understand a situation from many points of view.

A memory flashed through my mind. My father appeared, sitting at his desk, reading a book. His face lifted to look at me and smile. I snapped my eyes closed and reopened them, making the image fade as quickly as it had come. I straightened my back and took calculated steps until I reached his desk, setting my cooling coffee down on his custom coasters.

I rubbed my hand on the back of the oversized brown leather chair. Where my father had sat, so many times was worn.

Pulling the chair out, I took a seat behind the large wooden desk, stretching my palms along the sturdy oak. I traced my fingers on the long lines of the grain, the light tones of the wood reminding me of my father's hair. I shook my head, reminding myself that reminiscing wouldn't get anything done.

I moved the wireless mouse to start up the computer, and the screen flickered to life. I logged into my Gmail account, intent on emailing Ben. He had a final guest list for me, pending my approval, and a caterer lined up. For my father's rumination ceremony, Ben ordered cases of champagne to toast in his memory. Ben's email informed me I'd need to write a brief speech. He also wrote he'd selected my gown styles for the evening. There were five to choose from, I'd need only to pick one, and it would arrive in a day or two. He had the best seamstress contracted to come over to tailor the dress to my body. Kale's outfit would match mine accordingly. I nodded along to all Ben's emails as if he were here telling me all this in person.

Reading on, I followed Ben's directions, checking each of his attachments. I finished my email to him, giving him all the final approvals he needed. I thanked him again for his time and dedication to our family.

Lastly, I logged into our family bank account, transferring a bonus to Ben. He did not know how many overwhelming details he'd saved me from. Throwing money at someone had never been our way of conducting business, but I remembered what my dad had told me about showing gratitude and appreciation where it was due.

I selected 'Complete Transfer' on the screen and logged off. Pushing my chair away from the desk, I scrubbed my hands against my cheeks. All of this felt tedious, these frivolous tasks all done in the name of 'duty.' None of it brought me closer to finding out who betrayed us and where Xercarus's lair was.

Glancing at my phone, I noticed messages from Kale and felt disappointed. I'd been hoping to hear from Connor about the plate. He was busy documenting case files, but it couldn't hurt to message him and check in.

Any information on that plate yet?

Against my better judgment, I opened Kale's messages. I swiped back over, pulling up Kale's name.

BEST.PANCAKES.EVER. Can't wait to see you after dinner
You must be crazy busy
LMK if everything is going okay

Pressing my phone screen off, I huffed and tucked it back into my pocket. Time to go for a run. I'd run in human form. I couldn't trust my wolf to not chase Kale down, and right now, she and I were immaturely ignoring one another. At this point, it was a grateful relief, not having to fight her, too.

I made my way outside and found our track empty. The air was crisp, ready for the Winter Solstice and the snow that would come soon. It always intrigued me—how the faeries dispersed winter. In our schooling and under my mother's constant guidance, I learned the importance of nature's balance.

The Unseen housed all seasons, unlike the human world. We lived near what was Southern California—the land of no snow. But the Unseen didn't follow the same Earthly laws, and the fae took it upon themselves to divvy up weather based on geography. In the human world, you simply couldn't have snow where it was hot, but here it was like living in a bubble.

Soon the Unseen would have snow-covered rooftops and trees with silver frost, but once we hit the Barrier—green and sunshine. The more I thought about it, the more I respected the magic of it. It was a curious thing to know some people never experienced snow, each flake a tiny, crystal masterpiece. They were missing out on a wondrous happening, indeed. I thought of all the times my father had played with us in the snow, building forts, and never passing up a snowball fight. The frozen waters we'd ice skate on. There were days we'd come inside, sopping wet and chilled. Calliope and my mother would have hot cocoa with too many marshmallows ready for us. The memories welled up in my eyes. I sniffed, clearing my nose of the heavy sensation of tears.

I took my father's sweater off, smelling it again before setting it gently onto the nearby patio table. Putting my AirPods in, I queued up a playlist from my phone. 'Legends Never Die' blasted into my ears. I closed my eyes, breathing out, and set off running, more like sprinting. Wind whipped my face, threatening tears, but I didn't stop. My legs blazed around the track, my feet pounding the ground over and over. I ached to discharge my conflicted thoughts into the sky. Air hit my face harder, blowing up into my nostrils. Faster, I needed to go faster, to outrun my feelings. I closed my eyes, unafraid of tripping. I knew this terrain, every dip, and every curve. My eyes tore open, my neutral green seized by a vibrant jade, sparking like the inferno raging inside me. Smoke poured from my nostrils, and I surged forward, hitting new speeds in my human form. I grinned to myself, feeling the freeing rhythm of my body. My AirPods paused, the robotic voice of Siri reading an incoming text message:

Message from Connor: *Bad news, kid. The plate belongs to Jennifer Miller. Turns out she was working at Zephyr on and off. We actually interviewed her. Acted cagey. We found nothing and had to cut her loose. What's this all about anyway?*

Siri's voice stopped, and the music resumed. I dug my heels into the ground, causing deep craters as I did. I came to an immediate halt, ripping my AirPods out.

Jennifer Miller.

Jenny.

This wasn't intuition. I knew it. I could sense it, like a punch to the face. We'd advised her to go home, even got her an Uber, and in return, she thought running her ex down was a reasonable idea. I thought of the many ways I could kill her. A tiny fraction of me wanted to be the bigger person, but I'd already offered Jenny that option. This time, I didn't think I could. She tried to hurt Kale, my family, and for what?

Atlas launched into my thoughts. *Thea, what was that?*

I felt it as well, what happened? Anders tried reaching me too.

*The plates—they belong to Jenny, w*as all I responded. My hands burned. I grappled for control while my wolf and dragon battled me for influence, both wanting vengeance and me wanting to provide it. I reached for my phone. I had some calls to make.

Our hangar crew said the helicopter would be ready in fifteen minutes. The closest place for us to land was four miles away from Jenny's apartment. That was more than close enough. I'd run that in minutes.

I came barreling back into the house through a patio door. I needed to change. I jogged upstairs, opening my bedroom door with so much force it slammed into the wall, making a hole. I put my father's sweater down, digging in my drawers until I got what I wanted. I stripped down and clothed myself in all black —it hid blood better.

Atlas and Anders came flying into my room, their eyes wild. They intended to calm me down. That wasn't happening—not this time. My lip curled up in a snarl.

"Thea, you gotta take a minute and think about what you're doing," Anders tried first.

I said nothing as I pulled my hair into a high ponytail, the length dusting between my shoulder blades.

"Come on, don't be so damn hard-headed. Listen to for a second." Atlas threw his hands up, trying his luck with me.

Looking at their spooked faces, I felt a twinge of guilt over what I was about to do. I couldn't have them in my way.

"As your Alpha, I *command* you not to stop me," I spoke my words clear as a bell. They had no choice but to obey. A command was absolute and law by our nature.

"Dammit, Athena!" Atlas sputtered, fisting his hands.

Anders folded his arms, "Fine. We won't stop you. We're going with you to clean up the fucking mess you make."

"There won't be a mess. Just stay outta my way." They were

fuming at me. Their harsh glowers and tight lips changed nothing. There was no other choice. Compelling them wasn't enjoyable, but I had zero intention of being swayed, so why engage in an unnecessary argument? I had a mission. They were going to help me or get out of my way.

Atlas took out his phone, sending a quick text, likely to Kale. If they couldn't interfere, involving Kale was the best option. And on cue, my phone rang, vibrating pulses. Kale's name and face lit up my screen, insisting I answer.

Not this time.

I put my phone back into my pocket. "Nice try, boys. But if I don't answer, he can't convince me of anything. Are you coming or not?"

Anders and Atlas rolled their eyes. "Fuck! Yeah, we're coming," Atlas growled at me and kicked at the ground.

Anders clenched his fists, jogging to catch up.

Right on time, we made it to the hanger. The Agusta 109, our fastest helicopter, reaching speeds of 180 miles per hour, was gassed up and ready at our arrival. The loud whooshing of its blades cut through the air as we all got in, strapping our harnesses. We flew in silence. My brothers tested out a new tactic, expressing their fury by not speaking to me. I had too much going on in my head to care. I used this time to take a crack at calming myself, an impossible endeavor. Instead, I became more frustrated as time dragged on, and my fingers ached from restraining the fire I wanted to release. The only saving grace was traveling at these speeds made our trip quick.

The pilot gained final clearance to land. I exited the helicopter first, Anders following, then Atlas. I didn't bother waiting for them, bolting to the stairwell and hurling myself into a dead sprint. My feet hit the pavement hard, and I expertly dodged walking pedestrians.

My brothers both yelled, trying to get in my head, but I blocked them completely out.

Quiet.

Must be the perk of being full-on Alpha, you didn't get in my head unless I wanted you to, and right now, I didn't want anyone in there—no witnesses to my messy, clustered thoughts of Jenny's demise.

It didn't take long to reach the address Connor had provided me. I was almost there until I noticed doors opening on a white Chevy Equinox. Kale and Brody stepped out of the vehicle. Kale looked frazzled, the grimace covering his face telling me he was just as pissed off as my brothers.

Too bad.

I opted to ignore Kale, trying to zig-zag past him. A breeze blew, bringing Logan's scent to my nostrils. He was somewhere, hidden in the distance.

Kale stepped in front of me, absorbing the impact of my body colliding with his. He put his hands on my upper arms, and his angry voice broke my concentration. "What the hell are you doing, Thea?"

I scoffed, mocking Kale's tone. He didn't know how stupid it was to get in a wolf's way. "What am I doing? Are you kidding? Do you know what she did? Did either of them tell you, or did Atlas conveniently leave that part out?" I shot a harsh glare at my brothers.

"I guess neither of them explained. I know it's not because we dated. You're not petty like that." Kale's blue eyes went soft, and his tone fell flat.

I rolled my eyes, snorting with exasperation. "Of course, my dear brothers didn't tell you, because if they had you wouldn't be here trying to stop me." I paused for a moment, letting Kale put together the pieces. "She's the one who hit Brody. It was her car. Bet if we check, we'll find Brody's blood on it and see the dents. Doubt she was smart enough to wash it." I folded my arms across my chest, knowing full well Kale wouldn't take my disclosure very well. I hadn't been trying to ambush him with the information, but it happened anyway. His brows knit together, and he threw a glare at Atlas then Anders.

Kale didn't say anymore, and having been here before, knew where Jenny parked. He proceeded to the back of the apartment complex. We reached the parking lot, and sure enough, it was the car from last night. Her car. Silver Honda Civic, license plate 377 JCM. I assessed the car: smashed grill, tinted windows, broken headlight, and little splotches of red.

The smell of Brody's blood filled my veins with blind rage. I tore past the guys, heading for the apartment complex door. I paused to look at the buttons and speaker, searching the panel for her name. Jennifer Miller—D1. *Floor two, how convenient.* The lobby door required visitors to be buzzed in. I yanked the large wooden door open with ease, busting the metal lock. *Good thing I wasn't the average visitor.*

Reaching the stairwell, I heard stomps behind.

"Goddess, Athena, you broke the fucking door!" Atlas announced like I didn't already know. "What if there are cameras here?"

"There's not—old building. Landlord didn't wanna spend the extra money. I made sure of it when I called Connor," I answered him in a hiss. I was not inept and didn't appreciate being thought of as such.

Kale took me by my shoulders. "Hey, look at me, Thea."

Heat resonated from where his hands touched me. I couldn't look at him, not yet. I jerked out of his hold, my wolf growling at my behavior. I continued up the stairs and into the hallway until I reached D1. The door was ajar. I gave over to my baser instincts, putting my nose in the air, sniffing. A particular stench poured from behind the door.

"Thea!" Kale hollered and stopped in his tracks. His leaf chain was glowing a hot-red, like out of a blacksmith's fire. Anders's and Atlas's chests rumbled, picking up the same scent.

Anders's voice was lower, full of loathing, "One of them is here. We can all smell it."

"I can't smell anything," Brody said, sniffing the air. Sweat beaded his brow. *Fear.* He tried masking it by controlling his breathing, but it was no use. I could sense it on him, rippling like tide pool waves. His heartbeat louder and faster with each step.

"Humans aren't capable of smelling supernaturals," Anders explained, without going into more detail.

Atlas moved to get in front of me, putting his hand at my waist. "Thea, let me go in first."

"That's gallant, but I'm not here for chivalry," I said, looking Atlas straight on, daring him to challenge me. His goal was to protect me, and I loved him for it. But this was on me.

I nudged the door open with my foot. The unpleasant odor amplified as we entered.

Jenny's apartment seemed in order. She had neat, beach-style decor hanging on her walls and a small beige futon in the living room with a modest-sized tv. The kitchen hosted a retro table with paper scribblings on it. I picked up the papers, Kale's name scrawled on them harshly over and over. I tossed the paper, letting it fall to the linoleum flooring. Nothing else out of place, outside the stench giving away what lurked inside. I scanned the open room, noticing the closed bedroom. I heard low, scratching movements from behind it. Jenny yanked open the door, her mouth gaped open, and her eyes went wide at seeing someone in her apartment.

"What are you doing here?" she questioned. Her voice was a twisted mixture of repulsion and alarm.

I tilted my head to the side. "I think you know exactly why I'm here."

"Kale! You're alive! But how?" Jenny squealed, staring at Kale, who stood slightly behind me. "I hit you." Her confession made this all the easier and sparked Kale's rage. He moved past me in a blur.

"Hit me? No, Jenny, you didn't hit me. You hit Brody—almost fucking killed him," he spat at her, his previous concern long gone.

Jenny laughed deliriously. "Oh, how silly. You two look so much alike. I meant to hit you. He said she put a spell on you. That you would love me if I broke it," Jenny rambled.

"Love me? You didn't love me. You loved the fame. You didn't even care when we broke up. You've pulled some shit before, but this isn't you. This is sick," Kale yelled at her, trying to reach Jenny with truth, but someone poisoned her mind —broken it.

"Isn't me? What do you know about me, Kalen? What do you know about *her*? Maybe I don't love you. I wanted you because all the rest of them did, but you left me for her. He told me what she is. She's got you brainwashed!" Jenny pointed a condemning finger at me like she had at Zephyr. I snarled. That finger of hers was going to get her killed. My lip curled up, and I bared my teeth, feeling them inch down.

"When you left... I just wanted to see you again. For you to love me—but no! You let her trick you. We can fix this. I can fix this." Jenny stopped, the hand behind her back, pulling out a serrated kitchen knife. She snarled, lunging at Kale.

I pushed Kale aside, catching Jenny's arm in my hand. "Xercarus lied to you, Jenny. It's what he does. He's a deceiver. He used you to get me." I felt her bone break beneath my grip as she struggled against me, screaming and still trying to get at Kale.

Anders looked at me, his face contorted in dismay. "That bastard. He infected Jenny to get to Kale. Xercarus must believe if he kills Kale, he'll weaken you."

Brody's eyes were wide with disbelief as he watched this horror scene unfold. Frightened as he might've been, Brody remained silent and stayed out of the way. For a human, Brody handled himself and fear well, similar to Kale. They had a tolerant nature I didn't understand—either that or a death wish.

Jenny laughed again, and her eyes faded to black. This time, something distorted her voice; an insidious, deep rasp came from her lips. "Ah, Athena. My, aren't you pretty? Such a divine creature. Why do you protect these useless sacks of flesh? So fragile, so simple. Together you and I can create a world where humans crawl at our feet. You don't belong among mortals. You're a God, like me. Come. Come join me, Athena."

My lips curled up in the snarl, and my hands sizzled. "Think you're clever, do you? Taking the body of a young woman? You're no God. You're a coward! A demon thief, who skulks in shadows," I shouted at him, my eyes casting off flecks of green. I bit my tongue. I shouldn't taunt him, but fire rallied in my chest, urging me on.

"You dare call me a coward? You're a dog to humans. If you won't join me, you'll bow before me after I kill your precious mate, just like your father. I'll destroy everyone you love, one by one, until you have nothing to live for. Then you'll make me an army this world has never seen!" Xercarus boomed from Jenny's slight frame. Her skin cracked, oozing black mucus under the pressure.

I chuckled, letting my fingertips ignite, "I. Will. Never. Bow. To. You." I lifted my hands, concentrating on Xercarus inside her. I felt a surge of fire radiate into my limbs, begging to push him out. "Infernum Mortem."

Jenny's body flew backward; her body slammed with hot flames and blue sparks that sent her careening into the wall. Drywall crumbled, white and gray chunks hitting the floor and covering Jenny. I'd meant to force Xercarus out of her body, expel him from her spirit. Instead, she lay crumpled up, appearing lifeless.

"Holy shit!" Brody yelled, tripping over his own feet and falling over into a chair near the futon. "What was that? Is she dead?" Nobody answered Brody.

"*Shh*," I hissed.

I listened hard, trying to pick up her heartbeat. *Thump, thump, thump.* There it was, a faint rhythmic beat. Anders ran to Jenny, tossing caution aside. I reared my hand back, a fireball manifesting, ready to flame anything daring to touch Anders. Anders placed his hand on Jenny's head, trying to repair the damage I'd done.

Glancing up to me in awe, Anders his mouth gaped. "You did it, Athena. He's gone from her. In all the books, no one has ever released someone from Xercarus's hold."

Anders picked Jenny's limp body from the floor, pushing open her bedroom door and carrying her to her small bed. He kept her in a sleeping state as he finished clearing the unpleasant memories. While he worked his magic, I called Connor, giving him all the details. He'd make her car 'disappear' and have it reported as stolen. Jenny would have a new vehicle within a week. Within an hour, all the unsightly would disappear. All as Jenny slumbered, sleeping off this ordeal. She'd wake with no recollection of what she'd done under Xercarus's possession.

Kale reached for me. I tugged away, going to sit by Jenny's side on her bed.

"I know you can't hear me. I wanna say this shouldn't have happened to you. I was angry with you, thinking you'd done it out of spite. I intended to hurt you, Jenny, but I'm going to make sure he can't do this to you again." I kissed my fingertips, putting them on her forehead.

"Praesidium."

A small white crescent moon remained on her forehead, staying on her skin for a moment, fading until it vanished. I hoped the spell was enough to protect her from invasion again. I got off the bed, Kale approaching me. I went to evade him. Once he touched me, I knew my resolve would give way, and the determination to keep him at a distance would dissipate.

"Thea. Why are you avoiding me?" he snapped, catching on to what I'd been doing.

Atlas and Anders went to take a seat by Brody, ready to watch the fireworks. They wanted front-row seats to the show, but far enough out of my reach.

"I understand you're busy, but dammit! I had to text Anders just to see if you were okay. I respect that you have responsibilities, you know that. But this clearly isn't about your obligations. You're avoiding me, and I deserve to know why." Kale raised his voice, his narrowed eyes searching my face.

I met his eyes, captivating azure blue to my untamed green. I couldn't deceive him, not face to face like this. Kale was learning to read me like a book. He'd learned my body language over the weeks, understanding all the things I wasn't saying.

"I'm... avoiding you. The farther you are from me, the better. You'll be safer this way."

Kale snorted, pinching the bridge of his nose. "Keep me away. That's your solution? Is that supposed to be some kinda joke?"

My temper flared, and I threw my arms to my sides. "It's not a fucking joke. Nothing is. Is it so hard for you to see? Ever since I came into your life, I put you in danger time after time. I changed you. You're not even human anymore! I'm the reason Brody almost died, Kale. I was going to kill Jenny, and *oh*, Goddess, I wanted to, like really wanted to."

My heart hammered in my chest. "I'm—I'm the reason my father is dead. Me. That's all on me." My body trembled. "So, you stand here, asking me why I'm avoiding you? Because everything I seem to get close to goes to absolute shit. I'd run from my own brothers if I could. I don't wanna lose them, and I can't lose you. I just can't."

Kale stood still, watching my every twitch from a distance while I blurted the entire contents of my mind. Brody took a seat on the futon and rubbed his knees, likely waiting for an explosion of some sort. Anders and Atlas looked back and forth between each other, their pupils dilated.

My eyes crinkled, and I tilted my head downward. "What if something happens to you and Xercarus is right? Stay away from me, Kalen, just walk away. I'll find a way to cure you. You can live a normal life. One without demons and death." The last part of my speech tumbled from my lips, stabbing me in the chest as it did. My eye moistened, and I blinked away tears.

Shaking his head, Kale closed the distance between us, taking my face into his hands. "A normal life? What you're talking about is a life without you. You don't get to do this, Thea. That's not how any of this works. You don't get to change me so thoroughly, and just, just—leave."

Kale rubbed his thumb across my bottom lip like he often did. I inhaled deeply, and so did he. Our connection never dulled, always as grand as the first time.

"You don't get to light my life on fire, then try to keep me in the dark. I'll make you a deal. If you tell me right now that I'm not who you want, that you don't love me—I'll walk away, but not before I make this very clear. None of those things were your fault. Not your dad, not Brody, not Jenny. So, I'm gonna need you to say it, Athena. Tell me you don't love me."

Kale didn't blink. He gazed into my eyes, opening a window to my soul. Part of me reached out to touch Kale, knowing he was exactly what I wanted. "You know I can't say that. Because I do love you. I think I might've from the moment you didn't run."

Kale smiled, his lips and hands twitched. "Settled then. I was going to do this at the Solstice, but I don't think it'll ever be the right time." He backed up, rooting around in the right pocket of his jeans. He pulled out a small turquoise box.

"This is one of the errands Brody and I went on. If you don't like it, I'll get you any one you want." Kale paused, and in the middle of Jenny's living room, he opened the box with a click, displaying a brilliant emerald cut rose gold ring. It might have been the most magnificent piece of jewelry I'd ever laid my eyes on, or maybe it was the person holding it.

Like most human women before me, my hands clasped around my mouth. My blood thrummed in my ears. "Is that an engagement ring?"

"Yes, and no. It's more like a promise. I know we're mates, and this is trivial in your world, but it's time the human one understands I'm no longer on the market. Did you want the speech I rehearsed, or should we call it good?"

I almost laughed. "There's a speech?"

Kale grinned. "I'm nothing if not thorough." He cleared his throat. "Athena, from the moment I saw you, and every second since, I've wanted to spend whatever time I have in this life by your side—I vow to love you, in every way I can, to accept and have you in all forms. I'll remind you of your strength when you doubt it, lift you up when you're down. I promise to be your biggest supporter. And most of all, I promise to never watch an episode of Stranger Things without you."

I had no words. Kale saw me—*all* of me, and yet, he wanted to stay. This seemed far more intimate than I imagined. If we weren't already fated together a semi-proposal or *promise*, as Kale had put it, this would seem like too much. But what was a little marriage between mates?

CHAPTER 21

$\mathcal{K}$ale slipped the ring on my finger. It fit perfectly. All I heard were hoots and hollers. Brody scooped me up before Kale could. Excitement replaced his previous fear, and he had a tear in the corner of his eye.

As usual, our moment was cut short. The front door pushed open, and Connor and his team came in. Connor's face was all business as he headed straight for me, his team surveying the room and categorizing everything. Two guys started taking down the damaged drywall, while two others carried in a new piece.

"Trouble follows where you lead, huh, Athena?" Connor said, smirking at me in good humor, then set his gaze on Brody. "Another new guy. Interesting. Are you going to introduce us?"

"Yes, seems I've misplaced my manners. This is Kale's brother, Dr. Brody Ryan. Brody, this is Agent Connor. Connor handles the human end of this operation."

Connor extended his calloused hand, examining Brody with a dutiful eye. "Nice to meet you, Brody. Welcome to the circus," he joked, causing me to shake my head.

"I always liked the circus as a kid. Here's hoping I can teach Kale to jump through a hoop and juggle." Brody side-eyed Kale with a nervous smirk that ended with Kale punching Brody in the arm.

"Not a chance," Kale laughed.

Connor put his hands into his pockets, looking more solemn. "Well, we got her car loaded up; paperwork is all filed on our end. When she calls in, it should be just fine. She'll get the car replaced. Do me a favor, though, will ya? Try not to let any more humans you know get run down by cars," said Connor, putting a dry grin on his aged face.

"Will do." I offered a salute and headed for the door. "We good here?"

"Yeah, we're good. You let me know if you get any more on this Xercarus guy. He's shaping up to be a huge thorn in my side. I don't like it one bit."

Walking away to confer with another agent, Connor turned on his heels. "Oh, wait. Tell Logan I say hi, will ya? I'd like to take him to lunch sometime. Guess he snagged some clothes from one of our vans."

"I'll let him know." I nodded to Connor. *Logan, you sly wolf, stealing clothes from the Feds.*

Before leaving, Anders wandered back into Jenny's room. He put his hand to her forehead and then joined us a moment later.

"Wanted to make sure she stays out longer," he said while making his way out the apartment door.

I messaged our pilot, making sure he was ready to meet us. Upon putting my hand back in my pocket, it got caught on the newly present, sparkling diamond ring. I gazed at it one more time. I'd never been one to care about expensive jewelry. This ring symbolized more than what Kale had spent on it. It meant we were going to get married at some point, in a human setting.

"Don't go getting lost in that head, again. Come here," Kale said, gripping me by the waist. He put the front-facing camera on his phone. "Take a picture with me. I realized I had no pictures of you or us. I wanna be able to see that beautiful face of yours anytime we're apart."

I obliged his request, smiling and bringing my face closer to his as we paused on the sidewalk. Grasping my hand, he pulled it up, holding it in front of us. He gave me a kiss on the cheek, catching me by surprise, and snapping another picture as he did.

"That's perfect. That one is going to my mom," he said, his grin never fading. "I don't use socials much anymore, but you're going on Instagram—unless it's against the rules."

"No rules against responsible social media use. Share away."

Kale clicked away on his phone, posting our photo. "There. Now all my followers will know we're together."

I rolled my eyes and laughed. "Ah, does this mean I get to be head of the Kalen Ryan fan club, then?"

"Definitely. I'll get you a special pin." Another grin spread across his lips, and I nudged him with my elbow.

"Very funny."

Kale kept texting on his phone, glancing up at me momentarily while we made our way back to the helicopter. Brody was chatting with Atlas and Anders. Smoothing my hair reflexively, I felt my phone vibrate. Kale had sent me the photo he'd taken. I opened his message, pulling up the photo into a larger view. I looked at it, Kale's lips on my cheek. His eyes creased at the corners, holding a hint of a smile. He looked truly happy. My expression mirrored Kale's. Even caught off guard, sheer delight emanated from my entire appearance.

"Did I hear you say you're sending that to your mom? She knows about us?" I asked, not realizing his mother was aware I existed.

What would his parents think of a woman they'd never met having a rock this size on her finger? Maybe they'd hate me, which seemed fair enough considering what I continued to put

Kale through. I knew it wouldn't change mine or Kale's mind. Still, I wanted them to know how much I cared for Kale. I'd won Brody over easily enough. Then again, I'd also helped almost kill him and introduced him to a girl possessed by a demon. I wasn't exactly shaping up to be the best sister-in-law.

Tucking his phone away, Kale took me into his arms. "Yes, she knows about us. I told her a couple days ago. Truth be told, she's a little disappointed about not having met you yet. Wait, I have an idea. Come with me tonight?"

"Come where?"

"Dinner at my parents' house. After this spectacle, I was gonna cancel to go home with you, but this is so much better, say you'll come. Brody can drive us—they only live, like thirty minutes outside of the city." Kale rushed his words, waiting for my response. I noticed his eyes sag a bit, thinking I might decline.

I didn't need time to think. "The timing isn't the best. I still have—"

"Thea, you're always going to have some life-threatening scenario you need to save the world from, but we're allowed to have a life along the way. Otherwise, what's the point of all this?"

It was hard to argue when he put it like that. "Goddess, I hope not, but you win. I'll come, as long as it's not any trouble for your parents." Guilt pitted in my stomach over putting off my responsibilities again.

I wanted to meet his family, see where he'd grown up. So much of his life before me was unknown, besides what he'd told me and what was available on the internet from his tour days. This was a chance to gain more insight into my future *fiancé*—such a funny word. Wolves didn't use the term. We were old-fashioned. The thought made me shake my head.

Hmm, fiancé...

Kale gave an energized leap into the air, unable to contain

his exhilaration. "Yes! Oh God, no, they won't mind at all. My mom literally lives to cook. Meeting you is a bonus." Kale whistled, trying to get our brothers' attention, "Atlas, Anders—you up for dinner at my parents?"

The guys jointly looked at Kale. I could tell Anders and Atlas appreciated the invitation. They'd grown close over the days we'd spent together.

"I could eat," Atlas replied.

Anders shrugged. "Sure, just don't expect Atlas to be a gentleman."

Kale chuckled. "I wouldn't ask for the impossible." He took out his phone. I assumed to share the good news with his mom.

Brody pushed his hands through his hair, reminding me again of Kale. "How am I supposed to fit these two in the back of the Equinox?" he asked, looking my two larger brothers up and down. "We left the Challenger at my house."

"Don't worry about it; I can have a car here for us in ten minutes. Let me just make a few calls—get our plans changed, and Logan on the helicopter back home." I dialed up our car service.

Kale raised his brows, ready to interrogate me, but waited until I got off the phone.

"Where's Logan? I haven't seen him," Kale quizzed me, folding his arms across his chest.

I smirked, fawning naivety. "Full disclosure? He's been with you the entire time. Monitoring you."

Kale scoffed. "You've had Logan babysitting me?"

I paused before answering. I had expected Kale getting upset with me for having Logan trailing after him. I linked Logan, freeing him of his scouting, and gave instructions to get home. Kale kept his eyes trained on me, awaiting a response.

"Yes, I suppose I did, if that's how you want to put it, but—"

Kale exhaled louder than necessary, cutting me off. "I'm not angry, not about that. I might do the same thing in your position. I just want you to tell me things, talk to me. When you're scared, upset, all of it. I'm here for you, even the parts you think are messy. I want those, too." He brushed stray hairs from my ponytail off my face and kissed my lips. Again, my body bowed to his, as it had every single time he touched me.

"*Mm.*" Kale pulled away, his eyes staying closed. "That never gets old."

Atlas and Anders stood staring at the phone screens, sending what looked to be several text messages.

The vehicle I ordered would be here any minute. Kale sent Brody off ahead of us, opting to ride with me. Gazing at him and then at the ring on my finger, I never imagined I'd use the term husband. I let the word settle in my brain. Kale was going to be my husband, and for the life of me, I couldn't figure out why that term seemed more significant than *"mate."* A husband you could divorce—a mate, not so much. Yet to me, *"husband"* implied a critical step forward. Were we ready for another leap forward? A white Suburban with tinted windows pulled up against the curb in front of us, disturbing my train of thought.

Kale opened the passenger door. "Your chariot awaits," he said, adding a cheeky wink.

CHAPTER 22

The fast-paced city morphed into a calm suburbia. Tall palm trees lined the cul de sacs we passed. Children played outside. Their giggles and bicycles brought the manicured sidewalks to life. Kale told me about where his parents lived in Cheviot Hills. I learned they'd purchased their home before Kale was born, and they had moved in while his mother was pregnant with him.

Like any family, they'd wanted a pleasant neighborhood to raise their sons. Kale shared his parents had the house remodeled last year and how his mom was a huge Joanna Gaines fan. Never having designed or remodeled anything, I was unsure of what that all meant or who Joanna Gaines was. A fast search on my friend Google, and I understood HGTV had found a gold mine.

I heard a phone camera click; Kale snapped another photo of me. I rolled my eyes while continuing to read.

"What was that for?" I asked him, still staring at my phone, engrossed in learning about shiplap and crown molding.

Kale was chuckling again and rubbing his forehead. "My mom will never believe you didn't know who Joanna Gaines was. This is photographic proof—you Googling the home renovation mogul."

"Ha ha. Glad I can amuse you," I retorted, laughing along with him.

Kale reached out his hand, beckoning me to give him mine. He stroked each of my knuckles, then gently tugged on my ring finger. The tug reached all the way to my heart, and I knew it belonged to him, now and forever. I watched him stare down at the diamond. Even in dim lighting, it shimmered. Kale possessed excellent taste. He'd selected a timeless piece of jewelry. I'd have worn it if he'd given me a ring pop, though this sparkler was a welcomed addition. It reminded me of Kale's eyes, clear and brilliant.

Our car slowed, indicating we'd reached our destination. The driver put the Suburban in park right behind Brody's car. The outside of the Ryan family home was Cape Cod style and quaint for its larger size. The gray shingles matched well with the blue shutters, inviting you in. They had a small front porch, garnished with cream-colored Asiatic lilies and the pale pink peonies Kale had mentioned before. More tall palm trees and well-maintained shrubbery shaded the walkway.

"Ready?" Kale asked. I nodded.

Anders and Atlas waited at the front of the walkway for us, Atlas smoothing his shaggy blonde hair while Anders adjusted his V-neck knit pullover.

I told the driver he was free to do as he pleased. I'd message him when we were ready to leave. He nodded and pulled away, leaving us in front of the house.

"Their house is beautiful."

Kale took my hand and walked us to the front door. At the last minute, I tugged my hair out of the ponytail, shaking my head a bit and letting it fall loosely past my shoulders.

"Hey, you look gorgeous." Kale pressed a quick kiss to my

temple. Being with Kale had opened me up to a vast array of emotions, most unexpected.

Atlas and Anders followed close behind, keeping their banter to themselves as we made our way up the paved walkway. Little solar lights lined the path, casting small shadows. Reaching the large blue door, Kale opened it without knocking. I instantly smelled the aromas of their home: magnolia candles, rosemary, the seasoned grill going out back, and lavender. I smiled at the last scent.

"We're here!" Kale shouted from the entry as Anders closed the door behind us. I already heard footsteps coming in our direction. One gait I recognized belonged to Brody. The other was much softer, belonging to Mrs. Ryan.

A slender, graying woman rounded the corner into the foyer. Highlighted blond hair framed her eyes. She dusted her hands on a pink, flowered apron tied neatly around her slender waist. Smiling tenderly at Kale, then me, she quickened her pace toward us.

"Kalen, honey," she sighed out. "You must be Athena! Gosh, you're even lovelier than your picture. Please, come on in! Come in. Let me see you all." Warmth overflowed in her tone. "I'm a hugger, hope you don't mind." Mrs. Ryan grabbed Kale's face, embracing him. "I'm so happy for you. Now, let me hug my future daughter-in-law." She paused in front of me with open arms. I accepted her embrace. She felt as warm as she had sounded, full of life and kindness which radiated from her.

Mrs. Ryan pulled back, still holding onto me, and I saw the tears glistening in her eyes. "It's so good to meet you, Athena. Please pardon my son's manners for not having brought you by sooner. He's always been secretive about his relationships, but my, I've never seen Kale this excited and happy. I suppose I have you to thank for that." She used her apron to dry both eyes, then leaned back in to hug me again.

"I'm really pleased to meet you as well, Mrs. Ryan. Thank

you for having us all here on such short notice," I said, a genuine smile glued to my face.

Mrs. Ryan fanned her face. "Nonsense! It's no trouble at all. It thrilled me when Kale said you'd all be coming by tonight. And don't you dare 'Mrs. Ryan' me. Please call me Linda. I hear we're going to be family, darling." She winked like she'd just told me a secret. "I whipped up some cookies and got a pie in the oven before you arrived." Her eyes drifted behind Kale and me and landed on Anders and Atlas.

"*Oh*, heavens, these must be your brothers. Okay, who is who?"

Atlas stepped forward around me first. "Atlas Whiteridge. A pleasure to meet you, Mrs. Ryan." Linda reached to hug my brother, who was nearly double her size.

"Not you, too. It's Linda," she said, smiling and giving his arm a pat. "Your parents must've had their hands full with triplets, is it?

Anders came up front, introducing himself as well. "Anders," he said, leaning into Linda's open arms. "Triplets weren't enough, though. We have another brother, Lincoln. He's at home."

Linda gave a kind grin as she released Anders. "My, what a nice, big family. You'll have to bring Lincoln next time. We'd love to meet him."

When our introductions were over, we headed to the kitchen. I looked at all the greenery and rustic décor. Photos, along with hand-drawn pictures, were staggered on the light-painted shiplap walls. Kale's family home was open and bright. White bookcases framed their tv, filled with dozens of books and various potted aloe plants. The home had lots of greenery and flowers nestled in corners, giving their house a welcoming vibe. From the living room ceiling hung a modern wire and wooden chandelier, giving the room a soft glow that could make the most uneven of skin tones look flawless. Off to the left, through a wide sliding barn door, there was a black piano with a small bench.

I imagined Kale sitting at it, playing as a young boy. The picture collage on the wall behind the piano captured my attention the most. There were so many. I glimpsed one of Kale in his cap and gown, Brody's arm draped over his shoulder. There was another of Brody walking across a stage, a family photo on the beach, Kale holding a fish... So many of their memories covered this wall and shelves.

This was a home of uncomplicated love, of a family. I felt a pang in my chest, letting my mind pull me down another path. If Kale and I ever had children—what kind of life would they have? I wanted to give our hypothetical children a life of simple pleasures and memories, but that was beyond my control and not possible in the Unseen.

"Athena," Kale called my name, jerking me from my roaming thoughts. Summoning me closer to his side, he placed his hand on my lower back.

A smile took over my face again upon seeing Kale's father entering through the glass patio door. He had barbeque tongs in his hand, clicking them together like castanets and dancing to the upbeat music coming from outside on the deck. I had to hand it to the man—he had rhythm as he swayed into the room. He was of average height, shorter than his sons by a few inches. His hair was the color of both Kale's and Brody's except for the graying at his temples. Fine and deeper lines shone on by his eyes and mouth, the only real things giving away his age.

Putting his tongs down, Kale's dad continued to dance his way over, "My boy! Get over here and let me meet my new daughter-in-law."

"Dad. Nice." Kale said, smirking. Kale hugged his dad, clapping his back.

"Athena. Good to meet you. I'm Jonathon, this guy's dad. You be sure to give Kalen hell, alright?" He opened his arms, just as his wife had, pulling me into a snug embrace. "Good to have you, Athena. Kalen looks, well, he looks really good. I hope you know that."

"Jonathon, watch your mouth. We have company. Don't scare the poor girl away," Linda said, shooting her husband a mock glare.

Jonathon chuckled, similar to Brody. "Hate to break it to you, dear; they've heard and said much worse." He replied to his wife, grinning while he re-tied the strings on his cliche "Kiss the Cook" apron.

"You gotta be Athena's brothers. Glad to have you, boys. The more, the merrier we always say at the Ryan house." His tone was jovial and welcoming. Jonathan was clearly a man of generosity, not unlike his wife. Kale and Brody made more sense to me now, seeing the home and the people they'd grown up with. The kindness. The understanding—it all fit like puzzle pieces. My body warmed with content.

Brody slid open the patio door. "Let's take this party outside, shall we? It's beautiful out. Mom, I grabbed a couple bottles of Merlot. Is that alright?"

"Brody, you know you never have to ask about food or drinks in this house. Take whatever," Linda was beaming, in her element, her stove and oven going with both her sons home.

Jonathon made his way over to my brothers, shaking their hands and saying again how good it was to meet them. Kale snaked his arm around my waist, and a shiver moved up my spine from his unexpected touch. I stared at Kale again, taking in all his features as if they were brand new. Everyone told me how happy he was, but I was seeing it for myself. Every feature on Kale was lit up, giving off an almost tangible bliss. His dimples were on full display, and his eyes looked brighter and more energetic.

I realized this was his home, but he was mine, a place where

I felt safe and comfortable. Wherever he was, I'd find peace, and we'd build a full life together. He was the simple pleasure I wanted. I let inner guilt and panic drift away, not feeling the need to clutch onto it when there was much to enjoy at present.

I overheard Jonathon joking about how having two brothers would make me overqualified to tolerate Kale and Brody's crap. Kale chatted at his mom, touching her shoulder, as we all made our way outside per Brody's suggestion.

Their backyard was stunning. A giant pergola draped with vines and Edison bulb lights stood above our heads. They decorated the deck with more plants and a few lemon trees. Kale led us to a sandy-colored cushioned sectional to sit. Brody turned up the gas firepit, igniting the rocks with higher flames.

Linda had gone back in, returning with stemless wine glasses, while Jonathon took the corkscrew and opened the bottles. I could smell the deep undertones in the wine, rich and dark. Kale took my hand, looking at me, then kissed my temple. "Thank you for coming tonight," he whispered to me.

I mouthed, *"You're welcome,"* back to Kale, squeezing his hand in mine.

We both heard Linda sniffle. "Aw, now don't do that. You'll have me in tears all over again," she said, dabbing her eyes once more.

The night moved along at a relaxing pace. The food was delicious. Jonathon did wonders on the grill, cooking filet mignons to medium-rare perfection and roasting asparagus and zucchini until it melted in my mouth with its garlic butter and lemon deliciousness. Linda's raspberry pie tantalizingly combined sweet and tart, and Anders and Atlas both had a second piece. We ate and drank wine, laughing, often at one another's jokes.

His parents asked all the standard questions: What did I do for a living, how did we meet, had we given any thought to where and when we wanted to get married? It was the last set of questions that left me stumped and with my stomach in knots. I didn't know where I wanted to get married or when. The wedding part seemed unimportant, and a venue never occurred to me—nor did a precise timeline. When I failed to offer ideas, Linda was quick to add there was no need to rush and changed the subject.

Thank the Goddess for small miracles.

Sipping my wine, I let Kale do the talking for a while and let my mind wander. For wolves, we always held union ceremonies near a Solstice or Equinox to ensure good fortune and health. And always in three parts over two days: Gratia, Fiducia, and Coniux. Each part signified the most important foundations of a relationship: love and trust. I learned from shows and traveling past the Barrier how humans handled weddings. The thought of launching into full-scale wedding planning made me queasy, and I adjusted in my seat. I hadn't the foggiest idea how to be a bride and no real desire to plan such an extravagant event. I drank my wine faster, emptying the glass.

Kale rubbed my back, detecting my prickly thoughts.

Anders and Atlas explained how we worked at our family investment company, which wasn't a lie. We did, in fact, operate Lakeview Investments in place of my father.

Kale's dad grinned widely and patted Anders on the back. "It's nice to see kids staying in their family business," he told us.

Kale reached for the wine, refilling my empty glass. "Are you trying to get me drunk?" I teased.

He smirked. "Me? Never. Besides, I know better. It wouldn't work." He lowered his voice, putting his mouth to my ear. "Also, if you're implying that I'd need to get you drunk to get you in my bed, I know from experience that's unnecessary."

I blushed as I sipped my wine, hoping no one else heard him. To my satisfaction, no one had.

Kale set down his wine and stretched. "I'm going to give

Athena a tour of the house real quick, show her my old trophies." Kale stood up, offering his hand to me.

Trophies, my ass, Atlas laughed in my head.

I glared at him for a moment, then put a casual smile back on my lips.

Brody, Atlas, and Anders all continue to snicker like children. "Stop that now, boys, they're adults, and so are you," Linda chastised them, laughing as she did. "You show Athena the house, honey. I want this to feel like a second home."

Kale led me by the hand back into the house, and, again, the sweet smell of magnolias filled my nose. We reached a white and brown staircase. I stopped, running my fingers on a picture of Kale playing the piano. He must have been a teenager in the photograph; his build was leaner, but he had changed little.

"Second door on the right is mine," he said, letting me walk up the stairs, which were lined with more photographs.

"And what will I find in there?" I asked, pretending to be coy.

"A bed," he answered his tone lower and more seductive this time.

He leaned forward, opening the door. Shelves of music books and young adult fiction grabbed my attention. Catching sight of the book *Eragon*, I smiled to myself.

So, he always fancied dragons...

Neat stacks of sheet music covered various surfaces along with tattered, old notebooks—no doubt full of song lyrics. His walls were a light blue with concert tickets, pictures, and show pamphlets pinned to one wall like a collage.

I touched a ticket stub, so faded you could barely see the writing. Here lay all these pieces of Kale's youth, put on display for me to see, giving me a glimpse farther into his childhood.

I grazed my hand on an empty guitar stand and then a

small wooden desk with trophies. At the back of his room, a bed, as promised.

I stared at it, thinking about the things I could do to him right there, and then Kale took my hips in his hands, turning me about and gazing at my eyes, then my lips.

"I've wanted you alone since I put that ring on your finger," he moved his hands to grasp my face. "Kiss me?" he asked, his voice low, riddled with longing.

I lifted my chin to do as he asked, kissing him. It started gentle and sweet, digressing into something frenzied and raw.

I pulled back from him. "Is this part of the tour?"

Kale's eyes shimmered. "Only if you want it to be."

"What if someone hears us?"

"Does it really matter?"

I shook my head "no," letting my lips turn up into a smile as I placed them back on his full mouth. Kale let his hands wander to my bottom. He curved them around my backside and held me closer to him while pushing us until the backs of my knees hit his bed. We tumbled down, landing on his soft queen-size mattress. Kale nestled between my thighs, caressing my leg until it hitched higher on his waist. I arched against him, hard enough to make Kale groan my name.

Kale's breathing was heavy like mine. "I know we can't, but, god, I want to. If there are condoms in here, they're at least five years old and useless."

I exhaled, picking myself up, breathy, I whispered in Kale's ear. "We don't need one."

Kale moved his head, his eyebrows shot up above his wide eyes. "Thea, yeah, we do. We're not risking—"

I put my finger to his lips, trying to extinguish his fear. "Shh. I got a shot. Dr. Birch said it's effective right away."

"I just wanna do everything right with you." He pressed his forehead to mine, exhaling a cool breath.

"You are," I replied, not taking my eyes off him.

I touched his chin, then stroked up his cheek. Kale let his inhibitions go, placing his lips on mine again, then trailing them down my neck. He rose to his knees, taking one of my feet into his hands, removing my shoe, and tossing aside. He repeated the action with my other leg. Leaning back down to me, Kale tucked his finger beneath the waistband of my dark Lululemons, tugging down. Feeling him, I arched up, letting him pull them off. Kale bent to kiss my navel, licking at the dips on each hip. He tugged his blue shirt off over his head, dropping it to the floor, and undid his pants, lowering them to reveal all of himself to me. I swiveled my hips in readiness. Kale pulled at my shirt, revealing as much of my torso and chest as he could.

His mind flooded into mine. *I want to feel as much of your skin as possible.*

I leaned up again, kissing his chest, directly over his heart, and let my worlds move from my thoughts to his.

Você me completa.

"Tell me what that means again," he said while brushing my bottom lip with his thumb, his chain dangling above me like a silver star.

I used my voice this time. "You make me feel complete."

Kale closed his eyes, his thick lashes almost touching his cheeks. A sly grin took over his lips, and breathing intensified, like the amber growing in his irises. "I don't think I'll last long." He opened his eyes, looking at my mouth then back up to my eyes. His face held concern and lust simultaneously, each one rivaling the other for dominance.

I touched him, coaxing him onward.

He parted his lips to kiss me again, using his free hand to adjust himself. Kale eased himself into me, and I let out a gasp. The fullness was satisfying, as it had been the times before, yet different, almost like feeling more of him. Kale closed his eyes for a moment, reopening them to reveal his glowing gold irises. Kale moved, and I met his thrusts, feeling glorious sensations building inside. My emotions knotted low in my stomach. He reached for my hands, removing them from their hold on his back, and held them in his. The chain I'd given him dangled above me, grazing my cleavage as he shifted. The metal was warm from being near his skin and mine.

I met Kale's amber gaze. *Mark me.*

Kale stilled, his wolf hearing my plea. A soft but possessive growl rumbled up. Kale's eyes flashed brighter.

"I don't wanna hurt you," he murmured, his mouth descending closer to the sweet spot on my neck.

I grabbed his face to look at mine. "You won't. I promise." My heart fluttered faster with anticipation.

Kale needed little convincing, and his wolf required none. He moved his hips faster into me, finding a sublime rhythm. Matching his pace, I tightened beneath him. I watched his canines extend only slightly. I turned my neck, baring more of myself to him. Kale bent his head to me, placing a whisper of a kiss first, then I felt his lips part. His pointed teeth sunk deep into the place between my neck and shoulders. My eyes closed, dashing open to reveal my vibrant green.

The rest blurred together in a churning fury of desires and emotions as I tumbled into each sensation. Even rushed, the pleasure of being intimate with Kale had no equal, each touch running the gamut between hot and tender.

Kale collected our scattered clothing from the wood-paneled floor. After partially dressing, he wandered off to a bathroom across the hall, bringing me a warm washcloth to help us both cleanup. Then he led me to the mirror, where I attempted to straighten my hair, knowing it didn't matter. My cheeks were a sweet pink, my lips reddened. We could fool everyone else, but my brothers would know what we'd been up to. I frowned, then let it pass. I'd suffered similarly from their antics with their many counterparts. I would not let myself regret any more moments I had with Kale.

"Was it... I mean, did you enjoy it, like I did before?" Kale asked, using his fingers to tug my black shirt aside a bit, and found the bite already faded.

"Feels like every part of me is connected to you. It's intense." I flushed as I answered, my eyes flitting down. "We better get back."

Kale took my hand, pulling me to him again. He brought my knuckles to his lips, kissing them then kissing my cheek. "You know, every day since I've met you keeps topping the last for my best night. And yeah, we definitely better head down," he replied, trying to suppress his own flushing face.

As we headed back downstairs, Kale grabbed two photo albums from a shelf of a brown bookcase. Making his way to the kitchen, Kale tucked the albums under his arm and opened the built-in counter chiller for another bottle of wine to take outside.

I meandered over to the piano, touching a key with my index finger. It pinged, the note ringing in tune. I admired how meticulously crafted the wood was, running my hand along the smooth top. Kale must have been watching me, and I heard him set the albums and wine on the counter. He walked over, then stood behind me, placing his hand on the small of my back.

"Do you play?"

"Only a little, if you count 'Twinkle, Twinkle, Little Star.' I had a few lessons when I was nine, but my father sent my tutor to a different territory, and I never had another."

"So, there *is* something you can't do." Kale grinned like a Cheshire cat, his dimples consuming his cheeks. "Well, I can be your tutor now. We can teach each other as we go." He nudged us onto the bench and began playing 'Fur Elise.' His long, able fingers moved along the keys in nimble movements. It was an enchanting melody. Watching him play, I fell in love with him all over again, each note tethering me to him. Kale's face held a small absentminded smile, one that showed how passionately he loved music.

And then, Brody walked in.

"I thought I heard you playing. Here I was, on the hunt for another bottle, and you have it. Come on, Beethoven, bring your ass back outside. Or at least Athena's. Mom totally adores her. After two sons, she's dying for a daughter," Brody chuckled, grabbing the bottle of Merlot Kale had set down.

We got up from the bench, following Brody outside to find Jonathon and Linda dancing along to some older song I'd never heard, both of them smiling and laughing. Atlas glanced at us, smirked, and went back to chatting with Anders.

"There's our lovebirds!" Jonathon announced, grinning from ear to ear.

Linda swung around. "Kalen, you brought our pictures! You know I love looking at our old photos. Oh, that reminds me! Let's take a picture of all of us together. Document the moment. One of you boys has to have a long enough arm to get us all in."

Kale smiled brightly, pulling out his phone. "Anything to make you happy, Mom." We all did as Linda requested, huddling close together, and with some adjusting, all of us fit onto the screen.

"Now everyone say, *family,*' and smile!" Linda said as she hugged onto Brody's lean waist. We snapped the photo, and Kale sent it to his mom's phone. Kale nuzzled my neck, then took a seat at the table.

Linda rushed over, leading me to a table. She flipped through the album slowly, explaining each photo, showing me cousins and other various family members. Several hours passed as I got to know the Ryans more, growing to adore them like I had Kale. They were generous people with a long family tree. Again, I was compelled to think of how I'd altered Kale's life course and what or who we might contribute to their lineage in the future. Kale and I hadn't gone into an in-depth discussion on the matter of children, only that we had zero desire to have them soon.

It was getting late. The moon rose high in the sky, adding an extra twinkle to the lights on the pergola. Brody eyed Kale, mentioning he had to get back to work tomorrow. Linda cleared glasses and put the dark, empty wine bottles in the recycle bin near the corner of the fence as Jonathon made sure his grill was off.

I promised Linda that Kale and I would be back soon, and I meant it. I understood how Kale had become such a good man. His parents raised him with kindness and taught him compassion.

Our car pulled up, as arranged. Kale hugged both his parents goodbye one more time, then led me out by the hand. My brothers had already gotten in the car, settled in the seats. Kale and I climbed in after. I was quiet for a minute, letting tonight wash over me as I twisted the new ring on my finger. It shimmered in the dim moonlight.

At that moment, everything felt—*right*.

CHAPTER 23

*L*incoln was the only one awake when we arrived back home. He was in the living room, TV on, playing Call of Duty. Even with headphones on, Lincoln sensed us come in and turned toward the archway.

"You're back," Lincoln said while hopping up off the couch to greet us. "Did you give it to her?" he asked, waggling his eyebrows and directing his question to Kale.

Kale took my hand and hugged me close, showing a smiling Lincoln the ring on my finger. I couldn't contain the grin on my face. Seemed everyone was in on the surprise but me.

"I did," Kale answered.

Lincoln jumped up in the air, hugging us both. "I've never been to a wedding before." Excitement radiated off him. Lincoln's genuine response gave me an idea.

"Me either. Guess we'll both be in one now," I replied.

Kale offered a half-grin at Lincoln. "If we do finally get around to getting married, this will not be a traditional wedding by any means. I take it there won't be bridesmaids?"

I shook my head. "No, not really. My best friends are my brothers. But I can make them wear dresses if you really want," I laughed.

My eyes wandered over to Atlas and Anders, who had sprawled out on the couches. Their ears perked up as they felt my gaze settle on them.

"*Ha*, real fucking funny, Athena. Don't even try it," Atlas said, glaring at me.

"Fine. But I really hope you two didn't think you were getting out of wearing tuxedos."

Atlas faked a groan, rolling his eyes. "Ah, come on. You know we'll be right next to you. Don't be upset if I outshine you, though, 'cause I look damn good in a tux."

Anders chuckled from the other couch.

"If we do decide to do the big wedding thing. Will you—will you both walk me down the aisle?" I asked, feeling a strange compression in my chest, thinking of our father.

Anders pushed himself up off the couch and scooped me up into his strong arms. "Thea, it would be an absolute privilege to walk you down that aisle." I leaned my head up to hug him tighter.

"Thank you," I whispered.

Atlas gave the tiniest of sniffles behind me, undoubtedly trying to cover up the fact he'd gotten emotional. It was typical of Atlas; his humor and constant jokes were just part of the mask he insisted on wearing. The truth was, Atlas was sensitive and thoughtful. His exterior suggested he was unphased by most anything, but under that—under the bravado—there was a gentle giant.

The noise of the couch sliding on the floor made me let go of Anders. In a second, Atlas had me in his arms. All he did was hug me, his massive body and warmth consuming mine.

Thea, Atlas's voice crept quietly into my mind, *I know we're no replacement for Dad, and I should be more upset. But all we've ever wanted was to see you this happy.*

I responded to his thoughts, *I know.*

Lincoln folded his arms, letting out a small laugh. "Well,

this got super sappy, super-fast. I'm gonna get back to my game." Lincoln plopped back down on the couch, putting his headphones back on.

Kale shook his head. "Kids these days." He curled his arm around my shoulders, pressing another kiss to my cheek.

"Bed?" he asked.

I nodded, saying my goodnights to the boys, who were all invested in video games and fighting over the controllers.

Breakfast the next morning was full of hugging, too much food, and the repeated "oohs" and "ahs" at my ring. It was almost as if Xercarus wasn't threatening our entire existence. I wished it could stay this way, my family locked in this little bubble of joy, but I knew better. Now wasn't the time to be selfish or let down my guard, but I had.

After we finished eating, I excused myself to the office. I had some calls to make and emails to return. Ben had messaged me twice; the outfits for the Solstice were ready, and the tailor would be over this afternoon to fit both Kale and me. Kale had offered to come with me to the office, and we walked in quiet comfort down the hallways to the office. Kale texted on his phone, grinning on and off at the screen.

I took a seat at the desk as I had before. Stretching my hands on it, trying to sense out any traces of my father on it. The room still smelled like him, woodsy and comforting. Taking a deep breath, I started up the computer, jumping right into the emails. Most were condolences—the standard, "I'm sorry for your loss." I read them all, sending polite thank-yous back. I made my way to Oriel Reed's email. He suggested we invite Henri Pelletier and his family to the Winter Solstice. Oriel had done me the "kindness" of sharing the news I'd found my mate, and no union would take place between Henri and me. Oriel apologized once again. I knew it was well-intentioned, but that didn't save me the aggravation.

As expected, the Pelletiers didn't welcome the news, upset

over losing the opportunity to gain rank among the packs on two continents. I'd have to deal with Henri sooner than later, but I'd rather not. Hopefully, he didn't carry a grudge over the ignored texts and calls over the years.

To smooth out my father's blunder, I'd extend an invitation to the Pelletiers as my guests and said I was looking forward to working towards developing an agreement with them.

I sighed, rubbing my temples, knowing this news would trigger a possessive streak in Kale's wolf. Oriel was right, though; I'd need to ensure we maintained a decent relationship with the European packs, especially in this time of transition.

Kale's head popped up from his phone. "What's the matter?" he asked, his mouth turned down on his stubbled face. I chewed my lip, not answering right away. Kale got out of his chair, coming to stand behind me at the desk. "What's going on, Thea? Something wrong?" He placed a gentle touch on my shoulder.

I sucked in a breath, momentarily rendered still by his hand. Every single time he touched me, tiny sparks shivered from the point of contact. Kale's jaw tensed, feeling the same flare of sparks. I gazed up at him, then pushed out of the large rolling chair. I positioned myself in front of Kale, moving him until he was leaning on the desk.

Kale cocked his eyebrow, unsure of what I was doing. "This can't be good if you're trying to proposition me here, on the desk. Can't say I'd tell you no." He exaggeratedly waggled his eyebrows at me.

I chuckled at his immediate dirty thoughts. "*Ha*, no. Though, that's definitely not your worst idea. But no. I just want you in a more relaxed state before I run this by you."

"Something *is* wrong, then?"

"Nothing's wrong. Oriel just made a suggestion. I think it's best we heed his advice. So, in light of there no longer being a union between Henri Pelletier and me, Oriel recommended we invite him and his family to Winter Solstice. You know, try to keep as civil a relationship with them as we can."

I watched Kale's features, morphing from bemused shock to aggravation. "We're having your bullshit arranged marriage *fiancé* over?" He huffed out a breath that bordered on a muffled snarl, putting air quotes around the word fiancé.

"Firstly, you know he was never that, at least not to me. And yes. But there's something else. You wanted me to be honest with you, even the messy stuff." I tipped my chin up to maintain eye contact. "Henri wasn't just an arranged thing. I've slept with him. Only once. Well, technically twice." I swallowed between breaths. "It's the best option, not ideal by any means, but it's imperative we keep our contact with other packs as harmonious and united as possible."

Kale's eyebrows furrowed, pondering what I'd said. "I get it, Athena, I do. The fact you slept with him changes nothing. The idea just doesn't thrill me. Having some guy here, thinking he has some random claim on you because of a sketchy deal Oriel and your Dad thought up."

"Doesn't thrill me either. Then again, it doesn't change my mind. I'm issuing an invitation to the Pelletiers." I stared hard.

Kale raked his hand through his shiny dark brown hair. It fell down against his brows, strands almost grazing his bright blue eyes. "Fine."

"One more thing," I paused, realizing this was likely the hardest part. "We're providing their accommodations—here, with us."

Whipping his head back to full attention, Kale gripped his hands on the desk, digging in, "What? Now you can't be serious?"

I reached for Kale's wrist, rubbing my thumb up and down, trying to soothe him. I used my other hand to pluck his stray hairs from his face. Kale tensed, his jaw clenching. I felt a chill on my fingertips, stretching up my arm where my hand touched Kale. Looking down at our hands, I saw the desk frosting, ice crystals forming.

"Kale, it's…" I hesitated, not wanting to further stir what was inside him.

"Please, Thea. Just give me a minute." Kale's voice trembled low. "I can't. I mean, I'm not in control of myself."

He was struggling, his muscles twitching, trying to suppress the raging voices inside him. Kale's ice spread across the desk, covering the light oak with icy white sheets.

"No. I won't back away," I said, standing my ground. "You won't hurt me. And they won't either. Give me your hand."

Kale met my eyes, his blues taken over by amber. "Thea. Please."

"Trust me. Give me your hand," I said again, feeling fire coiling in my palm.

Kale shook a bit. "What if I freeze you?"

"You won't." I offered my hand for Kale to take. He hesitated again, his eyes darting from side to side, then shakily lifting his hand to take mine. He grabbed my hand, lacing his fingers with mine. As soon as we connected, my eyes snapped to life. Their intensity matched Kale's amber. Our bodies pulsated, vibrating together. The floor shook as our energy bubbled over. I remember a spell I'd come across in the books about the Fire people. I had never used it—until now.

"Ignis et Glacies." My voice took on the low rumbles of the spirits within.

Kale didn't take his eyes off mine. "What's happening?"

"Repeat after me: Ignis et Glacies."

"Ig—Ignis et Glacies," we said together, and Kale's dragon released its booming voice.

Our hands flashed red like fire, and white-hot sparks streamed from our connection. The windows in the room smashed out; the shards shot everywhere, then stilled mid-air. I felt weightless, rising above the floor. The books and artifacts flying off shelves, whipping around us like a protective shield. Magic cocooned in a whirlwind of papers. The smell of old pages and smoke surrounding us swirled in the air like a thick smog.

Atlas, Anders, and Lincoln came barreling into the room, almost taking the door off its hinges. They stopped so quickly they collided with one another, toppling Lincoln over. They stood below us, watching the swirling debris around Kale and me.

"See, you can't hurt me. Together we are two halves of the same piece. Equals," I said, feeling our powers intertwining, feeding off one another, growing larger than even I could comprehend. With Kale's power amplifying mine, I felt stronger than ever before—invincible even.

"We're equals," he said back, taking my other hand, bringing us closer together.

I knew Kale felt our dragons swimming about our minds, mingling together on an ethereal level. The force of their energies binding was an otherworldly phenomenon as they moved throughout our souls, stitching us together. Tawny, cherry-red scales from Kale's dragon chased after my dazzling white ones as if they were dancing. Her wings spread wide, welcoming Kale, the ice to her fire.

Strange that our colors should bear the opposite's element —my frosty lightness to his bright crimson.

A blast whooshed from us, knocking the desk and all its contents over. Kale and I gasped, the influences from inside us breaking loose. Kale pulled me closer, like I was weightless, letting go of my hands to cradle my face. The swirling around us quickened; crackling flashes of light emanated from our explosive link. I glanced down to see Atlas, Anders, and Lincoln pinned to the wall, fighting to move against our expansive energy.

"Subsisto."

All at once, the tornado of glass, books, and ice froze for a second, suspended around us again. Then, as suddenly as it started, the pieces zoomed back into their places. The glass flew back to the window frames—completely unbroken and clear like before. The room settled, neat, and tidy, untouched by the previous cyclone. Kale and I remained, floating together, near the ceiling, a fireball and ice globe orbiting around us. I could see the boys able to move from the wall, gaining their footing. Their faces were wide-eyed with disbelief.

Kale's lips twitched upwards. "That was—that was him, right? This is—you're amazing."

"We're amazing. Do you see now? Together, you and I are a natural harmony. The ability to create chaos and bring balance."

I descended to the floor, feeling the wood beneath my feet. Fiery electricity freely flowed around my body, pushing from my hands into Kale's and back through mine. The odds of Kale randomly being able to transform into the exact opposite of myself was no coincidence. And there was only one way to test my new theory.

"Holy fuck! What kind of shit was that?" Atlas hollered, bouncing towards Kale and me in odd fascination.

Kale didn't take his eyes off me, disregarding their presence. He clung to my hands; an intriguing grin stayed on his face as he observed me as if seeing me for the first time.

I was too excited over my revelation to stay locked in Kale's grasp. "I have an idea!" I said, talking much louder than needed and ignoring Atlas's question. I headed for the door. I needed to get downstairs to the lab.

Anders and Atlas looked at each other and then to Kale and me again. The confusion among them was palpable in seeing their still open mouths. They all clamored to follow me out of the office.

"Thea! Wait up! Where are you going?" Anders hollered, nearly losing his footing trying to keep up with me

"The lab. Hurry up. I need your blood." I didn't bother slowing down. If what I had in mind worked, this was a game-changer.

"What's this about Thea?" Kale asked, joining the inquisition. I heard his pace speeding up.

Not having the patience to wait for the elevator, I tore down several more flights of stairs, taking them three at a time. I felt faster and somehow stronger even without Kale. I made it downstairs in record time. I burst into the lab, loose papers scattering and hitting the tiled floor as I zipped by.

Before they entered the room, I had my arm tied off, the syringe ready. I poked at the bluish vein beneath my skin. The needle found its mark. I pulled back, dark red blood filling the syringe.

"Thea! You don't draw blood like that. Dammit. Be careful." Atlas leaped to me, placing a cotton ball and his fingers on my arm, where the needle had been. The gesture made me want to chuckle. He knew, as well as I did, I'd heal. I grinned, still on an energy high. I admired my brother's proactive thinking. Anders might have the power to heal, but Atlas would've made a fine doctor, his reflexes and passion for knowledge. He had to mend a body the old-fashioned way, with no supernatural help. I thought after all this, Atlas should pursue a career in medicine if he improved his bedside manner.

"Give me that," Atlas raised his voice, replacing my hands with his on my other arm.

Anders stood back, grabbing Kale's shoulder to keep him from rushing in. I saw Kale's chest heaving up and down quickly. Lincoln took a seat on a sofa, his eyes moving around the room. He picked up a medical journal magazine off the coffee table, fiddling with the pages. His nerves were still a mess, not yet settled from his own vampiric transformation or the in-home hurricane he'd just witnessed.

"Alright, Thea. We're gonna need some explanations here." Anders kept his tone as mellow as he could muster, fluffing his hair.

My eyes darted to Kale, then Anders. My thoughts were racing and hard to nail down, too amped up from our dragons merging. I let out a slow breath, attempting to bring myself back down.

I rushed to get up, pacing as I talked. "I don't think I can make just anyone a dragon. I can't explain to you what Kale and I experienced; it's everything. Okay, lemme—I think I was able to change Kale because he's my mate. After marking and giving him my blood, he became my perfect opposite. Ice to my fire, right?"

I concentrated my gaze on Kale as I spoke, "We can create balance, bring it back. Kale and I can defeat Xercarus together. Blast him straight back to the hell he crawled from."

Atlas finished putting my blood on slides and several vials into a chiller and cleaned the mess I'd made of his equipment in my hurry to prove my theory.

"Okay, Thea. Why do you need the blood, though?" Anders asked, his brows knitting together and his mouth quirking upwards.

Kale hadn't said a word, his eyes watching my erratic movements, causing his head to tilt back and forth like a curious puppy.

"I'm going to mix my blood with yours and Atlas's. I won't be able to change you," I announced.

They met me with an astounding round of rebuttals in unison, all besides Lincoln, who scrolled on his phone, oblivious to what I proposed.

"Absolutely not!" Atlas said, jerking his head up from the tablet. "No way."

Kale took unnaturally fast steps toward me, puffing his chest. "We're not trying that."

"You realize that's a terrible idea," Anders said with an exasperated sigh and dropped down to a sofa, his knees buckling under him.

I chuckled, cocking my eyebrow, and clicked my tongue. It was risky, but this was one fight I wasn't willing to give up. If I was right, my blood was useless to Xercarus, and more, we could cure anyone he afflicted with his demonic sickness. The pros massively outweighed the cons.

"Sorry, boys, I'm pulling rank. Look at you all, ganging up on me like big brothers. Hear me out, though. If this works, we have an alternative solution for Xercarus's horde. We wouldn't have to kill them; we could save them."

Kale lowered himself on his haunches, trying to steady his breathing and to stare me in the face as I sat in the chair again. "And if it doesn't work? What happens if you lose your ability to shift again, or worse?"

"That's obviously a possibility. But I need you to trust me— trust us. Okay? Fate put you in my path for a reason."

"I trust you," Kale said, pressing his forehead to my knee. My insides knotted again.

"Please, Atlas, Anders, do this for me?" I asked them, not wanting to use any more force.

My brothers sighed in unison, knowing they were about to do as I asked. Atlas cuffed up the sleeve of his green shirt, shaking his head. Anders approached the table where I sat, and pulled off his two-toned sweatshirt, setting it on the steel table.

"Athena?" Lincoln said, and I turned my head to give him my attention.

"Yeah, Linc, what's up?"

Lincoln dipped his head, putting his phone down, and twisted at his hands. "You'll be okay, won't you?"

"Hey. I will. I'll be fine." I softened, trying to reassure him, but not entirely certain who I was trying to convince more, him or my brothers.

"You better be, Thea." Atlas glowered at me; his brown eyes so dark they were almost black.

Anders and Atlas put their blood on slides, adding a drop of mine to each one. Atlas placed one slide under his microscope, adjusting the lens up and down. He was silent as he examined the samples. I could feel my anxiousness growing, eager to know if I was correct.

Atlas puffed out a large breath. "Thea, I almost hate to say this. But I think you're right. Nothing is changing. Our blood looks the same. Your cells don't appear to be compromising ours."

"That's great!" I leaped up on Kale, almost knocking him to the ground. That was odd, must have some residual power left from our exchange earlier.

Kale stumbled back, "Whoa."

"Yeah, sorry about that," I said, kissing his cheek, a lingering ember sparked against my lips.

On to part two of my theory.

"Anders, we still have the body, right?" I asked.

"What body? The mutated vampire? Umm, yeah, why?"

Atlas jumped from the chair. "Oh Goddess, now what?"

"Just *shh* for a damn minute," I grumbled.

I walked over to the wall, pulling out the cooler drawer. There it was, the mangled thing that had tried to kill Kale and the gaping black wound in its chest where Lincoln had ripped its heart out. I suddenly felt sorry for the creature, but my theory could make this reversible. Not for him, unfortunately, but for the others to come.

"Kale, give me your hand," I instructed, not taking my eyes off my experiment.

Kale walked over to me; his brows furrowed deeply, and his nose wrinkled. I took his hand in mine, opening my mind.

Fire spread to my palms with no fear of burning Kale. His body responded as soon as heat hit his hand. He didn't jerk away, only glanced down. When he met my stare again, his eyes flickered golden amber. Cool streaks intertwined with the blistering flares of mine.

I squeezed Kale's hand, triggering swirls of fluorescent sparks to fly out. "Do you remember what I asked you to say?"

"Yeah," Kale said, nodding again. I noticed his one eye flickering with a familiar green, and I wondered for a second if mine had traces of amber now too.

"Ignis et Glacies." We sounded together, putting our united hands over the corpse. A white flash of energy beamed like fire from our hands, hitting the body, jarring it from the table. I heard my brothers and Lincoln gasping. Kale and I looked at each other, pushing our power farther onward. The corpse jerked, the distorted skin reverting to its human flesh tone—the claws retracting back into single fingers. I watched, engrossed in the transfiguration, unable to take my eyes off the rapid changes occurring. The jagged hole closed, restoring the creature to its natural form. The body stilled. Its transformation was complete. There it—well, he—was, hair too long and dirty. He was a vampire, turned earlier in life, but not nearly as young as Lincoln. His face suggested he was nearly thirty, maybe a few years less. The more I looked at him, the more youthful he looked under the grit. He'd clearly been beautiful once, a strong jawline not unlike Kale's. His face was sculpted, the lips full and uncracked. Light, long eyelashes grazed his freckled, high cheekbones. The lasting speckles suggested he'd once spent days in the sunlight, and I continued to wonder about his life before.

My eyes wandered down his unmoving body, a sheet covered the vampire from the waist down, but I saw the muscles he'd once possessed, each defined line of his old body back for us to see.

Kale grinned, his white teeth shining at me. "We did it."

Anders and Atlas made their way closer to us, examining the reconfigured body. Lincoln took a chance and extended his index finger, poking the vampire corpse.

"Lincoln. Be respectful." I chastised him, swatting at his hand.

"Sorry, Athena." Lincoln looked down, but a smirk remained on his lips, like a child who'd been caught with his hand in a cookie jar.

"How's this possible? You changed his chemistry back to normal?" Atlas asked, rubbing his stubbled chin while Anders stood there, mouth gaping and shrugging in disbelief.

I looked back down at the body. He'd really been quite handsome. "I don't really know."

I reached down, picking a strand of long hair from the placid face. As I tucked it behind the ear, an arm shot up and grabbed me by my wrist tightly. I let out a yelp. The eyes of the vampire on the table before us flew open. Without hesitation, Anders and Atlas shifted into their wolves. Pieces of their clothing hit the floor like falling snow from the speed of their transformation. Their large white frames snarled and snapped their teeth. They'd gotten faster at shifting, less contortion, and almost flawless in speed. Kale grabbed at the hand, which remained clutched onto me. The vampire slowly shifted his gaze to Kale, continuing his observations in silence. I heard Kale growling, the animal inside fighting to break free, but it was the oddest sensation. I didn't feel alarmed. The cool grasp felt vaguely familiar. The vampire moved forward as if to sit up. I locked eyes with him.

Who was he?

"Let. Go. Of. Her." Kale enunciated each of his words through clenched teeth. His tone wasn't a threat; it was a promise of harm. The room chilled, and I watched ice form on each metal surface.

I'd meant for us to turn the creature back, removing Xercarus's bitterness, but Kale and I had not only restored him to his former self—we'd reanimated him. This was certainly an unexpected event and not quite the theory I'd been working on. With this power, Kale and I had some ability to reverse death, at least in supernaturals. I'd just gotten us into a whole new game, *yet again.*

CHAPTER 24

I held up my free hand, putting it to Kale's chest to stop him from removing the newly awoken vampire's limbs. "Kale, wait. I don't think he wants to hurt us. Look at your necklace. It's not red." My face softened, and my tone dropped an octave.

"You don't mean to hurt me, do you?"

His eyes showed no trace of redness from hunger or anger. They were an odd brown and glossy like we had awoken from sleep, not death. He nodded slowly, in agreement.

"Thea," Kale rumbled again, more menacing and unsure. Atlas shared Kale's sentiments, pawing at the ground and sniffing at the air.

The vampire tilted his head, plainly admiring my face. He released his hold on my wrist and sat fully up; his face was closer to mine. The vampire seemed too preoccupied observing my features and ignored Kale's warnings, along with my brothers' ominous growls. His hand crept up to caress my cheek. His fingertips carried a chill, and I shivered from the coolness. I moved back, not appreciating his unnecessary touch. A smile danced at the corners of his pale lips. Like all vampires, he was physically appealing, designed to lure you in.

"Is it really you?" he asked. His voice was smooth and low. Honey eyes poured over my face and features. The unwarranted fascination made no sense. He reached to graze his thumb along my bottom lip. I drew back, putting more space between him and me as fast as I could without creating a scene. The touch was too intimate, and a growl from Kale told me he shared the same opinion.

"My name is Athena Whiteridge. And you are?"

The vampire hesitated, tilting his head from side to side before finally answering. "Colin McCormick, at least, I think, Ms. Whiteridge. Seems I can't recall some things," he said, his eyes and mouth both sagging downwards at his confession.

Kale and my brothers ceased their rumblings, listening to him speak.

Colin sighed. "You're... magnificent. I remember your face —those green eyes so clearly—and his." He pointed to Kale. "How did I get here, in your care like this?"

Lincoln rushed back into the room, my mother close behind. I hadn't realized he'd left. He and my mother stood and remained silent, watching this unfold.

"That's a tricky question. One better answered after we get you all cleaned up. Does that sound alright?"

Colin took a survey of himself, blotches of black remaining in his hair and skin. He frowned, then his face perked up. "Yes. I'm a bit of a mess," he mumbled, his fawn-colored hair gleaming.

Kale stiffened next to me, and Atlas inched another step forward, rumbling on and off.

"I'll escort you to a spare room, get you all set up, then we'll talk." I gestured my hand to the two white wolves, who'd been baring their teeth.

Colin paused. "Wolves. You're a shifter, then?" Colin asked, focusing too much on me.

"Yes. We're wolves, and you're a vampire," I replied, keeping the composure Kale was on the verge of losing.

Stretching his arms upward, Colin inspected himself again. "Vampire," he repeated. "Indeed, I am a vampire. Seems that hasn't changed. But why am I not hungry?" Colin searched my face for an answer, his eyes falling to my lips.

I heaved my shoulders in a shrugging motion. "I really don't know, Colin. We'll do our best to find out. Now, why don't we get you off this table? Yeah?"

Colin lifted the sheet sitting at his waist. "Oh, my. I'm very much in need of good cleaning and perhaps some clothing." He smiled good-naturedly, taking this better than he should've. His demeanor was reminiscent of Kale's, along with his willingness to accept what was happening around him. Colin was a vampire, though; supernaturals were familiar to him. It struck me as off that he seemed to have forgotten a great deal about himself or at least recent events. Maybe the was amnesia due to Xercarus turning him. There was no way to truly tell.

The more he talked, I noticed Colin's voice carried the hint of an accent dulled over time, Irish perhaps, and in the limited number of times Colin had spoken, he'd been more formal. His face might suggest an age, but I understood as well as everyone else, a vampire's face told nothing of their true age. Immortality offered them a distinct advantage of having endless time, walking through the ages untouched by the years. I pondered how old Colin might be or what time he was from. He definitely wasn't a newly turned vampire. He was far too aware of his hunger.

Several more minutes of awkward conversation and introductions continued. Kale, my brothers, and I headed off with Colin to another one of our many guest rooms while my mother and Lincoln went to inform the guard of our surprise guest.

Once we had Colin settled in the bathroom, I dismissed my

brothers to have them shift back and return fully clothed. They'd be less hostile in human form, but not by much. I took a seat on the bed to wait as Colin showered. There was no way I'd let him out of my sight until I knew for sure he wasn't a threat. Kale took a spot right next to me. He placed a hand to my thigh, gripping it tenderly.

"Didn't expect that." Kale exhaled hard.

I shook my head. "No, definitely not. I proved my theory, though. Just worked a little better than I thought."

"Yeah, it did. I think he's into you too," Kale admitted, rubbing the back of his neck and rolling his shoulders.

I playfully shoved Kale's arm and stifled a smirk. "Seems unlikely. Colin just met me, and he was kinda dead for days."

"Nah, don't dismiss my instincts."

I took Kale's chin in my hand, feeling a buzzing tingle. "You have nothing to worry about. Mates, remember?"

Kale took advantage of our proximity, catching my chin in his fingers and placing a kiss to my lips. It started soft and inno-cent. His other hand reached for my face, cupping it between his hands. My body bent to Kale, leaning more into his kiss. Our connection was all-consuming. Time stopped and raced at the same time. He fisted his hands at the base of my neck, curling his fingers in my hair. I knew this was not the time nor the place, but we possessed a magnetism that was damn near impossible to ignore.

A throat cleared. I jerked away from Kale, leaving his lips in mid-air.

"I do sincerely apologize for my intrusion." Colin offered, retreating from the room.

My cheeks heated with embarrassment at my lack of restraint. "No. I apologize. It was inappropriate. Let's go downstairs."

Colin grinned; his eyes cast downward. "Young love is hard to contain. No apology necessary."

"Yeah, love is hard to contain." Kale took my hand, kissing my knuckles. It was difficult to tell if he'd done it more out of affection or possessiveness.

Colin leaned against the wooden doorway, and I finally got a good look at him all freshened up. He brushed his hair back, but the wet ends grazed his shoulders—such an unusual rusty blonde shade, almost bronze. He was tall, not quite Kale's height, and he'd dressed in some of Anders's jeans that sagged at the waist from being too loose. The white t-shirt he wore strained against his muscles. When I got to his eyes, I noticed Colin staring at me. I smiled uneasily. Maybe Kale was on to something. The way Colin looked at me surpassed friendly.

Colin looked down, rubbing his bottom lip as he thought. My brothers walked in, just in time for the unease forming between Kale and Colin. In my hurry, I hadn't even had a moment to invite the Pelletiers to Solstice, and now this landed in my lap. Technically, landed was wrong. This was another situation I'd gotten us in. My actions had been impulsive, rash even. If I wasn't mistaken, I heard my wolf let out several yips, mocking me. She was normally the one who wanted to charge headfirst into things. This time, the lack of control was mine, and it annoyed me.

"Are we interrupting something?" Atlas asked, holding up his hands.

"Not at all. I need to take care of one more thing, and we can get Colin up to date."

"Yes, please do. I'd be very interested to hear how I ended up on the morgue table, quite indisposed." Colin appeared to be getting livelier by the minute, his humor gaining confidence making his eyes brighter.

I lead our motley group back to my office. The room was certainly large enough to accommodate us all, and I could eliminate the Pelletier issue with a quick phone call while we discussed what to do with Colin, or rather what we had done to him. Kale was proving to be right; Colin was strange towards me. His eyes lingered on me too long as we walked, and my senses detected less than polite thoughts rolling around his mind. My wolf and I both sniffed curtly at the idea. This vampire didn't even know me. It was mighty presumptuous and a tad foolish to have such ungentlemanly thoughts about an Alpha.

We got to the office, and I took a seat behind my desk, scrolling until I found the contact I needed. I glanced at the time on the computer; it was an appropriate hour to call. Knowing the Pelletiers, they were likely finishing up a lavish late lunch full of champagne and rich foods. I clicked the digits, readying myself.

The line rang several times, a secretary greeted me kindly upon answering. My mother had required us to learn several languages, and I was finally grateful for her insistence. She always said, speaking to someone in their native tongue tells them you care and shows a certain amount of dedication.

"*Oui, bonjour. Je m'appelle Athena Whiteridge. Excusez-Moi d'être un peu en retard, mais j'ai eu une affaire urgente. Puis-je parler à Marcellus Pelletier?*" I replied, hoping to recall my French fluency like I was taught and not make a fool of myself. The polite woman put me on hold, saying Marcellus would be on the line shortly.

I heard Kale and Colin make light noises. It was obvious neither of them knew I spoke French. I glanced up from the computer screen, noticing both of them had wide-eyed captivated expressions on their faces, and a smile played on Kale's lips.

"You speak French?" Kale mouthed to me. An amused grin beaming at me.

I winked at him. *I speak many languages. Perhaps later I'll give you a demonstration.* I responded using our link. No one else needed to be aware of our cheeky exchange. Kale's grin widened, and I smirked as I held the phone. I saw Colin cover his mouth slightly upon noticing my smirk and divert his eyes away from me. What an odd thing to do.

"*Bonjour,* Mademoiselle Whiteridge!" A fake exuberant voice came onto the line, he continued, his French accent thick, "Terribly sorry to hear of your father. You must all be so stunned, not having an Alpha present. To what do I owe the pleasure of this call?"

Ah, the smugness was evident, masked under the façade of courtesy. Marcellus aimed to provoke me. It seemed Oriel was very much correct. The Pelletiers hadn't taken the dropped union proposal very well.

"Good afternoon, Monsieur Pelletier. Thank you for your condolences. It's been difficult adjusting to such a significant loss; my father was admired by so many. However, my transition to Alpha has been seamless, but we needn't discuss my title of Alpha Queen. You'd do my family a great honor by joining us for the Winter Solstice. It'll give you an opportunity to meet our future King, as well."

Marcellus sputtered. If he wanted to take jabs, I was happy to exchange in a verbal duel.

"*Incroyable!* I had no idea, Your Majesty." Marcellus responded, less conceit in his tone this time.

The French monarch proceeded, "It would be a divine honor to join the Whiteridges during the Winter Solstice. We'll make arrangements right away."

"Wonderful. That will be unnecessary, though. What kind of Queen would I be if I did not host an ambassador? Please say you'll stay with us at the Manor. We have more than enough room and access to any amenities you desire."

Atlas snorted loudly, putting his fingers up to his head, making a gun gesture, and sticking his tongue out. Clearly, he was keen as Kale had been over discovering my decision to accommodate the Pelletiers here. Anders elbowed Atlas before he could make what could only be a rude remark. Kale folded his arms, puffing his cheeks, pouting. Colin and Lincoln exchanged oblivious glances and shrugs, neither of them understanding what was going on.

"*Merci beaucoup*, Your Majesty. It is indeed a great honor you bestow to have us in your home. I accept your most gracious offer. Besides, your late father spoke highly of your *magnifique* wine cellar. I'd be much obligated to see it." Marcellus's voice almost seemed jovial. Maybe inviting them wouldn't be so horrible. *Ha, not likely,* I told myself. At the very least, I had done my political part to smooth over the botched arrangement my father had made.

I kept my tone even, not giving away anything, "The pleasure is mine. We look forward to having you. And our wine cellar should not disappoint, I'm sure. I'll leave the rest of the preparation for Ben, my assistant. He's most competent. We'll see you in a few weeks. Safe travels."

We said our goodbyes and hung up. The talking resumed before I could put my phone down.

"Queen? I was under the impression Alphas were all male?" Colin quirked his head at me. His eyebrows moved up, and I couldn't tell if his question was genuine curiosity or needling.

Kale raised his brows as well, pursing his lips and folding his arms across his chest again, looking to me for a reaction.

I simply inhaled a small breath, narrowing my eyes to almost slits while staring Colin straight in the face. "Well, Mr. McCormick, that's the old way, but things change, progress happens. I am the Alpha; my brothers are my Betas. After my father, the King's passing, I inherited this title, but don't assume I didn't earn every bit of it."

Atlas, Anders, and Lincoln smirked quietly, their eyes moving from one another, sharing their inside jokes. Kale was far less subtle, giving a chuckle and dropping his hands to his sides. I knew he was enjoying my terse manner more than necessary.

Colin took a casual stance, shifting his back to the wall and opening his arms, "I meant no offense, Your Grace. Merely trying to gain an understanding of whose presence I'm in."

I admired Colin's appearance of sincerity. Perhaps I shouldn't have gotten as snappy. The poor vampire was mutated, then killed. He deserved more grace than I had given. I was mildly ashamed for trying to chastise him over an innocent question. However, my wolf was less inclined to feel my shame, and snorted loudly in my head.

"No need to call me Your Grace. Athena is fine. I need to remember my manners as well," I replied, softer, with no malevolence in my tone this time.

Kale wasn't ready to offer civil behavior. "Alright, so now we have what you can call Athena settled. Can we move on to where you were just dead a bit ago?" Kale was eyeing Colin and shifting himself closer to me.

"Dead? Excuse me, Kale, is it? I'm a vampire; I am, in fact, *undead*." Colin's tone rose to meet Kale's annoyance, straining on his courteousness. Colin wasn't aware of how volatile a new wolf was, especially one with dragon blood circulating in their veins.

I decided it was wise to take charge of this discussion. It appeared Kale was in no mood, and my brothers were all too eager to follow his lead. I examined Colin again. He was leaning against a tall bookcase, arms folded across his broad chest. His hair was drying, waves becoming more apparent. Colin had these light, long lashes I'd noticed before, framing his russet-colored eyes, such a warm brown with flecks of honey flecks. He wasn't hard to look at. I rolled my eyes at myself. I'd never really found anyone appealing until Kale. Truth be told, I wasn't drawn to Colin, not like I was to Kale, and yet I felt guilty over finding anything charming about Colin. I pushed the notion from my mind and ground my teeth.

"Have you ever heard of Xercarus?"

Colin's hands dropped to his sides, and his jaw strained. "I remember little of my recent life, but I'd recall that bloody bastard anytime. Pardon my language. I was in Ireland when he first started his so-called plague, the killings. He's the reason I'm... this." Colin drew his hand down his body, gesturing to himself.

"You're from the 1300s?" Anders asked, leaning in, his attention peaked.

Colin adjusted his posture, too, angling himself toward Anders. "I am born and raised in Dundalk, Ireland. His uprisings reached us. Most died, and I barely escaped. I remember being bitten by what I soon found out was a vampire. He looked as though the devil himself had conjured him. I killed the filthy wretch, of course, but his bite was already on me. I fled Ireland, too ashamed of what I'd become. I'm almost grateful to forget some of my life, this existence 'tisn't as glamorous as your cinemas often suggest—killing humans for food."

Kale softened, easing his shoulders. Colin's tale taking effect. "Your history with Xercarus isn't gonna make this easier to tell you, man."

Colin's head quirked up, his hands going to the pockets of his jeans as he attempted to hide his fidgeting. "I want to know," he said, concentrating on me again.

I continued on, in place of Kale. "Colin, several nights ago, you and an accomplice came into our home. You weren't yourself as you are now. You were this mutated thing—a dark creation of Xercarus's."

"That cannot be," Colin said, putting his hand to his forehead. I felt even more pity toward him.

I swallowed. "Doesn't get any better from there either. Kale disabled you and Lincoln, well," I paused, fiddling with my hair, wanting to be delicate. It wasn't every day I told someone they had their heart torn out. Atlas, never one to be overly delicate, picked up on my hesitation and took over.

"Lincoln here ripped your heart out, buddy. You were *dead* dead, as Kale said. No coming back," Atlas told him, not skipping a beat.

Colin took a step back, visibly stumbling. "I was, one of them? One of his bloody hordes? Goddess, help me. How am I... alive then?" He put air quotes on the word alive, spitting the word out as if it had a bitter taste.

"My brothers, Atlas and Anders and I are the Triad. I'm not sure if you're familiar with the prophecy," I said.

Colin's eyes got larger. "The Triad. You're the—I didn't know, that's who you were. My mind is hazy. I should've put two and two together. I've heard about you; all the Unseen has." Colin bowed his head, offering me respect.

I nodded back at him. "As for how we brought you back, my gifts have expanded. Kale was human. I unintentionally turned him, and now he possesses certain abilities, like my brothers and me. I thought we could reverse Xercarus's effects on a mutant. Your body was available, and I used you as an experiment. We tried to remove his darkness with our energy. But we did a lot more than that." I closed my runaway mouth, realizing I divulged a great deal to someone who'd been revived less than an hour.

Way to go, Athena.

Colin froze, his hand holding his chest and rubbing where the gaping hole had been. His face contorted, and his brows furrowed together, taking in what I'd told to him. We all remained quiet, letting Colin absorb this new information. Looking at him, I felt a sorrow move into my chest. It grew when he moved his eyes to catch me watching him. He did us both a favor by looking away quickly.

Several minutes had passed before Colin spoke. "I suppose

I owe you a debt of gratitude for bringing me back. I'd hate to believe, as soulless as I may be, that I died serving such a despicable demon. I thank you."

Before I could even think, I reached to comfort Colin. "You're not soulless. Lost, maybe, but not soulless."

"Perhaps you're right. I am lost. I also have an obligation to repay you." Colin nodded.

Colin's words hung in the air. An obligation to me meant Colin had intentions of sticking with us. The idea of him maintaining a more permanent residence with us or me wasn't altogether unpleasant. I couldn't explain it. A little while ago, he'd been nothing but blackened, oozy flesh. Now, he was an old vampire with an Irish accent. There was something off with Colin or maybe me; I needed to figure out what caused this pull towards Colin I felt on and off. I knew how deep my feelings for Kale ran, mate, or otherwise. Kale was everything. His acceptance and kindness had virtually no limits. It didn't matter what arrant thoughts I had; I'd choose Kale. I'd always want Kale. Colin being around changed nothing.

CHAPTER 25

nders, fascinated by history his history, offered to show Colin around the manor. I suspected Anders planned to pepper Colin with as many questions as he was willing and able to answer. As they walked off, Colin looked over his shoulder at me, a sort of longing expression on his face and in his odd copper eyes. Fortunately for Colin, Kale hadn't noticed. As the room cleared out, Kale seized the opportunity to embrace me, tighter than usual.

He sighed into my hair. "I know I shouldn't be, but that guy really puts me on edge. I enjoy people admiring you. I always wanna be your hype guy, you know? With Colin, it's different. I can tell something is up. I just don't know what."

I held on to Kale, appreciating his ever-present honesty, another reason I loved him. He didn't hide his emotions. Holding him like this, his closeness always moved my mind to less productive ideas.

"I understand what you're saying. But you don't need to worry. You're the one, remember? That doesn't just change because I resurrect Mr. Brown Eyes back there." I kissed him before leaning back. "*Eu te amo.*"

Kale's eyelids fluttered, taken aback by my unexpected kiss.

A smile crept over his lips, curling upwards. I touched his cheek, moving my fingertips down to his jaw as his eyes stayed closed. His breathing quickened; his body responded to my touch—a buzz traveling between us.

I let my mind slip, opening Kale to my thoughts, *I should take you on the floor, right here.*

Kale let out a low, devious chuckle. No doubt he'd heard me. *I wish you would. I'd never deny my Queen pleasure,* he responded, letting his mind reach out while his hand traveled up and down my sides.

Every part of him made me feel more alive. "You know I'd love to act on my desires; however, once again, responsibility awaits. The tailor and seamstress will be here any minute with our outfits for the Solstice. If we miss that appointment, Ben may lose his mind."

The fittings went like planned, and as promised, Ben had selected a beautiful gown for the Solstice. The rose gold matched the color of my ring. It shimmered and glistened in all the right places. It accentuated my body's every curve, made my eyes look brighter; my hair even appeared shinier. This gown would showcase my accession to Queen, with a hint of sex appeal to turn every head. I became mildly anxious as I looked at my reflection, wanting to see Kale in his attire, but he'd gotten this dated idea in his head of how much better it would be if we didn't see each other's outfits until Solstice. I agreed to his suggestion. It took all my patience to not bust into his changing room and see how stunning he was in formal dress.

Instead, I let my imagination run with images of Kale's nimble fingers unbuttoning his shirt, exposing his taut chest. My wolf rumbled low. Kale taking clothing off appealed to her too. I ran my hand up and down the beaded fabric on my torso, almost forgetting the seamstress in the room. I apologized for my wandering mind. She smiled and patted my hand, telling me she was happy to see her Queen had found her mate and

King. She looked near my mother's age, maybe a little older. Sophia was her name. I realized I knew little about her besides the fact she'd altered my mother's gowns for years. The best in our territory in the Unseen. Her hands worked quickly while she pinned and unpinned, complimenting my figure. Our King is a lucky wolf, she teased. I smiled and blushed. Sophia was gifted and had the dress fitted to me in minutes, her hands delicate and fast.

Once I changed back into my clothes, I took out my phone and messaged Ben, letting him know the fittings had gone well and his taste was immaculate. I provided him with a list of items that needed to be shipped over before the Pelletiers arrived. Ben was already on it. The Pelletiers secretary had sent over a flight itinerary. They would arrive the day before Winter Solstice, in the morning, enough time to likely drive us all mad. It'd be a game of roulette to see which one of us cracked first under the pressure of strained niceties and royal formalities. My money was on Atlas or Henri.

Upon leaving my bedroom, I heard Lincoln yelling, then several loud crashes. I wasted no time, only taking a millisecond to remove my ring and put it on the dresser before launching my beast forward. I shifted in time to leap down the stairs in one bound, leaving my clothing in shreds on the steps. White fur blurred, scrambling through the house towards the racket. I heard Lincoln cry out again. My mind raced with terror. *Where was Kale—my brothers? Oh Goddess, my mother!*

Kale. Atlas. Anders. What's happening? My paws pounded on the flooring as hard as my heart, my claws causing me to skid into the wall with a hard *thud* on my way out. No hands to open the patio door, so I lowered my gigantic head, charging through it, glass flying everywhere, some nesting in my course outer fur. I shook my coat and let loose a snarl. I rounded the corner, nearing the track, barely hearing Anders's voice as I tried calling for him and Kale again at the same time. My adrenaline rose higher from their lack of response. I'd annihilate whatever was stupid enough to come near them.

Anders felt my agitation clearly now. *Hey, hey, Thea, everything is fine. We're just helping Lincoln train. Colin has been showing him how to use his vampire strength.*

Settle down. We're all good, Atlas jumped in.

I tried to slow myself, but I couldn't. I kept my blistering pace until I reached the course. I wouldn't stop until I saw their faces. My hulking body skid to a halt, sending dirt flying into the air. Lincoln laid on the ground, Colin above him, extending his hand down to him. He took Colin's calloused palm, a laugh escaping his muscled chest. Lincoln dusted himself off, Colin patting him on the back and offering praise. Colin got a look at me, tilting his head, while I pawed at the ground. A smile of appreciation inched onto this face as he observed the striking snowy form I'd taken. I found nothing amusing at the moment and snapped my jaws in his direction.

Vampires. Always thinking they could charm someone.

Kale turned to face me, and I panted heavily. It wasn't the running that tired me—it was the fright, the anger plaguing my chest. He jogged over to me, a small crease forming in his furrowed brow as he felt my stress. I couldn't focus on his face for long. All I could think was, they're fine. *They're all safe.* I sniffed a sigh of relief, pawing at the ground more rapidly and snorting.

"Thea, I'm sorry. Your brothers and Colin were teaching Lincoln and me some things. I didn't think to mention it. You must have thought... well, I know what you thought." Kale lifted his hand to place it between my erect ears, stroking my white fur. He glanced down, seeing blood on my paw.

"Fuck! You're hurt," he said, raising his voice as he bent down to inspect my paw and leg. He picked up the large paw, turning it until he could see the pads. Finding nothing, he let me set the 'good as new' paw back down. I stomped it on the cool ground, showing him there was no pain.

I shook my furry head. Kale had forgotten I'd healed moments after the injury. The blood was the only proof I had of the cut. It must have been the glass when I'd charged through it.

The glass. Dammit. I'd need to fix my mess.

It surprised me Mother hadn't heard me crashing around the house. But, of course, my mother wouldn't have heard me, she wasn't home. In my panic, I'd forgotten she and Calliope had gone out for groceries. My mother insisted on doing household shopping for our meals herself, even with the ability to have everything delivered. She preferred to go to farmers' markets, selecting the freshest produce and locally made items. She said it gave her an opportunity to connect with her people, strengthening our bond. That reminded me, as Alpha and new Queen, I should accompany her once in a while, up the morale. Another to-do on my growing list.

The rest of the guys trotted over, picking up on Kale's conversation. Atlas was shoving Lincoln, tussling his hair. It reminded me of the vision Kale had the night we'd met Lincoln. I warmed thinking about it and how much I cared for Lincoln in such a short time. He was so young and much more perceptive than I gave him credit for. I couldn't imagine someone hurting him; the thought stung. Kale flinched, sensing my brief unease. It was good they were teaching him proper defensive techniques. Being skilled with hand to hand combat would be beneficial for Lincoln, even if the thought of him being thrown around terrified and angered me. I realized I'd been trying to shelter him, treating Lincoln as if he were a fragile child, but he wasn't anymore. He was a vampire and proved right deadly when it came down to it.

"Athena." Anders bent down, kneeling on the grass to examine my paw.

I'm fine, Anders. It's repaired itself already. Don't fuss over me.

Anders looked up from my paw, kneeling. I used my wet muzzled to jab his shoulder and cheek, teasing him. He laughed, placing his hand to his knee to get up, then dusted off his jeans.

"*Mac Tire*. She's certainly something. Is she hurt?" Colin bobbed his head around Atlas to peer closer at me. His eyes surveying every inch of me. He tucked stray blonde locks of hair behind his ears.

Kale whipped his head in Colin's direction, narrowing his eyes, his previous appreciation for Colin's combat expertise fading fast. The breeze kicked up, moving Kale's agitated pheromones around with the drying leaves.

"She's fine," Kale answered, bordering on a growl.

I bumped my head against Kale's face, signaling him to tone down the aggression.

Colin certainly wasn't deterred and kept walking down the worn grass path closer toward me. "I've never seen a wolf of her size before." He paused, admiring my snow-white wolf form again. "And so white. You're quite a lovely creature."

Kale was scowling, fisting his hands in his jean pockets. Atlas and Lincoln noticed Kale's souring disposition and decided it was best to ease the growing tension. Lincoln shrugged his protective gray vest off and strolled over to Kale, giving his arm a pat. I understood the nature of Kale's possessiveness. It was in our temperament as Wolves to be overprotective of our family members, especially our mates. It wasn't so much Kale, but his wolf looking at Colin as a challenger. I knew all too well the battle Kale was waging to keep control over himself. I dipped and rolled my head underneath Kale's chin to aid in distracting him.

"You haven't seen a wolf like Thea over here before because she's an Alpha. She's bigger than other shifters and supposedly faster. What the hell is *Mac Tire* anyway? An Irish saying for holy shit?" Atlas shot me a wink, his brown eyes looking for trouble.

I lifted my muzzle and snorted. *I am faster than you,* I linked Atlas, only to hear his laughter in my mind as he tapped his dagger to his thigh.

Colin smirked, putting a capable hand beneath his chin, "No. Not at all. It's an old Irish word for wolf. Comes from human mythology about lycanthropy." He paused, looking me over further, "Hm. Are all Alphas white in color then?" he asked, his soft brown eyes staring into my emerald ones.

"No, they can be any color. But the three of us happen to be white, like our mother." Anders answered Colin's question this time. Anders cocked an eyebrow and shook his hand as he watched Colin's outward fascination.

Kale bristled next to me, and I brushed against him again. *I need your help fixing the door.*

Opening my mind to Kale was like second nature to me now, requiring little effort.

"Of course, Athena." Kale offered me a tight smile while glaring at Colin again before turning to walk with me back to the house.

Lincoln raised his eyebrows, stifling a laugh, and headed over to Colin, shaking his head.

We started making our way back to the deck. The ground felt natural on my paws, the dirt and gravel connecting me to nature. I lifted my nose to sniff the breeze that blew Kale's hair and his scent to me. *Sea salt and kindle.*

I was curious to see if Kale and I could use our energy without me being able to recite the words. We walked along the path, my head level with Kale's. He touched my side again, ruffling my snowy fur.

"You are beautiful, you know. Even as a wolf. Colin's right about that." Kale murmured as he kicked up some dried-up brown leaves.

I flicked my ears, sniffing his shoulder.

So are you, I linked back to him. At least that put a genuine grin back on his face.

We got to the patio, covered in glass and my bloody paw prints. Wood splinters and metal hung down from the mangled door frame. I heard Kale audibly gasp and stop short.

He looked at me, mouth gaping like a fish. "I know you heal. But damn, Thea. It doesn't stop me from worrying. You did a number on this door."

I know exactly how you feel. I'd like to tell you it'll get easier, but I'm not willing to lie to you. I heard Lincoln cry out. I thought... Goddess, I sniffed, picking my head up higher. I'd need to pay more attention, be more aware. I let myself get too preoccupied with the paperwork and duties and had forgotten to be present when it mattered. How did my father ever manage? The more I let it roll around my mind, the more I understood why he did certain things—including Henri Pelletier.

Kale rested his hand on my shaggy back, "How should we go about this?"

Our eyes connected, green to blue. Kale knew what I wanted to try. He stroked my fur again, opening his mind. His eyes switched from blue to a crackling amber, flickering with embers of light. I felt an expansion in my chest, the fiery warmth spreading from where Kale's cool hand laid.

"Ignis et Glacies," Kale said, putting his other hand out toward the glass and battered door frame.

The broken pieces of splintered wood and shards levitated off the ground, stilling in the air for seconds as if waiting for direction. In a lightning flash, the door and frame were repaired. My hunch was right again; we could be in any form and use our energy together. This made me curious. Atlas and Anders were of my blood. What if we could expand their power as well?

Over all the years we'd grown and trained together, it had

never dawned on any of us to try and band our abilities together. We'd always pushed ourselves in separate directions. My brothers had learned magic spells alongside me in our schooling, but when our tutor noted Atlas and Anders as not having the affinity for magic like I did, so their magic studies came to a halt. Perhaps, like everything else, their ability for magic could grow.

"I see you thinking again. Your head must be on lock down. I couldn't get in there." Kale said, his eyes losing their amber glow. I watched his ocean blue color returning.

Hmm, I was gaining more control of my mind, like a true Alpha. Only letting my thoughts out when I wanted to share them. A whine bubbled up my throat.

I'll shift back.

I felt my bones and body rearranging as I answered. The transition was quick. I'd gotten seamless in my forms, one easily interchanging with another. Kale took a step back, admiring the speed at which I was my human self again.

Atlas cleared his throat as politely as possible. *Thea, you might wanna cover up.*

Kale and I hadn't noticed our audience, absorbed in our own little world. I dropped my hands to cover as much of myself as possible, hunching over to reveal less. I noticed Colin's gaze linger on me for only a moment, then he too turned away from my full-frontal show. With a fluidity only a supernatural possessed, Kale positioned himself between me and the voices we were most definitely paying attention to now.

Lincoln had his eyes squinted closed, snickering like a schoolboy. Atlas and Anders had the back turned towards me. While they might be a thorn in my side, those boys were never anything outside respectful when it came to our necessity for nudity; I offered them the same in return.

When we were younger, our mother went to great lengths

to explain our bodies and our differences. We knew proper terminology for bodies as soon as potty training hit. Illiana Whiteridge, graceful Luna Queen, and a modern-day feminist in her own right. She told me to never be afraid of my body—that it was the home holding my soul, and I should never, ever be embarrassed about the home I lived in. I grew up not fearing the skin I lived in, though it still didn't help me enjoy the current situation. Poor Lincoln, this was the second time he'd caught me in a compromising position. Though it didn't appear to faze him, as he stood, laughing uncontrollably, his hair bouncing along with his cackling.

Kale reached a hand behind him, shielding me, as he turned. Kale looked down at my chilled body, all goosebumps and hardened flesh. He swiftly took off his pale green shirt, tucking it over my head like an oversized blanket. His scent engulfed me and bewitched my senses. Millions of inappropriate thoughts invaded my mind. *Kale...*

"Thank you," I mouthed to him. He bent to kiss my forehead. His lips did nothing to help contain the familiar warmth pooling down below.

Colin decided now was a good time to speak, "A modest she-wolf, how fascinating," He paused, "Most females I've met are more than willing to show off their—assets. Which it appears, Athena has many of."

I popped my head around Kale, facing Colin and putting a hand to my hip. I was about to open my mouth when I saw Atlas shift himself to look at Colin, eyebrows raised.

"Watch your mouth," Atlas snapped at him, his mouth landing in a firm line.

Anders growled in agreement.

"*Oh*, I meant no disrespect to Athena. It's quite refreshing, actually. Like traveling back to the old days," Colin said but pulled his brows together and looked down, realizing his mistake. Kale's expression became grim, his mouth in a firm line, and eyes dead set on Colin.

Colin stammered, lifting his hands in a 'hold on' gesture. His mouth moved, but the words stuck as he tried to race to recover.

"Not—not that I wish to see Athena or any other woman as a virginal bride or anything of the sort. I only meant that..." Colin trailed off in his attempt to backpedal. He backed up a few steps as if waiting for Kale to sack him. The thought of punching him myself crossed my mind. If I allowed this line of conversation to continue, I could guarantee a fight. We didn't have the time for them to act like children. There was one sure-fire way to distract Kale from the boiling rage. I'd need to use the only thing that ruled his senses more than his inner wolf—*me*.

As I predicted, Kale didn't give Colin time to finish speaking. "Colin, if you wanna see the end of today, shut your mouth. Athena's not a common wolf or woman. She's an Alpha. Her body, in any form, is hers to show or cover in whatever damn way she sees fit. This isn't the 1300s. And I think you've spent far too much time eye-fucking Athena as it is." Kale's voice wasn't hinting at a vicious rumble. It was full of the promise of harm.

Anders and Atlas moved in, putting themselves between Kale and Colin. Lincoln had stopped laughing altogether and reached his hand to Colin's shoulder to draw him farther away from Kale and me. Part of me was proud that Lincoln tried to protect Colin. What I didn't want was him getting caught in the cross hairs of Kale and Colin as they engaged in a pissing contest. *Males.*

I touched Kale's back, feeling him relax under my hand. His breathing slowed, and his chest settled.

"Hey, Colin, why don't I show you where they keep the

vampire friendly lunch around here?" Lincoln said, trying to diffuse the growing tension.

Colin backed away with Lincoln. Seemed he knew well enough to never turn his back on an angry wolf. With Colin making a wise retreat, it was my turn to grab Kale's attention away from the murderous acts he was contemplating committing.

"Come inside with me," I paused, letting my fingers linger on his back, then stroke up to his hair. Kale's body trembled in response. Appealing to Kale's more primal nature was the quickest way to distract him.

I leaned up higher and whispered as close to his ear as I could reach. "Why don't I show you exactly what my body can do."

Kale whipped around fast, letting his interest in devouring Colin melt away. His eyes softened and sparked, a wicked grin turning up the corners of his mouth. I knew what he was thinking without a link or words. It aroused him; I smelled it on him. Something about Kale's declaration riled my insides, stirring my ever-present desire for him. I wanted Kale so badly it felt like a need. I let out a tiny, low sound, provoking Kale and pulling the attention of his wolf fully toward me.

Kale sniffed the air. "You did that on purpose." His tone was gravel and rasp, like it always sounded when he felt lustful.

I grinned, letting my canine slip down to pierce my lower lip. A hint of pain mixed with the pleasure I knew was coming. Kale's chest puffed, his eyes flickering again.

"You don't play fair." He reached for me, taking the hand I'd offered to lead him into the house and to our bed.

Biting my lip one more time, then licking the top one, I gave Kale a wicked grin. "I never said I did." And I pulled him through the restored patio door, sliding it shut behind us.

I heard both Atlas and Anders muffled grumblings of "Gross" and, "Is this shit going to go on forever?"

Their feet hit the ground hard as they both ran off to catch up to Lincoln and Colin, putting distance between them and us as fast as they could. The old me would've been more reserved, doing my best to hide sensual thoughts. The new me didn't really care. I'd come too close to losing Kale to get uncomfortable by our extraordinary chemistry. As if reading my immodest thoughts, Kale picked me up into his arms, bridal style. His bare chest rubbing against the side of my clothed breast. Supernatural speed and strength came in handy, getting us up several flights of stairs to our bedroom quickly without becoming winded.

Kale kicked the door shut behind us, and I found myself on my back, flush against the mattress, Kale between my thighs. His kisses were hot and frantic. But I had more wicked things in mind. I pushed on his chest, his leaf necklace brushing my hand. He pulled away, knowing to lean upwards. His mouth left my lips and chin pink from his stubble.

"Yes?" he asked coquettishly, tilting his head. "Tell me what you want, Athena."

I licked my lips before answering. "I want you to get off me and lie on your back."

Kale's eyes went wide, and his mouth popped open with surprise. Without a word, he did as he was told. Sliding off me to let me up and then laid himself back down. I looked him up and down, taking in his every feature. His sculpted abs, rippling every time he moved even a fraction. Stubbled covered his angled jaw and roughed up my delicate skin. His eyes, still vibrantly blue, hinted of amber waiting to be engaged. He was a fine specimen of the male architecture, and mine.

All mine.

He was waiting for my next move, his brows knitted together, unsure of what I had in mind.

"Unbutton your pants."

Again, Kale did as he was told. His arms moved to his waist, taking the button of his jeans into his deft fingers. He undid them, then rested his hands at his sides, palms down. He'd caught on to my game.

"I want you to hold very still and be very quiet," I instructed as I tugged his t-shirt over my head, revealing myself to him. He grunted at the sight. I watched him strain against his jeans. The denim taut as his sizable length stayed trapped under the fabric.

"Do you understand?" I asked him. Kale nodded in slow-motion as I crawled on the bed to kneel over him, freeing his length from the laboring pants. He stood full and high. Taking him in my hand, I began moving up and down. I realized how smooth he was. The skin was soft, almost fragile for such an impressive size. I chuckled to myself, amused at this perceived power I had over him. This was going to be fun. He shivered under the touch, not breaking eye contact. He enjoyed me teasing him.

I moved my head down, kissing the muscled 'v' of his hips, and pressed more kisses down a thin trail of hair that indeed led to treasure. I let my mouth take the place of my hand. It was a beyond satisfying set of movements I was unaccustomed to; most were involuntary and visceral.

Kale quivered and trembled beneath me as I flicked my tongue over his tip and took more of him into my mouth. I peeked my eyes up to see his white-knuckled hands fisting the bed sheets. Soft moans and hisses escaped through his gritted teeth. I found a rhythm he appeared to take the most pleasure in. He was fighting to remain still or quiet. His hips bucked and arched adeptly against me. I was astonished by how much of him I could take in, pushing myself to find a limit. I drew back. Kale was slick with saliva and reddened with want. He opened his eyes, burning amber, like smoldering coals from a fireplace.

He groaned my name and hissed in a breath. His silken

voice was baritone and needful. "I'm trying so fucking hard not to finish."

I looked down at him lasciviously, stimulated by his response. "Don't. I want you to." Placing my mouth back on him, I moved faster. I lapped up his arousal, driven forward as he called my name, and squirmed while fisting my hair. Kale hadn't been lying—a few moments longer, and he came completely undone, pulsating between my lips. As he lay panting, Kale's hands reached down to grasp my shoulders and pulled me towards him.

Raised pink marks covered Kale's chest; I'd clawed his chest in our excitement. I continued to slide up his torso, watching it heal right before my eyes. Kale caught me staring and let out an amused, breathy chuckle.

"You'd think I might've noticed that." He caressed my shoulder. "But what I really wanna know is, where did that come from?" Kale stared at me, eyes wide and mesmerized. The blue swirled, making its way back.

I nuzzled his chest, smelling the sweet scent of his lingering excitement. One of Kale's best attributes as a mate was how he expected nothing of me, never pushing for sexual advances. He was a patient and thoughtful lover while I learned more of the little things that made him and myself tick, so to speak. With Kale no longer human, it made things easier. I didn't have to worry about overpowering him—unless I wanted to...

I'd often heard talk that females weren't often fond of giving oral. I knew the opposite of myself. I liked the control, having Kale completely at my mercy. Then again, what Alpha didn't get off on control?

Thea, he probed at my mind, trying to hear what I was thinking.

Nuzzling him again, then peeking my head up. He knew what I wanted. Shifting us to the center of the bed, he got on his knees, moving my body to wrap around him, positioning me atop him. He rhythmically rocked us, picking up speed. Amber eyes glistened to my green, Kale's lips parted, giving me a glimpse of his teeth. In between passionate kisses, he marked me. It wasn't prolonged, though that had little effect on its tenderness and climatic end. Kale's lovemaking always left me locked in between wanting and satiated. In my heart, I knew it wasn't a mate thing. This was specific to Kale, who he was as a person and lover.

After we finished, we held one another a while longer, listening to each other's breaths, and let the events from our day fade into the background. Kale finally pulled himself from the bed, heading to the bathroom, and ran us a hot shower. I stretched, feeling my unsteady limbs, and followed behind him.

He opened the shower door, helping me in, and let himself in behind me. He shifted through bottles, finding my fragrant freesia soap, and washed my back and then hair, tracing circles on my skin as he did. It was as if he was appreciating every inch of me, committing it once again to his memory.

We got out of the shower, both drying off. I wound my hair up in a towel, walking to my vanity for my lotions. Kale's bare feet padded to the bedroom, opening drawers. He slipped into some comfortable lounge clothes. I watched his reflection from the mirror, his body falling into view. He had to know what he looked like in sweatpants that fit him in all the right places. If he didn't, I intended to remind him again. A muted growl rippled up my throat, accompanied by a mischievous smile.

Kale winked. "Hey. I'm gonna round us up some snacks. What do you say to dinner in bed tonight? We'll face demons and the undead tomorrow, yeah?" Kale had an earnest look on his face, biting at his lower lip, which practically begged me to agree.

I knew I had things to attend to, but it was rare we had quiet moments to ourselves for any extended period of time. As

Queen, I'd always have something pressing I needed to do, but things weren't more important than family. I sighed, taking my hair from the towel.

Kale persisted. "Please don't overthink it, Thea. If they need you, they'll call with our freaky mind line."

I smiled, raking a brush through my thick hair, "Alright, alright. Only if you promise to bring up some cheese, crackers, annnd wine."

Jumping up and down like a kid, Kale left the bathroom, returning almost immediately. "Here, let's not forget this." He took my hand, slipping my engagement ring onto my finger. The sparkle of it still rendered me speechless. He kissed my hand while smiling, then bolted back out of the room. I clutched the towel tighter to my skin, a flurry beat around my chest, and I knew it was my heart, racing to match Kale's. I bit my lower lip, smiling to myself.

We spend the entire evening in our room, in bed with snacks of all kinds scattered across the duvet. Kale felt it necessary to bring up a laundry basket full of treats, trying to fulfill our every food craving. He prepared a picnic-style feast of grapes, sharp cheddar, and crackers on a tablecloth he snatched from the kitchen as well. He'd brought stemless goblets and a bottle of red wine and had even grabbed refillable water tumblers. The man thought of everything. We turned on Netflix and watched a delightfully sassy rom-com, per his request. He insisted the guy should've told the woman sooner how much he liked her.

We sipped wine and talked. The conversation was carefree and animated, like how I imagined Kale was before me. It was like we were a completely normal couple for a moment. Not shifters or supernaturals. No Alphas or Betas. *Just us.*

Kale told me to pick the next movie. I kept up our theme and picked a paranormal romance. Kale used this time to have me further dispel more myths about the Unseen while we cuddled and laughed. By the end, we sided with the girl rather than the too cautious human.

I interrupted our snacking to question him. "What would you be doing right now if you weren't here?"

He laid back on the pillows, propping his arms behind his head. "Hmm, good question. I don't know, sleeping?" A roguish grin crept up Kale's lips.

"You know that's not what I meant, smart ass." I threw a cracker at him.

Kale laughed and rolled on top of me, pinning me to the pillows. "Honestly, I don't know. I didn't have any long-term plans before you, but I do now." He kissed my nose and shifted off me.

"Like what?" I braced myself on my elbows.

His eyes lit up. "I sent some emails out to a few realtors, and I think I found the perfect space for the studio. You've got a lot going on, so I figured I'd go check out the location next week."

"That's great. Why didn't you say anything earlier?" I sat up and scooted towards him.

Kale rumpled his nose, his long body leaning into me. "We were helping Lincoln, then you distracted me with sex."

I bit my lower lip. "I may have done that, but still. This is big. Do you have any idea what you want to call your label?"

"I do." Kale rolled again and slid off the bed, grabbing pillows and the throws off the edge. "Come with me, I'll show you."

I shuffled off the bed. My eyebrows knitted together. "Where are you going?" His free hand reached for the balcony door. "I'll get it." I moved around him and sniffed the air, then opened the door for him.

He looked back at me, almost rolling his eyes. "Was that necessary?"

"After last time, yes?" The night air hit us both, leaving chill bumps on my skin. The trees swayed lightly against the star-speckled sky. Kale tossed the pillows he'd grabbed on the chaise and sat down.

"Sit with me." He patted the nook between his legs. I took a seat and curled into his warmth and the blankets Kale quickly threw over us. We both gazed up at the midnight sky, so dark and blue. The stars twinkled and danced like they shined for us. Two arms wrapped around me, and Kale nestled his chin near my head.

"Are you going to tell me what you want to name your label?"

"Lumen Records."

I turned my head, trying to look at him. "Lumen?"

"The other day, you said I was the light in your dark. Well, you're mine." Kale's lips touched my hair. I smiled, a warmness cresting in my chest.

We stayed huddled up together, staring at the navy clouds above. A shooting star streaked across the sky.

"That's good luck, you know."

We spend the rest of the night talking, making love on and off, exploring each other's bodies at our leisure without boundaries or care for time. I wasn't sure we'd sleep at all. And with Kale, I didn't care if I ever slept again. He was all I needed.

CHAPTER 26

The next day we came down for breakfast. The whole crew crowded in the kitchen area as usual. Colin and Lincoln used tumblers from the cabinet to hold their breakfast. I'd gotten used to the smell. Its earthy and livery aroma didn't trigger my previous suspicious response. We were becoming a very blended family as of late, though I wasn't exactly sure of what Colin's intentions were. Sure, Kale and I had resurrected him, and I wanted to investigate his biological response to our magic, but I wouldn't force him into tests or staying. Something told me that if I asked Colin for anything, he'd eagerly agree.

What I couldn't predict was Colin strolling across the kitchen and taking a seat next to Kale at the island counter. My mouth stayed closed, but Atlas and Anders stopped chewing, letting their forks hit my mother's favorite ceramic plates.

Anders stiffened, preparing to separate the two. Atlas put his hands behind his head, stretching out to enjoy the upcoming show.

"Good morning, Kalen. Mind if I take this seat?" Colin asked, his voice smooth. Kale looked at Colin, then at me. I shrugged, pouring myself another cup of coffee. It was too early for testosterone.

"Not at all," Kale nodded, uttering between bites of his garden omelet.

I could tell it was a bit of strain to keep his tone civil, but he managed. The room was quieter as we all waited to see how this would transpire. The only ones unaware of the tension were Calliope and my mother, chattering on the phone.

Colin cleared his throat. "So, you're getting married, then?"

Kale shifted, setting his mug down on the counter a little harder than necessary. I brought over the coffeepot, refilling Kale's mug, hoping to refocus his attention. I poured the steaming, black beverage into the blue ceramic mug. Kale, still staring at Colin, hooked an arm around my waist, giving me a tender squeeze. He released me quickly, letting me reach for the almond milk I knew he preferred in his coffee.

Kale exhaled. "At some point. Why do you ask?"

Colin set down his tumbler. "No reason—just trying to make conversation. Listen, you and I continually get off on the wrong foot. I'd like a chance to explain myself, if I could."

Chuckling lightly, Kale took a sip of his coffee, putting it down more calmly this time, "Please, by all means, explain to me your fascination with my mate?" My eyebrows shot up into my hairline. A fraction of me was concerned for Colin's safety, while my heart couldn't help but quicken at Kale referring to me as his mate. He didn't use the term often. It showed me how much he'd acclimated to my family and our ways. My pulse crept up; Kale eyed me, taking notice of the minor change.

You alright? His eyes gazed at mine. My brothers were unphased. They'd gotten used to mine and Kale's ever leaping heartbeats.

I smiled. *I'm fine,* I offered back, not wanting to make a big deal over terminology.

Colin watched our interaction thoughtfully, then continued on to explain himself, "I won't deny I find Athena... tempting. She's as striking as she is brilliant, though that doesn't excuse my behavior. I'll do better to respect my place here. I owe my life to you both; I don't want to appear ungrateful because I can't control my thoughts. I apologize to you and Athena; she just looks so much like her."

Her?

Kale sat straighter, almost glaring at Colin and his confession. I put my hand on Kale's shoulder. It was obvious Colin found me attractive. I just didn't think he was bold enough to directly say so. I'd be lying if I denied something tugged at me when Colin looked at me or spoke, drawing me to him. Nothing like Kale, but it was there.

That wasn't the most important part of what he'd said. Who did I look like?

When Kale opened his mouth, he'd apparently been wondering the same thing. "Looks like who?" he asked, his gruff tone telling us he didn't accept Colin's apology.

Sadness washed over Colin, and his eyelids fluttered with what I could only assume was a memory. "Her name was Caoimhe. It means beautiful or precious in Gaelic, and she was just that... a lovely soul, inside and out."

Caoimhe, I mouthed it to myself. I knew from books they pronounced her name nothing like how it was spelled. Her name made gentle sounds as it came off the lips. *Kee-va*, I repeated in my head. *Caoimhe.* I instantly knew who she was to Colin without asking. It came to be like an old memory. My cheeks heated, and I prayed to the Goddess no one noticed.

Colin continued on, his face squinting a bit, but he pushed past the difficulty and pain speaking of her visibly caused him. "She was my wife. Before I was this." Colin gestured to the tumbler of blood and then himself. "The only girl in the village to have black hair, like Athena's. Her green eyes. They were so bright and full of life. I knew the moment I met Caoimhe, I'd marry her."

Kale's eyes softened while he listened and Atlas, Lincoln,

and Anders all remained silent. "What happened to Caoimhe?" Kale asked, part of him knowing the answer.

"He killed her. Xercarus killed the only person I ever loved in this world. The men gathered near the moors, thinking they'd kill the beast who had stolen the children. It was a trap. They slaughtered most of us and took the village. I got away, making it back to the village. Not soon enough, though. Fire was everywhere, and too many of his monsters." Colin wiped at a tear he couldn't shed. "I know now, the villages would've been set on fire anyway, claiming the plague struck them. All of it to cover up what that demon had done and is clearly doing again."

"I'm sorry, Colin." My eyes stung from trying to hold back my own sorrowful tears. Why did his sadness have such an effect on me?

Kale lowered his head, raking his hand through his hair as he often did when stressed.

Colin gazed into my eyes until my face heated. "Don't fret, Athena. It was long ago."

"By why? Why did he kill her? Why not turn her?" Kale shook his head, trying to understand.

"*Ack*, that lass had a spirit made of fire and sheer will. I saw her, tried running faster, but my legs wouldn't carry me. She refused to bow in fear like the others. She clutched her belly and cursed him back to hell. The bastard laughed at her. Said he'd offer her the kindness of a pure death. *That was it*. The last time I ever saw Caoimhe. Until Athena, your face so much like hers. Fierce and compassionate all at once." Colin stared directly into my eyes as if he was searching for my soul. I looked away, hearing enough.

Colin cleared his throat, drawing attention away from me. "When I woke, seeing Athena, I thought I'd finally died, gone to a heaven of sorts. That's obviously not the case."

Colin's story took me aback, and my mouth trembled

lightly. It was strange he should end up here, in my charge. We were all so engaged in Colin's tale no one had noticed my mother and Calliope had gotten off the phone. My mother's face, gentle and soft, turned her mouth down as she rested a hand on Colin's shoulder, then hugged him to her.

"*Oh meu doce homem bonito.* I can feel your suffering, years of aching for her. The elven people I grew up within Brazil spoke of reincarnations. We can live a thousand lifetimes if your soul is made of light. Perhaps Athena is that for you. A representation of your dear Caoimhe. That's why you feel, *amor a primeira vista,* oh how do you say, love at first sight. Athena has always had a hand in deciding her fate and in this life. Her heart lies with Kale. He is her one true love, her mate. That can't be changed, no matter what you might feel for her." She touched his shoulder and gave it a knowing squeeze.

Moments like these were what had made my mother, such a great Queen. Her empathy had no limits, intuition guiding all her actions. She offered a warm embrace paired with honest words to anyone who needed it.

Kale pushed into my head with ease. *Thea, I'd never have—I mean, I wouldn't have been such an ass. I didn't know.*

Turning Kale's stool, I positioned myself on his lap, holding him to me. *How could you have?* I soothed him.

Can I ask you something? Even in my mind, his voice was shaking a bit.

Anything. I didn't let my eyes leave him.

Do you feel a connection with Colin? Like, your mom said. Kale observed my face.

His question didn't shock me. I looked over at Colin. My heart ached for his loss, no matter how long ago it was. I wasn't sure what connection I had with Colin; something drew me to him in a small way. Kale and I had promised complete transparency after I tried to push him away. If roles were reversed, I'd want to know his true feelings. I took a deep breath.

I know I love you. I feel it every fiber of my being. I don't know what connection I have to Colin, but, yes, a small piece of me is drawn to him, like a tiny string tugging. I don't know if reincarnation is real or if my spirit is tied to Caoimhe. Anything is possible in the Unseen. But it doesn't matter because I'm not her.

Kale stiffened under me; he leaned his forehead to mine, inhaling me. *That's all I need to know. If he's any kind of important to you, he'll be important to me. I trust our bond.*

He gave me a quick kiss on the lips, sparking us both. I pulled away, touching my lips and smiling.

Everyone was staring at us, including Colin.

"I don't want to be any more trouble. I should be on my way. You've all been good to me. I don't intend to wear out my welcome."

"Nonsense," My mother said, putting her hand to her apron covered hip, exactly like she always did when she was about to get her way.

"Colin, man, don't go. I still haven't learned how to use my vampire trance thingy." Lincoln lifted his gray eyes from his iPhone, focusing them on Colin.

Kale eased me gently from his lap, putting his hand on Colin's shoulder. "You don't need to leave on my account. I get it. If I lost Athena and thought for a second, I'd found her again, I'd do anything. I only ask that you try not to interfere with our relationship because she might've been the love of your life hundreds of years ago, but, in this life, she's mine."

Colin appraised Kale, his eyes and mouth drooped down, holding onto a bit of sadness, but he extended his hand for Kale to shake. "I understand, and I never want to intrude. But I think it's better if I make this a clean break for myself and go." Kale extended his hand to shake Colin's hand, both exchanging knowing glances.

Kale yanked his hand back, pulling his lips into a sneer like Colin had burned him. Atlas and Anders clambered to their feet, even Lincoln edged off his chair, all of them unsure of what happened.

Kale raised his eyebrow, narrowing his eyes at Colin. His mouth turned up in a sarcastic grin. "You're gonna kiss her."

Colin took a step back, his mouth popping open, looking beyond confused. "What? Who?"

"Kale," I whispered, reaching for his arm. I had no clue what he was talking about, but I knew Colin would not be kissing me. *Not happening.*

"Athena. You're going to kiss Athena." Kale's voice remained eerily relaxed as he shook his head, looking down to chuckle, and ran his tongue against his sharpening teeth.

I heard an ungentlemanly hoot from Atlas and him slapping his leg. "This oughta be good. Let me know when the fur hits the fan. I'd pay to see these two in a fight. My money's on Kale."

"Atlas, shame! Not appropriate," Our mother raised her voice to reprimand her youngest son, who was hellbent on adding fuel to the metaphorical fire. Typical Atlas, always prepared with matches and verbal gasoline. At least he was consistent—consistently an instigator.

Calliope frowned, shaking her head, then did one better. Striding across the kitchen, she stood next to Atlas, giving him a sturdy swat on the shoulder while scolding him softer than a whisper in Portuguese. Calliope tolerated rudeness about as well as our mother, which was not at all. Anders winced at me and shrugged in Atlas's direction in a *"why would you do that"* motion.

"No. That can't be right. We just discussed how that wouldn't be an issue." Colin furrowed his light brows and tried to argue. He was careful to avoid raising his voice. The rest of us had already figured out Kale had a small premonition.

What'd you see?

Kale ignored me, keeping his eyes trained on Colin. "Oh, it'll happen. Good news for you is, it changes nothing."

Colin took his turn, taking his hand to move the hair off his face. "How can you be so sure?" he asked, gritting his teeth a bit. "Because I have no plans to kiss Athena."

"Call it a hunch," Kale replied, his jaw flexing with each word.

I stepped in front of Kale, positioning myself between him and Colin. "Kale has the gift of premonition. When he touches someone, occasionally, he can see a glimpse of their future."

"I see," Colin said, pursing his lips and looking down at his tumbler.

Anders pulled Atlas back to his seat and gestured at Lincoln to do the same. They knew I had it under control.

"Colin, I'd appreciate it if, for now, you stayed. At least until we can figure out how much of an effect our magic had on you." Colin's face fell, his reserve crumbled under my request. I knew he'd stay, not willing to deny me. I should've let him go. I didn't need him, didn't want him—so why did I compel him to stay? I had to let it go.

I turned, angling my torso, so I was facing my ambusher of a mate, "Kale. Thank you for retaining your composure, but what you just did was unfair. You knew Colin didn't know about your ability. And no one kisses me unless I allow it." I raised my brow and set my mouth in a firm line as I finished, trying to amplify my point.

Kale put a finger beneath my chin, drawing my face near his. "I know," was all he said, his eyebrows cocked up as he released my chin.

What the fuck did that mean?

I felt a small ping in my chest for Kale, then Colin. Colin leaving bothered me, not nearly as much as Kale's vision and comment. Kale implied I'd *want* Colin to kiss me. That didn't seem right. I only knew a small portion of me wanted to know more about Colin, but nothing in me desired to kiss him. I had to assume the Goddess had another plan I was not privy to. Just like Kale, Colin's appearance here was too much of a coincidence, and I'd figure out why. Kale touched my waist before sitting back down, pulling me back into the moment.

"Colin." He turned almost too quickly at the sound of me saying his name. "You'll stay then."

As I was about to continue, my phone vibrated, and I glanced at the screen, assuming it was Ben again, but no—it was Connor. I had to answer his call.

"If you'll excuse me, I'm sorry I have to take this." I excused myself out of the kitchen and walked into the foyer. My brothers up again and trailing not far behind me. *Eavesdroppers.*

"Agent Connor, what can I do for you this morning?" I said, answering my phone.

I listened, gripping my phone tighter as he explained how they'd found several human bodies drained of blood and missing several organs outside another nightclub, Onyx. It resembled Zephyr entirely too much. My blood pressure rose. Connor and I both agreed; finding the bodies was merely a decoy. Someone placed them there to get our attention. If we went to Onyx, we'd be walking into a trap. I wasn't willing to sacrifice more human lives to save my own skin; that wasn't how my father taught us. The Triad wouldn't hide.

I told Connor I'd call him back after I spoke to my family, but what I needed to do was clear.

I hung up, seeing Anders and Atlas looming behind me, their eyes on me expectantly.

"What's going on with Connor?" Atlas asked, his tone dark, matching his eyes.

"Let's talk in the kitchen. It's best if I speak to everyone at once." I touched both their arms, guiding us back into the counter. Opening my mind, I linked Logan quickly, giving him specific orders.

Anders touched my back. *Yeah, this obviously isn't good. I can feel it on you.*

I didn't respond to Anders, only nodding. My mind was occupied with listening to Logan before I shared the news with everyone else.

The three of us reentered the kitchen, all the chatting ended, with everyone's eyes landing on me. Kale stood up immediately upon seeing my expression. I didn't want to put my family in danger but taking out another blood house was a necessity and would no doubt bring us closer to Xercarus. Colin and my mom's faces went stiff, trying to hide the concern welling beneath.

My mother clutched her hands together, wringing them. "Athena, *amor*. Who was it?" Her accented voice broke the silence.

"Agent Connor. He found human bodies outside another club, Onyx, it's another blood house. We both believe Xercarus left the bodies to draw our attention and lure us out."

Kale clenched his fists and closed his eyes, knowing what I intended to do.

We were going to take the bait; we just weren't going unprepared.

"Looks like we're going to Onyx then." Atlas stood behind me, crossing his arms.

"Yes, we are."

My mother's hands went to her mouth, gasping. She didn't bother questioning me. Just like her, she knew once I made a decision, trying to change my mind was a futile waste of energy. She wrapped her arms around Lincoln, who was closest to her. Lincoln, still sitting, tilted his head up and patted my mom's hands, his gray eyes peering up at her. I heard him whisper to her.

Colin got up from the chair, standing behind Kale. "That's madness! You can't seriously be thinking of going, Athena?" Colin raised his voice, questioning me. Colin's posture told me he wasn't trying to be confrontational. I could sense his desire to protect me, shield me from Xercarus, but that wasn't going to happen, nor was it his right. Kale turned slowly to face Colin, the hair on the back of his neck standing up.

"Are you suggesting we let them continue killing people?" Kale asked, giving a hard '*hmph*' at the end of his question.

Both Colin's brows arched up, and he shook his head lightly. "Well, no. Not exactly. I only meant…"

I interrupted Colin, deciding it was best to not test his and Kale's labored newfound tolerance.

"I'm sure that's not what Colin is saying." I tried to clear the air between them, ultimately, I knew I was only about to madden them further with my decision, but it was a necessary evil.

"Not all of us will go to Onyx tonight. I'm taking Atlas and Anders." I did my best to keep my face placid.

I reached for his arm. "Kale, I'd like you to stay with Lincoln and Colin. I want you three here at the manor, with our mother and Calliope. I'll inform the certain guard to run patrols all night, alternating shifts." I stared at Kale as I finished speaking.

Anders nodded, leaving the kitchen and heading off to get his gear ready. Atlas smirked, more amused than usual.

"Fuck, yeah! Just like old times. The *Triad* is back!" He whooped and fist-pumped in the air, exiting the kitchen right behind Anders. Atlas might have been pleased, but he knew Kale wouldn't be. And he wasn't sticking around for that fallout.

Atlas winked. "Good luck," he tossed over his shoulder. Why did he have to be so damn antagonizing? For such a thoughtful individual, he rarely expressed that side of himself. I let my palm tingle. It seemed a perfect time to remind Atlas exactly who he aggravated. I lifted my hand as if throwing a baseball; a pint-sized fiery orb sailed through the air, hitting Atlas squarely between the shoulders.

"*Ouch*, Athena!" he shouted at me, making his retreat even hastier. I grinned from ear to ear. He deserved it.

"Athena. That's not polite," my mother chided, and my grin fell a bit.

"No, it wasn't, but neither was he. Atlas is gonna learn to watch his mouth, one way or another."

"I suppose you're right, love. I'm going to excuse myself and Calliope while you four talk this out. I'll be tending to the garden if you need us." My mother bowed her head slightly then left with Calliope in tow. She didn't need to tend the garden, but my mother understood this was a conversation I'd need to have without an audience.

I turned my attention back to Kale. The grim expression on his face said it all. His chest heaved harder up and down. I didn't want to leave Kale behind. It was the best solution to spread us out and be protected on all sides. Until Kale, it'd always been my brothers and me. Colin and Lincoln stood motionless, reading the seriousness of the room.

"Kale, before you get upset," I started. Kale snorted and sighed, shaking his head as he raked his hand through his dark hair, then tugged at the chain hanging around his neck.

"Before I get upset? That's comical! You make an arbitrary decision that affects me without even consulting me, and you expect me to not get upset?" Kale didn't raise his voice, only changing his tone. He crossed his arms over his chest, waiting for me.

"It's not ideal, but it's the best solution. We still haven't found if there's a defector in the guard. This wasn't an easy decision." I reached for him, but he moved away. His eyes sharp and harsh.

Kale scoffed. "Huh. Really? Because you got a phone call and announced to the room your plans."

"Kale, that's—"

"No, Athena, we're not doing this here. I understand why. I'm not gonna argue with you about it. But I don't have to like it either. I'll stay here, do as you asked. And when you come home—you're mine. Now, if you excuse me, I'm going upstairs to clear my head."

Colin stood up, screeching his chair across the floor and opening his mouth, daring to speak. "You're going to let her go? Just like that?" He wasn't talking to me. He aimed his question at Kale.

Kale blurred past me, up in Colin's face. "Listen, old man. I know back in the days of cholera where you're from, women were possessions, and they were to do as they were told. That's not how it works here. Athena is my equal. She's asked me to do something, to help her protect our family. So no, I'm not *letting* her do anything. She gets to decide." With that Kale stalked past me, touching my shoulder on his way out. It was his way of letting me know he loved me.

Lincoln's jaw dropped. "Whoa... that was intense. I think I'll brave the sun and gardens with Illiana. It'll be less awkward than watching any more of this telenovela." He walked off, shaking his head, popping his AirPods back in, and slipped out the patio door.

I almost wanted to smile. Lincoln had spent too much time with Calliope and my mother. What teenage vampire knew about telenovelas, which were a known guilty pleasure of my mother's? It was then I realized Colin and I were alone. I should've felt more uncomfortable by our proximity, but I wasn't. I wasn't afraid of Colin—far from it. He and his story intrigued me.

Colin rubbed his neck, then tucked his hands away in his pockets. "I didn't mean to come off that way. God, what you must think of me? I don't even know what to think of myself. I can remember my life hundreds of years ago, see your face like it was yesterday. But I can't remember anything recent. I've lost track of years—decades of time unaccounted for. Who was I? What did I become, getting so close to Xercarus? Becoming a monster of his, like the ones who cut down—" Colin stopped, indecision making him fidget. "I think—I think, I did bad things, Athena, lost my way, let the years change me into something dark. When you brought me back, you washed it all away, giving me a second chance. I can't thank you and Kale enough for that. I'm trying my damnedest to make heads or tails of all this, to find my place. And I can't. I can only think of you. Protecting you, unlike last time. Athena, if you want me to stay, I'll stay. I will do my best to keep my distance." Colin's eyes drifted down, then back up. He searched my face for any sign of emotion.

"Colin, I—" I lost my words, backing away from his longing stare. "I wanna ask you to stay, but I realize it's wrong for so many reasons. This thing, between you and me..."

My mind ran through all the words and ways to tell him the truth of how I felt, but none of them would spare him, and even so, I'd ask him to stay.

Colin shook his head 'no' and extended his hand. His movements were graceful and calculated as he took my hand into his and placed it on his stone-like chest. "There's no heart here to break anymore, Athena. You needn't worry about that."

With that, he released my hand as quickly as he'd taken it. It appeared Colin was a liar. His sad, glassy eyes told me everything he wasn't willing to say.

I swallowed, my mouth feeling dry. "Listen, I don't know what this is. I can't really say what I believe, I can only feel. When you're near, I sense you, like I know you, yet I don't. And if I'm asking you to stay, I have to tell you—I love Kale. That won't change. Nothing will break that bond, and I wouldn't want it to. Anything I might feel for you doesn't compare. I don't want to hurt you. You've lost so much already, but—"

His warm brown eyes stared, his mouth twitching in the corners. "Shh." Colin blinked slowly, composing himself. "I'll stay."

Before I could stop myself, I had Colin wrapped in my arms, hugging him close to my chest. He was stiff, his body chilled and firm. He smelled familiar, almost floral, laced with notes of a finely aged wine. I held onto him a moment longer, and he relaxed, lifting his arms to return my unexpected embrace. Colin squeezed me, then tucked a hand on my neck. He pulled back ever so slightly to look at me. His brown eyes flecked with gold and bits of green looked livelier somehow. I wondered if maybe they were hazel, an ever-changing hue.

My body jarred like a startled cat, and I glanced down, embarrassed at my impulsiveness.

Colin half-smiled a crooked grin. He backed up, letting me go. "Thank you. That was—surprising," was all he said before pinching his bottom lip between his thumb and finger and retreating from the room and heading outside.

I stood in the kitchen alone, except for my thoughts, and I wondered if hugging Colin like that was crossing an invisible line. I rationalized that I hugged people all the time. Then again, most people not being a presumed former lover from lifetimes ago. My teeth clenched, and my lips twitched. I didn't have time to fret over Colin; my head had to be in the game. I wasn't sure what was waiting for us at Onyx, but first, I wanted to speak to Kale. We needed to be on the same page.

As I walked upstairs, I heard Kale well before I reached the top. He was in a guest room, or rather his room, the one housing all his instruments. His voice lulled me, making me close my eyes and drawing me to him like a siren call. The rise and fall of the notes, and dulcet tones of his voice, carried my body the rest of the way to him.

I knocked on the closed door, "Come in," he said, continuing to pick flawless strokes on the chords.

Kale sat on the bed, his long fingers strumming one of his acoustic guitars, singing softly. I hated interrupting. He looked content in the purest way, leaving his cares in his music.

I took a deep breath. "Hey, are you okay?" I asked, aware it was a loaded question. Kale had a lot on his mind. His thoughts spilled over the moment I asked, and I sensed it. Jumbled words and thoughts moved around my head. It made me want to mend this little rift of ours even faster.

Kale heaved a breath, setting his guitar down. "No, I'm not. I'm so fucking far from okay. I'm trying my best, Thea, to be fine with this, to prepare myself for you walking out that door tonight." His voice came out thick, muddled with the emotions he was trying to suppress. His eyes studied me, moving up and down my face. "Do you know what that feels like? It fucking hurts. It's like there's a weight on my chest I can't get rid of. And it pisses me off because I'm strong enough. I'm supposed to be your equal, and you won't let me help you— again." Kale bent, putting his head between his legs and his hands on his neck, his muscles twitching as he did. He blew out a breath. "I feel like I'm always whining at you. So many situations with you are black and white. Where are the gray areas? The compromises? You need to do this. I get it. I just wanna stop thinking about things that haven't happened yet or might never happen. Does that make sense?" Kale dragged his eyes from the white carpet to look at me. They were glassy and full of hurt. My chest tightened as I stared back at him.

I pushed myself onto Kale's lap, wrapping around him like a blanket. He didn't resist, letting me enclose as much of him as I could in my arms. His pain was tangible, striking me like a dagger. I sucked in a breath, exhaling fast. I tried to mentally push away his pain faster than it was seeping into me, but it raged and overflowed.

"Dammit, Kale," I whispered to him, my mouth near his ear as I hugged him tighter. "Of course, it makes sense. I wish I could take it away—Goddess, I wish I could. But I can't, and I'm sorry. I'm sorry for everything. When... when I think of losing you—" My breath and wolf fought against me, not wanting to say the words. "We have to be separate tonight because honestly, I'm not ready to put you in jeopardy again, not yet. We have this new energy, but when you're around me, I'm stronger and weaker at the same time. I need to concentrate, or I'll endanger us all." I shook my head slowly, casting my gaze off to the side, afraid if I looked into his eyes, my conviction would crumble. "I'm just not ready yet. I'm working on it. I want you all to myself a while longer. I can't have that if you're dead. So, for tonight, try not to see this is as black and white."

Kale took my face in his hands, holding my cheeks with care as he'd done many times before. "There's really no other way to see it," he sighed. "But, fine. You win." He kissed my forehead quickly, taking in my scent. My skin vibrated. "I hear you. I'll do as you ask. Just don't expect me to be okay with it because I'm not, and I won't be. Not tonight anyway." He picked me up off his lap, setting me back down on the plush bed. Kale kissed the top of my head one more time before walking out of the room. I saw him holding the necklace I'd given him, clutching it in his fist.

I was alone again, only Kale's guitars and sheet music to keep me company while I contemplated.

I'm taking a run; I'll be back in a bit. You go ahead, get ready with Atlas and Anders, Kale's mind touched mine.

Guess we aren't going to talk about your vision with Colin either, then? I got up off the bed to go after him, then stopped myself. Kale needed time. Hounding him wouldn't help.

Not now, was the last thing he said before I sensed him shift. Seemed he was taking this run as a wolf. I respected that. Wolves needed to be let out—to run free.

I raked my hand down my cheek, leaving pink marks behind. I'd wanted to get Kale and I on the same page. I'd failed rather miserably. We weren't on the same page—not really. He'd given in, shown me his belly, so to speak, to save a fight.

I thought back to what I'd said, trying to recall if I'd used any Alpha characteristics on him to sway him into agreeing. I was sure I hadn't. We kept coming back to these crucial moments, worrying about things that may *never* happen.

Kale continued to struggle with visions—or lack of. He wanted them to be more timed, but that's not the way premonition worked. Then again, I wasn't exactly sure how fae magic operated, but I knew a little. It was a complex gift, triggered by many things: touch, sound, emotion. Premonitions couldn't be provoked; they occurred, in an organic sense. Kale had gotten lucky with Lincoln, seeing a glimmer of our future with him. Kale wanted more premonitions like that, ones he felt contributed.

I put my palms on the bed, deliberating on getting up, and I noticed I'd set my hand on scratchy papers. Kale left notebooks out. I collected them, seeing notes, and scribbled words on each one. They were songs, his songs. I innocently read them, some about love, most of them actually, and several were about heartbreak. I came across lyrics from an older song of his. One he mentioned was the hit landing him on tour—"King of Broken Hearts." I'd heard it so many times before on the radio. It was about his relationships and not wanting to commit. I closed the notebook.

I lifted up another paper to put away. Like the others, it was covered with Kale's handwriting and scribbles. I couldn't help but read the words. It was a love song, but less about love and more about sadness. I sat back down to finish reading it.

I remember seeing your face for the very first time
The moment I heard your voice, saving me from the dark
Now it's all I hear, sweet words with little lies

A droplet fell from my cheek, hitting the ink and paper. I touched my face with the back of my hand. It was wet. Another stray tear trickled down. These were Kale's words, his feelings. He'd always been honest with me, but in his music, there was a raw side of him he hadn't shared with me yet. Kale didn't believe he was what I needed. Had I led him to feel this way? Given him the impression he wasn't enough somehow?

Without warning, I felt as if I'd invaded Kale's privacy, like reading his personal journal. I couldn't be sure if he'd meant for me to find his songs or if he'd been in a hurry to put some distance between him and me. It was likely the latter of the two. At this moment, I wished we were back in bed, tangled up together in blankets and snacks, drinking wine and laughing again.

It was no wonder Kale wanted real alone time with me. Colin's entrance into our already chaotic lives had made much more of an impact on Kale than he'd admitted. He wasn't jealous of Colin's presence. Kale worried he'd lose me to him. My wolf snorted, uneasy at the thought.

For the first time since Kale and I had met, I longed for the simplicity of being unattached. Everything was more complicated and erratic. I couldn't solely make decisions without second-guessing myself, factoring in someone's needs, and—most of all—safety. Before, it had been only my brothers, who didn't always agree but understood what we must do. We'd grown up as the Triad, with certain things expected of us. Now, I was Queen, had a mate and a demon to defeat, but I was caught up in events, fittings, and songs. I hardly recognized myself. I'd always prided myself on my ability to lead, to be decisive. Where was that Athena?

The wolf inside snapped, implying I was too busy being a bureaucrat and tiptoeing around feelings.

Ah, now you have something to add, I mentally retorted, putting my hand to my hip with annoyance over her sardonic manner.

Her dour mood and stomping around my head told me what she was thinking. She was angry about my behavior with Colin, snorting at the mere thought of him. She forced the words "likable parasite" to the front of my thoughts, making her feelings clear.

I grunted and started talking to myself out loud. "Likable parasite, that's rich coming from you. And bureaucrat? Ha, one of us has to solve problems without teeth. And that's a really unfair assessment. You're drawn to Colin, too, and I didn't mean —" A shrewd shaking of my wolf's head interrupted me from inside my mind.

Yipping one last time, she flicked her tail and wandered back into a corner of my mind and sat down in the shadows. I couldn't find it in me to be angry with her anymore. She'd been far more perceptive than me, effectively reminding and putting me in my place, as the Alpha. I was capable of compromise but never simpering around, hoping for someone else to solve my problems. Kale and Colin would have to wait.

I'd use this time to see if Atlas's and Anders's powers could be extended, not wasting it by sulking about males. Alphas didn't mull around over petty matters, but Kale wasn't petty. I shook my head.

Enough.

I called for my brothers, asking them to meet me at the library. Maybe we could pull out a few spellbooks and see what they were capable of when pushed by me.

CHAPTER 27

I scanned my finger, arriving at the library before Atlas and Anders, giving me an opportunity to get our transportation arranged and our gear loaded up. We weren't wasting time driving to Onyx tonight. We'd take one of our smaller charter planes.

After a quick phone call to Connor, I'd linked Logan, giving him instructions to head out immediately. Within an hour of taking one of the helicopters, Logan had gotten a rental car and parked outside Onyx, staking out the place.

Logan sent pictures. It looked similar to Zephyr. Large script-like letters on the outside of a brick and metal building that likely lit up and as soon as the sky dimmed and floodlights to draw more attention. Onyx had an even better location than Zephyr, more central to downtown. Meaning once this place opened, it'd be crowded—more so than Zephyr.

Great. More humans.

Logan had also established there were four entrances and exits, none of them hidden. We weren't going in or out without being seen by someone unless Logan located another point of entry, something concealed from inquiring eyes.

I called Ben, seeing if he could pull some blueprints of the building under the radar. He had them emailed over within thirty minutes. I looked for underground access, and, sure enough, an elevator shaft went below the storage level for maintenance. These complexes were all built the same nowadays, connected by pathways making it easier for workers to get around and make repairs. We'd enter from several buildings over, using the connecting tunnels to the maintenance bay. I forwarded Logan the email, giving him all the details he required to lay the groundwork for my plan. We might walk into a trap, but we weren't going in empty-handed. Conner would have his men strategically placed outside and in Onyx, waiting for my signal.

I set down my phone, finishing up with Connor when Atlas and Anders strolled in, both clad in all black.

"We thought you might still be battling it out with Kale," Anders said, sitting down across from me.

"Or kissing Dracula," Atlas sniped, giving me a proper jab. Maybe I deserved it, but the Alpha in me snarled at him.

Atlas lowered his head. "One fireball is enough for today. You ruined my fucking shirt, you know."

I ignored his shirt remark, rolling my eyes, and looked at the old purple book in front of me. It was one of many in our collection I'd used to learn spells when I was younger. I'd start with simple incantations, moving small objects, levitation, then see if they could manifest bursts of fire, like me.

"So, what's up, Thea? Why are we in here instead of getting ready? You plan on having us throw books at Xercarus?" Atlas quipped, never one to keep his head down long. A mischievous grin played on his lips.

Anders, always more patient, pulled the book from my hands and began reading, "Spells? You know most of these already."

"Yes, but you don't." I took the book back, turning the pages to where I'd been reading. "I've got another theory I want to try out. I think your powers have expanded. You just haven't tried."

Anders put his elbows on the table, his mouth dropping open a bit. Atlas gave a scoff, crossing his arms. I set the book down in front of Anders.

"Move the book." I waved my hand over the dark cover. "Inno," I commanded.

The books floated, hovering above the tabletop. I flicked two fingers, sending the book sailing through the air. With another movement, I had the book back in front of Anders, gently settling back onto the table.

Anders scratched his head, then placed his hand in front of the book just as I'd done. "Alright. You're the boss."

"Focus."

Closing his eyes, Anders repeated the spell. "Inno."

The book waffled, flopping in front of him. The clattering caused Anders to jolt forward and open his eyes. Atlas hurried to pull out a chair next to Anders and stared at the moving book.

"Well shit," he said, rubbing his chin.

I smiled outwardly, reveling in yet another correct hypothesis. The more magic Anders and Atlas were capable of, the better they could protect themselves.

"Try again. The more confidence you have in your words, the better the spell will work. It's all about intent."

Anders nodded, holding his hand out again. "Inno."

This time the book lifted into the air, hovering. Anders moved his wrist, sending the book way right, left, then higher in the air. After a moment, he set it down, flopping back in his chair, clearly impressed with himself. Our powers and affinity for magic were growing, as I suspected. I shuffled through possible reasons: Solstice being close, our twenty-fifth birth-days, father passing, Kale's presence. Maybe all of these circumstances contributed in small ways. I'd most likely never know for sure.

"Inno. "Atlas's voice brought me back from my ponderings. We all watched as the book levitated, following Atlas's hand and swaying gently in the air.

"How did you know we could do this?" he asked, wide-eyed looking at the book he had sailing around the room.

I shrugged. "I didn't. Only made sense your powers would strengthen along with mine and Kale's. Okay. Let's skip right to the difficult stuff—*fire*."

Anders and Atlas both cocked their heads. "Uh, fire is your domain, isn't it?" Anders questioned my idea.

"Not necessarily, being a dragon gives me fire, but I still use spells to create heat when I don't wanna burn a place down." I exaggerated out a breath. "I'm going to regret this, especially after this morning, but—" I swallowed, wetting my throat. "I'm going to teach you how to throw a fireball."

Atlas gave a hearty laugh. "Oh, this is rich! The idea of getting your ass burned by one of us must really get under that scaly skin."

"*Mmm*, Atlas. Fire doesn't burn my skin. You remember that, right?" My eyes rolled.

Definitely a mistake.

"*Hmph*. Well, shit."

"You know Atlas, she wouldn't throw fire at you if you weren't constantly such a prick. I mean, you do know you ask for it, right?" Anders clapped his hand on Atlas's back as he mocked Atlas.

Atlas lifted his fist, slugging Anders in the shoulder. "Whatever. I keep you two from being boring. Now, let's get this roast going."

"Alright. Get your breathing centered. The words are 'Ignis Pila.' You should feel a burn in your chest, where you're harnessing the fire, then it'll spread to your palm. Open your palm and hold the energy there. And for Goddess's sake, do not set the library on fire." I got up from the table, motioning them to rise too. They both shook their arms, closing their eyes to breathe as I had instructed.

"Ignis Pila," they said in unison. Atlas and Anders opened their eyes, and, for the first time, I saw flickers of emerald in their irises. Lifting their left hands up, they both opened their palms, and fire sparked, like a flame being flinted to life.

"Concentrate on the fire, the feeling. Let it flow through you." This was going to be easier than I anticipated. Their fireballs crackled, growing larger.

"It's an interesting sensation. To hold onto fire and not be charred." Anders tilted his head back and forth, moving his palm closer to his face. Then extending his arm, he tossed the fireball in the air, catching it in his hand like a baseball. He closed his palm, making a fist, and the fireball was extinguished. Atlas started tossing his fireball up and down, catching it without effort.

Atlas's brown eyes creased at me playfully. "Think I can hit you from here?" he laughed.

"Maybe. Care to try it?" I raised my eyebrows, challenging him.

He laughed, suffocating his fiery sphere in his fist. "Nah, I think I'll keep you in a good mood, since, well, actually—" he hesitated. "What's going on between you and McCormick? I mean, we know how Kale feels. Can't quite get a full sense of you, though."

I fussed with my hair, fidgeting. "Honestly, Atlas. I don't know." I tapped my fingers on the table, tiny flames sparking on my fingertips as I did.

Anders, who'd been reading, looked up from the book and sighed, cautious about putting his two cents in. "It's hurting him, you know... Kale's conflicted," he blanched, a paleness taking over his skin. A frown creased his brows and mouth, but

Anders continued, "We don't feel anything for Colin like you do. And I'm guessing it's because whatever connection you have to him isn't from you. You've got a lot on your plate, but you gotta clear the air with Kale. We don't know how Colin got involved with Xercarus, remember? I'm not saying he's a bad dude, but if I get a whiff of shady behavior from him, I'll stake him, Thea—without hesitation."

Anders bowed his head as soon as the words left his mouth, almost like he was asking for forgiveness. He had nothing to apologize for. Anders spoke the truth; we didn't know how or why Colin had wound up one of Xercarus's horde. Anders or Atlas had no trouble ending him if he put any of us in danger. I ground my teeth, questioning whether I possessed the same capability...

I touched Anders's hand. "Don't. It's fine," I said, not wanting his obedience. I needed to hear him. "Let's just keep going, shall we?"

We practiced for several hours. I taught Anders and Atlas three chapters worth of spells. Their capacity to retain spells was phenomenal, like mine. It'd been a long time since we studied together, so to speak. While exercising their skills, we found out the nearer I was to them, the stronger their spells were, almost like they were feeding off my energy. Moving objects came easy, despite the distance, but the closer I was, the faster objects traveled. When we had more time, we'd work to overcome the distance obstacle. They were strong enough to manage a few spells for now, and that would be good enough. It had to be.

"I'm gonna change and find Kale. Meet you at the hanger?" I started to leave the library and turned back around. "Oh, and can you grab a few non-lethals for the humans?"

Anders's mouth shaped into a lop-sided grin, and he gave a fake salute. "You got it, boss."

Atlas ignored me, busy working a water spell and sloshing it on the floor. I hadn't seen him this focused in a while, perhaps magic would be good for him, or at least it might keep him too occupied to run his mouth.

Doubtful.

Reaching my door, the ocean filled my nose. Kale was in our bedroom. I opened the door; to see Kale sprawled languidly on the bed, phone in hand, texting from the looks of it. A Bluetooth speaker on the nightstand played The Weeknd. The balcony doors were open, a cool breeze wafted his scent around me. He was like a spell, dazing me. I closed the door behind me. Kale looked up and set his phone down beside him.

"Hey," I said. My cheeks heated, seeing him barefoot and relaxed.

Kale smiled, picking up my flush. "Hey, yourself."

"I wanted to—" I started, but Kale sat up, patting the bed next to him. I walked to him, sitting down, so close our knees touched.

"*Mm.*" He raised his hand to stop me. His face was calm, his mouth smooth, as he touched my thigh, causing us both to shiver at the contact. "I wasn't ready to talk earlier, and I'm sorry. I thought about it, I mean really thought about it, while I was running. I even called Brody after to help get my head on straight. So, if you'll hear me out, I have some things I wanna say."

I shook my head. "Definitely. Yes. I want to hear whatever you have to say."

He exhaled. "Um, where do I start? Okay, I don't wanna ask you to choose between Colin and me because that's not even a thing—yet."

I raised my eyebrows. "Kale, it's not like—" I protested.

"*Shh.* Hey. Hey. I know. Give me a minute to explain, yeah?" he asked, touching my cheek to soothe me.

"Alright. Go on."

He forced a small grin, but his lower lip trembled. "What

Colin feels for you is just as real as what we have. I see it in his eyes. And in my vision." Kale tightened his jaw, visibly trying to coerce himself to continue the words he was failing to get out.

"Look, I've been with other people, and I know it's not the same, but I was in other relationships. You said it yourself—you felt nothing with anyone else. I know I what I want, but maybe you need time—"

I let out a stunned breath, my cheeks flaming scarlet from anger. "Are you trying to give me some kind of fucked up permission to sleep with Colin?" I realized my tone was shrill, bordering on offended. No way was I sleeping with Colin. I might be keen to figure out how we were connected but not morbidly curious enough to jeopardize anything with Kale. My palms burned with a pulsing fire.

Kale rubbed his hands together and huffed out a long breath. Guess he noticed I didn't appreciate his suggestion. "God, no. Not at all. I don't want that. I'm just saying—look, if I were him, I'd try anything I could to get you back. Anything. I'm only saying... shit—what am I saying?" He stopped talking, setting his jaw, raking his hands through the thick dark hair I loved so much.

Kale's eyes seemed sad, and he drew in another sharp breath. "I'm saying, I'll wait. If you need to explore what's between you two. I owe you that much."

My hand went to my throat reflexively and then touched where Kale marked me multiple times. I rubbed my collarbone too hard, making my skin burn. "Owe me? Stop. Just stop. We're mates. What about loyalty? I don't even know Colin."

"You didn't know me at one point, either..."

I instantly had a headache. What was I hearing?

Kale parted his lips to speak again, but I wasn't interested in hearing more. "Don't I get to choose? Don't I get to choose you?" I asked him, my face contorted with confusion and anger.

I felt my skin growing tight with tension, and my wolf snarled from her corner.

Kale grabbed my face in both hands this time, caressing my cheeks and thumbing my lips. "Absolutely. That's my point. You can choose whatever you want, but it's not like that. You're not being disloyal if we're open and honest about what's going on. I want you to choose me if it comes down to it. I need you to be one hundred percent about it. I wanna know you're in this with me with a clear mind and heart. Because that's what I want, your heart. Everything else, your body, the magic, the sex... they're just an amazing bonus. And if you need to flesh out what's with you and Colin, so be it."

I cast my eyes down. I knew what Kale was offering, a free pass of self-discovery with zero judgments and complete transparency. I had no interest in such a pass. Colin intrigued me, but not enough. At least, that's what I kept telling myself.

Kale continued, releasing my face from his tender hold. "Besides, I had Anders get me some reading material the other night." He bent over to the side, pulling a worn book from the nightstand drawer. It was from our library, another volume of wolf history, specifically one about mates. I'd read it once before, years ago.

"It says here, sometimes Alphas took more than one partner. For diversity in offspring, to, you know, strengthen the gene pool with different aptitudes."

My expression hardened, giving the book a dirty look. I couldn't hear anymore, my ears buzzed, and I put my finger to Kale's lips. "I don't even know where to start with all this. I wanna be perfectly clear when I say this. I appreciate the openness in everything you said, but I'm not interested. Colin doesn't know me. He knows Caoimhe." I took that Goddess-forsaken book from Kale's hand, tossing it to the ground. No book was going to sway me into antique practices.

"And as far as offspring, that won't be happening. Vampires

can't sire children; their bodies won't allow it. Even if Colin could, that's not an idea I'd entertain, ever. If you and I decide we want to extend our family, that remains between us. No one else."

We were both still. All this talk of being with Colin and hypothetical children had my nerves balled up like a spring trap, ready to snap. The silence between us roared with the words we weren't saying and emotions we both concealed.

"Goddess, Kale, I know you're cloaking your emotions from me. This hurts you. I know it does—even talking about it."

Kale let his eyes wander over my face, eventually settling on my eyes. "Not as much as it did before. I have to fight with the wolf about it. It's why I bailed on you earlier and took a run. He obviously doesn't agree and calls me weak, saying you're ours. But it's not weak to respect the free will of the person you love." Kalen gnashed his teeth. "I don't own you. I say you're mine because you let it be so. Just like that night at Zephyr. You wanted me to come with you but never forced me. You gave me a choice. That said..." he paused, trying to control his rippling features, shifting from human to animal, both vying for authority.

"Kale."

He shook his head at me, squeezing his eyes tightly shut. "Look, it's not like I want you with Colin. I'm not gonna lie and say it feels good to think of you with him or anyone else, but..." He trailed off for a moment. "I want your happiness. The wolf doesn't get to decide. We do."

Kale looked away, staring out the window. He cleared his throat, but his voice had still changed, gruffer and strained. "I think after tonight I'm gonna stay with Brody for a few days, to give me—us—time."

My wolf whimpered; this wasn't rejection. Why did it feel like it? I felt like Kale had struck my heart. Kale's feelings flooded out, bursting into my mind. The veil he'd been trying to keep up slipped, his wolf angry at him for being stifled.

Without thinking, I put my forehead to Kale's.

"Breathe," I whispered.

He took a deep breath, exhaling through his mouth like I'd taught him. He repeated the technique, his heart rate slowing. I realized I was breathing along with him.

"How long?" My mouth sagged open on the last word.

Kale's eyes glossed. "Just a few days." He let out a jagged breath. "I want some space. From all this, for a little while."

"If that's how you feel about it." Again, the bitter taste of sorrow swamped my mouth, making the words stick in my throat, hot and teeming with reservations. A combination of confusion and anger bubbled beneath the surface. Who was I angry with? Kale, Colin, myself? Kale sensed my poorly disguised seething. Even in his own turmoil, he tried to soothe mine.

"Thea. Please don't be that way. It's just temporary. I'm giving you space because I refuse to be together out of obligation or a bond. I'm an understanding guy, but being with you means nothing if you don't want it like I do."

This time I sighed, feeling wounded. "I do want you."

I took him into my arms, but he pulled back, putting his lips to my ear, humming to calm himself and me. Instantly, I felt the intimate, sensual tingle skim across my skin. I sat; arms twined around Kale. I replayed the first time I saw Kale, how my heart and mind knew him before I did. I listened to the sound of his heart beating. I felt Kale nudge into my thoughts, watching our first meeting play out like a movie in our minds. The corner of his mouth twitched, along with mine. Kale opened his thoughts, flashing his memories of bright lights above us, music blaring, his lips meeting mine. The vision clear as the moment it happened.

"Ainda me lembro do nosso primeiro beijo." Kale trembled as the words left his mouth.

I leaned back, my mouth dropping open, stunned. "You learned Portuguese?"

This time he pulled farther back, his breathing level and his face fully human. "I've been trying to."

I hadn't realized the effect Kale speaking my mother's native language had until I noticed I'd practically crawled further on his lap, wrapping my legs around his waist.

"That's... When did you even have the time?" I stuttered on words.

"I've been learning a little here and there at night, or when you're busy," he replied, looking down, not giving away too much.

I nibbled my bottom lip. "You showed me our first kiss. Remind me?"

Calm again, Kale let out a small chuckle, closing his eyes for a moment. "We're having a rather serious conversation. Had I known speaking a foreign language might've spared us, I'd have skipped to it sooner."

A warm crimson color returned to my cheeks. "You surprised me, is all. Your pronunciation is rather flawless."

"I have a patient teacher. Plus, Duolingo on my phone. Pair that with a newly improved memory." He let out another light laugh, then furrowed his brow, knitting them together. I could tell a thought crept back into his mind, throwing a haze over the moment. Neither of us had let go of what he'd said, the choices he'd presented, but I tried anyway.

Kale drew in a breath. "Speaking of kissing," he exhaled, "you wanted to know about my vision."

"Back to business, I see," I replied, linking my arms around his neck again, still hoping to sway him in a more carnal direction. If I distracted him, we could forget the conversation—fall into each other and make love right here and now.

His long fingers gripped my thighs. "There's not much to tell. I saw Colin cradling your face. You leaned in, asking him to kiss you." He closed his eyes, recalling the vision. Opening them as he continued, "And he did. You kissed him as if—" Kale stopped, breaking our eye contact, his lips parted, letting a quivering breath sneak out.

"As if what?" I pulled back, not understanding.

"As if he were me. After that, I didn't wanna see anymore. It's bad enough at night when I fall asleep. I see you with him, then the image changes, you're walking towards me in a golden dress."

I asked Colin to kiss me?

No. Not possible. That made no sense.

I sniffed, my guard off balance. The aroma of lilacs and seaside struck me fast, causing my eyelids to flutter.

I stumbled to push my words out, in need of a subject change. "I, um. Gold dress. Hmph. You gleamed my gown for Solstice. You still have broken visions while you sleep," I said, in an attempt to focus on the least offensive part of his disclosure. It was useless. Images of Colin's mouth on mine overloaded my mind. The unexpected interest to know what Colin's lips felt like rivaled my desire to apologize to Kale for even thinking it. I quickly opened my mouth to ask for forgiveness but realized it wouldn't make a difference. I shut it equally as fast. An apprehensive silence fell between us again.

I ran my fingers through my hair roughly, snagging them on a tangle. I'd insisted Kale tell me what he saw, and when he had, I wanted to ignore it. Push it away and forget it entirely. I didn't want it—the kisses, Colin, none of it. A kiss that hadn't happened made me miserable, and here Kale was, stuck beneath me, watching my anxiety bubble over.

When I was close to Kale, like this, I had to try harder to form sentences. I wanted to drown out the angst, show him how sorry I was. I clutched at Kale's neck, trying to influence him.

"Kale." I breathed out, scrambling for composure. "I'm..."

He shook his head, mouthing the words, *"Not now,"* then glanced down at his watch. "It's time for you to get going." His posture went taut. He pushed up, lifting us off the bed with ease, keeping me in his arms. With his hands supporting my bottom, he walked us over to the closet.

I didn't have the patience to wait for Kale to kiss me. I put my lips to his, frenzy skimming over my skin. Instead of welcoming my advance, Kale lowered his arms, setting my feet on the ground, backing away from me. Kale dragged his eyes from my mouth, a grimace spread over his features, reaching his light ocean eyes. He grabbed my upper arms. Kale was conflicted with himself—a tangible chaos, like electricity in the surrounding air. He wanted me in his arms, yet fought against his instincts, placing a quick kiss to my forehead instead. I lowered my eyelids, embracing his gesture.

Before I fluttered them open, Kale had turned on his heels, leaving me in the bedroom. I was alone, left with icy patches on my skin from where Kale's fingertips had been. I pushed my sleeves up higher, stroking one of the slowly fading frosty designs. I admired their beauty, swirling in delicate patterns. I traced them with my index finger. They were so beautiful. One of a kind, like the man who'd created them.

What was I doing to Kale? Pushing his limits, causing him pain, making him believe I'd bed another for the sake of genetics, or because I wanted Colin?

I don't want Colin. I don't, I repeated to myself. I was sure of it. I wrapped my hand around my arm, covering the last of the wintry scrawls Kale had left on my skin.

"Amare un Ignis et Glacies." My voice was quiet. White light flashed beneath my hand. I squinted in discomfort, feeling an unforgiving burn burrow into my skin. I took my hand away, looking down. Kale's snowflake-like figures remained, sketched into me permanently, glacier colored and cool to the touch. I'd carry a reminder of Kale with me, wherever I went.

Forever.

I changed my clothes. All black, fire-resistant custom material made to be lightweight and flexible. Pieces of leather armor fastened to my chest on top of a tight, fitted tank top and vest that couldn't fully compress my breasts, only hold me securely in place. I brushed my tangled, unruly hair, pulling back into a sleek, tight top knot. In the tops of my thigh-high boots, I tucked away daggers, miniature grenades, and holstered a specialty firearm from view. I strolled to the mirror, observing my reflection, glancing down to my left hand. I worried about the engagement ring between my fingers, twisting the precious stone back and forth. Finally, I slipped it off, setting it gently on the vanity counter. I wouldn't risk losing it if I shifted.

Tonight, I'd wear my bond to Kale on my arm—not my finger. A ring was easily taken off, but these—I touched the fresh white flourishes, bearing the icy chill of Kale's power. I smiled to myself.

Ice and Fire.

I put my hand palm up, pushing the burning energy from my chest to my hands. Fire cracked and churned in my open palm. I squeezed my hand closed, smoke seeping out from between my fingers.

"Candesco."

My nails shimmered a stormy gray, then black. The matte darkness colored my nails like polish. Shadowed and deadly. I'd be a wicked combination of both. I'd spare no one this time. If Xercarus wanted a battle—I'd grant his wish.

I caught my reflection and didn't even recognize the woman staring back at me. The face was mine, but the features were dusky, all smolder and shade. My natural green eyes, now so gray they were almost black, giving off a hollow sensation; lips, a deeper shade of rose. A rumble from the depths of my belly rippled and resonated out from my chest. My dragon swished her tail back and forth, signaling her readiness. I was done playing defense. Anything in my path would be wise to run or suffer a fiery blaze.

CHAPTER 28

I knocked on the door to my mother's room, letting her know I was leaving. Upon opening the door, jasmine and frankincense wafted around me. She looked up from her book and set it on the bed beside her. Her tan hand went up, covering her mouth, an unexpected gasp sneaking past her fingers.

"Athena. *Amor.* What is this?" She lifted off the bed and strode to me, touching my cheeks directly beneath my eyes, staring at their murky shade.

"Nothing," I replied, glancing away. I tried to push her prying hand away.

"*Nao.*" Her tone was serious while she pulled me to her, hugging me tighter than necessary. "Don't lose your light, Athena. The dark will pull you, try to consume you. Don't let it."

I sighed. I hadn't come to her for a lecture. "Mother, I'm aware of the allure dark magic has. I'm not using it. Let's just say I'm embracing all facets of my power."

She held me away from her, hands still resting on my shoulders. "Ack," she clicked her teeth together. "Be safe. You are my

413

most precious gift." Moving her hands over my forehead, she gave me an elven blessing of wellness and protection. Her words were quick and hushed. I'd never been as fluent in elven as my mother. She learned it as a girl and kept her belief in the potency of elven magic. I shared her belief in balance, but today that poise eluded me. All I felt was fire, simmering below my exterior, waiting to be unleashed. She continued her sanction while I grew uncharacteristically more jittery. My insides coiled and tight under an unidentified pressure.

"I'll be back before you know it."

She nodded at me, clutching her hands beneath her chin. I watched her eyes go glassy; a single tear leaked down her cheek. Regret pitted in my stomach over my impatience. My mother had given me no reason to be intolerant. I bit my lip, cursing my temper.

I hugged her again. "I shouldn't have been short with you. I don't know what's wrong with me." I confessed, closing my eyes.

"Sometimes, Athena, I forget that for as wise as you are, you're still young. Much of this is new to you. You and Kale are at odds, yes?"

I frowned, knowing what she said was true. "Yes. He..." I stopped, embarrassed to tell my mother of Kale's latest proposal.

My mother smoothed her hand down my arm, stopping when she came across the cool marks. "Athena. What are those?" she asked, lifting my arm to examine the feather-light scrawls that reached a bit past my elbow.

"I cast a spell," I answered, trying to mask the shame and disappointment poking around my emotions. "After the vision at breakfast, Kale believes I need to explore my options, figure out if there's anything between Colin and me. So, he's going to stay with Brody for a few days."

"And these marks?" she asked again, her eyes glued to them.

"His touch left such beautiful designs, but frost melts. I made them permanent, like a tattoo."

She stroked the cold outlines. "They're magnificent. You see, Athena, you and Kale will have many trials. True passion like yours goes in all directions. The physical kind is easy. The emotional is not so simple. It can be maddening, but in the end, you'll both find your way back." My mother patted my hand.

I half smiled, her words offering me a small but needed relief. "Love you."

"I love you." Her eyes wrinkled in the corner with gentle thoughtfulness.

With that, I got up and left her room, only to catch up with Lincoln shortly down the hallway. His demeanor carried an unexpected seriousness about his duty to protect the family in our absence. He'd changed into a dark, tactical outfit similar to mine with a stowed away knife and firearm stowed at his side. He looked older, more like the vampire he was, standing taller and with confidence. His short lessons with Colin had made him more comfortable in his skin.

"Athena. I knew you were up here. I could smell you. Colin taught me how to hone in my senses, really focus them, ya know." Lincoln tapped his nose.

I nodded in approval. "Good. Vampires possess excellent preternatural senses. Should you fight, you'll need them."

"And I will fight if it means protecting us. I won't let you down, Athena, not again."

And there it was, his child-like purity, trying to make up for an assumed failure. Even in my stormy mood, I felt inclined to embrace Lincoln, hold him close to my heart. I knew he was genuine, always wanting to please me, but he didn't have to. I knew I'd forgive him for anything when I'd first laid eyes on him that night beneath Zephyr. Lincoln brought out a maternal instinct in me I'd never experienced before. It bothered me to know he felt as if he still had to prove. He had spent enough of his life trying to fit into families that didn't appreciate him, but that was over now.

I patted his shoulder. "Be safe," I said, continuing to head downstairs as I heard Lincoln let himself into Illiana's room.

"Athena," Lincoln called after me. I turned my head to glance at him, seeing his head peeking out from the doorway. "You look badass."

I chuckled, jogging down the stairs.

By the time I reached the patio, Atlas bombarded my head, complaining about my lateness. *Any time now, Alpha.*

Shut it, Atlas. My face soured.

Someone's in a mood, he said in a clipped tone and left my thoughts.

I made my way down the path, walking past one of our greenhouses. Trellises covered tall glass windows on the inside. Fragrant wisteria climbed the framework. The amethyst petals laced around the lattice and weaved through pale honeysuckle plants. Something moved inside the greenhouse. I glanced up to the sky. The sun was setting. No one should be in there this time of day. I veered off the trail. My ears heard shuffling and a faint 'misting' sound from inside. Gently, I pushed the level down on the door.

The plants took over the space. The wisteria and salmon-colored bougainvilleas hung from the ceiling like archways, almost touching my hair. Another misting sound. Someone was watering the plants. An earthy scent moved around the flowers. I put my arm up to move a vine, a thorn dug into my skin.

"*Ouch*," I whispered and yanked my arm down. A drop of blood pooled on my skin.

The misting sound stopped. "Who's in here?"

Colin? What was Colin doing in here? "It's just me," I answered.

The greenery gave way, and Colin emerged from behind a wall of passionflowers that crawled up a small pergola.

"Are you okay? What are you doing in here?" he asked, dusting his hands against the sweater he wore.

I took a step back. "I'm fine. Just a thorn, and I could ask you the same question."

Colin glanced down. "Fair enough." I noticed several leaves nestled in Colin's hair, caught on one of his sandy waves. I stifled a chuckle. He looked a bit ridiculous.

"I assume you didn't come all the way in here to laugh at me." Colin arched his brow and offered me a good-natured smile.

I put a finger to my mouth. "Not at all. I saw movement, and it's—you have leaves in your hair." I gestured to my own hair.

Colin lifted his arm and fussed with his hair. The greenery didn't move. Another small laugh slipped past my lips. "Here, let me." Colin moved closer, lowering his head. I plucked the leaves from his now tangled hair. "There."

Colin moved his head up quick, his face closer to mine. "Thank you." His breath hit my face.

"You're welcome. What brought you out here anyway?" I let the last leave fall from my hand.

"Illiana said gardening helps her think. I figured it couldn't hurt to try it." He shrugged.

I grinned, thinking of my mother. "Ah, the wise words of Illiana Whiteridge. She believes nature solves most problems." I laughed lightly.

Colin grinned and pushed up his sleeves. "That's a lovely sound. You should do it more often." He gave me a soft look and turned to grab another spray bottle.

"What is?" I asked.

He looked up from the plant he was misting. "Your laugh." The smile I hadn't realized was on my face drifted away. Colin took notice of my fallen face. "I didn't mean—Athena, I didn't mean it as—"

My head shook. "Of course not. I need to be going. My brothers are waiting."

Colin set his lips in a firm line. "Right."

I rubbed the tattoos on my arm. "We'll talk when I get back." I turned to leave the greenhouse.

"Athena?" Colin called after me.

"Yes?" I glanced over my shoulder and caught Colin's eyes.

He reached up and grabbed at his shoulder. "Just be careful. Xercarus will try to destroy what you care for most in this world. Trust me—I know."

Glancing away, I thought of Kale. "I will."

And I left, closing the greenhouse door behind me. I leaned against the glass door. My chest thumped. I shook my head and rolled my shoulders. Colin was nothing more than a complication, one I'd resolve as soon as time permitted. *Just a complication, Athena.*

Pushing off the glass, I started jogging down the path. I picked up my pace, breaking into a sprint. The air hit my face, freeing me from the uncomfortable interaction with Colin. I looked up at the sky, the sun giving way to a glorious hunter's moon. Tonight, I'd be the hunter. Pressure sprung from behind my eyes, their glow lighting my way. In my head, I heard a howl, and an ominous grin revealed my sharpened teeth.

The notes of clean sea spray struck me, stopping me in my tracks. I skittered to a halt.

Kale.

I didn't see him, but I felt him nearby. I sniffed again, inhaling the air—citrus and sea. Twigs and leaves crinkled, giving away his position. He burst through the trees, barefoot and wearing only short joggers. Sweat beaded at his hairline and chest, glistening on his skin like water as he panted. Dark strands of hair clung to his forehead and temples. Even sweaty and disheveled, he was provocative, with his wet skin throwing off pheromones. My vision focused on Kale. Emotions threatened to take over my actions. I held my breath, willing myself to keep control. I held my breath.

Kale stepped towards me, but I backed away, shifting downwind to evade his scent. The thumping in my chest grew louder until it rung in my ears. My blood rushed and pounded the longer I stared at Kale in all his bare-chested glory. I needed a healthy distance from him to keep my thoughts straight. Kale's eyebrows creased in confusion. He inhaled, shimmering blue eyes intent on me. "You're different. I can feel it. It's in your eyes, they're..."

Maybe it was the darker, wild magic I'd invited in, but I felt my inhibitions disappear. My body hummed, vibrating with the words I wanted to say to Kale and the things I fantasized about doing.

Kale took another step forward. I held up my hand, not willing to let myself get caught in the blind eye of the storm of emotions that Kale provoked. "Wait. I need to say this before I go."

His eyes roamed around my face, but he didn't move. "I told you I wanted to know what was between Colin and me, but only to sever the connection. I'm not Caoimhe. I'll never be her, and I don't want to be. I can't tell you why you had the vision. I can tell you, a kiss from Colin wouldn't change what I feel for you. Bond or no bond. You're marked on my heart and on—" I moved my hand to my arm, showcasing the white flurries I'd made everlasting. The twisting, frost lines spanned from my shoulder to my elbow.

Kale's jaw went slack, and the color drained from his face, remembering how he'd touched my arms in our bedroom. Covering his mouth, he frowned. "Did I do that to you? You said I couldn't hurt you."

I rushed to him, my shoes crushing dry leaves beneath

them. "You didn't. Your power can't hurt me. Your touch left these designs, but frost fades, so I made them eternal. I cast a spell."

Kale's eyes glossed as he brushed his fingertips over the swirls. "They're cold."

I let a grin pull up the corners of my mouth. "Yes, like your gift. You're with me, always—ice to my fire. You told me I didn't have to choose, but I choose you. I choose you."

Atlas nudged into my mind, intruding on our moment. *Um, what happened to you? You were just on your way. Move your ass, Alpha.*

Dammit, Atlas, get out of my head! I snarled. Atlas didn't say another word.

I wanted to stay with Kale in this moment for a little longer, but we were out of time for tonight. I touched Kale's face. "I have to go. They're waiting."

"I know you do. Atlas is bitching at me too. Just come home to me tonight." He tried to give me a quick kiss, but I turned my cheek. The tension between us peaked. How much more self-discipline did I have? My hands shook. I wanted more of him and hadn't the time. If I kissed him now, I wasn't sure I could leave him.

Kale sensed my shift of thoughts and languidly pulled his chain around his neck. His mood had changed—a feral sharpness in his features and scent. Kale's eyes glinted amber. He'd given over to his more primal brain. "See something you like, Thea?" Kale taunted me, rubbing his bottom lip. He understood his effect on me. He quirked his head to the side. "What's the matter, Athena? You don't want a kiss goodbye anymore?" He knew what he was doing. Kale was toying with me, baiting me, to unravel my last thread of control.

I opened my mouth, daring to speak to him. "I didn't say that, but—" was all that tumbled from my mouth in a clumsier fashion than I was used to. I felt my lips and hands tremble.

Taking Kale right here on the ground consumed my thoughts. I wasn't sure what triggered this needful response. Perhaps my body knew something I did not, or maybe the darker magic brought my longings to the surface. Either way, it had ahold of me, and there was no way to shake it loose.

"But what?" he questioned. "I've always liked playing with fire." He inhaled, his changing golden eyes on me. "There really is something unusual about you. I can't put my finger on it… unless you want me to."

I wasn't the only one who was behaving differently. Kale carried an unfamiliar edge to him, and I would've been lying if I said I wasn't partially enjoying it. The recklessness of it washed over me like a tidal wave.

The thread of self-restraint I'd been holding on to so tightly snapped as Kale trailed two fingers down my arm, grazing the tattoo. The adrenaline coursed through me, and I bolted forward, catapulting myself onto him. With his enhanced reflexes, he caught me with ease but could not keep us from crashing into a giant hardwood.

Splinters from the trunk flew into the air at our impact. I pinned Kale to the giant sycamore, kissing him like it was the first and last time all at once. I let all my emotions flow into that kiss, telling him all the things I could not.

I knotted my fingers into his damp hair, nipping his lips. Kale groaned, keeping a vice-like grip that dug into the sensitive skin on the underside of my thighs. I kissed down his neck, tasting the ocean like salt on his skin. He wanted fire; I'd make him burn. I loved the smell of his mounting arousal and the way he now struggled to fight it.

Kale tried to lean back, his heart speeding in his chest. "We can't." His voice was breathy as he panted. "We can't do this here." He strained harder to get his words out between my insistence.

I eased up. "Why? I thought you liked playing with fire?" I

grinned as I slowly continued to kiss his neck. How amusing—he'd set out to tease me, subtly seduce me, yet here he was, prey to my predator; completely at the mercy of the chaos, I unleashed on his body and each touch that broke down his resolve.

He tried to set me down, but I squeezed my legs around him, making it impossible. "Thea." Kale attempted reasoning by putting space between us. I didn't like it. I didn't want to follow the rules or be polite. I wanted Kale. He'd started this game, and I planned to finish it. Being seen, or worse, caught, did little to sway my mind. All I wanted was to give in to this hypnotic feeling.

"You know why," he said, his eyes rolling back when I placed a kiss at the base of his neck, next to his collarbone. My teeth inched down. I let out a low hiss, adding more fuel to our inferno.

I moved my hands to hold his face. "Do you want me to stop?"

Kale groaned again, this time in impatience. "No. But—"

"But what?" I tugged his head to the side, blowing on his exposed skin. Kale closed his eyes, his lips parting to release a cool breath.

"This can't happen here, not in the open." He was trying to convince himself along with me. I lifted Kale's chin with my fingertips, pinning it tenderly as I could manage to the scratchy bark of the massive tree. My thumbnail dug into Kale's cheek, yet he didn't resist, offering up his full trust. I trailed fervent kisses down his neck and nuzzled at his mark. I felt Kale stiffen beneath me, his body tensed and ready.

For fuck's sake, Athena. Let's go! Atlas's voice rang in our heads, like a bucket of ice water. I pulled back from Kale, and he released me slowly until my feet touched the ground again. Damn Atlas. My temper bubbled.

"Punch Atlas for me when you get there." Kale exhaled and brushed off the bark that stuck to his skin.

Groaning in irritation, I stepped backward, away from Kale. "I will." I touched my fingers to my lips and placed them on my white swirls.

I turned and bolted off down the paved path into a run again, making my way to the hanger and to my not so patient brothers.

Be safe. Kale's voice rang through my head again as I was walking up to Atlas, readying myself to punch him in his smug face. Lucky for him, Kale's voice had soothed me before I could, and instead, I smiled to myself.

Atlas and Anders turned to me. "I didn't realize becoming Queen made you arrive fashionably late." Atlas wore an arrogant glower on his face as he took his jab.

Anders stepped in between Atlas and me, putting one hand on each of our chests, trying to defuse the hostility. Anders shook his head at Atlas. "Not now, Atlas, just not fucking now."

"He's right. I'm in no mood to bicker with you. I had to tie up some loose ends with—"

Atlas scoffed, giving a sarcastic chuckle. "With who, Thea? Your mate or the vampire?"

I snorted out a laugh that sounded like a growl. "That's what this is about? I'm not sure if I should be pissed or proud. You're worried about Kale. I know you linked him." The nerve of Atlas sometimes. He could never just say I upset him.

Atlas folded his arms across his chest. "He didn't answer me anyway. And yeah, I'm worried about Kale. Triad, remember, Thea? You bonded him to us, not just you. I feel the hurt—your indecision, your sadness. And, I get to sit here and absorb all this shit. Look, Colin probably isn't a bad guy, but Kale's is family now."

Indecision. The word left a bitter taste in my mouth. I wasn't indecisive. I put my fingers to my temples, trying to ignore the sudden, too-loud whooshing of the blades. "I'm glad you're in his corner Atlas, but you don't need to be. Kale's my mate. That's not changing for anyone. Now get in the damn helicopter."

CHAPTER 29

On the flight, we went over our plan again, hammering out the fine details. As we talked with our headsets on, I fiddled with my phone, scrolling through Logan's texts again. He assured me he set everything in place. Anders showed me his new skills. Always a reader, he'd dived into the spellbook with rightful tenacity and basically mastered control of fire and easily negotiated his powers in the tight space of the helicopter. Atlas for once remained quiet, flicking fire every time he snapped his fingers. I looked down at my phone again, pulling up Kale's contact.

My fingers swiped deftly along the screen. *"I choose you,"* is all that came to mind. My fingers flew across the keys. I gripped the phone tightly in my hand, waiting for three little dots. His message popped up in blue, making my heartbeat quicken.

I choose you, too

Before I knew it, we were hovering over the broken-down abandoned building I'd found on Google Maps. Logan had cleared the building hours ago, ensuring it was empty and structurally sound. I'd determined it was best to arrive several miles north and avoid drawing more attention than necessary.

When we landed, I unbuckled my harness, hopping out before my brothers. I looked at the city and streets from atop the building. Taillights and car horns; the city didn't sleep on the weekends. We'd get to Onyx faster on foot. Traffic on the weekend was unbearable, and we lacked the luxury of extra time. We'd carried our backpacks until we got to Logan's rental car and dropped our extra supplies. It was approaching dusk, the orange and pink sunset ushering in the night sky. In the dark, we'd be less conspicuous. I linked for Logan, alerting him to our presence. He appeared out of nowhere from around a corner.

Onyx was opening its doors. Noisy chattering filled the air from the barrage of young, unsuspecting club-goers, all vying to get in first. None of them were aware they may never come out. It was no coincidence Onyx was opened on a block with multiple vacated buildings; it left ample space to house his creatures during the daylight. In all the buildings Logan investigated, he had found rusty stains, black droplets, and smears consistent with blood and Xercarus's dark sorcery.

As we walked to the dilapidated, discolored brick building, I smelled mildew, the dampness of rotting wood, and the familiar, bitter odor of death like Zephyr. A growl pushed up my throat, recalling how I'd found Lincoln that night, barely alive. Atlas snarled alongside me; teeth bared. He fed off my energy, and all at once, his emotions came crashing onto me like a wave, coursing through my bloodstream. It made my skin feel clammy and my feet heavy. Atlas's nerves plagued me, and his anger—a deep, brewing anger. It needled at him, so also at me.

Atlas always played up his carefree attitude, making jokes, and instigating bouts between us. I'd never detected this kind of unease from him. Atlas could shield himself physically, but he often masked his emotions. He possessed an overwhelming need to show everyone how strong he was by pretending nothing bothered him. I saw glimmers through that façade. Occasionally, Atlas let his guard down, and I peered over the wall, but he didn't like to let anyone past—especially me. The truth was, Atlas remained a sensitive soul, soft as the brown of his eyes. Knowing Atlas the way I did, it was best not to say much. He preferred to be left to his thoughts, but the protective sister in me didn't agree and needed to calm Atlas.

I stopped walking and touched his shoulder without a word. Atlas's warm, sad eyes met mine, glass with a tear that threatened to fall down his stubbled cheek.

"You're allowed to feel. You don't need to shield your emotions." I stroked his face. The face of much irritation but still yielded a loyalty no one could replace.

Atlas pushed his tongue into his cheek. Embarrassment washed over his reddened face. He resisted, trying to cocoon his thoughts from me and shirk away from my grip. I shook my head no as I watched him struggling to try and put up the mental divider, but this time, I pushed back. He needed to feel, to release the terror tumbling within.

I held his neck tighter. "Hey, listen to me. Fear isn't a weakness. It's a strength, a motivator to fight harder. You hear me?"

He nodded, squeezing his eyes shut. Anders was behind us, observing in his typical quiet manner. He walked on by, unwilling to ruin a sentimental moment between Atlas and me.

Atlas sniffed, wiping his face with his rough palm. I gave him a crooked smile, patting his cheek.

I needed that. Atlas touched my mind, his resolution replenished.

I know.

Logan cleared his throat and put his hand in his pocket, removing three small devices. "Connor gave me earpieces for you three to keep us all connected."

I nodded, taking mine from his open palm, fitting it snuggly in my ear. Anders and Atlas did the same. The cool metal buzzed to life, and Connor's voice flowed into my ears. Everything was in place.

"Ready?" I asked. My body hummed, energy coursing through my veins.

Atlas glanced at me, adjusting his earpiece again. "Yup. All good to go. Let's kick some demon ass."

Anders draped his arm over Atlas's shoulders. "Let's do this."

Logan shook his head at my brothers. His face showed no sign of fear. It was blank. He'd gone on more missions than I had, a seasoned warrior. "Shall we get moving then, Athena?"

"Yes, let's go."

I walked in first, hearing pigeons cooing and their wings flapping. Some nesting on old beams, and broken-down walls, others walking along, bobbing their heads to see if we had scraps of food. Feces from rats and pigeons splattered the rickety floor. The mildew smell grew stronger, and so did the scent of blood. Almost all the windows were boarded shut, glass smashed out long ago. The bricks and cement crumbled and faded. The elevator shaft was unusable; we'd have to take the stairs. I snagged my phone from my side vest pocket and pulled up the blueprint on my phone. "This is the tunnel we're going in. You got those UV and silver explosives set up, right?"

Logan held up the small black device. "Press a blue button for UV and red for silver." Then handed me the remote. I took the remote, tucking in another pocket on my vest.

"The goal here is to sedate as many of Xercarus's creatures. If you can't—kill them. And do not, I repeat, do not try to take Xercarus on alone. We do this together. Understand?"

All three of their heads nodded. "Yes, Alpha."

We headed down the cement stairwell, stained with chunks missing. The stairs grew more hazardous after the first two flights. Anyone without enhanced senses would've tripped headfirst down into the black, sewer-like conditions that awaited us below. The space beneath the building was a cesspit, drainage pipes broke and leaking. The mixture of sulphury gases and vapors were enough to knock anyone over. I held my breath, listening to the dripping and scurrying in the distance. The scampering was too big for rats. Even rats wouldn't keep company down here with these things.

We kept moving, walking in silence, listening to bellows and snarls that continued from around the corner. I put my hand up, signaling everyone to stop moving. I pulled out my firearm, flipping off the safety, and used my thumb to press an orange button, switching my weapon to the non-lethal sedative rounds. Logan, Atlas, and Anders followed suit, unholstering their weapons and changing the settings. I nodded.

Let's go.

We rounded the corner in tight formation, our backs toward one another to keep from being attacked from behind. In the darkness ahead, three foul mutations, snapping and clawing at each other. There was no way to tell what kind of supernaturals they'd been before. To be honest, I didn't give a damn. I fired before they broke up their skirmish. One dropped to the ground, its body making a splash as it fell into a murky puddle of filth. The other two whipped their heads in our direction. Neither beast was fast enough. Atlas and Anders fired off two rounds, taking them down. They faltered, losing their balance and landing on top of each other. They grumbled, trying to fight the heavy magic-based sedative flooding through their blackened veins.

Three down. Atlas winked at me.

The commotion was surely going to attract the attention of any more mutants down here, and soon our scents would roll around through the tunnels.

I touched my earpiece. "Connor. Three, around the first corner. Sedated."

Connor's team would collect the bodies, load them into vans and get them out of here. If all went as planned, Kale and I would reverse Xercarus's effects on them.

We continued forward, the cave-like tunnels splitting off in different directions. A quick splash, and we were rushed from the right. A slimy hand grabbed my arm. I reached for its wrist and twisted. The creature flipped through the air and landed with a hard splash on the cement. Atlas threw up his shield before another could grab for me. Logan double-tapped a second aggressor, and Anders shot the one laying at my feet. Looking at them, I almost felt pity for what they'd become—hideous fiends with no mind of their own.

Anders updated Connor this time, informing him of two more. I heard loud screeches and howls. By the sounds of it, there were more than I'd anticipated, and they definitely knew we were here now.

Bringing my hand up, I pressed the earpiece again. "Connor, evacuate Onyx. Now."

My earpiece chirped with Connor's compliance. I looked at Logan, my eyes blazed green with vengeance. "Go with Connor. Get these sedated bodies out and go."

Logan narrowed his eyes, shaking his head at me. "I can't leave you all behind like this!"

"You can, and you will. *Go*. Get back to the manor and make sure our family stays safe!" I raised my voice. I didn't have time to argue. Those monstrosities would be here any second.

Logan's nostrils flared as he nodded. He dashed away, disappearing back down the tunnel.

Connor buzzed in my ear again, desperate for answers I didn't have time to give. I raised my voice, desperate to get my point across. "Just do it!"

The hostile screeches moved closer. I couldn't tell how

many were coming for us. Their movements were enough to rumble the surrounding walls. Dust and dead insects from the bricks fell onto our heads. We pulled up weapons. Sedatives would not to cut it. More debris fell as the horde barreled down on us. I stood straight, switching my firearm to lethal, and readied my Solus blade in the other hand. Solus blades, known as *"light-bringers,"* capable of killing most demons with one blow. Over the centuries, Solus blades were used in battles, sending demons to their true death, and tonight, I'd get to test one out.

I braced my back against my brothers, covering each other's blindsides. The horde charged us, squawking and clawing towards us. We dispatched each one with ease. Slashing blackened limbs and plunging the daggers deep into the chests of the mutants. The dying cries of Xercarus's horde sounded like a symphony. A cacophony of screams and gurgles. It'd been too long since we fought, actually battled anything, and it felt... good. Each one I slaughtered amped my lust for blood. Black entrails splattered across my face as I slashed another in half.

My eyes flashed dark, then glowing green as I sent another assailant and their limbs crashing into the wall. I moved faster, using my legs to launch myself into the air, flipping, and taking another gnarled head off as I came back down with a splash. A grin pulled at my mouth while I plunged my Solus blade into the eye of another miscreant. Its scream ended in a muffled gargle.

I wanted Xercarus to hear their death calls. I wanted him to come and face me—to make him pay for all he'd taken from me. Rage filled my vision as I took down anything in my path, striking each beast down. My hands were pasty with the black blood of the fallen. I dropped my weapon and plunged my fist through a boney rib cage. I drew back, holding the heart in my hand.

I swung my blade, beheading the gasping carcass.

Reaching for another weapon, I glanced at my brothers. Both of them stabbed and kicked at bodies.

Atlas's shield allowed him to make even faster work of the shrieking horde. They couldn't touch him, and if they couldn't touch him, he always had the upper hand. His ability to shield made him the most agile fighter between the three of us.

A talon swatted at me. I ducked and dodged from the mutant's unpracticed swings and set it on fire. The fire ached in my palm. I launched fire into their mass. They squealed louder as they burned, colliding with each other and setting more of them alight. I lifted my hand and narrowed my pulsing eyes, coaxing the flames higher. Their scarred skin bubbled as it burned under the blue and bright orange flames.

Anders shoved another corpse off him, his face smeared in black. "Thea, you've got a blaze going. We gotta get outta here!" Anders shouted, knowing we couldn't evade the smoke for long.

Atlas breathed heavily. "We can't leave yet! We need to find Xercarus. I know the bastard is here somewhere! I can smell him."

I stilled. A cold shudder crept up my spine.

We didn't need to find Xercarus. He'd already found us.

"He's here." My nostrils burned with sulfur and spoiled blood. Every bone in my body ached with fire, telling me to light him up.

"Looking for me, little wolves?" A furtive, hissing voice called from the shadows of the smoke and ash; a contemptuous sneer followed his heckling. "Ah, of course, you are. Enough with the games, Athena. Come to me, and I'll let them live." I heard heavy footsteps moving closer. I dodged my head, trying to focus on the movement through the smoky air. The reddish shape was massive, several feet taller than me.

"Iridescidi." Light orbed from my hand, lighting up the

dripping cement around us. Anders and Atlas repeated after me. Their orbs of light up illuminated the room further past the smoke. The clawed footsteps backed up, seeking safety in the shadowy smoke, but I saw his face up close. Mangled, blood red, and twisted. His soulless eyes and pointed teeth, black as charcoal. He was more gruesome than the illustrations. A grotesque red beast with an aura so dark it clouded the tunnel.

"Don't like the light, do you?" I taunted back, letting my lip curl into a severe sneer.

A screech erupted through the air. The shrill shrieking pierced my eardrums. My body shook, and I dropped to my knees; the light in my hand dimmed. Atlas and Anders scrambled to cover their ears. Xercarus was going to deafen us with the cries.

My hand trembled, taking the remote from my pocket and pressing a blue button. A UV light exploded through the cavern. The screeching stopped long enough for me to get to my feet. I charged into the shadows, pulling another Solus blade from my hip. I leaped into the air, only to be struck in the chest by a huge, taloned hand. The blow sent me flying into the cement.

Searing pain took over my chest, leaving me gasping for breath. He'd broken my ribs. The bones crackled, realigning to heal, causing more agony. I grit my teeth, not letting the scream make it past my lips. I pushed myself up, holding my ribs in one hand and my blade in the other. I twirled the sword, a growl tearing up my throat.

"Stupid wolf." Xercarus scoffed. "Just like your predecessors before you. You hide behind those asinine Barriers, letting humans run amuck, and for what? They are beneath us, and some have grown tired of pandering to them. Have you ever asked yourself how I was able to return?"

Xercarus gave a jarring, sardonic laugh. "Oh, you didn't. Too busy gallivanting with your new mate to pay attention. No matter. You can still join me, Athena. We can make the humans bow before us."

I wiped the blood from my mouth with the back of my hand. His words gnawed at me. "Never."

Xercarus hissed in a breath. "Have it your way. You can die with the rest, Athena. We only need your blood."

We? Before I had time to think, he waved his hand in the air, summoning more of his mutants. Another howling group descended on us through the tunnel. The roars and screeches were almost unbearable. Atlas threw up his shield and widened his fighting stance. He beckoned the creatures forward with two fingers as if to goad them.

I tossed the remote to Anders, linking him. *Take it down.*

Anders nodded, flipping in the air to catch the remote. Like a cat, Anders landed on his feet, pressing the last button. The cavern shook, rock and brick caving in around us. Onyx was crumbling, the explosives demolishing the blood house above. Xercarus wailed, searching for a way out as more dirt and debris tumbled from above.

With Xercarus's back to me, I pushed myself off the tunnel floor. I launched myself upwards, springing onto him. I stabbed my Solus blade to the hilt into his shoulder, bearing down on him as hard as I could. His screams made my head throb and twist. I felt blood trickle down from my ears, but I wasn't letting go. If I had to die to kill him—so be it.

A red arm reached back, grabbing me. His claws raked down my body as he threw me off of him like a rag doll. I felt my head slam into the brick wall. My vision blurred as blood poured from my scalp down into my eyes. I blinked fast, trying to see past the scarlet streams.

I watched my brothers swinging, wild and fierce, dropping mutants to the ground. They were screaming something at me. My head pulsed, hurting too much to hear them. I knew they were urging me to get up, and I was trying. I pushed at the ground, willing myself to get up. I pushed myself off a chunk of cement and rebar, getting to my knees. Dizziness knocked me back down. I smelled the crisp air of the ocean; it was a tranquil feeling among the chaos and bodies.

Was this death?

Xercarus stood in front of me, leering down at me. He reached his talons down to pick me up. Fire, I needed fire. I put my hand up.

A flash of brown fur streaked in front of me. Xercarus flew backward, pinned to a wall by snapping jaws.

Kale. No. No.

He wasn't supposed to be here. Anders broke away and raced to my side, putting his palms to my head. My vision snapped back, jolted to life by the thoughts of Kale. I got to my feet, and as I did, I heard Kale growl then yelp. His sharp-toothed mouth dug into Xercarus again and dropped a rancid chunk of red flesh from his jaws. The sound of Kale's cries seared my chest, like when my father had died.

Xercarus held the body of my mate by the scruff. Kale snapped and snarled, refusing to give in. "Is this what you want?" His disfigured nose sniffed at Kale. "Ah, such power in his veins. It'd be a shame to waste it. Perhaps I'll drain him. It's not every day I get my hands on old—" He shook Kale at me. Kale's body shuddered, and his teeth snapped again, latching onto Xercarus's forearm. The beast screeched and reeled back but didn't release Kale.

My blood boiled, and fire covered my hands. "Let. Him. Go."

"You can have him if... you come with me." An insidious black grin spread on his face.

Kale's panicked voice radiated in my head. *Don't you dare give him what he wants for me. Fucking fight.*

Kale's fur-covered body writhed, trying to snap the devilish crimson claws that held him.

Atlas finished off the last mutant, slashing its throat in exaggerated rage. He flanked my other side. Atlas slipped another Solus blade into my hand I had behind my back. The mutant's black blood was fresh and sticky on the blade's handle. I'd stabbed Xercarus already. Fortunately, the move weakened him.

"Don't keep me waiting, Athena." Xercarus squeezed Kale harder, blood matting in his brown fur. Kale refused to howl in pain, only kicking his back legs harder. Saliva pooled at the corners of his mouth and dripped from his canines.

My palms burned hotter, watching Kale struggling. The flames behind Xercarus got higher, raising with my emotions. Xercarus didn't understand love, the strength it held. I'd kill him for this.

Kale's amber eyes stared, never leaving mine. *Kill him. I know you can. Don't worry about me.*

My heart plummeted at Kale's last words.

No.

The thought of Kale dying compressed my lungs, making me short of breath. Anger fumed. My eyes blackened. The darkness I'd invited in battled to my surface.

I whipped the knife, throwing it as hard as I could. "Solaris!" I shouted with Anders and Atlas. The blade lit up as if the sun itself shined from it. The blade struck Xercarus in the chest, missing his heart. He wailed and reared back, causing him to release Kale. Kale's body tumbled to the wet, hard ground, and he scrambled to get up on his four legs. Kale bolted to me, nuzzling my neck with his cold nose.

Between his wretches, Xercarus threatened, black ooze frothing from his mouth. "I'll be back. They always bring me back." He laughed, a diabolical, unnerving sound. "We offered you a choice, Athena. Now, he's mine—" He lifted his arm, black nails pointing at Kale, who stood by my side, teeth bared and growling.

An obscure dark mist struck Kale, leaching into him. His eyes went black, and he collapsed. His body hit the floor with a splash. All three of us surrounded Kale, taking our eyes off our enemy, for a mere moment. Kale's body shook, convulsing in the dirty water. More dark laughter raged as Xercarus tried to make his escape, using Kale as a distraction.

Not a fucking chance.

I ran at his retreating form, launching myself onto his blackened body. We crashed into the ground. Xercarus screeched again. I used my rage, the ravenous darkness I'd summoned, and I turned it to strength. I rolled Xercarus to his back, snarling from a feral place in myself I didn't know existed.

There'd be no returning for him this time. No prophecy— only true death. "Bastard!" I reached my hand above my head, calling inner beasts. My nails sharpened into razor-like claws. My body burst with white sparks and a diadem of silver radiance and night shadows crowned around me in a halo. I felt their enraged power ebb forward and thrust through me.

I slammed my hand into his chest, smashing through his stone-hard skeleton. I wrapped my clawed hand around the pulsating organ in his chest, squeezing it, crushing it. Xercarus sputtered, more obsidian fluid pouring from his wretched mouth. "Thiiss...isn't..." he ghastly words died off.

I leaned down, closer to his ear. "Ignis et Glacies."

The squirming organ writhed in my hand, convulsing until it exploded into floating ashes and shards of light. Xercarus went completely limp. Blue embers and fire blasted from his chest, so bright it almost blinded me. I used my arm to shield my eyes. He was dead, at least, but it wasn't enough. I couldn't contain my fury. I tore at his neck, severing his head from his body, and blasted fire down his throat.

"Thea! That's enough. We gotta go!" Atlas hollered, the

cavern shaking harder, and more debris clamoring down. His voice was enough to bring me back from the shadows.

I threw the useless head into a slimy pool of drainage water and turned to Atlas. My satisfied grin vanished as I watched in horror while Kale's body contorted violently, shifting back to human form. His mouth was bleeding. Dried blood and black smudges covered his skin. Anders dropped down, putting his hands to Kale's chest, his power moving over Kale's flaccid body. Nothing happened. Kale didn't wake, didn't move.

A howl tore up my throat. My heart pounded like a drum in my chest, feeling like it might breakthrough. I ran to him, my knees hitting the ground so hard I knew I'd broken one, but I didn't care. The pain paled in comparison. I put an ear to Kale's chest. His heartbeat was weak and erratic, but he was very much alive.

I stroked his face with my filthy hands, smudging his cheeks further with debris and blood.

"Atlas, the clothes in your backpack! We need to cover him up!" Spare clothes were always a necessity on missions, helping us avoid awkward situations should we need to shift.

"Yeah, T. Hold on." Atlas clambered for his small crossover bag, pulling things out and throwing them to the side. He found his shorts. We moved Kale's body around, covering him. I pulled Kale's limp body up and over my shoulder. We needed to get out of this place. Like Onyx, this place was going to burn. I put my hand up. Fire pooled into a large ball of flames. I threw it behind us, willing the flames to rise higher. I felt the heat from the blaze I'd set.

I'd leave nothing but ash when I was done.

We got out of the building; rain poured down, pelting our faces. Thunder and lightning controlled the sky. I cursed myself for Kale having been there. He must have left right after we did. I certainly couldn't ask him right now what he'd been thinking.

I set Kale's body down, rain cleaning off the smears and grit from his body.

"We can take him home. The lab has—" Atlas said, pacing while rain matted his blonde hair to his forehead.

"No. If something happens to Kale, his family..." I sniffled. "His family can't cross the Barrier. I won't do that to them. I've done enough."

Atlas tried touching my trembling shoulders. I jerked away out of impulse, somehow convinced if anyone else touched me, it would interfere with getting Kale back.

I fumbled through my pockets, searching frantically for my phone. With trembling hands, I typed the four-digit code quickly as I could, smearing blood on the screen. I got to Brody's number, the line ringing.

"Pick up, pick up, pick up the fucking phone!" I realized I was yelling out loud, fear flooding my senses.

The line picked up, "Athena, it's not a good time. I'm on call,"

"Brody, please, please, I need your help. There's been—" I tried to finish. A sob mixed with a howl ripped up my throat. "Kale's hurt. He's unconscious. Anders healed him; he's not waking up. Brody... He won't get up, and we can't take him to a—"

Brody interrupted. "Shh, slow down. He's breathing, right?" His tone was insistent and clipped. I knew he was trying to calm himself as much as he was me.

I looked at Kale's moving chest, the rain pounding down on him. Anders and Atlas held Kale, trying to link him.

"Where are you?" Brody asked, trying to get whatever coherent information possible from me.

"This club, Onyx. Near downtown."

"The one on the news they won't let the public near? They reported it collapsed from second-hand steel, but no casualties. Oh god... That was you, wasn't it? You know what—forget it.

You're about fifteen minutes from the hospital. I'll grab some supplies and meet you outside. The address is in Kale's phone."

I sniffled and wiped my face again. "Alright. Kale's phone. Wait—I don't have Kale's phone."

Anders looked around, realization hitting him. "He had to have shifted when he got here. Kale doesn't go anywhere without his phone. It's gotta be around."

"Call it! Ping it..." I pleaded. I felt myself wanting to fall apart, to sink into despair. I growled, letting my ferocity move past my lips.

Atlas took out his phone, calling Kale's. Sure enough, a faint ringing and buzzing sound caught our ears, coming from Logan's car.

"Found it! We'll be right there." I hung up on Brody as Atlas raced to grab Kale's phone. He jogged back, handing it down to me to unlock. I pressed the code in, his phone getting wetter by the second. I pulled up the address.

I shoved the phone back into Atlas's hands. "Here. Get us there."

Kneeling over him, I picked up Kale's soaked body. The cool rain pelting my back, giving me a chill.

"Let me help you, Thea." Anders extended his hands to lift Kale with me.

I growled, then lowered my head. "Anders—I'm sorry. I'm so sorry." Regretting my reaction. I couldn't bear anyone else touching Kale, but it didn't excuse snapping at Anders, who was hurting along with me. "I didn't mean to," I said.

"I know you didn't." Anders put his hand on my cheek. "We'll figure this out, Thea. He's not dead."

Atlas fished out keys Logan had given him before leaving with Connor. He raced to the dark vehicle, almost slipping in his hurry. He opened the trunk while Anders helped me slide Kale inside. I climbed in next to Kale, cradling his head in my lap. It was a tight fit, but it didn't matter. I stroked his wet hair, fighting back my tears, but it was no use. They streamed freely down my face as I clutched Kale harder. I'd give anything to have him open his eyes, give me that signature smile.

I love you.

Anders shut the hatch, running to the passenger side seat. Atlas sped off, the tires squealing on the wet pavement. No one spoke. Atlas bobbed in and out of traffic, taking advantage of the other cars slowing for the relentless rain. Time blurred, but we made it to the hospital in under ten minutes. Brody, as promised, was outside, waiting and soaked to the bone. He jumped in the back-passenger door behind Anders, twisting over the seats to get a look at Kale. Brody's eyes went wide, and his face grew white; he struggled to subdue the hysteria which came over his features.

"What happened?" Brody asked, reaching over the seat, taking Kale's pulse, then ran a thermometer across his forehead.

"He wasn't supposed to be there, Brody. We went out on a mission. Kale showed up, and Xercarus did something to him."

"Who the fuck is Xercarus? Never mind. What do you mean, did something to him? Like supernatural?"

I nodded, wiping my nose. I hugged Kale's head, picking drenched strands of hair off his face. Droplets of water along with tears beaded to my nose and fell, landing on Kale's forehead. I whispered to him in Portuguese so low Brody couldn't hear me. Only Atlas and Anders could.

Brody climbed farther over the back seat, feeling Kale's limbs for broken bones. He wouldn't find any. What Xercarus had broken in Kale had nothing to do with his body—it was his mind.

Brody gave Atlas directions, the car making rights, lefts, and stopping at lights. It all went hazy—distorted visions of streets and cars blurred around me. I stared at Kale, caressing his cheeks, willing him to wake.

I don't know what time we pulled up to Brody's complex. To keep up appearances, I let Brody and Anders carry the heavy Kale to the elevator. Brody fell into a hallway wall under his brother's weight. Nosy neighbors popped their heads out of their condos, eyeing us suspiciously.

"No worries, Ms. Canik. Kale's had too much to drink; sorry for disturbing you." Brody smiled nervously as he made his false excuse. My wolf yipped, irritated at the lie. I didn't blame her. Having to lie about Kale made me sick. Being drunk would've been a blessing from the Goddess.

They laid Kale on the couch, his body taking up most of it. Brody gave him a full examination this time. I stood in Anders's arms, clutching him around the waist like a child. I felt helpless.

Brody blew out an exacerbated breath. "Well, if Kale was human, I'd say we wait. He's not, so I'm gonna shock him. See if I can jolt him awake. It'll momentarily stop his heart, but we're equipped to get it going again if need be."

I looked from Anders to Atlas. "Okay. Let me do it."

Brody wanted to argue with me, throw his credentials at me. But all his degrees and training weren't enough for this. Brody's procedures were for humans, not wolf-dragon hybrids. Brody nodded, deciding it was better to concede. He pulled out the portable defibrillator, offering me the paddles.

"Don't need them. I can push current through my hands."

"Athena. You've done enough." Brody eyed me angrily.

"Fine." My mouth twitched. I didn't want to upset Brody further. After all, I might've cost him his brother. I took the paddles from his hands. They were lighter than I'd expected. Brody put patches on Kale's bare chest, showing me where to put the paddles. Atlas and Anders stood behind the couch, motionless.

"Just one should do it." Brody cranked a dial on the little machine. "Ready?"

"Ready."

I steadied myself, taking a deep breath. The charge was complete. Kale's chest heaved upwards, his arms flailing from the abrupt shock. His upper body falling back on the cushions. We waited a moment, all eyes on Kale. His eyelids fluttered, trying to open, and my heart leaped into my throat. I felt like I could breathe again. The paddles dropped from my hands as I grabbed Kale's face, stroking his cheeks.

"Kale. Kale. Can you hear me?" I asked, frantic for a response. Brody tensed behind me, his hands resting on my shoulders.

Kale's eyes dizzily opened. He blinked rapidly, trying to focus.

"Come on, Kalen, wake up." Brody coaxed, reaching down to tap Kale's cheek.

Kale lifted his arm, wiping his face. He looked at his hand, wet from his hair. He finally locked onto my gaze, a smile curving on his lips. I returned his smile, still gently sobbing. He touched my cheek, wiping away a tear with his thumb.

"Hey. What's a pretty girl like you doing crying?" he asked, that memorable smile of his, shining at me even in his disheveled state.

I laughed at his attempt to joke. "I thought we lost you."

Kale sat up against the couch pillows, rubbing his eyes, and looked at Brody now. "Lost me? Nah. Didn't I just pass out? Must've been a hell of a party. I'm soaked. And, *uh*, you're a bit of a mess." Kale ran in his fingers through his damp hair, shaking his head a little like a dog would. I touched my cheek, realizing I was smudged with black blood and ash.

Anders shot Atlas a scowl, taking a step back. "Thea," they said together. Their tone carried apprehension, picking up on something I wasn't.

I furrowed my brows. I didn't understand. Kale was just a little confused—how could he not be?

"Why's everybody look like somebody died? Have another drink, don't worry about me. I'm fine—happens all the time. I totally rally." Kale chuckled, rubbing the back of his neck.

Brody put his fingertips to his mouth. I quirked my head to the side. Kale really wasn't making any sense, talking about a party. Picking up on the growing tension, Kale hissed in a breath between his teeth. "I'm sorry. I must be rollin' pretty hard. I don't recall your name. My bad." He gave a sheepish shrug.

My face went blank, and I felt like he'd stabbed in the heart. My head spun too fast. I was going to be sick. I got up, running for the bathroom. I put my hands to my mouth, trying to hold in the sickness taking over. I fell to the cool bathroom tile, retching whatever contents my stomach held into the toilet.

Kale didn't know my name. Kale didn't know *me*.

Oh, Goddess.

My chest burned enough to make me heave again and again. I heard Kale talking from the living room, asking if I was alright. Brody casually questioned Kale. I pulled myself off the floor, washing my hands and splashing my face with cool water. I didn't dare look in the mirror. My reflection would only add to my fright.

"What do you think happened?" Brody asked, not wanting Kale to suspect anything.

Kale stretched as he stood up. "Party after a gig. I got shit-faced and picked up a random girl."

Atlas let out an aggravated chuckle, putting his hands above his hand and down on his back. "Random girl?"

Kale looked at Atlas, lifting his brows and blowing out a harsh breath. "Sorry, man. No offense, if she's your girl, all apologies." Kale was talking about me like I was no one. The ache in my chest continued to grow, reaching my limbs. I felt like they were going numb, every part of me heavy with grief.

Anders was straining to keep niceties, his cheeks twitching.

"That 'girl' is our sister." Anders didn't take his narrowed eyes off Kale. Anders was the most understanding among the three of us, but even he had limits.

Kale clapped his hands together and whistled. "Oh, shit. I have this bad habit of picking the most complicated women."

Brody had listened to enough. He walked up to Kale, putting a hand on his back. "Kale. Athena isn't a random girl."

I walked up next to Brody, wanting to touch Kale, hoping our connection would become clear to him.

"Pretty name for a pretty lady," Kale said, trying to lighten the mood. He was turning on the charm to get himself out of what he perceived was merely a sticky situation.

I pushed past Brody, getting closer to Kale. "You don't remember me at all?" I asked him, reaching out my hand to lay it on his arm. My skin sizzled, like always. Kale felt it too. His eyebrows knitted together, but he backed away regardless, putting distance back between us.

Kale gave me a forced, roguish smile while removing his arm from my grasp as he'd done with Jenny. "I'm sorry. I really don't. I meet a lot of girls after shows, but I only take the hottest ones home, if that makes you feel any better." Another wave of nauseating pain radiated through my body, all the way into my bones. I felt my shoulder sag, and I shrunk back.

This wasn't the Kale I knew; this one was something out of a frat house. He talked to me like I was nothing more than a common one-night stand. Atlas came up behind me quickly, gathering me in his arms. Kale's comments were directed at me, but Atlas and Anders felt them, the words cutting through them just as sharply.

Brody broke the tense silence, putting his hand on Kale's shoulder again. "Kale, that's enough. Stop it," he chastised. Brody's face fell. He felt sorry for me. His pity was evident in his eyes and in how he'd reprimanded his tactless younger brother.

Brody tried one more time to help Kale understand. "Athena's kind of your fiancé."

Kale laughed, shaking his hand and rubbing his neck again. "There's no kind of. Funny man. I know you hate my partying, but this low—even for you. A fake fiancé." Kale clapped his hands together, then patting his shorts, looking for a wallet. "What'd he pay you for this? I'll double it for creativity."

Brody snorted and rolled his eyes. "Kale, this isn't a joke. What day do you even think it is?"

"I'm fucked up, Brody, but I know what day it is. December..." Kale's voice drifted off.

"What year?" Brody asked.

Kale laughed. "Don't be an ass. 2019."

Brody's mouth gaped wide.

My jaw dropped, and Anders about choked, dumbstruck, and turning white.

Two years. Kale had lost two full years of memories.

Anders was unable able to stifle a low rumble. I shifted out of Atlas's embrace, putting a hand to Anders's chest to soothe him. I wouldn't risk making Kale's mental state worse with a beating from my brother.

Kale's crassness jarred me, and it stung more than I imagined possible, like a punch to the face. This is what Kale told me about. The behavior he'd outgrown. Except the Kale in front of me hadn't kicked his habits of parties and women. Another digging pain cracked me in the ribs—I was nothing more than a groupie to Kale.

Forgettable and replaceable.

Brody looked at Kale, wide-eyed and stunned. "No. It's not. Look at your phone. It's not 2019, Kale. It's 2021."

Atlas still had Kale's phone. He pulled it from his pocket, handing it to Brody, who shoved it less than gently into Kale's hand. The phone lit up, Kale's facial recognition kicking in. His wallpaper was a photo Kale had taken of us. Those smiling, happy faces on his screen were long gone, replaced with grimaces and confusion.

"Why'd you even have my phone? I don't know who the hell you are, either." Kale spat out his question, eyeing Atlas with unblinking intensity.

Atlas clenched his teeth, losing patience along with Kale, and narrowed his eyes back, "I had it because we were trying to help you."

Kale stared at the wallpaper for a second, his eyes scrutinizing our photo. He touched my face on his screen. "Help me. Right. Sure. I could've called a fucking Lyft and not had my phone confiscated."

Atlas pursed his lips together and crossed his arms, struggling not to say more.

Kale kept staring at the screen. He shook his head fast and pulled up the calendar on his phone, then muffled a gasp. We stood by as he exited his calendar and opened his photo gallery. He became more upset with each swipe. The last pictures were all of us, and one I didn't know he'd taken. It was of me laying next to him while we'd watched movies in bed. My hair was tousled and falling over my shoulders. I had my hand resting on Kale's thigh, and there it was—the ring. The promise he'd made, sitting on my finger. Kale pinched the photo enlarging the diamond. He looked up, his face twitching, sweat forming on his temples. Brody opened his mouth to speak but thought better of it, seeing Kale scrolling, reading over all our messages from days ago. His pupils dilated, growing larger the longer he scrolled and swiped.

Kale's forehead creased, and he stumbled backward. "How is this possible? How can I not know her? And how *the fuck* did I lose two years, Brody? What is this?" Kale yelled. Distress radiated off him in charged waves—waves that crashed into me, each one more powerful than the last.

Kale couldn't bring himself to address his questions to me,

let alone look me in the eyes anymore. I wasn't sure which wounded me more. I rubbed the cool marks on my arm, then squeezed them, trying to comfort myself, trying to recall what Kale's hands felt like on me.

None of us were sure how to answer him. How did we tell a grown man who'd lost time he wasn't just my boyfriend? That he was a powerful wolf, set to rule a world he no longer remembered existed with me?

Xercarus couldn't change Kale's biology—or could he? We'd witnessed firsthand how he mutated supernaturals, Colin included. The dried, black blood from the many sorry creatures I'd killed remained on my clothes, a reminder of our battle and Xercarus's capabilities. But I ended him—ripped out his useless heart. Despite that, he tore mine out one last time.

I sniffed the air near Kale, not wanting to alarm him. His scent hadn't changed, fresh and wild. Kale was, in fact, very much a supernatural. He'd forgotten the inner voice, suppressed it somehow. This recent development made Kale dangerous. Too much stress could cause him to shift. If he shifted in his current condition, it'd fracture his mind and cause him to go into a permanent panicked state of fight-or-flight mode. Like a cornered feral animal, he'd attack anything perceived as a threat. Keeping Kale as calm as possible became the number one priority, meaning not overloading him with truths he wasn't mentally ready to accept.

Kale glanced back down at his phone, a message from him to me. "What is this?" He lifted the phone screen to my face. He knew exactly what it was and asked me anyway. I had the same photo in my gallery. It was the picture he'd taken of us with his family at their house. His mom's face with her welcoming smile that so resembled Kale and Brody's, his dad's strong jaw pulled into a gleeful grin. My brothers both looked happy. That moment felt so far away right now. I wanted to get back to it. To feel Kale's loving arms and kisses on me, but Kale just gaped at me, a vacant expression on his pale face.

"So, this is real, then?" he asked, looking away and gritting his teeth. His posture remained guarded as if getting closer to me would taint him.

I nodded, respecting his space. "Yes."

Kale glared at me, twisting his mouth in frustration. "Yeah? And what is that you want from me, huh? Money? Or just tickets to red carpet events?"

My eyes stung with tears. The pain ripped into me. I closed my eyes for a moment, trying to keep the agony from tearing the bond away. "Kale. It's not like that..."

Atlas pushed past me, pointing his finger in Kale's face. The angry reddening his cheeks. "Fuck you, Kalen. Don't talk to her like that."

I grimaced, and my stomach lurched. Kale darted his eyes away, his teeth gnashing together. "I need you to leave. Brody, please, just make them go." Kale's eyes went cold, almost lifeless in their vacancy.

The place on my neck where Kale marked me burned like being branded with a hot iron. Kale hissed loudly, snatching his hand to his own neck, feeling the same scalding sensation. His rejection broke down our bond, snatching it away from me. Kale stomped out of the room. I stood there speechless, clutching my neck. The pain, the sheer weight of it, pulled me down to my knees. Anders and Atlas got behind me, catching me as I collapsed. And there it was, throbbing grief reared its ugly head, causing my chest to seize up. I felt frozen with terror. My lungs clamped closed; I couldn't breathe. The man I loved looked at me as if I'd just ripped his heart out. It was torture, a stinging agony I had no words for.

Xercarus had done it. He'd taken what was most important to me. He let Kale live and wiped me from his mind. Kale didn't know me and remembered nothing about our time together. I was nothing and no one to him.

Hours ago, Kale had been willing to give his life to save mine.

Now... he had no idea *who I was*.

If you enjoyed Athena's beginning, please consider leaving a review on Amazon and Goodreads.

I was suffocating, surely, I was.

I couldn't breathe through the dry cotton sensation in my throat. *Let me out;* I tried to scream, but not a word left my lips. Out. I needed to get out, to get away. Burning from the lack of air, I clawed at my throat. My body boiled with a heat so intense I gasped harder and harder for the oxygen I couldn't seem to get. Hands shook my shoulders, and faraway voices called my name, begging me to wake up.

Fire and burning uncased my fingers, my skin aflame. Everything around me covered in a blaze.

So hot. I need air.

"Athena. Come on. Wake up!" The shaking got harder.

Where are you? My head stayed dizzy and my vision faded in and out as I struggled to keep my eyes open.

It's a dream. He's here. No. No. A nightmare on repeat. It raged through my body and burrowed so deep it bruised my bones. I begged. *If I opened my eyes, please Goddess let Kale be next to me, snoring, in a peaceful sleep.* My eyes shot wide open filled with fresh, hot tears that spilled down my cheeks and wet my nightshirt. Anders wrapped his arms around me, cradling me in his side, gently rocking me. My hair flattened to the sides of my head, sticking to my cheeks, soaked with sweat and tears.

It wasn't a dream—Kale was *gone...*

Athena's Journey Continues in Equinox...

ACKNOWLEDGMENTS

I need to start by offering thanks to my incredible friend, Keri. For the unwavering support, pushing me to continue, and reminding me exactly who I am. Your belief in me and mindset gave me an opportunity and nudge to open this door and walk through it. May you always know how wonderful you are.

The most significant debt of gratitude I owe goes to Lane and Sarah. There's not enough appreciation I can give to you both. Not enough 'thanks yous,' I can say. The hours of reading and rereading, you dedicated to Triad, to me, is more than I could ask for. Your time and opinions made this possible. You are part of Triad and part of me. The consistency of your support shows how lucky I am to be surrounded by such amazing, accomplished women. You make me better.

Mom, where would I be if not for your help in making me an avid reader? And my beloved Gram, who read me bedtime stories repeatedly and showed me what it was to stay strong and be myself. You both gave me a steely determination and smart mouth to carry me to my goals.

Samantha. What can I say? Dynamite comes in small packages, and you're just that! Your encouragement and thoughtfulness have been pivotal in my reaching this point. Thanks for being my coffee buddy and keeping my witty banter up to par. You've become the best friend I didn't know I needed —thank you.

Dad. You took on a responsibility many years ago and haven't let me down since. Thank you for choosing to be in my life and showing me how to be cool while driving.

Nick and Allie. I'm so glad to have found you. Internet friends are real. Allie, you're crazy supportive and basically never sleep—you're amazing! Both your comments, your support—make me a better writer. I wish you both the success you deserve. Nick, you share my love of Disney. Thank you for reminding me friendship is found anywhere and that humor makes most things better. You went above and beyond. You beta read Triad, then came in and helped me edit at crunch time. Thank you for not bailing on me when I couldn't figure out where to put a comma...

For Rachel and Hannah, having you in my corner has filled my life with memories and joys I cannot replace. Thank you for the name inspiration. I hope Lincoln Harper and Colin McCormick do you both proud.

To my husband, who tolerates late nights, and my Air-pods always being in. Thank you for your patience, good nature, and for creating experiences worth writing about. *I love you.*

Huge thanks to my entire family for listening to my nonsense, partaking in my shenanigans, and who inspired me to write this. Should you find little pieces of yourselves in characters, know it was purposeful. Thank you. May you be as proud of me as I am of all of you.

I'd like to include a special thanks to the artist behind Triad's character art and Portuguese translations—Bryan Camargo a.k.a Fall Out Bryan. Thank you for making sure my translations were correct and for bringing my characters to life in a whole new way.

Thank you to the readers, who gave me the courage to strike out on my own path and continue this story. I hope Athena and Kale bring you joy and *spice*.

Brittany Weisrock is a blogger turned author. Working at her family's business by day and writing at night, she's been published in *She. Magazine.* Triad is her debut novel. She lives in Wisconsin with her husband, Bryan, and their amazing daughter, so naturally, she enjoys cheese and the Badgers. When she's not got her nose in a book or writing her own, you can find her in a bathtub or enjoying a coffee shop. With a fierce love of fantasy and Mickey Ears becoming an author has been a long time coming for Weisrock. A self-proclaimed wine enthusiast and Netflix lover, Brittany enjoys falling into new worlds of fiction with a glass of red wine in hand. She hopes to share many more of her stories and help other authors grow with the start of her own publishing company, Lake Country Press & Reviews.

Please find me on the following sites:

Tiktok: britt.weisrock
Website: www.lakecountrypress.com